MAN-KZIN WARS X:

THE WUNDER WAR

THE MAN-KZIN WARS SERIES
Created by Larry Niven

MAN-KZIN WARS X:
THE WUNDER WAR

HAL COLEBATCH

Created by
LARRY NIVEN

MAN-KZIN WARS X: THE WUNDER WAR

A Baen Books Original

Baen Publishing Enterprises
P.O. Box 1403
Riverdale, NY 10471

ISBN: 7434-3619-9

Cover art by Stephen Hickman

First printing, August 2003

Library of Congress Cataloging-in-Publication Data

Niven, Larry.
  The Wunder war: Man-Kzin wars X / created by Larry Niven.
    p. cm.
"A Baen books original"—T.p. verso.
  ISBN 0-7434-3619-9 (HC)
  1. Kzin (Imaginary place)—Fiction. 2. Life on other planets—Fiction.
3. Space colonies—Fiction. 4. Space warfare—fiction. I. Title: Man-Kzin
wars X. II. Title: Man-Kzin wars 10. III. Title: Man-Kzin wars ten. IV. Title.

  PS3564.I9W86 2003
  813'.54—dc21

                                                          2003008635

Distributed by Simon & Schuster
1230 Avenue of the Americas
New York, NY 10020

Typeset by Bell Road Press, Sherwood, OR
Production by Windhaven Press, Auburn, NH
Printed in the United States of America

ACKNOWLEDGEMENTS

Thanks are due as always to my wife, Alexandra, for all manner of support and constructive criticism, and also to my friends, including especially historical novelist Michael Talbot, for many helpful suggestions.

—Hal Colebatch

CONTENTS

DEDICATION

To the memory of Poul Anderson,
friend and inspiration

One War For Wunderland

Prologue

The ship flew in like a drunken bat, an automatic distress beacon shrieking. It did not respond to signals.

When they came within visual sight they saw it was grossly damaged, and plainly not under maneuvering control.

When they boarded the ravaged ship with its crew of crumbling, desiccated, drifting corpses, some in strange costumes, the only survivor they found was a head-injured woman in coldsleep. They slowed it and stopped it just before it entered the deadly embrace of one of the outer gas-giants.

The ship had come a long way under its autopilot from the general direction of either Sol or the Alpha Centauri System. The oddly shaven-headed man who must have instructed it as he died still floated with a freeze-dried hand on the controls.

But they tested the hull metal where they cut their way in and found that, if it had come from Earth, it must have been a very old ship before it started.

There were many dead. Far more than a normal crew. This was as packed as a colony ship, more packed, indeed, for a large part of a colony ship's complement would have been frozen embryos. Nor did it carry the vast array of stores and supplies a colony ship would have had: almost nothing but people and hibernation cubicles and bare provisions for a skeleton crew of watch-keepers.

They were tough spacers who boarded the ship, and most had seen death in space before, but still this was especially horrible and upsetting.

Apart from the strangely costumed and coiffured men, a large number of the dead were women and children. The hibernation facilities could have just accommodated them all and

3

looked as if these had been being prepared for use when disaster struck, but only the one had been activated.

It was easy to see but difficult to understand what had happened. It had been sudden. Perhaps the ship had accidentally crossed a big com-laser near its point of origin. A laser—a big one—had burned through the rear of the hull and opened one compartment after another to space, punching its way through hull-metal and human tissue indiscriminately. But if that was what had happened, why had the ship or the station that had fired the laser not come to its rescue?

Anyway, it had stopped short of total destruction, and a few emergency systems were still working, including the beacon that had signaled its arrival.

The damage had caused short circuits and fires that had raged even in sealed compartments until the last oxygen in the life-system was consumed. The logbook was melted slag. The last minutes of life aboard the crowded ship were better not imagined but must have been mercifully brief.

The activated coldsleep unit was damaged and operating with a backup of questionable efficiency. They took the woman down to the surface, and tugs with electromagnetic grapnels moved the strange ship into a parking orbit.

Even if the woman had not been head-injured to start with, brain-death seemed a near certainty. When they checked the brainwaves' readouts with their own equipment they were astonished by their strength.

They were careful, and took a long time healing her and bringing her back to consciousness. The people of We Made It were sometimes painfully aware of being a colony, without the vast medical and scientific resources of Earth or even Wunderland, but their science was still good. The robots of twenty-fifth-century nanotechnology—comparable in size to some large molecules—crawled into her brain, and when a net of them had been formed whose neural connectivity made a whole that was far greater than the sum of its microscopic parts, they sought to trigger a memory. Sensors, receptors, cognitive and motor response units more delicate by far even than those used in normal reconstructive nerve surgery linked their impulses.

It was a new technology and imperfect. The watchers saw some of what little was left of her memory translated into flickering holograms. There was a jumble of images, including, quite clearly, a scene of a sidewalk café and a man with a lopsided yellow beard under an open sky.

It looked to those who examined it like something from a

picture book of old Earth, though it was not a Flatlander's beard. The tiny robots sewed and spliced and healed a little and crawled out of her brain. They would wait before applying nerve-growth factors so new neuronic connections would not interfere further with the grossly damaged, immeasurably delicate and diffuse network of connections that created the hologram of memory.

The woman's brain continued to puzzle them, even when they had repaired it as much as they might. There were few pictures but many abstract symbols.

They tested her DNA but that told them nothing save that she was of human stock originally from northern Europe. They brought her back to consciousness.

She could speak only in broken sentences when they began, gently, to question her in the hospital at We Made It.

Chapter 1

2367 A.D.

Some lead a life of mild content . . .
—Saki

Around me as I flew, the evening sky of Wunderland was full of light. Alpha Centauri B was so brilliant in its time as to cast its own sharp shadows at dusk and to fill the air with color, yet at an average of 25 AUs easily distant enough to be looked at with the naked eye.

There too was the red jewel of Proxima and the diffuse, braided lines of the Serpent Swarm. There, a routine sight in this system, was the sliding and flash of meteors, plus a couple of fair-sized moons and other smaller satellites, natural and artificial. There were other points of light that were in fact potato-shaped stony worldlets of various sizes, some carrying loads of instruments, the axled wheels of the old space-station, the squares and rhomboids of advertising signs (hardly used now—they proved unpopular and counterproductive), high aircraft and spacecraft, and, higher still and parked in their plodding orbits, the old slowboats that had brought the original colonists.

The towns and city too had their high points of light, not because population pressure in a limited space had forced them upward—Wunderland's chief cities were still quite small—but because .61 Earth gravity made for both high but easily conquerable hills and a few relatively inexpensive architectural flights of fancy.

Wunderland. Humanity's first interstellar colony was well-named, I thought, watching the landscape pass below me, high crests and ridges still lit by the rays of setting Alpha Centauri A, mountainsides glowing. I had seen pictures of Earth, and understood again the delight our ancestors must have felt in their first days and nights on this new world.

Not a new thought but still a good one. With its towering hills and mountains, sparkling seas and lush life, its forests, parklands and savannahs where the red-gold of the local vegetation now mixed with the green of Earth plants, its brilliant sky, a gravity that gave good health, good looks (if we exercised hard) and long life, it was impossible to imagine a more wonderful place. Someone had once compared it to the valleys of Malacandra in C. S. Lewis's ancient fantasy *Out of the Silent Planet*, and noted how Lewis, even if his Mars was a billion years or so behind the times, had anticipated the effects of low gravity on waves. The frustrations of my personal life could be seen in their proper perspective as I flew over that glorious landscape, under those stars.

I have often remembered the details of that night, and the contentment I did not then know I felt. In fact, I was relieved to be getting away for a few hours from my own thoughts and from the political intrigues and pressures that were becoming more and more obvious between Herrenmanner and Prolevolk on the one hand, and Teuties and Tommies on the other, with the *déclassé* jumping about on the edges.

Because of the frequency of meteor impacts, our fathers had been wary of building near the coast, but we had a good meteor guard force now, with sensors and big rock-blasting lasers mounted in spacecraft and also on the ground, and Circle Bay Monastery stood on a headland, high on the rim of an old crater.

To the west a wide swath of open parklike country swept down to merge with the outer marshes of Grossgeister Swamp. There were ponds and limestone caves, some with odd populations descended from sea creatures washed inland by ancient tsunamis. To the south-east were hills and, seeming far away but still just visible from the air, the diffuse glow of Munchen against the sky. As the night deepened the lights of scattered hamlets and farms were spilled beads rolling to the horizon. A sudden bright plume of orange smoke climbing starwards indicated a takeoff from Munchen spaceport. It had, I thought, been unusually busy lately.

Munchen had been called New Munchen immediately after its settlement, and its river the New Donau, but the prefixes had fallen out of use. The other Munchen and Donau were more than four light-years away, and there was little chance of confusing them.

There was the outline of the monastery ahead, dark walls and lighted windows, growing larger as the autopilot shifted into descent.

I brought my car down in the monastery courtyard. The abbot was waiting for me, visible from a distance as a spot of red light. He had taught me at school, and I had used the monastery as a base for collecting expeditions in the past. We knew one another well.

"That's where it was seen," said the abbot when I alighted and we had exchanged greetings. "It vanished down there." He gestured with his cigar to a grove of red Wunderland trees near the outlying margin of the swamp, dark in the night shadows.

"Did you watch the area?"

"Not continuously, I'm afraid. We thought the best thing was to call you. We kept an eye on the trees during the day, but there doesn't seem to be anything there now. Unless it's good at hiding. But it would have to be good. Some of the brothers aren't bad hunters."

I scanned the grove with my nitesite. There were a few dull red points in the dark of the trees showing the body heat of small animals. Nothing much bigger than a large rat or perhaps a Beam's beast, but some of the Wunderland reptiloids, even the big ones, were cold when resting. So close to the swamp, it was as well to be respectful of what might be out after dark.

"Well, I'm not going in there now."

"Of course not. But you'll take a drop of wine?"

The monks of Circle Bay Headland made their own wine in the old way. It was famous and expensive and part of the reason I had not waited and flown out in the morning. The abbot was a good host, and the guest rooms were comfortable in an old-fashioned style. We crossed the wide lawn of the courtyard to his study.

"Something like a big cat, you said. Who saw it?"

"Three of the Brothers. Peter, Joachim, and John. They'd been fishing in the marshes. They wrote down their impressions separately, as you asked. All emphasized cat."

I knew them quite well. Brother John was a trained reptiloid handler and had come collecting with me; the others were horticulturists with a good bit of botany and a good deal more zoology than most, even by the standards of an educated and intellectually curious community that lived largely by farming on what was still a comparatively new world with two competing and adjusting biosystems. All intelligent and reliable men.

"And it was how big? Not a tigripard?"

"No. Not a tigripard. It was big, bigger than a man, bigger than an Earth tiger, as far as I know, and far bulkier, and they said it ran differently. Sometimes on four legs, undulating like an Earth weasel, sometimes—and this is odd—on two legs. Nothing that they recognized as either a local or an Earth creature."

"And it didn't attack them."

"No. But it was plainly a carnivore. They didn't get to see it for long, but they said there was no mistaking the teeth and the limbs."

"And nothing local, you say?"

Some of the bigger Wunderland animals, like gagrumpers, were—appropriately for Alpha Centauri A's planet—centauroid in form, but they generally went about in herds and with all six legs on the ground. In any case, gagrumpers were herbivores and placid unless threatened. And as far as large animals go, even creatures as evolved as humans can generally tell herbivores from carnivores instinctively at a glance. It's deep in our genes.

"Definitely not."

"Everything we know about evolution says such a creature wouldn't evolve in this ecology," I said. "Predators don't grow bigger than they need, and the native prey-animals all around here are quite small. If there was anything big enough to jump on adult gagrumpers, we'd know about it by now . . . we'd have seen anything really big long ago. On Earth nothing preyed on elephants, at least not healthy ones."

"I know. But you said the *native* prey-animals. We've introduced equids and cows and sheep and pigs. That might attract visitors from farther afield. What's in the hills and the forests? You haven't got the whole planet classified yet, have you?"

Wunderland is smaller than Earth but a good deal bigger than Mars. The last I heard, even the surviving vestiges of Martian life had had their mysteries. "I might say: 'Give us a chance!' It is a whole planet!" I told him.

"And things can grow bigger in water, can't they? We've got both the sea and the swamp not far away . . . But they're sure this was not a water dweller. I told you I had something odd for you."

Something odd. It gave me a sudden queer shiver. Sometimes we remembered that, if Wunderland was wonderful, we were also still alien intruders upon it.

"The cat aspect is strange, certainly," I said, "Even a tigripard isn't *very* catlike. But this sounds more like the persistence of an Earthside myth than anything else. Many wild places on Earth had legends of solitary, wild giant cats that had no business being there—there were sightings, even photographs, of the Beast of Bodmin in England for centuries." Cryptozoology was one aspect of Earth history I had to know something about—the habits of a lot of Wunderland's fauna might be described as cryptic.

"They were probably actually big wild dogs that had turned sheep-killers, plus sightings of domestic cats that had gone feral and bred a bit bigger than normal, or surviving *Felis sylvestris* wildcats. Maybe there were one or two big felines that had escaped from captivity. But it would be odd to find the same legend here. And they are sure it wasn't a tigripard? They can be quite dangerous enough!"

"No. It was the first thing I asked them. They are quite sure. I don't want to overreact, but I thought it could be something special—which can mean specially dangerous."

"If it's unknown, it could be dangerous. What looks more harmless than a Beam's beast? They caused a lot of casualties before we got the measure of them."

We passed under an arched doorway, through an enclosed space I had learned was called the Garth, through another arch with a brass-bound wooden door in a lower wall and entered the abbot's book-lined study.

The Catholic Church, like some of the Protestant denominations, had been supported on Wunderland by a large and wealthy congregation once, including some of the Nineteen Families. The monastery buildings had some extravagant architectural follies from those days, including sections of battlemented wall and a high tower that could have come from Neuschwanstein. The monks' private quarters were austere while eschewing extremes, but the abbot had to be something of a politician now, and entertain. As the church's support declined, paradoxically, he had to show influential visitors more than a modicum of comfort.

Well, I wasn't sorry for it. The monastery's past generations of abbots or whoever had made these rooms had managed to combine comfort with a rare feeling of stepping into an almost museum-exhibit-like past. But it was part of a still-working institution with a life, a poetry, if you like, that no museum can achieve.

I was glad there was such a place on Wunderland, where every human structure was relatively new. There was an antique open fire burning in what the abbot had told me was called

a "grate," old chairs that one wouldn't want to sit on for long
but which reminded one of how our ancestors sat, as well
as comfortable modern ones, a *really* ancient ornate "clockwork" clock, a shelf of antique-looking paper books in red
and gold beside the computers, a crystal decanter on a side
table. It seemed odd to talk of unknown dangers in such
surroundings.

"You have weapons?"

"A few." He waved around the room: "You know we like
old things. There are a couple of antique shotguns we use
as fowling pieces, and the collecting guns." A ginger kitten
jumped onto his knee as he sat, kneading the folds of his
robe and purring raucously as he stroked it.

"Also, of course, we need them when we have to kill a
badly injured animal or one of our own beasts for meat. We're
old-fashioned in just about *all* ways, you know."

"I remember the first time you fed me meat from an ani-
mal you killed," I said. "It took me a bit of getting used to.
A useful accomplishment for a biologist on field trips, though."
We both laughed at the memory of my rush to the bathroom
the first time I saw—and then realized—what was on my plate.
"Sometimes I thought you were toughening me up deliberately."

"I was." There was something different in his voice for a
moment that snagged my attention. Then he resumed his usual
slightly pedagogical manner. Perhaps one's old teacher never
quite gets beyond teaching, I thought.

"I've said it is part of the churches' duty not to move with
the times, though not all the secular brethren agree with me.
Oh yes, and we've got some modern strakkakers in case we
encounter dangerous creatures like Beam's beasts or tigripards
at the sheep . . .

"Or, between you and me," he continued, "in case we are
attacked by humans, who could be much more dangerous.
We've got a few bits and pieces in the Treasury and round
about that might tempt thieves." The clockwork clock, I
thought, must be just about beyond price for some rich collector. But who would know how to maintain such a thing?

"Using strakkakers against thieves sounds pretty draconian!"
The strakkaker's blizzard of glass needles would turn a man
into an anatomist's instant diagram. Even police only carried
them in emergencies.

"We wouldn't, not in the first instance. But if anyone broke
in, we might have to defend ourselves. The Papacy has always
taken the long view about weapons technology. It was the Bull
Romanus Pontifex that gave the charter to the age of European

exploration." He loved to lecture, I knew. When I was a child he had spent a lot of time with me after school and guided me towards my career. "It was a pope who tried to ban the cross-bow. And it was a pope who tried to ban the sale of the noisy, inefficient stone-throwers called cannon to Africans in 1481. We knew they wouldn't stay at that state. But the ban didn't stick and the Moorish pirates were using them in galleys to domi-nate the western Mediterranean not much later. . . ." He took a sip of wine. "We're aware our isolation could make us vul-nerable."

"It's an isolation a lot of people would envy. I know I often do."

The abbot laughed. "I'm well aware of it. We're short of monastic vocations, but there's a long waiting list of people wanting to come on temporary retreats here. A lot of people seem to get something out of a retreat. But they want the tranquillity without the discipline—or without the religion at all . . . without the religion at all," he repeated, and the laugh went out of his voice. We were both silent for a slightly awkward moment. "They'd better make the most of it while it lasts," he added.

"I thought you were planning to be here forever."

"That's what I'd like, but I have to look at the demogra-phy. Christianity is dying on this world, as it is on Earth. Life's too easy for most people to feel the need of a religion . . . a little mild pseudo-Buddhism among some of the urban young, perhaps. But we've talked church history before."

I nodded. On Earth, when people mentioned the Holy Office today, it was generally a slang reference to one of the more secretive departments of ARM, Earth's technological police. Was I right in a vague notion that about the time the last slowboat-load of colonists left Earth, senior church figures had been taking up day jobs? Did it matter? Earth was a long way away. We Masons, who were required only to believe in a Supreme Being, and had a life of our own in our lodges, had an easier job surviving on the whole, but we too had had our lean years.

"I love coming here," I said. "I could never be one for the discipline of the monastic order, but a furlough among all this is pure contentment." He filled our glasses from the sparkling crystal decanter. The wine shone ruby in the firelight. Per-haps my too obvious appreciation of this luxury touched a nerve.

"We're not a very disciplined society, are we? Not a very tough one," he said. "Also," he went on, "there's this politi-cal trouble. How much do you know about that?"

"Not much. But more than I want to. We've got a whole world—a whole system—thinly settled. Huge tracts of land still for the taking, huge tracts still *unexplored* from the ground, if it comes to that. Habitable asteroids, Centauri B close by, even the Proxima system to settle if we want to live in bubbles under a red sky. What reason is there for us to fight?"

"The reason that we're human. It's not just Herrenmanner and Prolevolk. Teuties and Tommies fought systematically on Earth once, you know."

"I've heard about it," I said. "I don't know the details."

"Not many do now. Earth is censoring its history in a big way, and though we did bring some records of our own there seems no reason for us to advertise the story of Earth's past. . . ."

"It's not likely to come to fighting again, anyway. Not in this century. We aren't savages."

"Not in the old sense, I grant you," he said. "Not wars and armies and so forth." We both laughed at the absurd image. "But there are other forms of violence. Just lately . . . people have disappeared, you know."

"What do you mean?"

"Just what I say. Von Frowein, a senior councillor. He went on a camping holiday a couple of weeks ago and never came back."

"Didn't they search for him?"

"Yes, and they didn't find anything. He had the usual tell-tale beacon on him, standard equipment for lone campers, and there wasn't a peep out of it—as if it had been deliberately smashed. It gave me a nasty feeling when I learned about that. And there have been others. The police think we are seeing some organized murders—political murders."

"How do you know these things?"

"I'm not just an abbot, you know. I'm also a bishop—a priest in the secular sense. I hear confessions and . . . other things. My monks can retire from the world. I can't." He got up, pushing the kitten gently onto the padded arm of his chair, and began to pace the room.

"Did you ever read Saki?" he asked, looking at me with a sudden curious expression, "An old Earth writer. A heathen, as far as I can gather, but he had a hand for verses:

"Some lead a life of mild content:
Content may fall, as well as pride.
The Frog who hugged his lowly ditch
Was much disgruntled when it dried.

"He didn't write them as poetry, but as literary artifacts in a short story. Still, they can set one on a certain train of thought." I knew enough of his manner of rhetoric to know that when he spoke again it would be to quote something he had picked for a reason.

> *"You are not on the road to Hell,*
> *You tell me with fanatic glee:*
> *Vain boaster, what shall that avail,*
> *If Hell is on the road to thee?"*

Did he let that last line linger in the air between us for a moment? His glance turned to the blank faces of his computers, and in the soft lighting I seemed to catch something strange there. But it passed. "We—the church, that is—have survived by being ultra-orthodox, archaically conservative," he said musingly. "Heresy comes too easily if you give it a chance, especially when it takes the fastest message four and a half years to travel between us and Rome. And heresy means disintegration.

"We know our own history. The church very nearly died of tolerance once. Space travel and the scientism that went with it looked like killing us, but it may have been the saving of us instead. We religious weren't backward in getting into Space, you know. The first religious figure to set foot on a new world was an Episcopal lay preacher named Buzz Aldrin.

"As for us, there's a stained-glass window in our chapel with a likeness of Father George Coyne, the director of the Vatican Observatory, who applied for astronaut training in the 1960s. His Provincial is said to have muttered, 'If I let you become an astronaut, George, every priest will want to.' He had a point there. A priest, Georges Lemaitre, first postulated the Big Bang. No, we've never been hostile to space and space travel, far from it. But perhaps that renewal was a miracle, an unlooked-for one, like almost all real miracles."

"You believe in miracles?"

"Officially."

"But not actually?"

"We've been here a long time. And I'm not young. The faith flickers sometimes. But you can't cross space without feeling the vastness of the Creation and the insignificance of mankind compared to whatever made it.

"Also," he said after a moment, "conservatism justifies my own comfort."

"It's a good life cut off from the world, you mean?"

"Yes. Not so much better here as it might be on Earth, I suppose. Wunderland still has plenty of room. That's partly how I justify it and don't think I'm just a fat selfish old man. We are keeping something alive."

He fell silent again. I nodded.

"The Church didn't only come to Wunderland to minister to the people here," he said suddenly, "though of course that would have been more than reason enough. Some hoped we would renew ourselves. I know some say we're in the pockets of the Nineteen Families, but we came here independently— at very considerable cost. I'm told it almost bankrupted the Vatican. It had to be done, particularly as we knew our . . . competitors . . . were aboard the original slowboats."

"What? You mean the Protestants?"

"No," he said, with a sudden harsh bleakness in his voice that I had not heard before. "Not the proddys, who we've got on with fairly well for centuries now. And not you Masons either, by the way."

"You know about that?"

"Of course. And the church's anathema still holds, you damned syncretist! I also know most of you are well-intentioned, though if you'll forgive me saying so, some of you may in sober truth be playing with a hotter fire than you know. But I'm getting off the point: when we left Earth, some of us thought it would be for our own good as well as that of our new flock . . .

"We did renew ourselves, I think, for a while, but . . . Of course, I have to run this place in the world. I've some idea of the political stresses gathering now. But they are hardly enough to drive people back to the church."

Although machines and farming robots grew or manufactured most of our food, land which had appeared unlimited when the first colonists had arrived had made for a largely rural culture: a gentle, easy one unlike the hard work and bloody realities of farmers of ancient times, but one that kept us in touch with seasons and open spaces. Despite our heritage of space travel and our modern technology, it made us conservative in many ways—worse than conservative, according to some, though others applauded it. Cities had grown slowly and were still tiny compared to the megalopolises of Earth. But with the establishment of those cities, land values had changed. People had changed too.

The rural life was fine in theory for many but city life was more convenient and exciting in practice. When, after its long gestation as a mere landing field and administrative headquarters, Munchen had begun to look like a real city (it had taken many years for the permanent population to reach a thousand), it had begun attracting natural urbanites and had grown faster and faster. However good communications and virtual reality might be, people wanted to be close to things, and some people wanted to be close to other people. An ancient expression about "rural idiocy" had been resurrected.

The university had been one of the first people-magnets. Some students had wanted cafés and classrooms with other students rather than computer screens in solitary farmhouses. For an eighteen-year-old, the best VR communication with girlfriend or boyfriend lacks a certain something. The university population alone was more than twenty thousand now. Of course it was mainly science subjects that were studied, both pure and applied—the new mathematical transform alone had caused a whole new department to be set up—but there was a growing culture of the humanities as well. A colleague in the literature department had told me that a new poetic movement was writing of rural life with nostalgia. With an urban population growing rapidly, a growing business and professional class and stronger unions, the Nineteen Families were feeling their hegemony challenged as never before. Threat was making them tighten their grip. We still, if one looked at Earth history, had few police even for our population, but I wondered that night how long that situation was going to last.

The increasing political bickering seemed foolish and far away in that pleasant room.

"You won't go out to the people?"

"Do you mean us monks or the church as a whole? That's work for the secular orders. But the Church can't compromise too much on this world. We went that way once on Earth and nearly lost everything. Still, we've lasted twenty-four hundred years and more. Just. I have faith we'll survive. . . . Faith, after all, is my business. Mark you, without being too hypocritical, I do feel the absence of any sort of . . . test."

"Test? I don't understand."

"I'm not sure I do, either," he said. "Just that I sometimes know things are too comfortable here."

"I didn't know they could be *too* comfortable."

"It's not a material thing. Not necessarily."

I noticed now an unrepaired crack in the stonework behind the abbot's head. It looked deep and old. Through the window behind him I could see what I knew were the monks' living quarters. Half at least of the rooms were empty now and dark. There was a small pane of glassine missing in the window. I wondered if the old man's faith in their survival was misplaced and hoped it wasn't.

We were proud of our differences from Sol system's rather coldly technological order, from the Sol Belters and their descendants in our own Serpent Swarm, with their slightly inhuman efficiency, and from Earth's crowding and regimentation and its—albeit we were told, largely benevolent and inevitable—control. We esteemed a lot of our own archaisms, including a freedom that Earth would probably have considered anarchical, but were we doing enough to preserve them?

Wunderland, I thought again, would never be a dull world, but it would lose something special if it lost the monks and their quaint, kindly, old-fashioned ways. That thought, I realized, had a patronizing feel about it. This place was more than pleasant: in some odd way it was precious. The whole place was a relic, and in many ways a decadent one—the monks' simplicity was more complex and expensive than ordinary modern life. It would not weather a real storm, but it had charm, and in the world of Wunderland, young, expansive, ripe for the taking in a hundred ways, there were no real storms on the horizon.

I went to bed warmed by that splendid wine, which no chemist could duplicate, and despite the coarse, woven bedclothes, slept well as I always did there, with an herb- and flower-scented garden just beyond my open window. I did not, of course, know it was my world's last night.

Chapter 2

The next morning I woke with the birds and a chapel bell. The monks had already prayed and broken their fast, as they put it, but they were indulgent towards sluggard guests, and there was something put by for me in the refectory. I had trimmed my beard, eaten, and was just finishing a pot of what was surely the best coffee in the Alpha Centauri system when I felt a tap on my shoulder.

"Good morning, Professor Rykermann."

It was Brother Peter. He was already carrying a collecting-gun, and thrust into his belt was a dust-gun with which someone with quicker hands and eyes than mine might shoot down collectible insectoids on the wing. I was a little surprised to see he had one of the monastery's strakkakers slung over his shoulder. Behind him stood Brothers Joachim and John. They were armed as well.

"And a-hunting we will go!"

"Aren't all these weapons rather . . ." I knew there was an antique word, and it came back to me from some history course. "Overkill?"

"No."

Normally the monks would be in thoroughly good spirits at the prospect of helping me on a collecting expedition. That part of my work was most people's idea of a holiday. But there was something serious in their faces that morning. I knew them as friends, and behind their politeness and what I thought of as their professional serenity I sensed tension. They didn't argue about the strakkakers but kept them.

There was no point in taking the car. The place where they had made the sighting was only a few hundred meters from the main gate.

Inside the walls were fish ponds and gardens with many Earth as well as Wunderland plants: a lot of these (netted over, as were the ponds, against various large and small flying pirates) were grown for their fruit, but some were purely decorative: casurina trees, cape lilacs, the scarlet of bougainvilleas and nodding palm fronds. Along with the flutterbys, Earth bees were loud. Near the gate the kitten was sunning itself in a patch of marigolds. A couple of bright flags flew on the higher towers.

We walked through the parkland-like meadow of red and green grasses star-spangled with flowers. The monks had a small business making perfumes from nectar, and perhaps that encouraged the flutterbys. They rose about us out of the grasses in glorious multicolored clouds.

But there was an undercurrent of something else. The usually tame animals in the meadows seemed nervous. Apart from the more usual domestic animals, the monks had raised a small herd of zebras for decorative purposes, and their black-and-white variations and heraldic profiles as they grazed usually provided a pleasing contrast with the riot of colours. Today, I saw, the zebras were clumped together, standing in a circle as far away from the swamp and the grove as they might get, the stallions facing outwards.

"This thing we saw," Brother Joachim told me again, "it's big. Bigger than a tigripard."

"So the abbot said. But three strakkakers? I hope you're not leaving your house defenseless."

Brother John, I knew, laughed a good deal. He wasn't laughing now.

"It's not only big. It's dangerous."

"How do you know?"

"Just because I wear this robe doesn't mean I'm not a hunter."

"Hunter's instinct, you mean?"

"More than that. Instinct usually whispers. This was screaming: 'Run! Run for your life!' That was even before we saw it. . . . The creature was nightmarish. If we'd told the Father how *terrifying* it really was, I don't think he would have believed us."

"I hear what you're saying, and I respect it. You're a hunter, but you're a scientist, too. What was so terrifying about it?"

"It's not easy to put into words. But part of it was that it shouldn't have been there. Look, Professor, a tigripard makes sense ecologically. But this didn't. It was too big."

"Odd, I told the abbot that last night. But size can be hard to judge at dusk."

"Not this size. There are the bushes where we first saw it."

"Yes?"

"It stood twice the height of them."

"We all agree on that," Brother Peter added.

"That's more than the height of a man."

"Much more."

"It looked like . . . like a cross between an oversized tiger and a gorilla. There's something else. Something hard to explain. It was . . . *monstrous*. It loped away a few moments after it saw us, but—and we're all sure of this—in those moments it was weighing up whether to attack us or not. And it had us at its mercy. If it had decided to attack, we were dead. We *knew*." The others nodded.

I thought I understood what he meant. Not from experience but professional observation. A hunted animal knows when it has been marked out as prey. There is a sort of subtelepathic thing, an ability to terrify prey by projecting intent, that is part of a certain type of predator's stock in trade.

And yet . . . the serious settlement of Wunderland had begun with the arrival of the first slowboat carrying the Families and the core of settlers three centuries before. It had been surveyed before the colonists unpacked, and the most obvious types of big fierce animals, in the immediate area at least, had been found and either eliminated or moved to islands. Since then there had always been natural scientists at work classifying, dissecting, ecologizing. . . .

But relatively few of them, and much of their work was directed to practical matters—agriculture, husbandry, mariculture, genetics, conservation, toxology, biological physics—rather than the fairly self-indulgent pleasures of pure zoological research.

I was only the second to occupy my chair. As the abbot and I had said, we were a long way yet from knowing even all the larger animals on the principal continent of Wunderland—it would be a sad day for me if we ever did!—but this was Circle Bay, only a short flight from Munchen. The Abbott had complained to me that light pollution from the city would soon be affecting the monastery's little visual observatory (a telescope in orbit was beyond the monastery's modern budget and not its style anyway).

The monastery's nearest neighbors were small niche farms, worked by vigilant, reliable robots under minimal human supervision. Grossgeister Swamp was large, not fully explored, known and rumored to be the abode of odd things as well as odd people. But as a scientist I thought it highly unlikely that it contained some kind of giant tiger.

Or was it? Tigers, I remembered, had lived in swamps as well as jungles on Earth. The Sundabands at the mouth of the Ganges had been so infested with them that towers were built for stranded sailors to shelter in. At the southern end of the Malay Peninsula, as late as the mid-nineteenth century, they had regularly swum the Johore Strait to the new city of Singapore to eat workmen. Water would support a big body, too—but the swamp had its own large assortment of strictly water-dwelling predators, including some analogous to Earth crocodilians. I doubted anything like a tiger could compete with them in a watery or muddy environment.

Apart from aerial and satellite surveys, and the expeditions of scientists and fishermen, there was a small population of humans, marshmen and swampmen—"characters," some fairly dubious—who seemed to like living in the swamp and often made some income as hunting and fishing guides. The swamp was undoubtedly dangerous for the ignorant, and these "characters" would have to be well-acquainted with it. Hard to imagine that a big land-dwelling predator had managed to live so near a populated zone for so long quite undetected.

But was it impossible?

Sometimes, when we were not taking it for granted and speaking of it as our home, even we, the Wunderland-born, tried to make ourselves realize how alien we were. It was good, I thought suddenly, that the first colonists had come in large numbers and, though we were thinly scattered on the planet still, our population was now in tens of millions.

I was glad that when I was born there had been a good scattering of settlements. A small, single colony, like some of the later ones on more distant planets, might well be a terrifying place to be. What was it like for a settler to look up at the night sky from the single settlement on one of the new colony worlds—assuming they *had* a night sky—and feel himself so utterly alone beyond that single pool of light?

We, and the tough loner humans of the Serpent Swarm, descendants of the tough loners who had first colonized Sol's asteroid belt, were, if we thought about it, quite alone enough.

Reduce the Sol system to a scale model on a large field: Sol is a ball nine feet in diameter. Walk away from it for about five minutes, a fifth of a mile, and you come to the orbit of Earth, a little ball about an inch in diameter. Earth's moon, the size of a small pea, is about two and a half feet from it.

Wunderland, *on this scale*, circling the nearest of all major stars, is 50,000 miles away.

No good. Draw what picture you like. Know that our ancestors made the journey. The mind still can't really take it in. But we should not be surprised by strangeness here.

Brother Joachim dropped on his knees and pointed to a patch of bare ground.

The tracks were of four-toed, clawed feet. The claws of a carnivore, I was sure. And they were *big*. Bigger than a human foot, and sunk farther into the ground than a human foot-print would have been. Something very solid indeed appeared to have made those tracks. Unless this was some sort of hoax— and I could not imagine why these monks might be hoaxers— it was a creature that was still very heavy in Wunderland's gravity.

Now I saw it had left an obvious trail. A wide swath of vegetation, including small trees, was broken and beaten flat. Its tracks pointed straight for the swamp. I cocked the collecting gun with its tranquillizer darts, meant to be good for both Earth and Wunderland animal physiologies. The monks unslung and cocked the strakkakers. Brother Joachim moved in front of me.

Following the trail could hardly have been easier. As we descended into the marshy ground the prints grew deeper. Clawed-up divots of dirt confirmed the creature had been moving at speed, and here and there were the marks of fore-paws . . . very curious forepaws.

Near the borders of the swamp proper the trail turned aside, towards the grove of Wunderland trees. It entered the grove.

And ended. There was a wide circle of disturbed ground, nothing more. I wondered if the creature had somehow buried itself or tunneled out of the grove. That seemed contrary to everything we knew. And those prints were not from the claws of a digging animal. But Wunderland was not Earth. . . .

I got the car then and we examined the site from the air. The car's ground effect obliterated the trail as it went but we filmed it first. The track from the grove to the spot where the monks had seen the creature became obvious, as did the track back to the grove, and the wide circular disturbance of the ground and bushes there. It appeared plain that the creature had left the grove and proceeded to higher ground near the monastery as if to observe the buildings.

There was no indication of how it had entered the grove in the first place or where it had gone. There was no disturbance to indicate a tunnel or burrow. This was not the cave country of the limestone ranges, there were no cracks or sinkholes, and radar had charted the location of all the shallow local caves long ago. We flew over the swamp's margins, and saw nothing new. Even the normally teeming flying and swimming creatures of the swamp seemed unusually silent and scarce.

The monks and the abbot seemed almost apologetic, but any biologist learns to bear with frustration and delay in fieldwork. I asked them to keep their eyes open and not to hesitate to call me if they saw the odd creature, or any other odd creature, again, and then I flew back to Munchen. But if I was reasonably philosophical about it, some disappointment remained. To have captured an unknown species of large animal, carnivore or otherwise, would have been a very big thing.

And the monks had been good witnesses that there had been *something* there. Something big and catlike. I was sure they were telling the truth to the best of their ability. Before leaving I had examined them separately and their accounts remained consistent. I wondered if I would ever see one.

The voicemail on the instrument panel lit as I approached the city. I thought it might be the Monastery calling to say they had seen anything new, but it was something that struck me as a good deal odder: the mayor's office. They wanted me right away.

Chapter 3

*The whole aim of practical politics is to keep the
populace alarmed (and hence clamorous to be
led to safety) by menacing it with an endless
series of hobgoblins, all of them imaginary.*
                                        —H. L. Mencken

"I'm frankly somewhat embarrassed to have called you like
this, Professor," Deputy-Mayor Hubertstein said. "I understand
you've been on a field trip today."

"Not much of a trip. But I can't think what this is about."

"We're setting up rather a rushed conference to put a number
of experts in the picture, including a biologist.

"A bit of a possible problem has come up. I've got to tell
you straight away, though: this meeting and its . . . subject
matter . . . are, well, potentially embarrassing at the moment.
I know you are a responsible man. You'll keep secret about
this?"

"I still don't know what 'this' is, but yes, I suppose so."

"All right. Come this way, please."

There was Police Chief Grotius, Captain von Thetoff and
another, more senior, officer of the Meteor Guard, with both
spacer and Herrenmann written all over him. Others joined
us in the capsule that took us up to the Lesser Hall. Most
of the seats there were already filled.

A string of my colleagues from different departments of the
university. There was Herrenmann Kristin von Diderachs,
spokesman (dictator, some said) to the City Council for the
Nineteen Families, smooth, confident, plump and complacent,
radiating pride and authority, who I had been presented to

but who would hardly have deigned to acknowledge me. There was van Roberts, his opposite number for the Progressive Democrats. Some other politicians had cross-party friendships but I knew these two hated each other and were said to be barely on speaking terms even in the Council.

Others I recognized as political figures and industrialists. And in a majority of them the dress, features, and unmistakable body language of the Nineteen Families.

There was The Markham, there was Freuchen, there was Thor Mannstein, there was a representative of the Feynman clan, and there were others: Montferrat-Palme, of an old family coming down in the world, Talbot with his defiantly symmetrical beard, The Dunkley of Dunkley, Schleisser, The Argyl, Mannteufel, Franke, Johnston, Buxton, von Kenaelly, Lufft. Golden or flaxen hair and those mobile ears. A more than usual number of asymmetrical beards with their own subtle identifications and codings of status. But there were other people too: as well as professionals of nebulous status like me (our beards asymmetrical but not blatantly so), there were a couple of obviously wealthy and successful prolevolk and a good number of the new *déclassé*. Also a man who I knew slightly as one of the town librarians.

I had been vaguely annoyed at having my evening interfered with, and further by being sworn to secrecy by someone like Hubertstein. I hadn't had anything like that done to me before.

As we entered the hall annoyance gave way to curiosity. Not just because of the caliber of those present. With modern communications, any sort of large face-to-face meeting like this was rare. And there was something in the body language of some of those already gathered: Grotius, who called us to order, and Mayor Larsen, who took the podium.

I had met the mayor socially a few times. I had even heard her speak formally before. But never like this. She opened new buildings and presided at civic banquets. She was another mouthpiece for the Nineteen Families. Her speeches were as a rule long on sonorous bromides and short on content. She normally began by working through the titles of the more or less distinguished ones present. This time she did not.

"We have had a warning from Sol system about hostile aliens in space. They have been attacking Sol ships."

There was a long moment of echoing silence.

"It seems the aliens have no interest in negotiation or communication. They have some kind of gravity control that gives them acceleration and maneuverability which no conventional ship can match. They have matched velocities with ships travelling at .8 lightspeed."

There was a brief hubbub of exclamations. She waited for it to subside before continuing to state the obvious.

"Of course, this message is more than four years old."

The hall was on a column, high above nearly all of the city lights, and had a plexidome for a roof. The designers wanted to make the most of Wunderland's sky. Sol was there, easy to pick out as part of a constellation in the new Wunderland zodiac, the Tigripard, made principally from the great "W" of Cassiopeia.

Both Alpha Centauri B and Wunderland's prime moon had set, so that the sky above us was as dark as it ever got. There was the white point I knew was Sol, and Earth was somewhere hanging in that blackness. A blackness that was suddenly strange. Somebody spoke.

"What are these aliens like?"

"Something like big cats. We have pictures."

The mayor clicked a switch and a holo appeared.

"This was sent back by a colony ship called the *Angel's Pencil*. It encountered one of them—one of their smaller scout ships, Earth now thinks, and got lucky with a drive mounted in tandem with a big com-laser. It escaped and destroyed the alien ship." She clicked through other holos. "These pictures have come a long way. They've deteriorated a bit, but you get the general idea. This is the wreckage of the alien."

She paused. There was a thick, heavy silence as the pictures stood there. Not shock, not horror, I think, not then. We were simply finding ourselves, too suddenly, in the presence of something too large and strange to understand.

"What does a whole ship look like?" That was von Thetoff.

Grotius answered. "We've got that." The holo changed and flowed into a red near-ovoid thing. "But I guess that if you see something coming at you at .8 light and making inertialess turns, you won't have to ask."

There was another dead silence in the hall. Whatever we had been expecting, it was nothing like this. Then a score of voices began to rise. The mayor held up her hand.

Another figure stood. I didn't know him, but he looked like a Herrenmann gone physically somewhat to seed and certainly to low-gravity fat. (That was one thing about Wunderland that irked us then: with workouts we could be the handsomest people in the universe but in later life without frequent sessions at the gym most of us tended to become either elongated stick figures or balloons. No world was perfect, some of us thought.)

"Do Tiamat and the Serpent Swarm know of this?"

"They will have got the messages as we did."

"Have you contacted them?"

"Not yet. Why?"

"Might it not be a good idea. This is surely going to mean some . . . special executive action."

"That is the purpose of tonight's meeting." said the mayor. "To decide what action." She looked us up and down and there was something curiously hesitant in her manner.

To decide what action! They don't know what they're doing! I realized suddenly, looking from one blank and bewildered face to another. *They're making it up as they go along.* A sudden, unexpected moment of panic for me, and then a reflection that was somehow calming: *Well, the situation is pretty unprecedented.* And then I thought suddenly and quite certainly: *She's lying. They're all lying.* And I remembered my thought of the previous evening of how busy the spaceport had become.

I suppose I'm at the making of history, I decided a few moments later. *This could be a late night.* The next question, when it came, seemed almost bizarrely irrelevant:

"What do they call them?" Instead of telling the questioner not to waste everyone's time, the mayor answered seriously.

"The aliens? 'Dinofelids' was one idea, but apparently there's already a Dinofelis among Earth's fossils. Not something one would have wanted to meet, by all accounts. The *Angel's Pencil* crew officially named them *Pseudofelis sapiens*, and the Earth term now seems to be *Pseudofelis sapiens ferox*. Bit of a mouthful. However, computers have translated some of their script, and it seems they call themselves"—she had difficulty in pronouncing it—"Kzin."

Another man on his feet now amid the flurry of whisperings. Without knowing his name I recognized him as a politician. One of van Roberts's allies in the Progressive Democratic Party who had weakened the grip of the Herrenmanner on city politics and were moving to weaken it in the countryside.

"You say this will mean special executive action. What exactly does that mean? More power for you and your friends?"

"It's obvious we'll have to do a number of things. It may mean radical measures. Obviously government must have appropriate powers to deal with an emergency! We are looking at questions of military security."

"Military!" Another hubbub. It was a bizarre word.

Van Roberts was on his feet: "This is all very convenient for you. What do we know of the bona-fides of this message?"

"You know what interstellar communication costs. Who do you think would send it but the authorities?"

"You mean the precious ARM! Since when have they been friends of democracy? And how do we know the message is real at all?"

Quite obviously people did not want to believe in such a message. There were sudden shouts from all over the hall: "Yes! how do we know it's real!" I saw some Herrenmanner joining in. *Somebody should be taking this in hand*, I thought. And then I thought: *Who is there to take it in hand? Us. Only us.* I think it was easier for us than it would have been for Flatlanders to take it in, but a lot of us were stunned, all the same.

"Excuse me!" That was van Roberts again. He pointed to a date at the corner of one picture.

"These are more than *four* years old. Much more."

"They were taken light-years from Earth. Then, apparently, they were dead-filed for years. It was thought they were some sort of hoax. About the time it was decided that they weren't, other ships began disappearing. Closer to Earth."

"And if these aliens are real," someone was saying, "when can we expect them here?"

There was a moment's silence. It was, I thought, one of those stupid and meaningless questions somebody had to ask. The mayor replied:

"Well, obviously, they could be here . . . now."

Grotius turned to the Meteor Guard officer with von Thetoff. "Commander Kleist, have there been any . . . anomalous events that . . . are worth commenting on in this context?"

Kleist was a tough, fit-looking young man, typical of the somehow almost feral deep-spacer type. But he spoke carefully now.

"There are always anomalous events in a system as full of debris as this one is."

"The Sol reports say the Aliens have gravity control. Do you know of any gravity anomalies?"

"There have been things on our mass detectors, yes. And we have seen new monopole sources."

"When and where!" That was Grotius, with a snap in his voice I had never heard before.

"Continually. But more so lately, I must say. As a matter of fact, we've got extra ships on alert now. We can predict meteors fairly well but we thought gravatic anomalies might herald a comet shower. There is an increase in anomalies. Out in the cometary halos at first. But they are moving closer."

"How long has this been going on?"

"A few days. That's all." His hand went up to his mouth and his eyes darted to Grotius. I knew he was lying and was not used to doing so. My major feeling was total puzzlement.

"Can't we reason with them?" That was Peter Brennan, much taken up with good works and a bore of planetary and possibly interplanetary reputation, a leading light of the local Rotary Club and also of my lodge, a purveyor of pharmaceuticals.

"With whom?"

"These people?" Only Peter Brennan, I thought, would refer to threatening aliens as "these people." One of his more futile projects was publishing a small Internet newspaper called *The Friend*, retailing stories of acts of kindness between Herrenmanner and Prolevolk and between Teuties and Tommies. But he had inherited money and had a good business sense and could afford his hobbies.

The mayor was speaking again.

"One way or another, we here represent the leaders, responsible people and relevant experts of Wunderland who could be gathered quickly. I don't need to tell you that we may be facing a situation that is unprecedented. As soon as the message was received—earlier today—I called Chief Grotius, Commander Kleist, Herrenmann von Diderachs and others who I could reach quickly. Hence this meeting." I was sure she was lying too.

The mayor continued: "We have agreed that the first thing to do is form a group of interlocking committees to formulate aspects of policy. Recommendations will be implemented by an executive committee composed of representatives of the Nineteen Families, the existing exco including special interest nominees, and the City Council."

"Point of order, Madam Mayor!" It was one of the politicians. "Giving executive powers to such a committee without the normal procedures is simply unconstitutional!"

"Yes!" From another part of the hall, "With due respect, Madam Mayor, what you are proposing sounds like a simple exercise in administrative lawlessness!"

"We have both a Constitution and a Constitutional Court. Any proposals of this nature should go to that court for a ruling. To side-step Constitutional procedures for administrative convenience is simply the way to chaos!" That another dark-haired, professional-looking man. "I've never heard anything like it."

"None of us have heard anything like this!"

"That's just the point!"

There were voices rising all over the room. The mayor banged her gavel. I saw her ears were flat and wondered if that was an uncontrollable sign of anger or a deliberate reminder to us that she too was a Herrenfrau of the Nineteen Families. Yet she was speaking in broad hints of the Platt dialect—was that to remind us she also had a foot in the Democrat camp?

"I note your objections. But the point is, I think, that putting some administrative structures into place to deal with this matter may be *urgent!* The best I can do to reassure you is to suggest that we entrench a provision that the situation be reviewed—radically reviewed if necessary—after one month. By that time we should have more information from Sol and know a bit more about what we are trying to do to solve this tanj snafu."

That last was Tommie slang. Was she putting that in deliberately also? There was a lot of muttering. Then Grotius played a trump card.

"Before the resolution foreshadowed by Madam Mayor is put to the meeting," he said, "I should point out that it is envisaged that all invited to be present here tonight will have positions on at least one of the committees. Therefore if anyone is unhappy about policy he or she will be in a position to make a direct input in policy direction."

That quieted a lot of objections. Most of the people at the gathering were not going to do anything to compromise prospects of their own power, I thought. No politician or Constitutional expert myself, I found I was on something called the Biology Committee and something else called the Defense Committee. Peter Brennan had us set up a Friendship Committee.

It went on a long time. At length I got home for a few hours' sleep.

Chapter 4

*"No passion so effectually robs the mind of all
its powers of acting and reasoning as fear."*
—Edmund Burke.

I found Dimity Carmody at the Lindenbaum Kafe, sitting at
her usual table between the chess players and coffee addicts.
With her better-than-fashion-model looks and quietly correct
if obviously Tommie clothes among the eternally scruffy students, she was always easy to find, even, or especially, hiding behind those sunglasses she generally wore. I hoped I could
talk to her now.

I hadn't always been able to. We had almost been lovers
once, and would have been if it had not been for the difference in our intelligences. It was not a good idea to have a
gap of more than 40 IQ points between oneself and one's
partner. A few halting conversations between us had made
that difference painfully clear. She enjoyed coming on field
trips with me occasionally, but interaction in the deeper aspects
of life was a different matter. I was a professor of biology
with some chemistry and physics, and she was . . . what she
was. Well, to use an old phrase, she wasn't exactly a rocket
scientist.

Born with an abnormal brainwave, thought to be something
in the Asperger's syndrome family, she had now learned to
adopt a protective social coloration. It hadn't always been that
way. Her father told me she had hardly spoken till she was
seven years old. He was an outstanding mathematician and
physicist—late in life he had worked on Carmody's Transform—
and to have such a child had hurt him badly then, though

33

things improved eventually. Now she could just about cope with normal people. Among her more normal socialization activities, she loved music boxes and had a little collection of them.

She was sitting drinking coffee, something she did a lot of. She didn't play chess, though, and I remembered the embarrassment when the president of the University club, an Aspirant Master, misled by her appearance of normality, had offered her a game here. He thought someone had set him up. She was doodling on some paper, one of her music boxes tinkling quietly on the table beside her. She signed for me to sit down, and stretched absentmindedly, staring at what she was doing. There was an ordinary notebook in front of her on the table, with many Brahmabytes of capacity available and connection to a really big brain if needed, but she was using pen and paper.

As she stretched I was reminded again that, despite the tricks Wunderland's gravity can play on the bones and tissue of the lazy and careless, she was near the epitome of human standards of beauty. Her body was a living version of the marble Venus of Cyrene, loveliest of all the statues of antiquity, who makes the Venus de Milo look heavy and clumsy by comparison, but as she stretched her attention remained fixed on the paper. Behind the sunglasses her face looked vacant. "Big tits and little wits/Do often go together" a rude old poet had once written. But it was not as simple as that. She had a pink hibiscus flower in her hair which, I thought, really made me understand what was meant by that term *overkill*. It seemed to attract the flutterbys, and there was a small cloud of them round the table, their delicate multicolored wings brushing the gold bell of her hair with its pink headband.

I broke an awkward silence. "What's this?"

Dimity had an almost squeaky voice. A Dimity voice, I called it privately.

"Sums. Difficult sums."

I was sorry I had asked. Her idea and mine of difficult sums reflected our respective intelligences: embarrassingly different. She went on, with that inevitable tone of patience:

"You know the theories that have been explored here and in Sol System about the ancient stasis fields? That they are somehow uncoupled from the entropy gradient of the Universe?"

"They haven't got anywhere, have they? It's all still just speculation."

"No. Not unless there's been anything new done in Sol System. But it gave me a notion. It's . . . difficult to explain . . . but it's to do with gravity as a function of time. . . ."

"*N*-space?" I hesitated.

"No. But as you know they learned to open a stasis field long ago on Earth with relatively primitive time-retarding technology."

"Yes. But the result was a disaster. I'm told there were a lot of casualties. And apparently it was nearly worse."

"That wasn't the fault of the technology. It was because there was something dangerous inside the field that got out. If we can make time precess at a different rates . . . well, my theory is that within a gravity field we can't, or not at the scale I'm talking about. But outside a gravity field—I mean a gravity field like the singularity associated with a star . . . The singularity acts as a massive governor. . . . Look, does this explain what I mean?"

I recognized some conventional mathematical symbols on her paper along with others that appeared to be her creation. Her father had told me once of how, one day at the end of a childhood that had been near-silent near-inactivity, he had found her playing with the keyboard of his computer, and of his flash of hope that she might grow into a normal child after all ("Who's a clever little girl, then?") which had died as he raised his eyes to the screen. They had published her first paper jointly. After that she had been on her own. His work on Carmody's Transform had brought him praise and when she was given her own department he had helped set it up but he had been little more than her assistant.

"What's that?" I asked, stabbing at random at one esoteric symbol to cover my embarrassment.

"It stands for the occurrence of Miss Bright's Paradox."

"Miss Bright?"

"Yes. You know:

> There was a young lady named Bright
> Whose speed was much faster than light.
> She went out one day
> In just such a way
> And arrived the previous night.

"But you see"—she pointed again—"I've eliminated it. Or rather I depend upon it: upon the fact that the universe will not permit such a paradox to occur.

"I have always thought that, doing what the tnuctipun did, time could be made to precess at different rates over a much larger scale," she went on. "You need an engine to generate your second field, of course, which is a problem. Caught between those fields you would be squeezed away from them, like a wet orange seed squeezed between two fingers. I calculate one of the results would be negative mass."

Stanley the waiter brought us two coffees. The Lindenbaum had de luxe human service in this section and put its prices up accordingly. Gazing at Dimity, he tripped over a neighboring table as he backed away. She went on:

"Within a gravitational singularity, that would be the end of you. You might become something like your own wormhole, millions of miles long, the length depending on how much mass you originally had, and less than the width of a subatomic particle. But beyond the singularity, and if you had a certain velocity, you'd move. *Without an increase in mass*. If what happens then can be described in terms of physical structure it might be called creating your own *big* wormhole. A sort of *shunt* rather than a drive . . ." She saw she was not getting through and made another attempt. "A matter of getting away from a greater impossibility by being pushed into a lesser one if you like."

"I don't understand." But I believed her.

She gestured at the symbols again, as if it was all obvious. She had, as I had thought that sad day when I realized our brains couldn't match, given that phrase "not exactly a rocket scientist" a whole new dimension of meaning.

"If you were moving at sufficient speed already . . . I think you'd be projected out of the Einsteinian universe. . . . Greenberg was able to tell us a bit of what happened with the ancient drive, the preconditions, but of course he didn't know how it worked, except that the speed had to be sufficient to affect the average mass of the universe. I think the two major achievements of the ancient technologies were connected. The stasis field was a byproduct of their drive technology, or their drive was a byproduct of the stasis-field technology . . ."

"Does that mean . . . ?" I couldn't say it, somehow.

She paused, and then there was something new that was hard and defiant in her voice, a challenge: "We know the tnuctipun could do it! There would be a bending effect of space and . . ."

"How fast?"

"How fast do you want?"

"Where do you get the energy?"

"From the Big Bang. Space is still full of it . . . Look at the rest of the universe as the norm, and the singularities as the exception. In terms of getting from one singularity to another, I calculate—it's on the computer at home—a light-year in about . . ." She paused. I think she felt herself shy of what she was about to say " . . . about three days . . . It doesn't break the light barrier, it shatters it, because once you move into that . . . dimension or aspect of space you can keep accelerating!"

There had been theories before. The first major modifications to the Special Theory of Relativity were more than four hundred years old. Things happened, or were thought to happen, at the edges of black holes. Nothing practical so far . . . but it has been done before, once before, by a race within an empire which, it was thought, had controlled most of the Spiral Arm at least and which had vanished before life emerged from the seas of Earth.

"And . . . that's what you've got here?" My own voice sounded somehow very small. The thing I had sought her out for suddenly seemed almost unimportant—until I put two sets of implications together and then it suddenly seemed more important than ever. I heard another tinkling sound besides that of the music box and found my hands were shaking as I held my coffee cup.

"Not yet. Not for years, I think. Maybe never. We know that with the tnuctipun drive they had to be moving close to lightspeed anyway. Greenberg told us it was the average mass of the universe that was the critical factor. But I'm getting somewhere. So far, the computers support my theorizing. Of course, I had to instruct the computers, but if there's a fault in my instructions I can only believe it's a very subtle one.

"This is the wrong place to do it. A double star means the combined singularity is huge. And the engineering is huge enough anyway. The tools are beyond our technology."

"Could you build such an engine . . . eventually?"

"Eventually is a long time. I think I could . . . *recognize* one. That's not very helpful, is it?"

I wrenched my mind away from the vision that opened up. I felt I needed her brain's connective powers for something else at the moment. "Could you come with me for a couple of hours?" I asked her. "I want to show you something."

The markings in and around the grove hadn't changed. "There it is," I said. "What do you make of it?" I had told her on my abortive expedition of the previous day, though not of the meeting that followed it.

She put away the calculations she had been scribbling at. "An aircraft landed there and took off again," she said. "That's the most probable thing. A fairly small one, but a good deal bigger than this. Not an ordinary private car. It landed and took off vertically but without chemical rockets—there's no sign of burning—and without jets or sufficient downdraft to damage the vegetation. But it hasn't left a ground-effect trail. That is very strange. In fact impossible."

"Yes. I thought you might say that. I wanted someone else to confirm it."

"Maybe it took your specimen."

"Yes. What I'm worried about is the possibility that my specimen was flying it."

Anyone else would have been brought up short by that. She took it in instantly.

"In that case it would hardly have made just one landing. Have you looked for other sites?"

"Not yet. There's too big an area to search."

"Perhaps we can narrow it down. Why did it land here? What's special about this place."

"The monastery."

"Yes. Let's say your specimen landed near the monastery because it was curious. Maybe it's landed near other human dwellings. What about the marshmen's shacks? And perhaps the marshmen have seen something."

I would have asked the marshmen the previous day, except that they tended to be highly unapproachable. On Wunderland, with plenty of good farmland for those who wanted it and good communications, hermits were hermits from choice. We were proud that here, unlike Earth, we respected individuals' privacy. But things had been different the previous day.

I pulled the car's nose up and we headed across the swamp. There was a bit more wildlife to be seen below us today, but it still seemed unusually shy and skittish.

There was old Harry's cabin on Hook Island. Or rather, there had been. There were a few pieces of walls and roof now, scattered about. There was a disturbed area about the same size as that in the grove.

The island had no trees, no cover anything could be hiding in, I thought. I did a couple of cautious passes and we landed.

The monastery garden had been silent but for the insects. This was a silence that was not perfect but of an utterly different quality.

There were the prints, obvious in soft ground. Very big, clawed prints, made by something very heavy. Water oozed into some, and one already had red froggolinas swimming in

it. There was a kermitoid with markings I had not seen
before. . . . Most of the small creatures around seemed ordinary enough, even if I couldn't name them all. Grossgeister
teamed with life in a huge variety of kinds and sizes, including
creatures on the larger islands who occupied the ecological
niches held on Earth by bear, swamp deer, or cougar. At any
other time my professional interest in them would have been
more intense. *I must get on with my great project of classifying all this*, one part of my mind remarked. My work in the
caves was a preparation for the greater biological treasures
of Grossgeister. . . . I jerked my mind back to what was in
front of me.

Tigers in the muddy Sundaband Islands. Swimming tigers.
We were standing on a permanent island made by channels
less than fifty meters wide. On the other sides of those channels
were tall reed beds and other islands with higher vegetation
that might hide anything. Part of the wonder of Wunderland
was the variety of its animals, descendants of survivors of
successive catastrophes caused by major meteor impacts. And
the fauna boasted its full share of opportunistic predators.

Could something charge out of that vegetation and across
the channel before we could get back to the car? *I get the
feeling we are babes in the wood here*, I thought. I hadn't even
a gun. The headland where the monastery stood was only a
few kilometers away, but here in the channels of Grossgeister
the vegetation hid any other horizon.

The swamp was silent, but, as it were, not quiet when one
listened: water rippling and bubbling, the grunts of mudfish,
the queer singing of the froggolinas and insectoids. But were
these ignorable, day-to-day swamp sounds covering up any
others? The sounds of something approaching? Cats stalked
silently.

There were peculiar smells in the air, some of them natural odors of swamp vegetation, living and dead. Others that
I didn't know.

There were the eyes and nostrils of a couple of small crocodilians in the still water, looking like pairs of floating Bob's
Berries or drifting bubbles. In a way the sight was reassuring: the presence of adolescent crocodilians meant the probable absence of big ones. A twin-tailed serpiform thing sailed
by with head held high like a periscope. Something very large
and white and curved floating just under the surface brought
me up short, heart jumping, until I realized it was the
marshman's boat. Or part of it.

There has been violence and disaster here, I thought. I had occasionally had dangerous moments on field trips, but that had been different. My assistants and I had always been equipped and prepared. Here I felt prepared for nothing. *What am I doing bringing Dimity into a place like this? The unknown is always dangerous. Get her out now! And not just because I love her!*

"Nils! Look at this."

Something metal glittering in churned-up mud, almost buried. A heavy automatic gun, the sort the marshmen used to kill the big crocodilians whose back armor might deflect even the needles of a strakkaker. Useless for specimen collecting, it would leave little of any specimen.

It was smashed. Twisted into junk.

It had been loaded with high-explosive bullets and set for automatic fire at 300 rounds a minute. Three rounds only had been fired. There were the casings on the ground. And there were stains on the recoil compensator and pistol grip that looked like blood. A predator?

"Nothing that powerful fits the ecology."

"I know."

"And this is the longest-settled part of the planet. If there was a predator like this here before we'd have known it. You would have seen it in all the other animals. Things would be faster, more powerful, better defended."

She was confirming what I had thought. But I had needed her to confirm it. I didn't want to damage the evidence before any investigation, but now that I had handled the gun already I thought I had better take it back. It would be easy enough to separate my DNA from anything else that might be on it.

I saw the honker, an electronic fence device to keep crocs and other possible intruders away, including humans if necessary. Honkers were a good deal more potent than their name might suggest, and like most modern electronics they worked perfectly when they were in one piece. This one was in many pieces, strewn in the mud.

Then Dimity pointed again. There was something different in her walk and stance, as though she had changed into something like a hunting predator herself. The café coffee-drinker was not there. Her ears were laid flat back. I had forgotten she had that much Families blood in her. There was a dark pool of what I was now sure was blood, surrounded by froggolinas and covered with small insectoids, scraps of cloth, and, gleaming pinkish-white among them, what I recognized at once as a human femur, cracked open at the lower end, part of the pelvic socket still attached at the upper.

I dropped the broken gun as we ran to the car. I saw another bone fragment in the mud as we passed: it looked like part of the zygomatic arch of a human skull, but I didn't stop to examine it. There were other scattered fragments too, I now saw. I wanted to get back to the city fast, but was still unable to recognize the voice of my own survival instincts. We gained a reasonable height and turned a little farther into the swamp.

"The monastery looks like a fort," Dimity said as we approached it. "High walls round the courtyard, no windows, the tower, the edifacium like a castle keep. It looks quite defensible. You've even got that." She pointed to a tall, smooth-lined metal spire that rose out of a small wooden chapel some distance away. "It looks like a rocket or missile ready for launching. And the marshmen's shacks?"

"Nothing like that. You saw what was left of them. Just thin walls and the honkers."

"That may be the point: it *looked* defensible."

The abbot might be a friend and glad to see me on the occasional evening when there was a bottle to be shared. But the monastery was a working organization, and my arrival unannounced in the middle of the working day, and with a woman, might well have been thought inconsiderate. All he said was: "What's wrong?"

"Is it that obvious?"

"You look terrible."

"There's trouble. We've been to six of the marshmen's cabins. They're dead. We've found . . . evidence. The cabins destroyed. We're on our way to the police. But first I need to ask the Brothers something. About that thing they saw."

I showed them a small copy of one of the holos I had been shown the night before. "This is a dead specimen, and not a very good picture now. But is that the same species?"

"Yes." Three yeses. Three nods.

"Without a doubt?"

"Without a doubt."

"And it ran from you. I wonder why."

"It didn't want to alert the 'fortress,'" said Dimity.

"We had no weapons when we saw it, no guns."

"It's not scared of guns. And it had already eaten. It didn't want to be discovered, and it probably thought there were too many of you in a building of this size. . . ."

"It thought . . . ?"

"I can only tell you what you have probably guessed for yourself," I said. "These creatures are—obviously—highly dangerous, fearless of humans, and, we have reason to believe, intelligent."

"How intelligent?"

"Highly."

"Where do they come from?"

"We don't know." That was only too true.

I guessed the abbot must be a clever administrator to maintain an institution like the monastery in the modern world. I had not noticed before how penetrating his eyes could be.

"Let me put it this way," he said. "Are they going to come horizontally or vertically?" The other monks were hanging on the question. Dimity looked as if she already knew. I didn't see the need for secrecy, but it was still a condition I was bound by.

"I'm not at liberty to say what I think," I told them. "I'm sure if there is a continuing problem you'll be put in the picture."

"Thank you. I think that answers my question. . . .

"Before our Order left Earth," he went on, "the Vatican gave us instructions on what to do if we met aliens. What the theological position was. Did they have souls? It's a very old question, predating space travel by centuries. Saint Paul was quite definite: The Resurrection applied to 'everything in the Heavens and everything on Earth.' The early church writers said we need not worry until we actually knew if they existed or not. To insist that 'God could not have made other worlds' was declared a heresy in the thirteenth century—and that covers alternate or parallel universes as well! Good aliens may have already experienced 'baptism by desire.' Still, it's an area of imprecision."

"But if aliens do exist, good or bad, you do have precise instructions?"

"We got some pretty comprehensive manuals when we set out. As far as that precise situation goes, I've never had cause to look, though no doubt it exercised our Founding Father when we first landed, along with a lot of other concerns. I'll have to get Brother Librarian to find them. But we have to be orthodox. We're too far from the Holy Father to risk departing from his instructions. Perhaps he'll send us a laser message."

If Earth's lasers aren't all busy with another thing, I thought.

"Don't go out at night," said Dimity. "Keep your lights on and your doors locked. Don't go out unarmed even in daylight. Don't go out alone."

"Now there's something odd," said Dimity as we flew toward Munchen.

Although ground-effect air cars were common, there was still plenty of wheeled traffic, particularly for heavy hauling. The road we were passing over turned south and led to the industrial districts of Glenrothes and Gelsenkirchen, then on to Dresden (still sometimes Neue Dresden), which had been created deliberately to recapitulate the history of its famous namesake town on Old Earth, and was famous for its experiments in low-gravity baroque architecture and artistic china.

Glenrothes and Gelsenkirchen shared a small landing field well out of the way of the main port's traffic and had some industries based on recycling redundant or obsolescent space material, the equivalent of old-time ship-breaking. Old, material-fatigued or overly damaged spacecraft were disassembled there and their component parts generally taken to Munchen for resale. A spacecraft life system, for example, had all sorts of uses for someone needing a habitat when establishing a new farm, whether on land or sea, and their complex computer hardware and powerful engines always found plenty of uses in things like industrial process control and mining. Sometimes, of course, old ships were cannibalized for new ones.

There were plenty of spaceships getting hard wear in our cluttered and dusty system, filled as it was with minable asteroids, and ship-breaking was quite a busy industry. It reminded me a little, and unpleasantly, of the way criminals had been dissembled for organ banks until modern medicine made such customs unnecessary, which was silly and irrational of me. But possibly others felt the same, because, apart from the fact that it was often a noisy business, it was kept well away from the city.

We were passing over a column of transports carrying parts of spacecraft, the bulk of main engines, including toroid sections of what looked like a ramscoop collector-head, being the most obvious. But on this road it was an everyday sight.

"What's odd about that?" I asked.

"The direction they're traveling," said Dimity. "They're taking those engines *to* Glenrothes Field, not *from* it."

"I heard there had been a special meeting called last night," said Dimity. "Would it have been about what I think it was about?"

"I can't say." Again, that was all the answer needed.

"I told you about the Sea Statue."

"Oh, yes." We had talked for a long time after returning

from the monastery. She had told me more about the near-catastrophic attempt to open the ancient stasis field discovered on Earth many years ago. I had had a vague idea: What had been learned as a result of "opening" the Sea Statue was knowledge similar to the knowledge in the Dark Ages that the Earth was spherical: A lot of educated people knew about it but didn't talk about it much. "What's the connection?"

"It appears likely that the ancients seeded this part of the galaxy at least with common life-forms."

"Yes." We had both studied what was known about the two-billion-year-departed ancient races and their omnicidal war, which wasn't much.

"That's probably why our plants and animals can grow on Wunderland, and why we can eat a lot of Wunderland plants and animals."

"Yes." I was beginning to see where she was leading, and didn't like it.

"Tigripards eat our sheep. Beam's beast bites poison us. Advokats eat our garbage. Zeitungers eat our garbage and affect our moods as well. . . . Something that the old SETI people could never have foreseen, but we should: Beings from at least two different star systems have biochemistry alike enough for them to be able to eat each other."

"So it seems."

"It puts some of my . . . mathematical speculations . . . in a rather different light, doesn't it?"

I had thought that before. But the full implications of what she was saying took a moment to hit me. Then it was like a physical blow. "We've got to get you out!"

"That may not be so easy. Where am I going to go?"

"We've got to get you back to Earth."

"How?"

There seemed no answer to that. I was beyond regretting that I had basically confirmed to her what the previous night's meeting had been about.

Chapter 5

*That fatal drollery called a representative
government . . .*
— Benjamin Disraeli

Despite the seriousness of what I had found, several days
passed before I got a chance to see Grotius. I filed a report
with the police but received a mere mechanical acknowledg-
ment. Grotius, when I did see him at a meeting of the committee, was abstracted and uninterested. He looked weary and
surprisingly aged. My report of evidence of multiple homicides
produced little more than a shake of the head.

"I've no officers to spare now," he said. "Most of them are
busy trying to find out how to reinvent the wheel. Or they're
at the spaceport, working on the meteor guardships.

"And I need them in the streets, as well as everywhere else.
One thing we've learned already is that a bunch of fifty people
can't keep a secret. There have been rumors in the streets
for days. It'll be on the newscast in a few hours. We can't
stop that. . . . We could, actually, but it would do more harm
than good. My cops are so busy that I'm expecting crime too.
There are almost no police on patrol. We've got a few extra
strakkakers in store and I'm issuing them. At least that will
look threatening if there's an emergency. "

"How many strakkakers have we got?" That was Talbot.

"I don't know, exactly. We had the one batch made for police
needs, plus replacements and spares."

"When?"

"Years ago. The factory's closed down now."

"Don't you think we should open it again? Fast!"

45

"What for?" A pause, then, "Oh, I see."

"There are police message-lasers, too. We can dial them up to weapons."

"Really?"

"Of course. It was always in the design."

"Yes. I see."

"I should clear it with the council."

"Later."

Grotius looked at him, then opened a hand-phone and began to speak fast. The Defense Committee had taken an executive action.

"I've been at the library all day," said Talbot. "Reading every book on war I could find. There aren't many."

"ARM went through our library before we left Earth. There are some records of old wars in a general way, even some copies of ancient visual films. There are a few books. But so little that is actually of practical use. They didn't want us building armies."

"No."

"I found one on a Japanese attack on some American sea-ships at Hawaii, *Day of Infamy*. The American ships had guns to defend themselves against flying engines, covered by awnings. An officer on one began untying the lines that held the awnings in place as the flying engines attacked. A cook ran up and cut them with a knife. We have to think differently.

"Grotius, we don't want one factory making strakkakers. We want every factory we can get on line. We want factories making factories making strakkakers. Now!"

"No! Strakkakers aren't the be-all and end-all. They are police weapons of last resort. We may want battlefield weapons, space weapons! Tie up too much of our industrial production in one thing and you lose in other ways."

"What are battlefield weapons? How are they different from other weapons?"

"I don't know. But I gather they used to have them, on Earth. I've found references to something called a main battle tank."

"We'd better ask the meteor people. They use big lasers, don't they? And bomb-missiles."

"Are you seriously suggesting . . ."

"Yes. Of course I am! There are old launching lasers on Tiamat and down at Equatoria. They're got to be brought back on line."

Other voices raised.

"Think of the cost! Runaway inflation! We've only got one economy to play with on this planet!"

"We don't want factories for strakkakers! We want factories for plutonium!"

"Whatever for? Plutonium's dangerous . . . Oh, I see."

"It's already happening. The Meteor Guard . . ."

"Shut up, you fool!"

"What trained fighters have we got? Only a handful of cops. They should be training instructors to train recruits!"

"Don't you think they've got enough to do already?"

Grotius turned to me: "Did you overfly the whole swamp?

"No. It's big."

"We should overfly it. I said we haven't time to consider homicides, but there may have been other things, things left behind."

"Aren't we jumping to conclusions?" van Roberts said. "This could be a completely purposeless panic that will do nothing but damage if we let it go on."

"But the monks saw—"

"The monks could have been mistaken. Or worse. The monastery has always been friendly to the Families, hasn't it?"

"I suppose so. The Order got the land as a deed of gift from the original Freuchens, before they moved out to the Norlands."

"And I imagine the old records will show that Families paid their passage here!"

"As a matter of fact, they don't." I happened to know that, because while waiting I had combed the old passenger lists looking for people whose occupations or profiles suggested might have brought useful books or equipment that their descendants might still have. A couple of the Families had brought private chaplains, but there was no record of the monks aboard the original slowboats. He ignored my interruption.

"And they've survived on handouts from the Families since. All that's left of the Church has. It's been very handy for the Families. Keeping people docile by promising them a pie-in-the-sky Afterlife, and at the same time getting rid of landless younger sons by putting them into skirts."

"That's propaganda, and utterly false! Anyway, there's plenty of land left!"

"Then why do you restrict the sale of it?"

"So there will be someone to work it. Do you want a planet all of landowners starving for lack of labor?"

"That argument might have made sense six hundred years ago. There are such things as machines now! I suppose you spend so little time on your own estates you neither know nor care whether they are worked by robots or peons. You keep the land of a nearly empty world locked up to preserve your own hegemony, and your own rents!"

"Then go to the High Limestone! Go and settle in the badlands! Some people do. Tougher, gutsier people than you, Teutie prole!"

I waited for Grotius to intervene. Then I saw he was asleep at the table. *We'll have to bring back electro-current sleep*, I thought. *Natural sleep is a luxury we may not be able to afford soon.* I was tired myself, I knew, and my thoughts were jumping about ineffectually.

"All right," van Roberts was saying. "So you admit the monastery is in the pocket of the Families."

"I admit some of the Families have been friends of the Church. That's hardly anything to be ashamed of."

"And your monks will say anything they're told to, including corroborating your story of hostile aliens!"

"This is preposterous!" I intervened. "They are trusted friends of mine. I saw the tracks, I saw the destroyed shacks, and found human bones."

"I assume you are telling the truth," said van Roberts, "but what does it prove? People have lied before. The Families may have got rid of the marshmen one way or another. What evidence are bones of anything—bones you didn't even bring back with you for testing? Apart from more *obvious* possibilities, they could have come from a cemetery, or a medical school, or even a plastics factory. Didn't monasteries once keep what they called relics of saints?"

"Why should anyone do such a thing?"

"Because the Nineteen Families are losing power. Bring in a police state, a regime of strict social control, and they can keep power forever. In the meantime everyone is panicking."

"Do you really believe that?"

"The whole tendency of political progress here has been evolution toward a less hierarchical, more representative form of government. This is profoundly regressive. It means increasing coercive authority which means giving the Families further powers."

"Who do you want in authority? The Families and the council on which you sit or cats with six-inch fangs?"

I looked around the faces. The Defense Committee did not want to believe in the—what was the word?—the Kzin. I did not want to believe in them myself. But I had stood in that swamp. My collecting clothes were stained with the mud and blood of the place . . . unless . . . I grabbed my own telephone and shut my house down.

I know the body language of animals professionally. A majority of the members of the Defense Committee were looking at van Roberts as a leader. Not because they all agreed with him politically, far from it. But he was presenting reassurance of a sort.

"We've got our families' futures to think of," said van der Stratt. "I have a little daughter who I want to grow up in a free and peaceful world. Some of you have children too."

Grotius woke up. "I'm sorry," he said. "Too much to do. I've also been reading all the military literature we can find. So many new terms. Everything from electronic battlefield management to caltrops. I really need a whole staff to help me."

"What's Electronic Battlefield Management?" asked van der Trott.

"What's caltrops?" asked Apfel.

"What's a staff?" asked somebody else.

"I don't like the degree of emotion that's getting into all this," said Lufft. "It's an unprecedented situation, certainly, but that doesn't mean we can't make decisions rationally. Let's bear in mind the fact we are twenty-fourth-century Humans, the children of a high science, the star-born, and guided by science and reason. We are not primitives and we shouldn't behave like primitives."

"All battles and all wars are won in the end by infantrymen."

What on Earth (literally what on Earth?) did it mean? It was attributed to someone with the odd and cumbersome name of Field Marshal Viscount Wavell.

Infantrymen? Infant men?

We were in a dusty back room in the warren of the old Mechanics' Institute, which had once served as Munchen's public library. Hermanson had opened it and was rummaging through boxes of old disks. We were lucky to have an almost equally antique computer that could display them. It had been standing under a dome as an exhibit in the entrance hall.

When the first slowboats had set out from Earth to Wunderland they had carried libraries of Earth historical material. Not much military historical material, though. ARM didn't approve of that even at first. We gathered that things had got even tighter by the time the last slowboat left.

Not that anyone had cared much. Some of the first generation had missed Earth, but why study its history when we had our own world, a wonderful, beautiful and exciting world?

We had our own history to make, and life to live on a scale flatlanders could only dream of. The Belters had been humanity's first proud space-born. We, in exalted moments, sometimes called ourselves the Children of the Stars.

Weight and volume had been critical for our migrating ancestors, too, even in craft the size of the slowboats. Practically all books had been reduced to computer disks. Some, over the years, had been lost or corrupted. Some had been reprinted in conventional book form, but these had been largely textbooks of strictly practical matters, of which there were many, or the literary classics. There were books published on Wunderland, certainly—this library and the new and bigger ones were a matter of some pride—but they were *our* books. And after the frontier, pioneering days, librarianship had largely had to be rediscovered.

General Earth history—unlike the histories of agriculture, ecology, oceanography, physics or computing—had become largely a matter of oldsters' tales, a unit in junior high school. As a university course it had never been popular and soon faded away—it was obviously useless, and most of us had enough scraps of family traditions to think we knew it anyway. Even oldsters who found themselves homesick for Earth had done themselves no favors by brooding over it.

Now we were looking at scraps. And many of them seemed to make no sense. Scraps like "infantry" and related words. Infants? There was something that seemed like a sort of song:

He'll attack in the face of murderous fire
On flat sand or through craters of mud.
He'll smash through the lines, over wire and mines
On the point of his bayonet is blood.

If you meet him untidy, begrimed and fatigued,
Don't indulge in unwarranted mirth.
For the brave infanteer deserves more than your sneer,
He is truly the salt of the Earth.

It was English. We all knew English. It was one of Wunderland's main official tongues, but this was also like a foreign language. Wire and mines? Mines? What had mines to do with military matters? There were plenty of mines on Wunderland: the more modern used biologically engineered worms to digest and process rare minerals. "Infanteer" again? Or this: "The niche-warriors of the future will wage information-intensive warfare." That seemed to be saying something. If only we knew exactly what. And this, that had come up under "weapons":

Whatever happens, we have got
The Maxim Gun, and they have not.

We had all been tired when we arrived, and this seemed utterly futile. "Let's see what's in the archives, under 'Military Science,'" von Diderachs had said, almost light-heartedly. Now half a dozen of us were staring disconsolately at a few boxes of rubbish and fragments. I had been scheduled to fly down to Castledare to address the Rotary Club, and though someone said unkindly that Rotary lunches had not changed in four hundred years and four and a half light-years, I wished that was where I was.

"Here is a fragment from someone called Gerald Kersh, from a book, *They Died with their Boots Clean*, published about . . . 1942. Listen:

"We came of the period between 1904 and 1922 . . . Those of us not old enough to remember the war-weariness of the century in its 'teens, are children of the reaction of the 1920s, when 'No More War' was the war-cry. . . . If only our own propagandists took a little of the blood and thunder that the peace propagandists so effectively used to move us!

"From page after laid-out page, the horrors of war gibbered at us . . . stripped men, dead in attitudes of horrible abandon . . . people (were they men or women?) spoiled like fruit, indescribably torn up . . . shattered walls that had enclosed homes, homes like ours, homes of men, men like us . . . cathedrals shattered; the loving work of generations of craftsmen demolished like slum tenements . . . children starving, nothing left of them but bloated bellies and staring eyes . . . trenches full of dead heroes rotting to high heaven . . . long files of men with bandaged eyes, hand-on-shoulder like convicts, blind with gas . . . civilians cursing God and dying in the muck-heaps of blasted towns . . .

"Oh yes. We saw all the pictures and heard all the gruesome stories, which we knew were true. We were the rich culture-ground of the peace-propaganda that said: 'If war was like this then, what will it be like next time, with all the sharpened wits of the death-chemists working on new poison gas and explosives, and the greatest engineers of all time devoting themselves to aeroplanes that can come screaming down like bats out of Hell?

"When we heard that first siren on the Sunday
of the declaration of war, things like damp spiders
ran up and down our backs. . . ."

He paused and drew breath.
"Damp spiders . . . I'm not surprised."
"It goes on:

"And then . . . we went out and begged . . . Men of
60, who had seen the things at the pictures of which we
had lost our breakfasts, and who had spent twenty years
saying: 'never again!' declared on oath that they were 40
and beseeched the authorities to give them rifles. . . .
Because it couldn't take us all at once, we cursed the
War Office."

"It seems there is a good deal about our ancestors we didn't
know."
"Blind with gas . . . blind with gas . . . I wonder how that
would work."
"On them or us?"
Up came something headed "strategical matrices"—rows of
outdated mathematical notations. "Axis of advance"? "Maginot
Line"? "Cones of fire"? Was that something like a Bunsen
burner? And what did they want it *for*?
Among the scraps the search of "war" had found us was
another piece, of no immediate value, but which I would
remember much later:

In one Japanese prisoner-of-war camp in World War
II a prisoner was caught stealing supplies from the Japanese guards. Other prisoners had been brutally beaten or
tortured to death for the most petty infractions of discipline
or for slow work, and hundreds were dying of starvation
and other ill-treatment. The Japanese authorities, however,
decided to make a real example of this man: The punishment they devised was so hideous that even the ordinary
Japanese guards were sickened and ashamed by it, and went
out of their way to give the victim extra food and otherwise try to compensate for the atrocity. The punishment that
so horrified them was this: the prisoner was compelled to
wear an armband saying "I am a thief."

Yes, I remembered that later.
"I'm worried," said Peter Brennan. He too had been perusing

old texts, trying to sort fact from fiction and put it all into some sort of coherent order. "Listen to this: ' "See what you have done!" cried the King, "Cost us a proven warrior on the eve of battle." ' "

"Why does that worry you?" I asked. It seemed an odd thing to arouse his concern among so much else.

"Because . . . because when I read those words, I realized I would like someone to refer to me as a 'proven warrior.' I don't know why. I'm very uncomfortable about it."

"Don't worry," said von Diderachs, "the occasion is hardly likely to arise."

I looked again at one of the first things I had collected:

> *Pale Ebenezer thought it wrong to fight.*
> *But roaring Bill, who killed him, thought it right.*

I had been too late shutting the house down: The cleaner had got to my clothes, but there was some mud from our shoes on the floor of the car. None of the police forensic laboratories had people available, but I had my own laboratory at the Institute.

Analysis produced DNA fragments: mine and Dimity's, other human DNA that might have come from the island or from previous passengers, a mess of countless Wunderland microbes, nucleic acid fragments and other microscopic biological debris, and a single hair, origin unknown, of an orange color. I had Dimity coopted onto the Defense Committee.

We would be moving into permanent session, I was told. Apparently it had been decided that Defense was a full-time job.

I was advised to get my senior graduate students to take over my basic teaching. The best of them wouldn't like that, I thought. They had research projects of their own. Or perhaps the best researchers were those who loved teaching too.

I was told to tell them it was the first step to tenure. And, anyway, it was an emergency. I called Leonie Hansen first. It is a dreadful failing for an academic to have favorites, but one can't help picking out the brightest. I told myself my good opinion of her was entirely due to the quality of her work, and not at all because she reminded me a little of Dimity.

Chapter 6

*It is useless for the sheep to pass resolutions
in favour of vegetarianism . . .*
　　　　　　　　　　　　　—R. W. Inge

"I've worked out what a general staff is. That's another spoke of the wheel reinvented."

"I've found a table of military ranks. I guess we should make our police chiefs and so forth generals."

"No!" said van Roberts, "It's easy enough to see what's happening: destroy every bit of Constitutional law and reform that has been achieved here and install a military or military-industrial dictatorship under the Nineteen Families worse than anything in the first settlement days! For what? An alleged signal from Sol and perhaps an alleged sighting of something by people who are virtually employees of the Families! Flap your ears all you want, but that's what it adds up to!"

"Rubbish! Irresponsible rubbish!"

"Is it?" That was Gretchen Kleinvogel. "We know the Nineteen Families like to think of themselves as the bearers of traditions. What greater ally and reinforcement of tradition is there than militarism?"

"What do you want next, flags and trumpets and regiments?" Van Roberts took this up. "We came to this world to make a new start, remember!"

"The Families formed the consortium that paid for the ships. You came courtesy of us!"

"As your hereditary underlings, so you thought!"

"No one compelled you!"

"The Families and their attached clans make up about eight

percent of this planet's population. They have half the places on these committees. Is that democracy or a naked powerplay?"

"It's not a question of democracy."

"No, it never is, is it?"

"It's a question of leadership, and necessity."

"And of raising taxes! This proposal to lift lasers onto our moons! Have you any idea what that will cost!"

"The Serpent Swarmers are already installing lasers on their asteroids. We should do the same!"

"If they are doing it, why should we need to? *They* don't have to haul them out of a gravity well. It's just duplication of effort. Unless, of course, it's your ships that are contracted to do it, your factories that are contracted to build them. . . . I suppose you'll say the *emergency* means we have to bypass normal government tendering processes."

"In any case, it's a fait accompli. The ships are gone."

"There are too many tanj faits accompli. Again and again we hear something has already been done before we're told!"

"Personally, I'm not too happy about the Swarmers having any assets we lack."

It went on. But a few wheels seemed to be turning now.

"We've got the strakkaker factory back in production."

"And are we building more strakkaker factories?"

It broke up at last. The various factions on the committee departed separately, several barely on speaking terms with one another. I thought again that a sleep machine would be useful. I had not foreseen how quickly production priorities would change. A whole range of technical and electronic goods had disappeared from the shops.

I was buzzed. It was Leonie Hansen. A dozen others were standing around her. All my graduate students had been working on the orange hair.

"When we took it apart, its cell structure was radically unlike any Earth or Wunderland form," she said. "Nor does it match anything we have from Jinx, Plateau or the other new colonies."

"So what do you think?"

"It looks as if the Grossgeister felinoid may have been some sort of scout. It would be better for us all if I'm wrong," she said. Excitement and exhilaration sparkled in her eyes.

A rosette of light began to blink at the corner of the screen, a signal that someone with a Defense Committee comlink was trying to reach me. I thanked the students and told them to organize a report for the next day.

It was van Roberts and Gretchen Kleinvogel, calling from the lobby, asking to see me at once.

I was not identified with any traditional political faction. What little Herrenmann blood I had would never give me privileges or an estate, but my academic position gave me a place more or less outside the system, not Herrenmann, not Prolevolk, not even middle-class in any conventional sense of that much-misused word. Of Teutie background but speaking Tommie and in love, even if hopelessly, with a Tommie too, if it came to that.

Mainly, I had the good fortune that, unlike many on Wunderland, class position did not need to interest me. This wasn't due to lack of snobbishness, simply to my own circumstances. I was comfortably paid, I had absorbing work, and few personal grounds to either resent the system or become involved in it. The one thing wrong with my life it couldn't change. I had watched the political conflict with a good deal of detachment until recently my position as a witness for the reality of the aliens had aligned me with the Herrenmanner.

"We're facing a big challenge," said van Roberts. "Also, it's probably the biggest single opportunity we'll ever have."

"I don't understand."

"These creatures are intelligent, we can agree."

"Yes."

"And scientifically in advance of us. We've got various technologies for air and space flight that are good enough, but we've got nowhere with gravity control. Electromagnetic ground-effect technology is a dead-end that way: It only works on small masses close to the surface."

"So?"

"Creatures technologically advanced should also be politically advanced. They won't have any sympathy for the sort of neo-feudal society we have here. Obviously the entire structure of governance in Wunderland has got to change, and, if approached rightly, they could be allies in that change."

"I saw old Harry Bangate in the swamp after one of them had eaten him! A couple of bones and pools of blood! I still dream about it."

"Didn't you also say you also found his gun? And that it had been fired? Perhaps the creature was acting in self-defense. Also, your monk friends said it didn't attack them when it had a chance. That sounds like reasonable behavior to me."

"Except that as far as we can tell all the other marshmen's cabins had been cleaned out as well."

"And all marshmen are hunters. They carry guns and live by them. If these aliens *look* ferocious, *look* like large predatory animals, then the marshmen would have attacked. I'm not saying I blame the marshmen—I wasn't there—but isn't that a fact? Perhaps the aliens just defended themselves."

I supposed it was. There *were* dangerous creatures on Wunderland, and no question, yet, of endangered species. The humans living beyond the well-settled areas had no compunction about being quick on the draw as far as animals were concerned (more than once I had regretted it, finding an unusual specimen blasted into bits). Could these aliens—if everything hung together and there truly *were* aliens—be, if not like us, still motivated by something no more malevolent than scientific curiosity, and have been attacked?

I sat and thought. Van Roberts had a point. Indeed a better one than he realized: surely a spacefaring culture *had* to be both cooperative and scientific. Interstellar flight was not for primitives or for what had once been called savages.

Eating bodies? A different culture. It had taken humans a long time to understand the values of cetaceans who were relatively close kin. Dolphins could be savage and ruthless enough, and while their values and ethics were very real to them, studying and understanding them was the work of human lifetimes.

And it didn't, after all, hurt the dead to be eaten. Perhaps it was even some sort of compliment. I had read very recently of the Gallipoli campaign in the early twentieth century. The British and Australians had buried the dead, the Turks had left their bones to bleach on the ground which they had died to defend. Each side in a different way, the author said, was trying to honor them. Honor? It was an odd concept I had never got the hang of, except that it seemed to mean doing the right thing when things were difficult. But there was something more there.

And there had been another old classic author, the great Geoffrey Household himself, who had written that being eaten might be considered "the last offer of hospitality to a fellow hunter." After all, we were dealing with *aliens*. Maybe they *had* killed reluctantly, in self-defense, and eaten the dead to honor them. Maybe—for we had not lingered to investigate the sites thoroughly—those had not been pieces of human bone we had seen, or so I tried to tell myself briefly. But no, I was a professor of biology and knew a human femur when I saw one.

The creatures *looked* terrifying. So said the monks and the crew of the *Angel's Pencil*. Well, so did gorillas. And very nearly too late to save the last of the species, gorillas were found to be gentle, intelligent vegetarians, handicapped by lacking a voicebox. Right at the dawn of archaeology the shambling, bestial Neanderthals were found to have been altruistic, caring for grossly deformed and helpless individuals until they died at advanced ages, sometimes burying their dead poignantly with flowers.

Even carnivores that were bywords for savagery in Earth folklore, like wolves and killer whales, were found by scientific investigation to kill no more than they needed. Further, throughout nature on both planets some harmless creatures had evolved a threatening appearance as protection. And sometimes it worked the other way: our poison-fanged Beam's beast looked like a cuddly toy.

They had tried to cook the crew of the *Angel's Pencil* with some kind of heat induction ray. A tragically mistaken attempt to communicate? No alien had survived to explain. There had been Belters in the *Pencil*. Sol Belters, like our own Serpent Swarmers, were regarded by flatlanders as paranoid.

I remembered an old lit. course story, a "sequel" by another author to H. G. Wells's late-nineteenth-century classic *The Time Machine*, which revealed that the horrible, cannibalistic Morlocks had in fact been benevolent scientists trying to communicate with the panic-stricken and homicidal time-traveler. And Wells himself had written of 1914: "Nothing could have been more obvious to the people of the early twentieth century than the rapidity with which war was becoming impossible." War and science did not go together, and, we were told, never had—until we started reading those old fragments.

Appearances were against the felinoids, but . . . surely when humanity established its first interstellar colony it had brought with it some wisdom and experience, some humble recognition of past wrongs to other species and some sense of responsibility to the future? And I remembered that automatic gun twisted into scrap, and human bone in a puddle of blood.

"So what exactly are you saying?" I asked.

"These creatures could be allies in advancing democracy here. We should be communicating with them. Instead of which we are turning out panic-measure weapons. All right, let us say we know they react violently to provocation. Surely, Professor, you can see we may be standing on the edge of either a great hope for this planet or a terrible disaster—perhaps for two species. Civilization is a reality. You're a biologist. You know the mechanics of natural selection. Capabilities don't evolve in excess of needs. How could a carnivorous felinoid get enough brain for space travel? That's not how evolution works."

That was a point, certainly. But there was an answer to it:

"How could an omnivorous savanna-dwelling ape get enough brain for space travel? That's surely equally impossible."

I felt vibration through the floor. Another big ship taking off. They were lifting heavy material. From my window I could see construction crews at work on hilltops beyond the city, erecting new launching lasers built from old plans. We were moving now, and by all accounts the Belters of the Serpent Swarm were moving faster.

"The unions are behaving very shortsightedly," he went on, "A lot of their leadership sees the rearmament program simply in terms of more labor demand and more wages and so are supporting it. I think they're in for a rude shock. Do you know what a bayonet is?"

"I do now."

"It was described centuries ago as an instrument with a worker at each end. Even capitalists like Diderachs and the Herrenmanner should see the point: money spent on production repays itself and perhaps more; Money spent on armaments may give employment but in the long run it's wasted."

"It's a lot to think about," I said. I wasn't lying. The cetaceans that mankind had once hunted and experimented upon and drowned wholesale in driftnets were now trading partners and friends. There were pods of dolphins breeding in one of our smaller enclosed seas, arrivals on the last and biggest slowboat, waiting till their numbers and the numbers of Earth fish grew and they took possession of Wunderland's oceans.

"Think fast. We may not have much time."

I knew I wasn't going to get much sleep again that night. Pills, I knew by too much recent experience, would only make me groggy the next day, and the doc wouldn't dispense anything stronger without better reasons than I could give it. I called Dimity after a few hours, using a selector so I would not wake her if she was asleep. She wasn't.

I told her my major concern and hope: that a spacefaring race had to be peaceful. This was not a matter entirely of wishful thinking but also of the logic of technology and education. Cooperation and peace were needed to create cultures that could support the knowledge industries—the stable governments, the institutes and universities, the individual dreamers and inventors, and the workshops and factories, as well as the surplus of wealth—that made space flight eventually possible.

"Have you heard of the Chatham Islands on Earth?" she asked.

"Vaguely."

"In the Pacific, off New Zealand. Very late in pre-space-flight history, in the nineteenth century, a shipload of Maoris got there and ate the inhabitants. The old Maori war canoes had never gone that way, so the islanders had been left in peace. But these Maoris stole a European sailing ship and its charts."

"I see. Stolen technology."

"Think of the ancient Roman Empire. Or the ancient Chinese."

"I don't know much about them."

"Very low tech, but in their way great achievements. They were built up, one way or another, in periods of relative peace and order. Then savage barbarians came: but they didn't destroy them, they took them over.

"Indeed the Romans themselves seem to have been primitives who took over the heritages of the Greeks and Etruscans, so that you suddenly had a warrior culture, disciplined and armed and organized at a level far beyond anything it could have achieved on its own.

"Human history is full of such cases if you look: technology taken from somewhere else. The point is, human culture or civilization and technology have often been out of step. For all we know, this may be the same thing, on a bigger scale."

"For all we know . . . We have so little evidence of anything." I repeated van Roberts's words: "Civilization is a reality."

"We wouldn't be the first . . . Egyptians, Babylonians, Greeks, Romans . . . They all had civilization as a reality. Where are they now? I'm only saying it's a possibility that these creatures are out of whack too. I wonder how the Chatham Islanders felt when they saw the clipper ship. But that's something we'll never know."

"I hope you're right about that last bit."

Chapter 7

It's reasoning that ruins people at the critical hours of their history.

—Pierre Daninos

"You know, Professor," said Kristin von Diderachs, "there's an aspect of all this we haven't fully considered. These aliens may be an opportunity as well as a threat."

"*You've* no doubt they are real?" I had been doing another broadcast for the Defense Council. The contents of the script I had been given were reassuring and optimistic, but I was tired and did not feel reassured.

"No. Whatever van Roberts and his merry band of cranks and radicals may say, we didn't fake those transmissions or anything else. And between you and me, I understand things are happening in space already. But even setting that aside, surely you can see that we are treating them as a genuine warning. What else have we all been sweating over? Do they think *we* want a high-tax regime?"

"Possibly. If it keeps *them* down."

"Nonsense. We pay more tax than they do. And how can it help us to increase popular discontent? Have you any idea what the costs have been already?"

"I think I've got some idea."

"I doubt it. Practically every aspect of industrial production has been disrupted. War production helps create an illusion of prosperity but in the long run it's money thrown away. We are treating these aliens as potential enemies because it's the sensible thing to do. But there's a chance they are not enemies. We should meet them—as far out in space as we can travel—and negotiate. I know there are people in Sol System thinking along the same lines. They've sent us accounts of negotiating games they've set up."

"How useful are they?"

"They are putting a lot of thought into them. Think what the cats could teach us!"

"Oddly enough, I have been thinking a bit along those lines. So have some other people."

"That could be hopeful. They could be a big positive influence for order and stability. And order is what we need at the moment. Human occupation of this planet is still vulnerable."

"I'm well aware of it."

"This could give us a chance to work together."

"You mean that in times of crisis people turn to the certain things?"

"Well, yes, partly that. But what I really meant was that . . . these outsiders could be allies."

"I don't see . . ."

"You don't build spaceships without cooperation. That means you don't build them without respect for ideals of order and discipline. Somebody has to give the orders. I've studied Earth history. Would the Greek democracies have got into space? No, they spent all their time squabbling among each other until the Romans took them over and organized them. Remember Shakespeare: 'Take but degree away, untune that string, /And, hark, what discord follows!' That's a universal truth. If they have space travel they have a scientific civilization, and that means a class-based civilization."

"I certainly hadn't seen it that way before."

"The defense preparations are obviously necessary, but for more reasons than one. The Prolevolk leaders aren't all wrong in their appreciation of the situation. Things are starting to break up here. They've got to be set to rights. I'm telling you this so you'll know who to side with when the time comes—if it comes.

"I've studied and thought about history. When the ancient explorers on Earth discovered a new country, it was the people in control they naturally allied with. When Europeans reached the Pacific islands it was the local kings they went to. If the Polynesian kings played their cards sensibly, they could do all right. I've been studying the records. The kingship of Tonga goes on today; there is still a Maori aristocracy and a restored monarchy of an old line. We could learn from their experience, and last longer, perhaps become stronger than ever. If we handle these newcomers properly and have them for friends."

"They kill people. I've seen the bones."

"Possibly there have been unfortunate incidents. Tragic incidents. After all, if the creature allegedly seen near the monastery was the same species as were on the *Angel's Pencil*, they may have reason to approach us warily. The behavior of the *Angel's Pencil* has rather committed us to a certain situation."

"Yes, I suppose so."

"And after all, can we know what *really* happened? Who attacked first? They have to be something like us . . . don't they?"

"I don't know." It was an argument that had been going on in my own head ceaselessly. Reason said yes, something else said no. I brushed him off and got into my car.

Six weeks had passed. The most obvious change had been the number of ships taking off from the Munchen spaceport around the clock and the number that seemed to land by night. But there were other changes too. We seemed to know as little about keeping security as we did about anything else military. Everybody knew. But there was a strange taboo about speaking of it.

There were new looks on the faces in the Munchen streets, everything from excitement to haunted terror. There were people who walked differently, and people who looked at the sky. There were a couple of ground-traffic snarls, and no one seemed to be attending to them. The Muncheners stuck to some old-fashioned ways, including one or two cops on foot with the crowds. Not this evening, though. The police seemed to be somewhere else.

There were also, I noticed, people lining up at certain shops. Food shops mainly, but sporting goods, hardware, camping, car parts and others as well. I had not seen that before except at the Christmas–New Year's sales.

That reminded me of something else, and I took a detour past St. Joachim's Cathedral. Its imposing main doors were normally shut except when Christmas and Easter produced more than a handful of worshipers. Its day-to-day congregation, such as it was, went in and out through a small side door. Now the main doors were open, and there seemed to be a number of people going up the steps.

There were also some new street stalls set up near the cathedral, and they seemed to be drawing a crowd, too. I stopped to investigate, and found they were peddling lucky charms, amulets and spells.

"This is the plan for something called a Bofors gun. From the twentieth century. One of the Families boasted an eccentric collector who brought it as a souvenir of Swedish industry. It fires exploding shells, but we have calculated that shells loaded to this formula wouldn't damage even the material of a modern car, let alone what we might expect of enemy armor."

"So?"

"We're building it anyway. At least we have the plans and drawings, and we've modernized it as much as we can. We've strengthened the barrel, breech and other mechanisms and hope they'll take modern propellants without blowing apart. We've rebuilt something from the old plans called a sabot round that may pierce very strong material. We've been able to speed up the loading too, and of course we have better radars and computers for aiming. We'll put modern mining explosive and depleted uranium in the shells and hope for the best."

"It looks slow."

"We're linking it with modern radar and computers and powering up the traverse. For a long time the tendency in war seems to have been more speed with everything. But that comes to a plateau. It may be different in space with decisions being made electronically, but infantry fighting can only get just so fast. Even with every electronic enhancement, it seems human beings—and I hope others—have some sort of limit to the speed with which they can make complicated battlefield decisions. And of course it may be that you're often fighting without electronics.

"Further, your own speed can become a weapon against you: run into something too fast and your speed exacerbates the impact. Also you lose control. That's the theory, anyway. At the moment theory is all we've got. The same collection as gave us the Bofors gun gave us this—it's called a Lewis gun. Not as powerful or as futuristic as it looks, but it's quick and simple to make.

"There's something else called a Gatling gun. We were very puzzled by the descriptions until we realized they referred to two guns with the same name, about 120 years apart."

"The later is likely to be the better."

"Well, we're trying to build the one we've got some drawings of. We're not sure which one it is."

"There's another message from Sol System," said Grotius. He was wearing new clothes now, a gray outfit with an old-fashioned cap and badges at the collar and shoulders. An archaic concept called a "uniform," meant to make hierarchy obvious and facilitate decision-making and enforcement. Several other Defense Committee folk were wearing them too, chiefly Herrenmanner.

"There's been more trouble. Scientific vessels, ferries to the colonies, robot explorers, have just stopped transmitting. There was still no full public announcement on Earth when this message was sent, but of course they've got ARM to organize things. They let us know so we can do what we 'think best.' They've reminded us about the Meteor Guard and its weapons potential, as though we hadn't thought of that for ourselves. Telling *us* doesn't compromise ARM's precious security."

"Decent of them." We "Star-born" had a somewhat patronizing attitude to the flatlanders of Earth—to all Sol Systemers in fact—but I had never heard them spoken of with such bitterness and anger before. "If they'd told us a couple of months ago it might have been useful."

"ARM has useful inventions suppressed long ago that they *could* tell us about. It's like the Roman emperor's reputed last message to Britain as the legions withdrew to defend the Roman heartland: 'The cantons should take steps to defend themselves.' That means: 'Good-bye and good luck!' for those of you who aren't ancient historians."

"We're setting up distribution points to hand out strakkakers, jazzers, ratchet knives and anything else that can be used as a weapon. But the factories can't keep the supply up."

"We've said it again and again: tool up more factories."

"We're trying. There are still so many bottlenecks. All our professionals at this—police, security guards—are being used as instructors. Those that haven't run for the hills. Some have. As for our industrial effort in general—well, we haven't made this public, but more than nine-tenths of our efforts are going to the Meteor Guard forces."

"In what form?"

"I don't know. I don't need to know." Another new phrase. There were a lot of new phrases now. "But from what I gather . . . they are already in action. They have been for a while."

"So when can we field an 'army'?" Like "uniform," that was an ancient word that still sounded odd.

"How good an army do you want? We've got armed people at the main landing field now. We're hoping to get cover for major government buildings, roads, bridges, factories, arms depots and so forth next, and then we think we can begin to start with a field force." The Argyl raised his haggard, sunken face. He had been Tommie-Herrenmann-handsome not long ago. "Meanwhile our General Staff are still trying to speed-read every book they can find that mentions a war. They've worked out why armies were traditionally divided into cavalry, infantry and artillery, and what skirmishers were. Quite a few things like that.

"We're also trying to move assets out of the city. We think that, and the spaceports in particular, will be their first objective."

"We should be getting machines away. We'll need machines to make weapons."

"Do you know how complex a modern factory is? It's not a matter of piling parts in the back of a carrier. And we can't spare any. We need weapons *now*."

"We've seen nothing more," said the abbot.

Things had changed in Munchen. The monastery had changed too. If it had looked a little like a fortress before, it looked more like one now. There were new bars on the main gate, and small gaps in the courtyard walls had been repaired with stone.

The lower parts of the windows had stones piled about them, too, and in the tower I could see watchers, presumably armed. Repair work was still going on, with human workers as well as machines. Another strange, archaic spectacle: It seemed indecent to watch humans at this type of labor. I knew the monks did a lot by hand, but these workers were new to me.

"Possible novices," said the abbot, when I remarked on this. "We've had a burst of applicants recently. We'll see how they like tending a concrete mix for a while."

"It looks very . . . quaint."

"Suddenly new machines aren't available. Anyway," he went on, "we've seen nothing more, either there"—he pointed to the slope of parkland and the swamp beyond—"or there."

He pointed to the sky. Another orange column was rising from the Munchen spaceport. Another ship lifting some cargo to the Serpent Swarmers or the Meteor Guard. I didn't know the details any longer. There were new faces on the Defense Council and I was being sidelined, though I was still being given statements to make for broadcasting. In any event, even for people at my level there had been a blackout of real news for more than a month.

And every night now there seemed to be unusual numbers of meteors, even by Wunderland standards, and other strange lights moving in the sky. No one was quite sure when this had started, but many had remarked upon it.

More importantly, while the Spaceport had never seemed busier, all passenger space traffic to Tiamat and the Serpent Swarm, and all other scientific and commercial flights, had stopped. That had caused a lot of anger, and possible reasons, all of them highly discreditable to one or all factions of the ruling powers, formed a staple of the new industry of streetcorner and public-square oratory.

Security was getting tighter, and political disorders, I had heard, were getting worse. There were rumors of rioting.

"You know what we may be up against?" I asked him.

"I think so, Nils. We're not flatlanders."

"No, we're not flatlanders. We don't live on a tamed world and we're used to dealing with dangerous beasts. Our farmers still have guns. But if we're right, *these* dangerous beasts have gravity control and spaceships that make inertialess turns. They have beams and bomb-missiles. It's rather a different order of things."

"I know."

"Then why bother with this? Strengthening your walls won't hold them off. With the wrong wind, the radiation from one fusion point detonated over Munchen, not even aimed here, could obliterate you."

"If they want to destroy this world, there's not a lot we can do about it. But why should they? And as for the walls, I might say that if they settle for something less than total destruction, we still have our fellow humans to worry about, as always."

"Yes," I said. "That's been brought home to me rather clearly lately."

"Paranoia is not only believing in nonexistent enemies. It's more commonly believing your enemies are more organized and efficient than they actually can be."

"At the moment, I'm wondering who our enemies actually are."

"And wondering what your place in it all is, I suspect."

"Yes. I was put on the Defense Committee when it was formed but I know no more about defense than any of the others."

"But probably no less than any of the others either."

"I don't know that van Roberts and von Diderachs see things quicker or slower than I do. What has a biologist got to do with defense, anyway? Oh, I might think of some weapons to use against an alien enemy—biological weapons, I mean, I've read a little about them lately, but I have precisely one hair to work on."

"I thought you were getting data from Earth."

I hadn't known he knew about that. But I realized he must have many sources of information.

"It's stopped. Or at least, I've had nothing lately."

"Ours, too. Some time back."

So they weren't as determinedly medieval as they let on. That linked up with something else in my subconscious, but I could not pursue it at that moment. It filed itself away somewhere. He went on:

"We're staying, of course. It's human to want to run, but it seems our vows must have meaning after all. When I've spoken of the people of Wunderland as our flock, you know I've meant it more than half in jest—an amusing archaism from the pastoral days when the Church had a more definite mission and when human beings could really be thought of in terms of sheep needing a shepherd. But it's a poor shepherd who deserts his flock and runs when the first real wolf appears."

"A wolf?"

"Know that I've also asked myself: 'What if it's more than a wolf? This might be a tiger.' It might also be a poor shepherd who commits suicide. If that's what staying means."

"And I remember a verse," I told him.

> I was a shepherd to fools,
>   Causelessly bold or afraid.
> They would not abide by my rules.
>   Yet they escaped. For I stayed.

"Who said that?"

"An old poet called Kipling. It was meant as a war epitaph. It was in one of the old books I've been reading lately."

"I've not heard of him."

"ARM didn't like him. He'd just about disappeared from public libraries before the first slowboat lifted. But he was one of the craft, it seems. Our lodge has a small library of its own. . . . Reading! . . . I feel useless. I make my contribution to the committee—try to say something, but when I do I feel it's a waste of time. Too many cooks spoiling the broth. There's nothing special I can contribute. If I were an engineer, I'd be far more use. Speed matters, and I might be able to enhance human reflexes with biological engineering, but the point is academic. To do anything meaningful in that direction would take years and resources I don't have."

"I'll have to say I'm glad of that. The Church doesn't approve of BE, for humans most of all. And yet things seem to be happening. I've never heard so many ships taking off. And there are new factories."

"They are happening with little help from me."

"Think carefully. Act honorably. And pray. That's all I can tell you."

Chapter 8

"Can you destroy your work?" I asked Dimity. I could imagine how any other scientist might have reacted to that question. She took it calmly, a little sadly. She understood the implications before I finished asking it.

"I haven't published yet. I can burn the papers. I can clear the computers' memories. I can't forget it. But it's far from finished. Years. And what I've got is only part of it."

"And we are more years from building such engines?"

"Oh, yes. If we diverted every scientist and engineer we have away from the defense effort, still years before the first proper experiments. And we would need deep-space ships."

"That's what I thought. We'll never get the resources now."

"I know."

"And now I think I know the best thing I can do for Wunderland. We've got to hide you. The caves will do for the time being."

"I'd like to play my part. Do something more active."

"I think we'll be active in good time. Right now, you are frankly too dangerous. I think it's time to go. And there's no one we're directly responsible for."

Dimity was an orphan, thanks to the misprogramming of an air-car's memory for altitude a couple of years previously, and an only child. I was in a similar situation and for the first time in my life I was grateful for it.

We got up. Many shops were shuttered, and one or two burned, the detritus of the previous two nights' riots. There were few people on the streets, apart from the new armored and heavily armed police.

Dimity and I had been the only customers at the Lindenbaum. Stanley, the human waiter who had given it its

71

cachet, waited no more. He and Otto, the proprietor, were doing something that I had also seen at the monastery: filling bags of fabric with sand to build a kind of extra wall. There was something obsessive or mechanical in their movements, and they hardly turned their heads as we left. I thought of the first time Dimity and I had sat here, and the last time, with the flower and the flutterbys. *I won't see our café again*, I thought suddenly. *I'll not see Munchen again. Even tomorrow it will be gone.* It gave me the feeling of a sad dream. Somerthing small and dark flashed along a gutter and out of sight down a drain: one of the native animals turned scavenger which we had previously kept out of the city. I had the car loaded with extra supplies and tools, slung in nets all over it. I had also loaded several extra lift-belts. I had kept it at the university, hidden. Some of those supplies would not have remained there long otherwise.

Munchen already looked different from the air. I saw gardens neglected and dying, uncollected garbage. The rioting had been more serious than we had been told. There were more burned-out buildings. The lawns and trees of the Englischergarten looked dry and dying, and its fountains were gone. Near my own house, water still reflected in the system of ornamental pools, but there too the fountains no longer played. On the streets I saw new, heavy vehicles with the word POLICE on them. But the rioting was not the only thing that had changed the city. For all the infighting, some other things had been done.

Haze drifted from factories thrown up in the last few weeks and put into operation without environmental impact statements or pollution controls. Smoke from heavy, crude rocket boosters hung in clouds. Some lakes and streams were bare brown mud, and I saw garden swimming pools that had been covered over. The householders who had covered their pools tended to have piles of stores in their yards or heaps of raw earth indicating hastily dug shelters.

Once I saw a line of hellish green glare slanting into the sky as a smoke plume drifted across the path of a test-firing laser—at least, I supposed it was test-firing. Heavy power-cables snaked across open ground, some of them superconductors running from hot, crude, hastily built lasers to a Donau that steamed and boiled around them, and there were radio-wave towers whose archaic shapes hinted at the hand and mind of Tesla. On roofs I saw the snouts of the new super-Bofors guns.

Once the city was behind us I flew low to avoid being seen, and not in a straight line.

Eastward there was empty country still fairly close to the city. We flew past the Pergolas Caves, well-known and visited by tourists, past the checkerboard of farms and orchards. The air was clear here, and below us little irrigation ponds and dams, and the fused glass of surface roads, glittered in the sunlight.

There was a brief second of darkness as something passed between our car and the sun. I looked up with a start, but it was only one of the big leather-flappers. There came into my mind another line from H. G. Wells: "Only a rook," he said. "One gets to know that birds have shadows these days." Which of the classics had that come from? Of course! *The War of the Worlds!*

That set my mind running on the old master's work, and its end, so cleverly foreshadowed with subtle clues, in which the invading Martians die of disease germs against which they have developed no immunity. For a moment I wondered if it had not been prophecy, and whether a similar inevitable fate awaited the invaders of our own world. But no. We were invaders here ourselves, and we had flourished and bred and grown. For the universe had been stranger than even the old genius had realized. We knew little of the ancient races that had exterminated one another in space during Earth's pre-Cambrian period, but we knew they had seeded many planets with common microbes and other life from which the more complex forms had eventually arisen. Modern docs could handle any odd exotic bacteria we had encountered.

Wunderland food, both vegetable and animal, was not ideal for us, but we could eat it. So we knew from at least this sample that the life-forms of different planets could eat each other. That brought my thoughts back full circle. "One gets to know that birds have shadows these days." I had swotted up the old classics for my university entrance, had learned passages by heart. As undergraduates we had dramatized *The War of the Worlds* as a play. I had been the artilleryman. What had he said, whose lines had been written before men flew at Kitty Hawk, of the humans faced with interplanetary invasion by technologically superior Aliens?

"That's what we are now—just ants. Only——"
"Yes," I said.
"We're eatable ants."

We sat looking at one another.

"And what will they do with us?" I said.

The first men to reach Earth's moon had gone there unarmed. Even the Slaver-Tnuctipun War, when we discovered traces of it, had not shaken the assumption that space-faring races would be by definition peaceful: It had been too long in the Galactic past to bear any relationship to the universe we knew. But what if Wells had got it right, not that these creatures were savage or barbaric, but that they were so advanced that they simply brushed us aside? I would have laughed at the idea, or rather not given it consideration, a little while ago.

If only Wells had not had such a mind for detail, like the passing reference to the multitude of crows hopping and fighting over the skeletons of the humans the Martians had consumed and left in the abandoned pit!

We passed over the long sprawling lines that marked Manstein's Folly, the remnant walls of a fortress and outworks some of the Families had begun in the early days of settlement as a defense post against alien enemies that did not exist on Wunderland. Recently the Defense Council had voted to complete the works with "hardened" defenses and weapons and install a "garrison" there, but it had not been high on an ever-growing list of competing priorities. Now I saw there were some people there, with machines and vehicles.

The sight was not very reassuring. We flew on to the Drachenholen, the great cave system in the Hohe Kalkstein four hundred kilometers farther east.

I had begun exploring the caves with students years before, one of a number of long-term projects, and the university had kept their location unadvertised. But if I had begun exploring them, the emphasis was on the word "begun." They were not high priority and if they were full of interest for a biologist (one student party claimed to have found footprints of a tripedal creature in one well-concealed cave), so was the rest of the planet.

Thanks to Wunderland's gravity, they dwarfed the Carlsbad Caverns on Earth. And thanks to the many Wunderland lifeforms that flew and brought protein into them, they had far richer ecosystems. In a society without modern chemistry, their vast guano deposits would have made rich mines. As it was, they were mainly mined with deep-radar beams, X-rays and collecting-spoons for fossils and theses.

Cave ecosystems on Earth were among the oldest and, if Man left them alone, the most stable on the planet: caves in

Australia and the Caribbean islands had similar insectile life-forms, apparently unchanged since both had been part of the ancient supercontinent.

The Wunderland cave ecosystems were old too, I knew, and variegated, but the knowledge gleaned from my small scratchings was tiny. There were largish carnivores in there, including the biggest, which we called morlocks, quasi-human-oid in shape. As far as I knew they did not venture onto the surface or far into the twilit zones near the cave mouths, though they had eyes, large, unpleasant eyes. Still, the uni-versity expeditions had been careful. In the twilit zone of the Grossdrache we had established a secure accommodation module along with what should be tamperproof stores of food and other supplies.

We had an outfit of guns in the air-car, personal strakkakers clamped to the doors and a couple of heavier ones mounted on the body. Other things, too: experimental sonics, a bullet projector that was a more powerful version of the monastery's collecting guns, a couple of ratchet knives. All products of the new factories.

The mouth of Grossdrache was partly hidden at the end of a long winding canyon but big enough for us to fly into. I had once thought of putting a gate on it, but decided that it would attract too much attention. Within, it opened into a grand ballroom before dividing and running off into vari-ous darknesses. The module, deep in this ballroom twilight, was camouflaged, partly for aesthetic reasons and partly to hide it from any rather stupid hiker or camper who might pen-etrate this far. I had the doors' combinations but had removed them from the University's computers. A key seemed safer.

The annex module, also camouflaged as a group of large boulders, was big enough to hold the car. I was glad to see a colony of crepuscular-nocturnal batlike creatures (some classicist had called them "mynocks" in tribute to the old *Star Wars* films) had established a colony on the roof of the storage module and among the columns of artificial stalactites that hid some of its fittings. Unlike their fictional namesakes they could do no harm to us or the installation. They rose in a squawking cloud as we landed, but soon they settled again. They were messy crea-tures but excellent protein suppliers for the cave food-chain and had stained the roof and sides of the module with their drop-pings in the most natural manner. There was no reason for an inquisitive human not to think the whole complex a scatter-ing of rocks. Already a drift of guano and dead Mynocks had built up on the ground beside the module, and segmented vermiform things, red and white-banded in our light, were industriously moving this material a link up the chain.

Apart from the chattering mynocks and rustling worms, the cave was still and silent but we kept our weapons ready as we crossed to the accommodation module. The trenches we had dug when collecting fossils were undisturbed.

Everything inside seemed to be in good order. The module had originally been built for space—an asteroid mining project that never went through—with space-standard backup and recycling systems that would have been unnecessary except that they cut out pollution in this delicate ecosystem. When I turned on the main desk I found the kitchen, storage bins, computers, lab tables, bunks, bathroom, and laundry all checked out. It was the best base and hideout I could think of.

"How long do we stay here?" Dimity asked.

"I don't know yet. You stay here until the situation stabilizes."

"I understand. But alone? I'm not sure that I'd like that."

"Not alone yet. But I can't think of a safer place for the moment. There are hundreds of feet of rock on five and a half sides of us, and these walls were designed to be proof against meteors and vacuum. I don't mean we have to live inside here long. This is just the retreat."

"Retreat?"

"An idea I got from the abbot. Somewhere to go when it's a good idea to get away from the world for a while."

We dialed some food.

"What's going on at Munchen?"

We dialed the news channel. Someone was denying there had been further rioting. She looked drawn and nervous, and twice people crossed in front of the studio camera. Then the transmission failed briefly.

"What's going on in space?"

There was nothing coming from Tiamat, the Serpent Swarm, or any of the satellites in low orbit. The other ground-based channels had a recorded chess tournament, a junior-school model of continental drift theory, a singer, a head talking on dolphin legal concepts, an ancient documentary on Beam's first zoological expedition to Castledare, an exhibition of Neue Dresden China, a Rotary-Masonic luncheon. This wasn't ordinary television.

"It looks as if things really are starting to break up," Dimity said. The screen flashed with a lightning logo and an audio alarm blared. We knew what that was. An emergency override announcement, usually for the evacuation of some area threatened by a meteor strike.

Karl van Roberts had been arrested. Police were searching for Gretchen Kleinvogel. Emergency powers were being extended.

I keyed into one of the university's own low-orbit satellites, used mainly for ground surveying. (Its deep radar had helped discover the shallower part of this cave-system.) Munchen was easy to find, and with higher resolution I could see fires burning. So it was on again. This looked worse than before.

I had done the right thing getting Dimity away, I told myself. Then I saw other things. The brilliant, flaring green of lasers firing through a clouded atmosphere. I punched the keyboard frantically, trying to get better focus. The satellite's cameras had unlimited focal length. As the picture shimmered I caught the flash of explosions somewhere off-camera. The transmission stopped, and the screen went utterly blank. It was as if the satellite wasn't there any more.

A local fault? I didn't think so. I fiddled with the keyboard for some time, without result. Then a local alert on the desk flashed and beeped.

I clicked to the modules' own security camera, mounted in the cave roof directly above us, which gave us a view of the whole ballroom.

A cloud of mynocks. A red telltale flashed. Something large moved quickly out of the picture into the darkness of the tunnels. I tracked it with nitesite but it was gone. Replaying the film showed nothing distinct.

"I don't know what it was," I told Dimity. "Something attracted by our movements, I guess. One of the bigger cave animals."

"A predator." A statement, not a question. Cave food-chains have little vegetable matter in them apart from fungus, and few vegetarians, and in any case it is predators that are attracted to movement.

The darkness and walls of rock about us had felt like safety, but I remembered with a creepy feeling in my spine the words of an ancient Earth tale, *Rogue Male*, again by the underground master Household, that I had studied in the Classic Literature course: "Darkness is safety only on condition that all one's enemies are human."

"Whatever it is, it can't get in here. You *did* lock the doors, didn't you?"

"Oh yes."

"If necessary, the car can fly out and shoot it under control from here. I'd rather not have any shooting here, though."

"Nils, what exactly are your plans?"

"Fluid."

"Does that mean nonexistent?"

"Not at all. I suggest we wait hereabouts till the disorders in Munchen are settled. There's nothing useful you or I can do there. Nothing more useful, that is, than keeping you out of danger."

"What about your students?"

"They are all adults. They know as much about the situation as I do. They're younger than me and I guess on average a lot fitter. My job is to teach them biology, not lead them in rioting."

"You think they'll all be safe?" She didn't include any name in particular, and such is the human mind that even there for a second or two I dwelt on the implications of that.

"It's out of my hands."

"Nils, how bad do you think the rioting is? Cameras can lie . . . give false impressions."

"Bad enough for us to sit it out here. You might be a prize for either side—Herrenmanner or Prolevolk."

"And here I'm a prize for you, perhaps?" But she smiled as she said it.

"I'm afraid I'm a little too keyed up to think in those terms." The desk-screen was flicking from one channel to another, the sound muted. There were the Munchen studios, the blank screen where the satellite had been, and the module security camera.

"Rioting isn't all that's going on," Dimity said. "There's something happening in space."

"Our satellite's gone."

"There's been something happening long before that. I've been watching. A lot more ships have taken off over the last few weeks than have landed again. And some of the ships that have landed have been damaged. When did we last hear anything from the Serpent Swarm?"

"I've not heard much at all lately."

"I have. You may have been on the Defense Council but I'm a better hacker than you—or a more unscrupulous one. The messages are in code, but I could work out that we and the Swarm have been losing ships. Lots of ships."

I remembered the fragments of military science and history I had sweated over so uselessly in the preceding months.

"It doesn't make sense. If you mean losing ships to aliens, why put the messages in code? Aliens aren't going to read our language, surely."

"I don't think it's to stop aliens reading them. It's to stop us reading them. Nils, why do you think you were put on the Defense Council?"

"Why not?"

"What was the point? It was all set up in a hurry, sure, and people were given seats on various committees partly to keep everyone who mattered quiet, but you're a biologist! What were your qualifications? Not anything to do with biological warfare; you can't even start that until you know what the enemy is like, and for all we know these aliens, if they exist, use nerve gas for underarm deodorant.

"You were there because you're Mr. Nice Guy. How many news features have there been, over the last ten years, on your expeditions?"

"Lots."

"Exactly. You are a celebrity. More than that, a celebrity who is also a scientist. And you've been given statements to make to the media over the past few weeks."

"Because I'd been on TV often enough before, yes."

"Because you are reassuring. Those statements were handed to you, weren't they?"

"Yes. I know what you're going to say next, Dimity."

"You haven't the least idea of the real situation. You were a handsome talking head, who was not identified with any political faction."

"That's why I've no qualms of conscience about quitting without much notice now. I realized I wasn't doing anything real. Look around you. That's why I'm here. Why you're here."

"Our culture hasn't much experience of this sort of thing, has it?"

"But we've got plenty of experience of politics, it seems. I thought of us as a young, innocent world."

Suddenly, I found myself crying. Dimity took me in her arms and I clung to her until the fit of sobbing and shaking had passed. I did not tell her I was crying a little for my own uselessness and a great deal more for fear for her.

Suddenly there were tiny chimes of music in the air. Dimity had brought a little music box from her collection. Heaven knows how she had thought of it, but those single notes, falling one by one, calmed me.

"You need some sleep," she said. "And you know we're safe. Nothing can reach us here."

I hadn't cried since I was a child. It seemed (or so I hoped) to release stress of whose intensity I had had no idea. I needed her arms round me to get to the bunk. I must have been asleep before she finished undressing me. "Nothing can reach us here" were her last words in my ear.

Chapter 9

Amid a multitude of projects no plan is devised.
                                        —Publius Syrus

Mechanical sounds. The hummings and clickings of an electronic habitat. I woke with the instant rush I have learned to hate. When I am at peace I wake slowly.

I remembered how much I had broken down the night before, remembered Dimity feeding me some sort of pills and liquid during the dark hours. I had not realised how vulnerable to strain I was. There was, of course, an autodoc in the module, and my first temptation was to make for it. But we might need to learn to exist without docs. I unwound Dimity's arm, got up and went to the desk. I dialed myself something to eat and drink. My beard was suddenly angering me and I cut most of it away.

I didn't want to look at the news just yet. I brought in the security camera instead.

I should have stayed with the news. The drift of guano showed big footprints. Not mine, not Dimity's, not human. But I had seen prints like them before.

I already had too much adrenaline in my system. I brought my pulse and breathing under control. Panic would do no good. We knew there were large animals in the deep caves, not only morlocks—I wished now that we had given them another name— which seemed to have rather more intelligence than dogs, but the modules, built of spacecraft hull-metal, were more than strong enough to keep them or any known Wunderland animal out.

Any known *Wunderland* animal, I thought, remembering the wrecked defenses of the marshmen's camps.

81

Would the aliens seek out a place like this? I didn't know how they thought. The behavior of terrestrial felines and Wunderland tigripards gave us two samples of felinoid behavior, investigating holes and caves, stalking before leaping, but these were allegedly felinoids with weapons . . . weapons that could burn through the hulls of spaceships or these walls around us.

I felt Dimity's hand on my shoulder. She too was looking at the footprints on the screen. One of the troubles with Dimity was that she could so often tell what I was thinking before I said it.

"Do we take the chance it's just a morlock?" I knew it wasn't.

"I don't think we can. And if it's not a morlock . . ."

"It could be back any time. We can't just wait for it."

Now that we were looking for them, it was possible to make out more of the footprints on the cave floor. They could be tracked into the deeper passages, but the drier blowing dust near the entrance showed nothing. We followed them to the limit of the camera's range. Then we tooled up with lights and weapons, and took a couple of fight-or-flight pills. Not generally legal, but I had permission to keep them for hazardous expeditions.

We didn't like locator implants as a rule—too much like the sorts of thing Flatlanders went in for—but I had insisted on them for all cave-exploring students and so of course had had to accept one myself. It was in my left arm and about half the size of a grain of rice—no trouble. There wasn't much point in it when there was no potential rescue party anyway, but I made sure the desk was keyed into it in case Dimity and I somehow separated and she got back without me. It showed where I was anywhere on Wunderland.

We left a beacon blinking and beeping on the module, and with electronic locators the danger of getting lost was at least minimal. I was not planning for us to be in the caves long, but I also took some concentrated ration packs, largely from force of habit.

Lower gravity than Earth's meant huge ballroom chambers could form with fewer roof collapses. There were taller, sharper stalagmites, broader stalactites, and shawls, heligtites and fields of flow-stone more luxuriant than any terrestrial cave could show, vast majestic frozen waterfalls frosted with crystal, glittering, mineral-colored wings and curtains and flowers of stone. Limestone-dissolving streams flowed more slowly than on Earth and in less straight lines, with more complex intertwining labyrinths resulting. Bigger caves also meant more and bigger cave animals.

Crystalline surfaces flashed in the light. Insectoids and other small creatures were swift shadows. We turned a bend, and the pulse of the beacon and the faint glow of the twilight zone disappeared. Oddly, I felt far less frightened than I had in the module the night before, and I was still scientist enough to notice the fact. Something to do with an ancient hunting reflex, I suppose.

We had artificial aids but we waited for our pupils to dilate naturally, then splashed through a cold stream, bubbling to a waterfall. We were still in the area of my previous expeditions. There was another ballroom, and several branching tunnels. We had erected a signpost there once, and a small depot with beacons and locators to help the lost. There was little left of it. Morlocks might have broken into the food stores, but electronics should not interest them. They could be all too cunning and intelligent for animals, but as far as we knew they had no real sapience in anything like the human sense.

We saw in our lights a human skull and bones on the cave floor at one point, not recent and all much gnawed and broken, possibly the property of some fool who had ignored the first rule of caving and gone in alone. I knew I had never lost a student, but . . .

There was a story to be written on humanity's relationship with great caves, I thought. On Earth in classical times and later they were thought to be the abodes of trolls and other monsters, yet tens of thousands of years before that our Cro-Magnon ancestors had penetrated them miles beyond the reach of daylight to create art galleries. Had something happened on Earth, deep below the light of day about 30,000 B.C. that had changed man's relationship with the underworld? Mankind could hardly have guessed then that one day it would find real trolls underground, in caves under another star.

Another star . . . and that reminded me why we were here, and that morlocks were very much not the only things we had to fear.

I thought of Geoffrey Household again, and wished I did not remember so clearly his words about another man in another cave: "He liked to have space and plenty of light around him and was continually turning round in case the unknown was following him. It was."

Onward and downward. A long curving passage, through glades of glittering flowstone and rows of stone shawls, stone spears, trumpets, swords, flowers, and fans. There was an

unmistakable stink. Our light showed a jumble of jagged holes
with piles of bones and rubbish. A morlock "town." We began
to back away as quietly as we could, but nothing seemed to
be moving.

Dimity grabbed my arm and pointed. There were eyes in the
torchlight, close to the ground, staring, unblinking, unmoving.
I spread the beam to flood.

A dead morlock. Very recently dead. And largely eaten.
Looking farther, I saw bits of others, all very dead and scattered. So something had destroyed a community of the biggest and most intelligent carnivores that we knew of in the
cave-system. And the morlocks themselves, like their fictional
namesakes, could be dangerous enough for two humans.

We already had our weapons on full cock. *I've been really
smart bringing Dimity here,* I thought. *Well done, Professor
Rykermann! Straight into the dragon's lair!*

Get on or get out? Whatever was hunting here hunted by
smell and sound. It would be silent, and if it was anywhere
nearby it would be well aware of us.

The torchlight shone upon it could be a blinding weapon.
A literally blinding weapon, I realized, for it had laser options.

"Back away," said Dimity. "Back away toward the entrance.
We can watch each other's backs."

"Yes," I said. I had never realized how slow a process
backing away would be. Through the stony glades, with
their myriad darknesses. There was the stream, the noise
of the fall. Then there was another smell, a peculiar,
gingerlike smell.

Eyes. Not morlock eyes. Much higher off the ground, two
pairs, and the eyes of each pair farther apart. There was a
snarling scream that hurt my ears and pale bodies moving.
Had I not been keyed up for fight-or-flight, that scream would
have paralyzed me.

Our strakkakers whirred. One mass fell, another came at
me, hit. I jumped back, rolling under it, still firing, and it
went over the fall with an indescribable cry.

Not dead. I heard it shrieking. I headed toward the fall ready
to fire again, but it fired first. A bolt of colored light smashed
into the cave roof, sending a shower of stone and crystal
crashing down after it with a lot going down the fall. The
screaming stopped. The creature must have buried itself.

There seemed to have been only two. I bent to examine
the fallen creature. The strakkaker had left plenty of it. It was
much bigger than a morlock or a human.

Not a cave dweller. The eyes, or eye sockets, were large

and could be those of a nocturnal hunter, but they were not a cave dweller's eyes. And I knew what it was.

A big catlike thing, tiger-sized and orange, though with a shorter body and longer limbs than a terrestrial tiger. The bare skull, stripped by the strakkaker's needles, showed a braincase bigger than a human's. *Pseudofelis sapiens ferox.*

I had known the theory of what a strakkaker could do, but had not seen the fact demonstrated at close range on a large living creature before. But I was used to dissections. This looked like the surplus material after a ham-fisted undergraduate class had been hacking at something for a week, though even then I thought the bare bones were odd: the ribs, for example, went all the way down, and there were bones that formed struts and braces in a manner that would, I thought, be immensely strong and had no Earth or Wunderland analog. What turned me suddenly sick was an unexpected detail.

It was wearing clothes. A wide belt holding tools and weapons, and a vestlike garment with webbing. That had turned the strakkaker needles and was intact.

"Get the belt," said Dimity as she stood waving her light about the cave.

Maybe with steadier hands and more time I could have done more. As it was, the torso was sufficiently smashed for me to get free the belt, with weapons, a huge handgun and a knife, as well as some packages in the webbing. As I bent above it I saw spots of dark blood appear suddenly on the naked bone and realized it was dripping from my own chest. Four parallel cuts, not deep and only now starting to hurt, but made by claws that had sliced through modern explorer-gear fabric and which would have parted my ribs had they been deeper. Our belts contained basic first-aid packs. Dimity sprayed the cuts with a bandage, disinfectant, anesthetic, nu-skin combination.

"I should take some samples to study," I said. "Tissues, organs . . ."

"I wouldn't worry about that too much," she said. "I think we'll be seeing plenty more of them. If we get out."

"What do you mean?"

She pointed with her light. The rock-fall had not all gone down to bury the alien. Our entrance tunnel was blocked.

"It'll take us hours to clear that," I said. She cocked her head on one side, gazing at the great mass of shattered crystal. We soon saw it would be a huge job to clear it and probably not possible at all.

"It may not be too bad," she said, "There must be other entrances that the aliens use. Otherwise, we'd have seen their transport and they would probably have moved on the modules at once."

That was a less cheerful thought than it might have been, but it was something. She twitched her ears.

"The air's still moving. And you can still hear the stream. And we have the locators."

The locators might be some use. They would tell us where we were in relation to the entrance cave and the modules in the labyrinth, but that was little use if we were cut off from them by tons of rock and they did not tell us what lay between. I did have some memories from previous expeditions. They were unreliable—I had depended on maps and instruments—but all we had now.

We set off, carrying the alien tools and weapons as well as our own. I also carved a few steaks from the carcasses to eke out our rations.

Morlocks tended to travel the caves in packs, and I knew they had a nasty habit of clinging to high stalactites and dropping down on prey from above. However, there seemed to be none around. Unfortunately they were among the least of our worries, and I could guess why they had disappeared.

It is notoriously hard to keep track of time in caves, but when our watches showed several hours had passed, we rested, taking turns to sleep. We dined on pills, soup to nuts in a mouthful. The stream was still flowing somewhere in the background. We should have kept watch, but I knew so little in those days, and we slept.

For years I had thought that to hold Dimity sleeping in my arms, on the edge of sleep myself, would be perfect contentment, which showed how wrong it was possible to be. The idea of sex then would have been a joke—I associated it with calm, relaxation, and good spirits. Sick with fear for both of us, and for what might be happening on the surface, several times I heard sounds far off that were not like the noise of water on stone. I fiddled with the alien weapon, trying various settings without pulling the trigger, and tried not to think about what I might need to use it for.

We pushed on. There was a sort of moss slide which took us, easily enough in that gravity, down a long passage to a ledge above another ballroom cavity filled with tunnels and rock-holes. I flashed a light briefly around it, then doused it quickly and we forced our way back up the slope. The place was another natural morlock "town," and it stank of them.

They were alive this time. Behind us as we climbed I heard morlock barking and scrabbling sounds.

I turned and saw the dim shapes closing upon us. I discovered the alien weapon's trigger needed two pressures, but the first blast from it cut down the first of the morlocks.

The second time I fired at a set of formations in the roof. It dispersed the rest of the Morlocks and more importantly brought down some of the roof behind us in a shower of glittering spears, but anyway we had no inclination to linger. When we paused at the top of the slope, bruised and scraped by sharp and sliding stone, I found I had lost the ration packs.

Two mornings later, by our timepieces, we were hungry enough to try the meat, cooking it with our light. It tasted foul, rank and gamy, but if one did not think about its origins it was possible to choke it down. I remembered C. S. Lewis's *Prince Caspian*, where children had had to eat cold, and as I remembered, raw, bear-meat, and pretending I was one of them helped. Dimity, I think, could use her mind to override her nerves.

But whether it was the meat of the morlock or the alien or both, we were sick and weak the next day.

I tried to count our mercies, and could think of four: there were plenty of pools and streams of clear drinkable water, our lights, unlike those available to cavers of previous days, would last virtually forever (a less cheerful thought: they would still be burning long after we were skeletons), with Dimity's memory and sense of direction we stood little chance of getting any more lost than necessary, and none of the creatures we feared came near us, though several times we found cave insectoids and vermiforms on our bodies. They have much the same position in the caves' ecology as vultures on Earth, and their increasing friendliness was an omen I did not like.

Two days later a swarm of mynocks flew past us. I had a hard time holding the alien weapon steady in my hands by then, but by waving it about I brought a few down in flames. We ate them ready cooked, but they also tasted vile. Time went on. We played Dimity's little music box, and I think that helped keep me sane.

Once, I was sure, I saw in my light a dim, strange creature of some size disappearing rapidly into a dark hole. I glimpsed it only momentarily, but its odd gait reminded me of the story of tripedal footprints. Once it would have excited me. Now I was only concerned that it was neither morlock nor alien and did not seem to either threaten us or provide food. I followed it cautiously but the passage ended in a blank wall of rock, so smooth it could have been artificial. A hallucination, perhaps.

A few days after that we found ourselves back at our starting
place. The dead morlock and the dead alien were still there,
the cave insectoids and vermiforms swarming over them. They
had just about finished the job of baring the Alien's bones
lying in a bed of orange hair. I was thinking a lot about food
by that time, and crushed up a paste of them. We were past
objecting to the taste.

Dimity tried hypnotizing me to see if I could remember any
passages more accurately. No good.

"The air's fresher than it might be," she said at last. "Is
it daylight outside?"

"I think so. Unless our clocks have gone wrong somewhere."
She scrambled up the rockfall. I tried to follow but my chest
and arms were very stiff now.

"I think I can see light!" she called. "There's a way through!"

There had been none before. We had searched thoroughly
the first day. I got to the top of the rockfall with her somehow. Indeed there were now a few distant chinks and shards
of dim light. Perhaps it had settled over time, or perhaps
something had interfered with it.

"We can't move any more now."

"What about the gun? That brought it down originally."

I didn't know how much charge was left, but there seemed
no harm in doing my best with it. I think I would have got
us clear eventually but before I had got very far a jarring
impact shook the cave. I thought at first of earthquake, and
saw myself and Dimity buried under a rockfall. But it was
something else. I got clear, dragging Dimity with me, as the
glittering crystal boulders spilled and settled further. More rocks
fell around us, but there was little we could do about that
except press against the wall. Dust hung in the air a long time,
but when it settled we saw a gap above the rockfall.

"That was an explosion," said Dimity.

"Someone after us."

"No. A long way away."

"It must have been a big one."

"Let's go!"

Chapter 10

"Do you know how many entrances these caves have? This whole system, I mean?"

"Lots. A dozen within a few kilometers. But why haven't they just come barreling in? Why did they hole up in these caves at all?" We were splashing through the stream now, back to whatever temporary safety the modules offered.

"I can think of several reasons, she said. "Watch a kitten with a ball of wool. Cats enjoy stalking until they are ready to leap. They may have found the caves with radar. Maybe their radar is better than ours. Also, they want to spy out the land. Remember the monastery. They don't give themselves away until they're ready. If they are like terrestrial felines, won't silent stalking until the pouncing strike be instinctual? They enjoy lurking, stalking, pouncing. Also, we don't know what's been happening in space. Maybe they *are* barreling in up there."

We were back at the modules, fed and rested. We had slept for the better part of two days, and done nothing for a few days more. But their walls now gave little feeling of security. We would have to flee farther, I thought. But where? Just how do you flee from an alien invasion of your world?

Perhaps one of the city political factions had succeeded in making contact with the aliens. The first-aid foam on my chest had now been hardened for a long time, but I guessed further treatment was needed. I placed my hands in the autodoc and it began to click and blink. Probably, I realised, too late to release my hands, it was putting a sedative into my system. It left me feeling as a sedative would: better but lethargic. I sat down heavily and watched Dimity at the desk as some time passed.

"This is no good," I told her. "I thought this was a refuge. It isn't."

She was flicking across the channels on the desk. Nothing from space at all now, nothing from Munchen but a brief flicker of a talking head mouthing without sound.

"Our lasers could burn through this wall. So could theirs."

"I know."

We had, in a curious way, been happy here in the last few days following our escape from the rockfall: perhaps what the abbot had called a retreat. Irresponsibly or not, I had kept the desk and the television turned off.

"Time to go."

I turned around in the chair. Dimity set the music box—such a tiny, delicate thing!—on the desk, and its crystal little chimes floated into the air. She was standing in front of me. We reached out to each other and came into each other's arms without a word. She nestled into me and I found myself kissing her hair, her throat, her lips.

On the security screen the mynocks rose in a shrieking cloud.

"I think we have company," Dimity said.

"We'll get to the car and fly it straight out."

"Can you manage now?"

"My legs feel a little weak. I can force them."

"Let's go."

I found my hands were shaking.

"You take the keys, for the annex and the car. I might drop them."

"No. Tie them around your neck. I'll need to hold the gun. . . ." She turned the light on the beacon up to flood. There seemed nothing more to do. We opened the door and ran.

I don't recommend running with a system full of medical sedative and an anesthetized chest. I was stumbling like a drunk and thought I would fall at every step. Dimity, holding a strakkaker at the ready and laden with other gear, couldn't help me.

No movement yet but the flying creatures. A horrible fumbling at the annex door, and we were in the car.

We were in the air when we saw it. It came staggering out of the tunnel, bent over one side, one arm and shoulder maimed and shredded. It must have climbed the fall.

It leaped at the car as I pulled the nose up. The claws of its undamaged forelimb scrabbled at the metal, dragging us down, tipping the car. We had not had time or the thought to fasten our seat belts. The car flew lopsidedly for a moment with the creature clinging to it as I wrestled with the controls. Then Dimity fell out.

It had nearly dragged us down by then. We were only two meters above the ground. Freed of Dimity's weight the car rolled up, gyros howling, throwing the creature off. There seemed no sedative in my system now. I wrenched the car around in a tight circle.

Dimity was getting up. She seemed unhurt. The creature was standing on its hind legs. Between Dimity and the circling car it seemed undecided what to do. I dropped the nose of the car and fired the two heavy strakkakers I had mounted on it.

We weren't used to fighting, and certainly not to killing. Whatever this being was, I didn't want it dismantled like the other. I fired into the cave floor in front of it. Then I brought the strakkakers back to bear on its head.

It couldn't have misunderstood. I knew it was fast, but I was also sure that, injured as it was, I would be faster when pulling a trigger was all I had to do. It was "at my mercy" as some old book put it. It took a step backward.

I brought the car toward Dimity, keeping the strakkakers trained on it. She jumped aboard and I gave thanks for Wunderland gravity. The creature seemed to have lost its weapons and equipment. I took the car up to near the cave roof, higher, I was sure, than it could jump in its present condition. It stood staring up at us, with those huge intelligent eyes, and suddenly I realised what I had done.

We had killed—yes, and even eaten—one intelligent alien and maimed another. They had, it was true, snarled and leaped at us in the cave, but . . . that might have been self-defense. It might even have been an attempt to communicate. Many a peaceful, herbivorous gorilla had died on Earth because its chest-beating display warnings to "leave me and my family and our territory alone" had been taken by humans as a signal of attack, and they had shot. As I had.

The dead morlock? But morlocks were aggressive predators. Who had attacked first? But there was something else there too. I thought again of H.G. Wells's Morlocks, the originals, and the fact, intentional or otherwise, that there was no real evidence in his story that they were really hostile. I thought of ancient science-fiction films like *It Came from Outer Space*, in which it had turned out that grotesque and horrifying aliens had only wanted to make repairs and depart, and had attacked only in self-defense. We had shot without trying to negotiate or make peace. This creature, or some creature like it, had not attacked the monks when it came upon them in the night.

Perhaps they now viewed the human race with as much terror as we viewed them, and with better reason. Perhaps these were peaceful creatures that had found themselves on a planet of horror. If so, no wonder they had not shown themselves! What would we have done in their position? It was armed. Well, so were we, and we had used our arms first and lethally. All this went through my head far quicker than I can tell it.

They looked carnivorous. Well, I had once had a cat, a gentle old female who moved in with me and whose main desires had been to be petted, to curl up on my lap, and to share my bed, and had who brought me gifts of food filched from neighbors' barbecues as offerings of affection. She had had pointed teeth, too, and claws and, until age overtook her, had been a terror to balls of wool. I am a scientist and I don't anthropomorphize animals or their emotions, but I remembered how, purring and kneading me in bed, that tiny-brained creature had gone against her own instincts and kept her claws sheathed. She sometimes bit my fingers in play, but took care never to break the skin or draw blood. Carnivores, even such perfect carnivores as cats, need not be cruel. Humans' front teeth were for meat-eating, but we were not . . .

The warnings from Sol? They might mean anything. What had happened light-years away in space might have been an exact parallel to this situation: panicky humans attacking first. We weren't sure what Sol humans were like now. And this creature was in a terrible way, injured and starving—I saw the bones starting through its wasted frame.

It all went through my mind in a few seconds as I circled in the cave, guns trained on the creature. I began to wonder miserably how many laws I might have broken, beginning with the one against murder.

I can't kill it, I thought. *I don't know that it even meant us any harm.*

It would be right, I thought, to land and try to negotiate with the creature, treat its terrible injuries, make amends. But that was impossible. Too much damage had been done.

Whatever its original intentions, it saw me as an enemy now. I had maimed it and killed its companion, or, for all I knew, its mate. It was much darker than the other creature, almost black, though with a white pattern like an old scar on one side, where its stripes did not match, and some part of my professional mind wondered if this was a sexual differentiation. My clothes were still spattered with its companion's blood. And there might be others coming up the cave system.

There was one thing I could do. Round my neck was the belt I had taken from the dead *Pseudofelis*, the "kzin." I had learned little from examining it, but it looked sufficiently like our own equipment for me to guess that it contained utility supplies, including, if there was any parallelism is our species' thinking, medical supplies. I held the belt out and dropped it at the creature's feet.

I had no idea whether or not it could eat our food, but I dropped a package of explorers' rations as well. I raised my hand in a confused gesture of salute, and we headed out of the cave. I felt a deathly misery and guilt as the car shot into the sunlight, like a stake of ice at my heart. "Are you all right? That was a bit of a fall."

"No permanent damage. I know how to fall. But it was no fun being on the ground with violet-eyes."

"What else could I have done?" I burst out.

"We're alive," said Dimity. "We might very easily not be. Those claws were sharp."

Perhaps I had read too much. I thought of the Ancient Mariner and the albatross, and suddenly knew what he meant by "a woeful agony." He had confessed his crime to a holy man and begged forgiveness. In the abbot I had an official holy man for a friend. I was not a Catholic, but would it help me to make confession?

Not far away to the north a vast cloud of black smoke was rising into the sky, an intense red flame at its core. Smaller fires were burning around it. Once before I had seen something similar. It looked as if something had smashed into the mountain range from space. That, I guessed, was what had caused the shock and the rockslide that had freed us from the cave.

I gave thanks as the ground flashed away below us and the scarp of the Hohe Kalkstein, looking ominous and threatening now rather than wild and fascinatingly myserious, dwindled behind.

Briefly I gave thanks. A red warning light blinked on the dashboard fuel gauge. Behind us in the sky was a white cloud. Pierce a liquid hydrogen system and it vaporises fast. I wouldn't be able to keep the car in the air for long.

Chapter 11

Again we had reason to be grateful to Wunderland gravity. Cars have limited gliding qualities. I kept the car flying as long as I could, putting more kilometers between us and the caves. We landed on a low mesa in arid, deserted country. The Hohe Kalkstein and the Drachenhohlen were a blue line on the eastern horizon, the farmlands still far to the west.

The damage was obvious. The kzin's claws had opened the metal at the rear of the car and at one point punctured a hydrogen fuel line. It was a tiny puncture, barely visible, but with liquid hydrogen fuel under high pressure it was enough. I doubted the puncture could be plugged reliably. The line and its fittings would have to be replaced. We had been lucky to get as far as we had. I had loaded the car with all sorts of spares, including, of course, spare fuel cells, and mercifully I had secured them thoroughly. But it would be a long job.

As I looked at the evidence of the power of those claws I realised again how lucky we had been. Suddenly we seemed to be still all too close to the Drachenhohlen. I had loaded a camouflaged biologist's field tent among the stores and we draped this over the car. It didn't cover it entirely but I hoped it might break up the silhouette. I would like to have had us both checked by the car's doc, but was not sure I could trust it after the rough time it had had.

Perhaps it was thinking of that which caused the sedatives still washing round in my system to kick in again just as the flight-or-fright was wearing off. I began to remove the damaged panels but started fumbling and dropping tools. Finally I gave it up and mumbled that I would have to rest again. When sleeping out in Wunderland it is ingrained in us to search out any cuddly little Beam's beasts and other small but dangerous creatures. I just about managed to inspect the neighboring small rocks, and we placed a couple on the car to break up its silhouette a little more.

Our elevation gave us a good view in all directions but also made me feel unpleasantly visible. We crawled under the tent and Dimity covered me with a blanket. When I next woke up it was night. My chest felt as if it was on fire. Even for Wunderland, I thought, there seemed once again to be an unusual number of meteors in the sky. I felt my head wasn't working well, but Dimity, sleeping apparently peacefully beside me, was something to cling to. The western sky was particularly bright. I could hear thunder and see distant lightning flashes.

Meteors *and* lightning storms? Lightning storms in a cloudless sky? Meteors visible in a cloud-covered one? I shook Dimity awake just in time for us to see the familiar rhomboid pattern of one of the bigger low-orbit billboards explode in golden fire.

Were there black shapes passing against the luminous band of the Serpent Swarm? They must be either huge or very low.

A burning thing like a tiny comet fell out of the sky and hit the ground with a fierce explosion a few miles to the north. We heard it and then felt the shock-wave.

The mayday alarm on the car began to howl. An emergency call close by. There was still plenty of battery power for the dashboard display. A spacecraft's escape module was descending almost on top of us. With the dashboard telltale to guide us, I picked up its blinking beacon visually with binoculars.

The sides of the mesa were partly eroded, and it was easy enough to jump down from rock to rock. The module landed as we approached and the hatch opened. We saw the pilot jump from it and run. I started toward him, but Dimity grabbed me.

"Wait," she snapped. "If he's running away from it, don't run towards it."

She dragged me partly behind the cover of a boulder. The pilot was running more or less in our direction, presumably because our car's alarm unit had fed back to him at least a rough position for us.

A dark wedge-shaped thing flashed out of the sky, swooping low. There was no time to make out details. I saw greenish points of fire flashing under stubby wings. The escape module exploded in a fireball. The dark thing was gone. We heard debris falling out of the sky.

Now we hurried to the pilot. He wore the insignia of a member of the Meteor Guard. He looked about as one would expect a crash survivor to look, and, his first energy gone, needed some help to walk.

"That thing will be back!" he croaked. He was breathing with difficulty. "Get under cover fast."

"Can it track our receiver?" asked Dimity.

"I don't think so. Not yet. But if they see us moving in the open we're dead."

Bearing a good deal of his weight and breathing shallowly made it difficult for me to talk as we shuffled back toward the mesa. Dimity asked: "Are they the cats?"

"Yes."

Burning wreckage was scattered over a wide area. As we climbed into the shadows of the mesa, the same black craft or another swooped down and fired another missile into the biggest piece. We were far enough away not to be involved but the explosion threw us flat.

"Heat. Don't give them heat to home in on," he told us. Then he added, "If they're shooting up ground targets like that now, it must be just about over. . . . Well, we gave it our best shot."

He told us to turn off the battery power and all electronics. We laid him in the back of the car under the cover and got his pressure suit off. Space pilots are scrupulously, fanatically clean. This man stank as if he had lived in the suit for days, for weeks. Many spacers are funny colors, often starkly piebald unless they are born black. This one had the space pallor in his face overlaid with dirt, sweat, oil and blood. He looked in terrible shape and again I wanted to use the doc. Again I decided against it. *We're all in bad shape,* I thought. *Munchen hospital will be our next port of call. I wish I had thought to fit a portable shower setup in the car.* I sponged his face with a cleaner and something came off, dirt or protection. I recognised Commander Kleist of the Meteor Guard.

At least I had some explorer's brandy. That and a meal was something we could use. Then he began to talk. He was exhausted, shocked and bruised, but he talked.

"We got notice of Outsiders long before even you were told," he said. "The powers that be on Wunderland didn't tell us too much and the public heard even less. Apparently the idea was that negotiation was a possibility. We were under orders to say nothing."

"You said little enough," I said, "when the first Defense Council meeting was called."

"That was orders. They said there had been some 'unfortunate incident' with Sol ships and if these were the same aliens we would have to approach them carefully and diplomatically.

By the time that first meeting was called the fighting had already been going on for weeks. 'There must be no panic'. . . . That was what they kept saying: 'No panic. But let them see we are aware of the problem and are doing something.' Were our people insane?"

"Inexperienced, anyway," said Dimity.

"We had the meeting you attended, and saw the various committees set up. We know now they'd been landing small parties for some time."

"We know that too."

"Not what we'd been watching for. We thought—I don't know if we knew what we thought, but we had some idea they'd approach us with some sort of *ceremony*. But the overall idea of everybody was that with a little talk they could be friends.

"When something was first detected coming in some thought it might be a new comet. But comets don't maneuver.

"We were excited, of course, and one ship didn't seem to be all that threatening. Some argued that the fact they had sent a single ship was an indication that they were peaceful. Our mass detectors didn't record it as very large, and it never occurred to us that its true size might be cloaked. We took what we thought were precautions. We sent a team of four ships, the anti-meteor lasers ready in case of trouble. I'm alive, so you can see I wasn't with them.

"It was quick. The Outsider ship dropped its cloak. Grew into something huge on the screens, travelling at comet speeds, then with other blips streaming away from it. It was a carrier, full of war craft.

"Our ships didn't last long. The Outsider craft could make turns without losing velocity, where ours had to maneuver with attitude jets. No answers to our signals, no negotiations. That time, none of ours even lasted long enough to get off a shot.

"The only thing that saved the rest of our ships was the distances of space. That and the orbiting laser stations. The outsiders evidently didn't know what those were, and came in range. They had good people on the stations, used to picking off meteors.

"We had fusion-pumped lasers to fire in the paths of meteors, as well as the big cannons. But meteors move in predictable lines. They hit several of that first flight of the Outsider ships before the Outsiders realized what was happening and began jilling around.

"At .8 lightspeed and more, with inertialess turns, they easily evaded any bombs or beams we could throw at them except at short range. The stations went on fighting and got a couple more, but they were all destroyed in a week. Suicide attacks by our ships did no better.

"Then we found at least one sane thing had been done . . . or I suppose it was sane: The Serpent Swarmers had been alerted, and they came in strong. They always said their meteor defenses were faster and better than ours, and they proved it over the next few weeks.

"But the real point was, the Swarmers had ramjets with them, which we'd never use so close to a planet, and they used the ramscoop fields as weapons. They also had a tactic of turning away with really large attitude jets that they had lashed on and using their drive flames like swords. A lot of them were robots—humans couldn't stand the G-forces. They made a sweep too fast for the outsiders to dodge, but it was the ramscoops that saved us.

"We didn't know if the ramscoop fields would affect the Outsiders like other chordates, but they did. The Outsiders had learned not to attack from behind, and seemed to prefer head-on attacks anyway. They'd come barreling in, and until they wised up the Swarmers had a real turkey-shoot. A squadron of Outsider ships that passed through a ramscoop field was suddenly manned by dead Outsiders."—He gave an odd laugh.—"Or inside-out-siders as we called them. Look at one and you'll see why.

"Off Tiamat a Wunderland–Serpent Swarm force boarded one of these dead squadrons. They had no time to find out the principles of their drive, though we know it affects gravity fields. But the Swarmers learned to fly the ships and use their weaponry, and they counterattacked. They destroyed more Outsider ships and even damaged the mother-carrier.

"That bought us time. The mother-carrier hauled off and we had a few weeks' breathing space."

"We didn't know any of this," I told him.

"None of the craft we captured and used survived the attack on the carrier," he went on. "But at least with what we had learned from them we were able to duplicate some of their more esoteric weapons—things like bomb-missiles whose detonation, as well as pumping lasers, could be lethal across a huge globe of space, for example. They have a heat-induction ray but we don't understand it. It's too slow for a military weapon anyway.

"We learned another tactic that cost them a lot of ships: strap big attitude jets on our craft and use them to spin like catherine wheels with the main reaction drives still firing. Not only did it give us better maneuverability, but it turned the reaction drive into a swinging sword even they could hardly dodge. We couldn't do it with manned ships—the inertial forces were too great—but we did it with drone craft. We began to win some more. If we'd had more motors, and more craft, and more resources, and more time . . . but that stopped them for a while.

"We studied their tactics, and an odd thing was, some of their behavior seemed almost as amateurish as ours. More than once they came straight at us, in an undeviating line, when a straight-on attack was the one thing we could meet with a good chance of hitting them. At the Second Battle of Tiamat's Lead Trojan, their big ships came at us in a column. It looked pretty frightening, seeing ship after ship closing with us like that—but what it meant was that we could hardly miss them. It was as if they were unimaginative. Or inexperienced. It didn't make sense."

We sat in silence for a moment. Something that might have been a meteor but probably wasn't streaked by far above. The scattered wreckage of the crashed ship had just about burned itself out.

"It might make sense," said Dimity. "Maybe they *are* inexperienced. At least in dealing with humans . . ." Her face went slack in a way that I had seen before.

"We took it for granted that space-traveling races would be too intelligent and civilized to fight," she said. "Perhaps we were *nearly* right. What if peaceful, civilized space-traveling races are the norm? Or were the norm. There may not be any others left now.

"Given that, the Kzin wouldn't have much experience of war. You need a fighting enemy to teach you to fight. What if when they meet other races they simply devour them. There's no more *fight* than there is between a tigripard and a lamb."

"One of the first human ships out of Sol that they attacked was able to beat them," Kleist said. "It used a com-laser as a weapon. Some of us in the Meteor Guard actually think aspects of our missile technology are as good as theirs or better. It suggests they come from a much cleaner system than this.

"Or sometimes it seemed as if they were not in control of their own minds," he went on. "Sometimes they seemed *undisciplined*. We analysed our own successful tactics, and realized that when we had been, almost unconsciously, *provoking* them to attack, baiting them, they would often leap and take the bait. Our ace pilots had been doing that, it seemed, by instinct. Someone said it was the instinct of the monkey to tease the leopard.

"At other times they would stalk us like cats. A particularly weird thing was that one of the larger enemy command ships had behaved at times as if its crew or something aboard it could actually read our minds. When that ship was destroyed the tactical efficiency of the rest fell off appreciably.

"We salvaged more of their wreckage, and began to study their drive and everything else. We were putting improvements into our ships. Reinforcements were coming from Wunderland and the Swarm. We got more confident.

"There was even talk of finding where they had come from and chasing them—counterattacking. We thought we had a superweapon in the ramscoop.

"Then they came back. If they had been inexperienced, they had learned from experience like us. They'd got more cunning.

"They avoided ramscoops, and seemed to flee from them. That lured us in. Then we found it was a trick. They generated magnetic fields of their own to distort ramscoop fields, or simply dropped things into them.

"We know they had taken human prisoners and perhaps they had learned things from them. Not just in space. When we killed one of their ships and boarded it we found bodies of human civilians from Wunderland.

"Apparently the Outsiders have been landing scouts in small cloaked ships for some time."

"I'm surprised. If they are so aggressive, why didn't they just attack in force?"

"Cats stalk their prey. They study the ground before they pounce. It's after the pounce begins that their control goes. This may be the same thing. Some of the humans they took had kept hidden records, hidden in their cages. Apparently the Kzin didn't care. Why should they? They aren't nice reading.

"Our eggheads are puzzled. These creatures are something out of a nightmare: cruel, man-eating, killing, but with science that is in so many ways ahead of ours. It shouldn't have happened, but it has. I'm told there have been quite a lot of suicides among our eggheads. . . . Oh yes, and from the prisoners' notes we found out why they sometimes behaved as if they could read our minds. They can."

"What!"

"They can. Or a few of them can. Apparently it's rare. But you can tell when they are doing it: a sudden violent headache.

It also explains how they came to know our languages so quickly—which they do."

That hit me like a physical blow, though it took me a few moments to realize why.

"Can it be resisted?" asked Dimity.

"Don't know. The prisoners we know they tried it on were terrorized, injured, starving, tortured already. In no shape to resist. Anyway, that's the war, and it's been going on for weeks. . . . I don't know how long. . . . I think it's nearly over now."

"We've heard nothing of this," I said again. "We've been told nothing."

"What was the point of telling?"

"It might have meant better war production."

"I think so. Others thought it would lead to 'a collapse of civilian morale.' I think it was their own morale that was actually collapsing. They said there was as much material getting up to us as could be reasonably expected."

I remembered my speed-reading of the last few weeks, and the attempted defense of Singapore in the Second World War. As the Japanese advanced down the Malay Peninsula towards it, the defending general had refused to construct field defenses in case they lowered the spirits of the civilians. It had not been a good decision.

"If people knew too much, I gather, it was feared they would simply flee into the hills, or mob the slowboats," he went on. "And then there was that . . . that one brief shining moment . . . when it looked as if we were winning.

"There was another matter too, which we found out late in the day: Some of our politicians minimized the threat because they hoped to enlist the Kzin as allies for their own factions in our internal disputes here."

I wished I could have said I found that unbelievable, but I knew too much.

"Maybe, if we could have duplicated their drive," he went on, "got factories into production, maybe if we had had a few more months, or a year, we could have fought them on equal terms. As it is . . .

"Wunderland is their prime target, of course. Anyway, the Swarm is more difficult to subdue. Dozens of inhabited asteroids, with defenses now. But we haven't much left here. Those drives and weapons are too good for us. And they've got reinforcements too. More of the big carrier ships have arrived."

"They could hardly have been alone," said Dimity. "With

drives like that and what we know about them from Sol. Where there was one ship there would be more coming . . .

"Tell me," she asked him, "Is there any suggestion, any indication, that they may have got through the light-barrier?"

"No. They get close to the speed of light. They can match velocities with any of our ships, and of course they are much more maneuverable."

"Could they have a superluminal drive in outer space and drop into subluminal close to star systems?"

"I don't know. We've not been in a position to observe. There's no evidence of it. Anyway it's impossible. Why do you ask?"

"Nothing."

"I only saw a bit of what was happening. I'm just a meteor jockey. The fighting was spread all over the system."

"You must have learned a bit about these creatures. Language, that sort of thing?"

"A bit." The pilot took a red disk from a pocket. "It's here, what we know. The spoken language is hard to understand, even with a computer, at present impossible to imitate, although some people are trying. The written is a little easier, at least when it's not in war code. It's another of those things we might have got better at with time."

"Can I play it?"

He shrugged and passed it to her. "I don't see why not. But what do you intend to do now?"

"Repair the car as soon as I can," I said.

"You can't show a light or heat source. They're still around up there."

"Well, we can't trek very far on foot, and we can't stay here. In any case, there are almost certainly a group of aliens in the Hohe Kalkstein caves. We know there's one."

"Kzin," he said. He pronounced it differently, a snarling cough it made my vocal chords ache just to hear. "They are called Kzin. Plural and possessive *kzinti*, we think."

"Oh yes, I know."

Kleist's nervous excitement was running down now. We were all pretty beaten up, and he and I sank into a sort of doze. Dimity had earphones on, and was playing the disk, staring at the screen. More than once I saw dark shapes, too sharp-edged to be cloud, driving high and silent across the luminous bands of the Swarm and the Milky Way, and more sliding lights that might have been meteors.

Chapter 12

*"If I am the Scourge of God, you must be truly
wicked."*
                    —Attributed to Genghis Khan

I woke in daylight. Modern cars have complex machinery and
neither Dimity nor I were practical mechanics.

"I guess we're walking out of this one," said Kleist. He
added: "That's a Spacers' joke. It's got a bit threadbare lately."

Repairing the car was an even longer job than I thought.
I soon saw that without Kleist we would never have done it.
We hoped the daylight heat reflected on the rocks of the mesa
would mask what we were doing. We spent most of that day
and the next working on the fuel line and its feeder controls,
freezing when we saw flying things. We kept a watch in the
direction of the Hohe Kalkstein, but though we thought we
saw some distant activity on the escarpment nothing emerged
from it to come our way. We also thought we saw an ordinary air-car flying well to the north close to the ground, but
had no safe way of trying to signal it. It never came back.
Alpha Centauri A had set by the time we were finished, Alpha
Centauri B rising and casting long shadows in the purple
twilight. And in the direction of the escarpment our glasses
were definitely picking up lights and movement.

Where to go? I had tried to get Dimity away from Munchen
partly to protect her from rioting and chaos and also to protect her knowledge. But there seemed no obvious safer haven
now. Kleist insisted he must get back to Munchen, which in
any case was the planetside center of the defense effort. (Had
it been stupid of us to place our defense headquarters in our

major city? I wondered, and came to the conclusion that it had been very stupid indeed.) Then Dimity recalled something.

"You said 'mob the slowboats.' What did you mean?"

"The old slowboats are still intact," Kleist said. "The Kzin haven't bothered with them for some reason, at least they hadn't a few days ago, and I saw them in the sky last night. Presumably because they are deactivated they don't see them as a threat, or a high-priority target. But they are being reactivated. We're getting people out."

That they *could* be reactivated had been firm policy, and every Wunderlander knew it. It was part of our history that when humanity's first interstellar colony was established, the pioneers laid down that the huge spaceships would be kept fully fueled and ready to fly if some unforeseen disaster on the new planet compelled evacuation. They were still there. Closed down and in orbit they required little maintenance, but it had been necessary at first to resist a temptation to cannibalize them. By the time it was obvious that we were here to stay and in any case the population had grown far too big to evacuate, we had factories supplying everything we needed without them. Besides, we might always want to get to Proxima or Alpha Centauri B. Why break up expensive assets unnecessarily?

"Do the Kzin know that?" asked Dimity.

"I think so. Their mind-readers know a lot. . . . During the breathing-space, the happy time after the Swarm reinforcements came, we got crews and fuel into them," he said. "It seemed the unforeseen disaster was well and truly upon us, and we could at least get several thousand people away. They're virtually useless as warships, anyway."

"Where would they go?"

"Back to Sol, I guess. Sol System should have been able to cobble together better defenses than we have. They've had more time and they've more people and factories, and their Belt has good technology, even if flatlanders think like sheep."

"Wouldn't the . . . Kzin just destroy the slowboats?"

"They haven't so far. But maybe it's a cat-and-mouse game. We found in one of our own old texts—Sun Tzu's *Art of War*—that an enemy should always be left with an *apparent* escape route as a disincentive to fighting with the courage of despair. But they're hard to understand. They fight without any concept of mercy, but they've also pulled their punches a few times. They could have smashed Wunderland's cities from space, or vaporized the major bases in the Swarm, but they've held off. They seem to be trying to do as little damage to infrastructure as possible. We don't know why."

"What do you know," asked Dimity, "about their concept of humans?"

"Very little."

"You say they have no interest in negotiation. Do they accept surrenders?"

"They have, yes. They have taken human prisoners. We think . . . It's horrible and bizarre, but we think they eat them unless they've promised otherwise."

"When do they do that? Promise otherwise, I mean."

"Perhaps sometimes if the humans have useful skills. Once or twice when humans have been in relatively strong positions they have bargained and seem to have kept their bargains. But that hasn't been often."

"So they don't look on humans simply as vermin to be exterminated?"

"That's hard to say. We've got a little of their language. Their word for human is *kz'eerkt*, which seems to mean 'monkey.' There must be monkeys or analogs on their homeworld. They refer to our ships as 'monkeyships.' " Kleist closed his eyes for a moment and frowned as if remembering something difficult.

"There was one odd incident: One of our ships was cut off and surrounded by a kzin squadron. It had expended its major weapons and the kzin boarded it. It was a big ship, a Swarm passenger liner originally, and they fought from cabin to cabin for days. At the end the surviving humans made a last stand on the bridge deck. Some of the com-links were still working and broadcasting what was happening to the fleet. We saw and heard the last fight when the kzin broke through.

"They killed the humans pretty quickly. In hand-to-hand fighting we don't stand a chance against them. The last surviving human detonated a bomb. Only a small one, but he must have taken a lot of kzin with him.

"That put the picture out, but we still got sound for a while. We *think* we heard one of the kzin say something we translate like 'brave monkey' or 'worthy monkey.' But I'm not sure."

"As far as we can gather, they honor brave enemies, if not to the extent of sparing their lives. Is that what you mean?"

"Perhaps a little. But if you were about to get control of an industrialized world," said Dimity, "would you smash up its factories and industrial plant?"

"No. Of course not."

"And nor do they. That means they're coming to stay. Their build suggests they come from a world with heavier gravity than Earth, and a lot heavier than Wunderland. This would be pleasant for them. They can breathe the air. Of course they are coming to stay—what price a whole habitable planet with industrial development ripe for the taking, with light gravity and meat on the hoof as bonuses? They landed scouts. They know something about human biology and morphology. They want to keep our planet, and it follows that they also want humans to work it. . . . Do you have any evidence, or any intuition, that they act more or less independently than humans?"

"More independently, definitely. Tactically they sometimes fail to cooperate with each other to a surprising degree. We'd all be long dead otherwise."

"Cats are generally independent-minded. And you think they know what the slowboats are for?"

"I think they probably do. Does it matter?"

"It could. If they think they are industrial assets of some kind—major asteroid miners or something—they might be reluctant to destroy them. And if they think they are refugee ships . . ."

"Once they see them leaving the system they'll be after them," I said.

"Not necessarily. Not if they got a long enough start. I'm trying to think like an intelligent cat, with a cat's independence. Go after a slowboat and yes, assuming you found it, you'd catch it. A slow obsolete ship technologically inferior to your own and useless except for its own specialized purpose. You might have a feed. But then you'd have to turn around and come back. Meanwhile, the other cats are all grabbing the choicest parts of the planet.

"Like terrestrial lions at a kill, or tigripards here: Would one leave a big kill that was already warm and bloody on the ground, with the rest of the pride lined up and feeding, to chase after a rabbit? Probably not. At least, we might as well think that way."

"I hope you're right," I said. "Anyway, you're going to be a slowboat passenger."

"Me?"

"Your drive theory. Humanity's got to have it. The Kzin must not."

"There was talk of drawing lots or something" said Kleist, "but I don't know if there will be time for that. What drive?"

"No, it may not work," said Dimity. "Besides, if you don't know, you can't reveal it under torture." I had been about to tell him what I knew of it.

"Yes," he said. "They're good at torture, except they don't seem to understand shock. As far as we can gather they tend to kill the victims too soon. That annoys them. But I suppose they are learning."

"So we head for Munchen and the spaceport. And hope we get there before they do."

"Fly as low as you can," said Dimity. "We don't want to show up on radar and get shot down by our own people." The subject of torture had left me rather preoccupied. "Don't head straight for the city. Hug the contours of the hills and trees."

"We'll have to slow down," I said.

"We should slow down anyway. Both sides will be looking for war craft, and they travel fast." It was a relief to be moving again, anyway.

Sunset seemed unusually prolonged for the season. There were also sounds in the air that puzzled me. As we headed toward Munchen we saw lights streaming up from the surrounding hills, lights in the sky, rising orange blossoms of fire, with the diffuse background glow of that strange slow sunset behind them.

It was like no light I had seen before: a wavering, pulsating orange glow.

Something moving in the sky against the glow, something black. Kleist grabbed my arm.

"Kzin aircraft!"

I wrenched the car round in a tight turn. The dark shape turned too, with a deliberation that was somehow terrifying in itself, and began to move towards us.

"What weapons do we have?"

"Personal strakkakers, a couple of big ones mounted on the car, some bullet projectors. Flashlight lasers."

"No use. Glass and teflon needles won't stop that thing."

"Ram it!" said Dimity.

"That means the end of us."

"We bail out with lift-belts. Keep the strakkakers by you."

Instinct had taken over my fingers. I had the car close to the ground, jigging violently from side to side. Our pursuer had lost height too, and was closing with us. I estimated it would be on us in two to three minutes.

"They like to get in close," Kleist said.

"Then get belts on, fast!"

Desperate fumbling. I programmed the car to fly steady and stop in two minutes. Then we stepped out, three hundred feet in the air. We fell for another two hundred feet or so and then the ground effect of the lift-belts operated and we hovered. There was the alien craft, big and black and *fast*.

Some instinct made me shut me eyes and throw my hands in front of my face. It hit the car with an explosion that deafened us and painted multicolored light across my eyelids. A blast of hot air knocked me spinning away.

There was the alien craft, stopped in midair. There were flames curling up out of its front part and its nose was dipping. It was sinking, quite slowly, toward the ground.

A hatch opened in its side, and we saw dark bulky shapes emerging. So they had lift-belts too. Of course they would, and with their gravity technology they would be better belts than ours.

There was the whirr of a strakkaker in the air behind me and a hideous scream. The first of the creatures became suddenly fuzzy in outline, and then disintegrated, leaving a half-skeleton hanging in the air.

Two others followed, fast, and they were shooting as they came. The exit port was their point of vulnerability. Kleist and Dimity had their strakkakers trained on it, and though the aliens were fast, they couldn't get through the glass needles.

But a strakkaker has a limited magazine capacity. I heard theirs fall silent, and brought up my own, ready at the movement I could see beyond the hatch.

More alien shapes, horribly bigger than men, were maneuvering something out of the hatch, and leaping onto it. It was rectangular, and I thought idiotically for a moment of a flying carpet, realizing it must be some sort of evacuation vehicle.

Whatever it was, it seemed to be an emergency device only, like a sledge. The aliens on it must, I thought, be dazed and injured by what had happened, but there was no opportunity for mercy now. They were still carrying weapons, and, though the flames of the burning craft in the air beside them must have affected their night vision, they would surely be able to see us soon. I fired the strakkaker again in a long burst, and swept them off the sledge as the two craft separated. I realized the fact that the strakkaker, unlike a beam weapon or bullet-rifle, had no betraying flame might be a great advantage.

The main alien craft was falling faster now, and breaking up, pouring fire from several ports. There was an internal explosion, and it dropped like a stone, exploding again as it hit the ground and scattering wreckage.

Our own lift-belts were bringing us down, too. They were emergency devices only, with limited power, intended at altitudes like this to slow a fall more than to fly. One of the floating aliens was still firing a beam weapon, but it was either dead or badly wounded, for the bolts were flying at random. I raised my strakkaker again to finish it.

I fired a burst of a second or so, and the gauge clicked on empty. But the thing dropped its weapon. I thought I heard it scream, but between the deafening explosions and the flames

I couldn't be sure. I marked where the weapon fell, though, as my own feet touched the ground. The others landed nearby. I was amazed we were all alive.

Kleist and I lifted the alien weapon between us and we staggered away. There seemed to be something still moving in the wreck of the alien craft, and I thought there might be explosions still to come.

"They were trying to capture us, weren't they?" said Dimity. "That's why they didn't shoot at first."

"They often try to capture if they can," said Kleist. "It's better not to let them . . .

"Well," he continued after a moment, "at least it should be difficult for them to find us now. Have either of you got any metal prostheses in you?"

We hadn't. The small locator implant in my arm was plastic.

"Good. Get rid of the belts, and any electronic gadgets you've got on you. Watches, calculators, pocketbooks. They can detect electronic activity in space. I don't know how much metal their detectors need, but why make it easy for them? And they can use the heat-induction ray to cook any metal parts you have inside you while you're still alive. I've seen it happen. . . ."

"Are we worth coming after?" I wondered if it would affect plastic and decided I could cut the locator out if I had to. It had already buzzed and vibrated once, which I did not like at all, but then had stopped.

"If another ship saw anything of what happened, they'll come. They're big on revenge, we've noticed."

The alien weapon had an orange light glowing on one side.

"I hope that's to show it's charged," he said. He broke off suddenly to cough. "I hope it isn't calling them. . . . Funny, it's got a trigger like a human weapon. Convergent engineering . . ." His voice was becoming rambling.

"You're hurt," said Dimity. "I ought to look at you."

"No time now. We're dead meat if the pussies find us here. Got to get out of the area."

"Where do we go?" My question. I was feeling numb and stupid. The caves had proven no hiding place. But we were still in arid open country. I wanted to get away from the terrible sky.

"We still head for Munchen."

"Where is it?"

"There." He pointed to the glow in the sky. "See the flames."

I suddenly understood what that glow meant. It looked as if the whole city was burning. Now that I looked, I saw shifting green lasers passing through smoke-clouds. We were still on high ground, and had a long view and wide horizons.

There, too, apparently crawling across the ground toward us, were lights. In my glasses they swam into focus as a column of vehicles.

"They're fleeing out of the city," said Dimity. "But why don't they scatter?"

With higher magnification we could make out details. Some of the vehicles had laser and other weapons mounts and some of them were shooting beams and bullets.

"They must be holding together on purpose. Strength in numbers. They're still fighting."

"Not enough strength, not enough numbers. The kzin can pick them off at leisure."

"Why don't they, then?"

"They're cats. They like a bit of sport," said Kleist. "Sometimes, and until they get tired of it. See there!"

There were other vehicles on the ground moving toward the human column from the north. Quite different vehicles.

"Those will be kzin ground forces. As far was we can gather, they like a bit of personal combat. I'd guess they'll call in a strike from space when they've had enough."

The kzin vehicles were advancing in a broad line. They seemed to ignore natural cover, and they were in a relatively concentrated mass. They were pouring out fire but lasers and guns firing from the more dispersed human line were hitting them. The area around Manstein's Folly was also sparkling with gunfire.

"I've seen that in space," said Kleist. "It's another reason we lasted as long as we did. They play around for a time and then something snaps and they just charge in headlong. No sense of tactics, once an attack actually starts. If we had aircraft to give support now we could make a real mess of them."

"We have an aircraft," said Dimity. She pointed to the kzin sledge, still floating above the wrecked vehicles on the ground, dead kzin hanging in the air around it. "There should be enough power left in three lift-belts for one of us to reach it. I'm the lightest."

"Could you control it?"

"It must be simple enough."

"No," said Kleist, "I'll go. I've seen some of their instrumentation."

"Some of those dead kzin have weapons," said Dimity. "Get them if you can."

Chapter 13

Let every Greek contingent
Meet the fury hand to hand.
But none of it will matter
If the Spartans cannot stand . . .
                                    —Peter Kocan

The kzin sledge was simple to fly. Its small motor was controlled by a wheel and joystick: left, right, up down. Even a monkey could understand them, especially a monkey used to flying aircraft. The motor was making a loud purring noise, but we had no idea if that was normal or not. It was a lot more stable and powerful than a human ground-effect car, further evidence of a terrifyingly advanced technology.

The sledge was armed, too, with a beam projector heavier than a personal sidearm. If we had not shot the kzin before they brought it into action we would have been wiped out in short order. The kzin sidearms we salvaged were heavy enough.

"I think we can make one pass," said Kleist.

There were recognizable kzin and human lines now, and enough smoke to show the shafts of beam weapons. One end of the human line seemed to be anchored at Manstein's Folly. As we approached it the human fire increased. We still had our pocket-vision enhancers and they showed some details.

There were recoilless guns, copies of an ancient design, mounted on small vehicles and firing rocket projectiles, firing and moving. A few of the human super–Bofors guns, hunkered down behind rocks and gully walls, were throwing out lines of shells as well. Some of these glowed in the air. Their explosions looked feeble, and I couldn't think they were

113

doing much good, but perhaps the sight of them was cheering. There were a number of kzin vehicles wrecked and burning but most were the victims of beam-weapons—probably the adapted police message-lasers. Beams passing through swirling clouds of smoke created a surreal effect in the night.

I remembered a statement in my hasty reading on strategy that for a general to retreat into a fortress was an act like grabbing hold of the anchor on a sinking ship. On the other hand, this half-repaired straggle of ruined walls and ditches was hardly a fortress.

The human fire seemed to be concentrating on the kzin machines. The higher these flew the easier it was for them to fire back, but the better targets they became. Mostly, they kept very close to the ground. We could just make out the shapes of the aliens leaping down from some of the nearer ones. We saw two or three get hit by fire, crash, and burn.

The kzin were throwing missiles and beams the other way, and to effect—the human line was being torn up from end to end, and the route of the human army was marked by the burning wrecks of vehicles. I saw the white flash of a molecular-distortion battery rupturing among the explosions, a big one that must be near full charge. Not many near that would survive. And as we approached there were more of the smaller dark shapes—kzinti advancing on foot. Either they didn't notice the sledge against the night sky or took it for the kzin vehicle it was.

Then they did see us. I can only guess they sent some identification call or challenge to which we did not respond, but a second later they were firing at us. Kleist fired back and took us down in a steep dive into a dead area behind a long rock ridge, beams passing above us.

"No good," said Kleist. "They've too much firepower. We'd never get through. And, in case you didn't notice it, the humans were firing at us as well."

"We've got to do something to help."

"Let's get to the human lines."

"Won't they see us coming and shoot us?"

"Try the communicator. Let's hope they've got one functioning at their end."

During a partial lull in the bombardment we found Grotius, von Diderachs and van Roberts in the ruined "keep" of Manstein's Folly. There was an odd flag flying from a pole above them, an outline of a man holding a lightning bolt and standing on two feline heads.

Neither party recognized the other at first, not merely because they were still wearing the filthy remains of those "uniforms." We had all changed. Von Diderachs with a bloody cloth bandage around his head, his proud beard cut away, looked Herrenmann leader no more. They were huddled around a table with an old-fashioned paper or fabric map, spread on it. Van Roberts was shouting into a communicator.

"Fire and move! Fire and *move*! Their radar can track your launching points!" Something must have happened because he stopped shouting and shook his head. "Fools." Then again, "Disperse! Disperse and fire!"

Human were running and firing from widely separated points, never staying in the same place after they had fired. Still some did not move quickly enough to avoid the returning fire. There were heavy automatic guns in armored cupolas that rose, fired, and retracted, installed as part of the restoration of the fortress. But none seemed to get off more than a few shots before the kzin fire found them and destroyed them.

Another group of humans rushed up to the wall and leveled a heavy beam weapon but didn't fire.

None of them looked surprised to see us. I suppose no one had any emotion left. Von Diderachs took in what was left of Kleist's pilot's outfit with the comment, "A professional. But we're all becoming professionals now."

"What are you doing?"

"Buying time. Time for the evacuations. The lucky ones get to the slowboats. The less lucky may get out of the city. Peter . . . Colonel Brennan is taking some guerrillas to the hills."

Whump! Whump! Whump! Three muffled sounds, almost like implosions, from somewhere farther down the human line, followed by the white light of MD batteries exploding, then a much louder explosion from the same direction. Van Roberts spoke into the communicator again.

"They got under cover in time. That was a human team. We're running out of smart automatics. Three rounds off from the mortar and they're still alive." Then: "Disperse! Disperse! Let *them* clump together!" I could see more humans scattered up and down the line now, crouched behind rocks and old walls and too scattered to be picked off easily.

"How long can they last?" I asked Kleist.

"I told you. Till the kzin get tired of playing."

"The Tesla Towers did some good at first," said Grotius. "The waves seemed to upset their motors. Then they knocked them all down. They found the naval base we were trying to build at Glenrothes Field and nuked it, but they fought for a while on foot at the perimeter first. . . . The last of the garrison got a message out . . . and it was a low-yield nuke . . . nice of them."

"You see we're cooperating now," said von Diderachs. "A little late in the day. Herrenmanner and Prolevolk, Teuties and Tommies. And I'm a general, like some of my distant ancestors. Do you know how recently we didn't know what a general was?" He laughed and laughed and then began to weep. Grotius slapped his face.

Suddenly the fire from the kzin heavy weapons stopped.

"Thank God!" gasped Kleist. He too was looking all in now.

"Don't be too quick to do that," Grotius told him. "The only reason they'd raise the bombardment is that they're sending in infantry. They like a bit of that," he added, evidently for me.

"Call in the picket! It can't do any good now!"

"Too late! Look!" From a depression in the ground beyond we saw a confused fight: bombs and beams. There was a hammering of gunfire.

"Poor bastards, poor tanj bastards," muttered Kleist, ceaselessly.

"Artillery!" van Roberts was shouting into a communicator. "On top of them! Put it right on top of them. They're dead men already." The whole depression seemed to explode as human heavy guns converged on it. I saw kzin and human bodies, whole and in pieces, hurled into the air.

"Here they come!"

"Stand to!" shouted von Diderachs, his weeping fit gone. "Infantry, rally to me!" To my surprise a man nearby began to beat with sticks on a little drum slung on his hip. It must have been a prearranged signal, because other humans sheltering behind scattered rocks and ruins began to converge upon it in crouching runs. Something that could not be blocked electronically.

A couple of robot guns and lasers, very new things that sought their own targets and took their own cover, were jumping and blazing, their muzzles dancing faster than the eye could follow. If only we had had more of them!

There were bigger lasers than I had realized, crude, strapped-together things, some with hideously dangerous unshielded conduction cables snaking across the ground.

The weapon at the wall began to fire. Other humans dashed forward, some bent in a crouch, hunched over the weight of the Lewis guns that they fired as they ran. There were a lot more humans scattered about the rocks and ruins than I had realized, and for a second I felt cheered.

There were the huge forms of kzin, carrying heavy arms, dashing across the open ground toward us, firing and snarling as they came. And they were *fast*.

Most of them seemed to be naked but for equipment, and under the light of Alpha Centauri B their brilliant orange fur made them stand out as targets. Human fire met them, strakkaker needles—which seemed to do little good against whatever the clothed ones were wearing but made straw and skeletons of the others—exploding Bofors shells, beams, bullets. A human would have tried to dodge that fire or to take shelter behind some ridge of ground, but the kzin kept coming straight at us. I thought at that moment that any space-traveling race would have a science of hard materials and wondered that they did not all wear armor. With the primitive and makeshift propellants we had, largely copies of antiques, our missiles would have bounced off modern armor like raindrops. Further, it would have camouflaged their brilliant coats.

There were a few coils of barbed wire and razor wire in front of and among the human defenses. The kzin for the most part leaped over it or charged through it, but some were funneled between lanes of wire into compact masses and into killing grounds where fixed guns were targeted.

I found that without conscious thought I was firing the heavy kzin sidearm. Dead kzin were falling and wounded kzin dragging themselves along the ground. Von Diderachs's mouth was open and he was screaming something, but the only thing I could hear in the explosions and the feline shrieks and roars was the scream in my own throat. There was one kzin in glittering armor ahead of the rest: I fired futility at the armour as it scrambled over the rubble and then at the junction of head and neck, decapitating it. I saw another kzin staggering and screaming, its feet transfixed by what I had learned were caltrops.

There were another mass of kzin, funneled by lanes of wire into a compact group.

"Clear the front for the claymores!" came a mechanical shout.

A moment later I found out what this meant. Directed explosions shredded the mass of kzin. But more came on, dodging the killing ground. They died in heaps, but more charged in.

The close-packed kzin leaped the wall and crashed into a counter-mass of humans that swirled apart to let them pass.

Evidently expecting the humans to stand and fight, the kzin seemed momentarily puzzled. The humans were around them, pouring fire into the mass of them from every side, slashing with beams. It lasted only a few seconds, but by the time the kzin leaped scattering into the humans there were far fewer kzin. I saw more kzin leaping the wall, and Dimity, Kleist, von Diderachs and I shot them down. They seemed obsessed with charging into the battle and hardly even looked about them. Certainly they did not count the odds, though now the humans were swarming in.

Nor did some of the humans. I saw one human, a huge man, a giant, rushing at the kzin swinging a farmer's sledge-hammer. But he seemed less of a giant as he approached the towering kzin. His blow with the hammer hit one in the ribs. It staggered back but did not fall as a man would have, then it grabbed him with one hand and took him apart with a few slashes of the other.

I saw two other kzin charge from behind one of the human gunners manning a recoilless gun. The human had no time to swing the gun round but fired it anyway, blasting one kzin to bits with the rocket exhaust, leaving the other burned black, eyeless and screaming.

A heavy industrial earth mover smashed through the rocks, driving into the kzin, guns firing from its windows and from a cupola on its cabin roof. The kzin charged at it. Some were mashed screaming under its blade, others boarded it and smashed their way into the cabin. The driver must have had a self-destruct.

More kzin crowded on flying sledges like ours. Bunched together like that they were impossible to miss, and a rapid-firing gun on the hill behind blasted them away. One sledge crossed a laser beam and exploded, the others flew on, empty.

Thought is too quick to describe, and somewhere in my mind flashed the memory of Kleist's words: "They don't have much experience of war."

One group of kzin still advanced in a purposeful body toward the ridge and ditch behind us. I saw van Roberts waving his arms in another signal.

"Now!" shouted van Roberts.

The kzin reached the edge of the ditch and hesitated. Humans hidden in it shot them down as they stood against the skyline. Strakkakers whirred and were drowned out by the ear-splitting rattle of the Lewis guns, human and alien screaming and the smashing blasts of the kzin sidearms and the claymores. There were dense clouds of steam from weapons' cooling-systems.

Another mass of kzin charging up a trench became jammed together. A pair of humans jumped in front of them, firing a Lewis gun and a beam weapon into the mass of them, back and forth, up and down, like two gardeners with hoses.

I saw a group of kzin and humans hand-to-hand, the humans flung and falling in explosions of slashing claws. The group reeled onto the naked conduction cable of one of the big lasers and died in a flash of blue-white fire.

Another fight was going on around the flag, kzin hacking with knives, the huge blades whirling quicker than sight among the humans clustered there. I saw the flag sway on its pole and fall, then a green beam waved through them and another human rushed forward into the dying mass to raise it. Another kzin leaped at him and a strakkaker beside me—Dimity's— dismembered it in mid-leap. In hand-to-hand combat a kzin could tear any number of humans apart, but they seemed unable to realize how much weapons evened the odds.

There were exceptions. "So you're a smart one!" I heard Dimity's voice as she spotted and picked off a Kzin avoiding the battle and advancing in the concealing shadow of wall.

The fighting had dissolved into a series of savage, shrieking brawls and blastings among the wreckage. In glimpses as I ran from cover to cover I saw a human and kzin rolling together, the human actually attempting to bite the kzin's throat for a second before he was shredded by its claws. I fired into the mess, then got to the now unmanned weapon on the wall and began firing up and down the kzin line. I reckoned that if they saw us still firing back they would think their attack had failed and not send in more support. The kzin bombardment resumed but half the casualties it caused seemed to be among their own.

Behind us something was happening. In the flash of an explosion I saw more kzin leaping up another approach trench. They had taken the defenses in the rear. I shouted and grabbed at the man nearest me, with one of the Lewis guns. He fired off the antique weapon's entire drum of ammunition, checking them till I managed to drag the big modern gun from the wall around and join in. Another kzin charged at me and, spinning the gun desperately, I cut it in two. Another conduction cable took out a line of them, the screams of the burning kzin briefly drowning all other sound.

I don't know how long it took. Finally the firing stopped. The kzin were down and dead. So were most of the nearby humans, though they had begun by considerably outnumbering the kzin. I seemed unable to take my eyes away from naked protruding white bones and worse things. This part of the line at least was largely depopulated. Someone was beating the drum, irregularly, and a few more humans were stumbling up to the breach. Others were collecting the human and kzin weapons and dragging them up to the wall. Clouds of steam and the stenches of burnt flesh and disemboweled bodies.

Van Roberts, Grotius and Kleist were nearby. I won't go into details, but only van Roberts was alive, and he was plainly dying. Even after all that had happened, up to that moment I had not realized what the felinoids' claws could do. I think it was because I was used to dissection that I didn't vomit. I still had some pain-killers in my belt and gave him most of what I had. Dimity and I tried to tie him together, though it was obviously pointless. I thought to hold his head so he couldn't see what had been done to him, but he had no strength to move it. Von Diderachs came and squatted by us. He was pouring blood where a couple of fingers and half a hand had been sliced away, but I don't think he noticed till Dimity stuffed some sort of dressing against it.

"Goodbye, Rykermann," said van Roberts. "Look after what you can." He took Dimity's hand and stroked it for a moment. "Fly!" he told her. She was soaked in dark liquid and I thought she was bleeding profusely but then it showed purple in the light and I realized that it was kzin blood.

"Time. Remember buying time is what it's all for. But when it's finished get out! Head for the hills!" van Roberts told von Diderachs. "Save yourself!"

"What for? I'll be with you soon, Roberts."

"You're not a bad fellow for a Herrenmann," van Roberts said. "God . . . God be with you and all of us."

Von Diderachs nodded. He touched van Roberts's cheek for a moment, then walked back to the wall.

Van Roberts plucked at my sleeve. We knelt beside him, clutching his hands.

"Remember, Rykermann, they're not good tacticians." he said, "They're too hasty. They can be fooled."

He struggled to raise himself and shouted in a stronger voice: "Don't send the colors to the rear yet! They are still our rallying-point! Don't let the kzin capture them!" Then he died. We pulled some cloth over him.

I heard single shots and saw humans walking about killing wounded. Human wounded as well as kzin. They were stripping the bodies. Less hideously wounded humans tied up in bloody fabric were making their way back to the wall and the guns.

"Use strakkakers, you fools!" shouted von Diderachs. "Save your heavy ammunition for the kzin!"

I saw two small humans struggling to lift a huge kzin side-arm and realised they were young boys. A kzin in gold armor, obviously one of their leaders, horribly damaged by an explosion, unable to leap or use a weapon, stood propped against a wall screaming as if inviting someone to kill it. Presently someone did. Another kzin, dying, used its last strength to hack at the ears of the human that lay dead beneath it. A heavy gun was firing in the direction of the kzin lines, but the gunner's hands that squeezed the triggers were attached to no body.

I saw a man, a politician who I recognized vaguely from the early meetings, standing in front of a pile of containers. Another man seemed to be arguing with him.

"I can't release more ammunition without the authorization of a competent officer," he was saying.

"No, sir, I understand," said the other man, "but this is an emergency." Something in his voice seemed to alarm the first speaker.

"These are all the supplies we have. Show me some credentials and I will release them."

"Yes, sir. Will this do?" asked the other politely. He pulled out a small folding gun. The first man began to back away, hands raised to his face. Then he turned to run. The man with the gun took deliberate aim and blew him to pieces with a single exploding bullet. Then he returned the weapon to his belt and began loading containers methodically onto a dolly.

How long has it taken us to go from the twenty-fourth century to the fourteenth? I thought as the strakkakers whirred and the screams of the wounded diminished. How long ago had I been dining with the abbot and had we been reflecting together over his wine upon the too complacent state of our world? I couldn't remember.

"We beat them! We beat an infantry attack!"

"One. Look at our casualties! We won't beat the next. They'll be forming up for the final attack now."

But I remembered something else the abbot had said.

"We still have the aircraft!" Dimity seemed to be giving von Diderachs orders now. "An attack from the air could do them a lot of damage. Create a diversion! Fire everything you've got at them while we attack. They won't be counting on air support."

"One pass," said von Diderachs. "One pass and then get out of this. That is a direct order and I give you no discretion in the matter. You'll do no good by throwing your lives away, and there's little more time to be bought here."

"I can't leave you like this," I said. Something primitive, atavistic. I had no idea what the emotion I was experiencing might be called—it was counter-productive to my survival and Dimity's, whatever it was—but it went against the grain to leave them.

"Then let me make it easier for you," said von Diderachs. "Wunderland needs you both. But if you try to return to this doomed battle I'll shoot you down myself. There! I said you had no discretion. Wunderland will need you, Rykermann. Will need you both."

I looked at his haggard glaring face and shrugged. I had no discretion.

"Cheer, you bastards!" I heard him shout into the communicator as we mounted the sledge, and scattered cheering came from up and down the line.

Our drum was beating again. From the kzin lines we heard answering drums—a deep booming. I realized the drums were more than signaling devices: they must also be to encourage one side and terrify the other.

I flew, firing the big beam-gun as we swooped low over the kzin lines, Dimity firing the sidearms as she could at the infantry. The humans were throwing everything they had at the kzin, suppressing their fire while our beam tore into them. And our beam was *hot*. We saw ground tearing up and vehicles and aliens mixed in it, burning kzin flying through the air like comets. We heard alien screams of rage and agony. I thought I also still heard distant cheers from the human lines.

The humans had established some guns on an outcrop behind their main line: These too poured fire into the kzin lines, but as a stationary position they had a short life. We saw them hit by a heavy missile, possibly summoned from space.

One pass and we climbed hard away. A squat cylinder flew in an arc through the air, slow enough to be visible, and exploded in another soundless disk of blue-white light, another following—someone on the human side was still firing molecular-distortion batteries at kzin as missiles. Our sledge rocked as something hit it from below.

I banked, and we came in again, north of the end of the kzin line. We fired a few more bursts into the end of the line, setting off a chain of secondary explosions. No kzin seemed to have a thought of taking cover, and the beam-gun on continuous fire knocked them down in flames until it overheated and shut off. The whole kzin line was burning and the human cheers were unmistakable. There was still a pack of kzin vehicles, and we fired our remaining weapons into that.

Some Kzin had survived. They weren't firing much but what fire they had left was concentrated on us. Beams were coming back at us now, fast and very close. Something hit a corner of the sledge in a spray of fragments, throwing it about wildly and nearly overturning it. The beams—as I should have realized with our own gun—seemed to use so much energy that they could only be used for very short bursts, but I saw one swinging like a scythe. We avoided it narrowly but plainly a couple like that would finish us. There was nothing more we could do.

Had we bought the human army a respite? For what it was worth, I thought we had. The last I saw, every human gun was firing into the kzin lines without answering fire. But I also saw lights descending from the sky farther south. It looked like a kzin landing that would take the human forces from behind.

Our heavy ammunition was finished. I kept us low, following the contours of the ground. Behind us were more explosions.

"They'll get sick of that sooner rather than later," Dimity said. "Then they'll detonate a fission or fusion device."

"More to the point," I said, "why don't we use them? The Meteor Guard have them—and used them against the kzin in space, Kleist said. We could break up their landings and concentrations."

"I guess if we did they would retaliate massively. They control space. Munchen and the other cities would be obvious targets then. There's lots more both sides could do: use plasma gas, run a ramscoop in atmosphere, fire a spaceship's reaction drive downward into the infantry and melt them in one pass. If I can think of that, why can't they? Things like that have been happening in space."

"They're holding back for the same reason hunters don't go after game with strakkakers," I said. "Where would be the sport in it for the kzin?"

"It's interesting," she went on, as though discussing a problem in astrometaphysics. "Both sides are holding back from using their ultimate punches. I wonder if there is any hope in that? My head hurts. I hope Diderachs or whoever is in charge has got the sense to scatter before the kzin bring the nuclear devices in. They might get a few away into the hills. They might. I think the kzin will have to pull back before a strike." There was something wrong with her voice.

Munchen was a sparkling patchwork of fires, lasers still lighting up the dense rolling clouds of smoke. Here and there shellfire from heavy guns climbed in strangely slow and graceful arcs into the sky, evidently following kzin aircraft. But the devastation seemed less than I had expected. There were still large patches untouched. In some of them the lights of streets and houses were still burning, and other lights showed traffic movement. It was a weird reminder of a remote and vanished world, until we got closer.

Chapter 14

Pray not for aid to One who made
A set of never-changing laws,
But in your need remember well
He gave you speed, or guile—or claws.
                                        —Saki

As we approached, I saw in amazement the reaction flames of ships taking off from the spaceport, apparently unmolested.

Dimity saw it too. We skimmed between the high buildings, setting down a few blocks from the university. "There seems to be some areas still under human control," she said. "We'd better not fly a kzin craft here."

I had been thinking the same thing.

"But I don't understand this," I said. "What are the kzin doing? They could have walked all over any resistance."

"They don't want to smash the place up too much," said Dimity. "They can see it's an industrial center."

"Wouldn't that make it a prime target?"

"It would if the issue was in doubt. But they're sure of winning."

"And why are they letting those ships take off? They must control everything in space by now?"

"We'll find out, I guess."

We landed at the outskirts of the city. I still had a strakkaker and, wanting my hands and arms free and not psychologically prepared to expect trouble from fellow humans, hung it in a pouch on my belt, which I buttoned closed. It was secure even if I could not reach it quickly. Never have I done anything I was to regret so bitterly forever after.

There were people in the street now. Few and furtive at
first, but as we approached the spaceport they became thicker.
There seemed to be some sort of order. We even began to
see police directing them. There were vehicles, ground-cars
moving in their regular traffic-lanes, an oddly normal sight
against the multicolored fire and smoke filling the sky. But
there were dead bodies lying in the street, and groups of
humans in strange clothes running crouched over weapons.
The streets grew more crowded as we went on. And everyone was moving the same way. I found blood smeared on my
hands and saw it clotting the back of Dimity's hair. She had
had some sort of small head-wound, presumably when the
vehicle had been hit by kzin fire. Neither of us had noticed
it and in that light I could see nothing more.

Ahead of us at the approach to the spaceport was some
sort of bottleneck. Police—"soldiers" perhaps—were manning
heavy weapons mounted on vehicles, pointed down into the
screaming crowd that had now congested and slowed. All order
seemed to have broken down. I had no choice but to use my
body as a battering ram to try to get Dimity through.

A kzin craft tore up the street, a few yards over the head
of the mob. It didn't fire and seemed to be simply toying with
them or herding them. The crowd parted somehow, many
people fleeing into side streets, but leaving bodies still on the
road and pavement. Dimity and I huddled in a doorway as
we saw the bulky shapes of kzin leap from the vehicle and
pursue the fleeing mob up one alley with deep-throated, leonine
roars that carried above the screams.

The soldiers cowered down, not touching their weapons as
the kzin disappeared down the street. But as I got Dimity to
the checkpoint they returned to them. The frenzied mob were
pouring back into the street again. The soldiers fired two bursts,
the first in front of them, the second directly into them. That
cleared them again. We reached one of the vehicles and a
soldier swung a weapon onto us. I shouted up at him.

"This is Dimity Carmody! The discoverer of Carmody's
Transform! You've got to let her through!"

It didn't matter if he believed me or not, or if he had heard
of her.

"No one beyond this point without a pass."

"But . . ."

He raised his weapon.

"There are a lot of people who want to get on the slowboats.
I've no time to argue."

I could have tackled him. It would have been hopeless but

I could have tried. But the other police were taking notice of us now. There were other people behind us with passes. One chance:

"Help us, then, for your mother's sake as well as mine."

He stared at me blankly, then shook his head. The crowd behind pushed us to one side. Dimity stumbled and I grabbed at her. To fall here under the feet of this mob would be death for her, after all we had been through. Pushed and stumbling myself, my feet off the ground, I feared we would fall and be trampled together, but somehow I fetched up against a barrier. It was giving way and I was going down, Dimity with me. And another man stepped deliberately out of the crowd to us.

"I heard you," he said, gripping my hand. "For my mother's sake as well as yours, I will. . . ." He pulled us back onto our feet. Another swirl of he crowd took us into an alcove, entrance to an office block. There was a passage and he helped us down it, though it only led to another street.

"Don't think too badly of them," the man said. "The first evacuations were better. I've seen some real nobility in the refugee queues. But this is the end." I was no longer surprised that in the midst of Ragnarok a human being should try to morally defend his fellow creatures.

The sky to the east turned white, then orange and red. Some time later the shock-wave reached us. I guessed that, as Dimity had predicted, the Kzin had tired of the human resistance at Manstein's Folly. All I could hope was that it was a clean bomb and the wind would be from the sea. We were clear of the crowd now. I shook the man's hand, and we parted. There were plenty of trampled dead to show how we could have been if he had not helped.

Another kzin craft appeared. This time the troops fired at it. It was a mistake. Four more appeared, following it, and dived on the gun vehicles.

We ran, pelting down the approach-way. The checkpoint was no longer relevant. Ahead of us was the landing field and a single craft, ringed with weapons. There was more order here, it seemed, and a line of people were running aboard with some sort of organization.

A kzin aircraft, a vast red wedge-and-ovoid, hurtled low over us, fire spitting from weapons. It was heading straight for the shuttle. We threw ourselves to the ground with the explosion reflex that was becoming instinctive. Wreckage and debris fell about us. The kzin aircraft soared away.

"They've had enough, evidently. No more shuttles."

A little less luck and we might have been on that shuttle now burning on the field. A crash wagon with some brave people aboard was heading out to it, siren wailing. I felt I had had enough. I was unable to think. I took told of Dimity's hands as we sat there.

"Now what?"

"No slowboats now for us," she said. "Someone may tell them to get away while the going's good. I'd say it's all over here."

"We've got to get out of this crowd. This is too much of a prime target."

The front of the crowd had seen the shuttle destroyed. They were spilling around the now purposeless police block. But the crowd behind was pressing on. We saw more people going down underfoot. Then we heard the ripping-cloth sound of more kzin vehicles, and this time they were shooting as they came. We heard the whirr of strakkakers briefly between the roar of the kzin weapons. On one of the roofs a Bofors gun was still putting on a fireworks display.

There was a manhole in the pavement, its cover knocked loose. Someone had tripped and was kicking and scrambling free. Dimity pointed and we dropped in. We fell a couple of meters, nothing in our gravity, and splashed into a stormwater drain. Above us were screams and gunfire. Others fell or threw themselves through the manhole into the drain behind us. There were a few permanent tracer-lamps glowing dimly on the walls, and by the light of these we saw steps and a narrow path running above the water.

"Underground again," said Dimity.

"At least it's not crowded, and somehow I don't think it's the sort of place cats would enjoy poking their noses into."

"Let's get away from this part, all the same. They might think it too easy to pour something nasty down here."

It was too dim and slippery to run, and we were too tired, but we set off at the best pace we could. I still had my night glasses with a built-in compass, and Dimity had a sense of direction which she had proved in the caves and which I trusted rather more. There was a roar, and the slick walls and the liquid around our feet glowed orange in reflected light. We looked back and behind us we saw flame boiling down the manhole, but we had already made some distance. I was alert for Beam's beasts but we saw none. I knew poison had been put into the drains regularly to keep them down.

We covered several miles, heading north, then took some stairs to the surface. The streets in this part were deserted.

We reached my house about dawn. It was running on its own auxiliary power, and the door recognized my retinal patterns. It didn't matter much since someone else had gained entry earlier by driving a vehicle through the front wall. There was an almost unbearable smell of decay inside, but all we found of the source were a couple of severed human fingers. The kitchen and the autodoc had been used.

We slept for a few hours, huddled in the basement in a nest of blankets. Dimity's head wound was still bleeding. I cleaned it as well as I could but thought that after our race through the drain the best thing to do would be to let it bleed and hope any infection might be carried away. Before modern autodocs I would, I thought, have had a medicine-chest with a bottle of disinfectant for injuries such as this. As it was I was worried about the shaking-up that nearby explosions had given my own autodoc, apart from possible tampering, and dared not use it. A lot of people would be having to learn to get by without docs soon, I thought.

I did find some acid in my laboratory, weakened it greatly with water, and cleaned the wound cautiously with that. Later I also rinsed some fabric in it and made a clumsy bandage, cursing the fact that modern fabric was almost impossible to cut without proper tools. There was still food in the kitchen and I dialed us a meal late in the morning. The windows were opaque and I left them that way apart from a few small spy holes. We had a view of deserted streets and smoke, with plenty of background noise. Television and Internet were all dead.

"How are we?" Dimity asked.

"Worse off than before we started. We've lost the transport, the kzin are here, and the slowboats are gone. We've achieved precisely nothing." There was something else wrong: Dimity's question, though basically meaningless, would have been a natural thing for a normal person to say. But the Dimity I knew would not have bothered asking it.

"The slowboats are gone." Nor did Dimity normally repeat things pointlessly. I felt something cold inside me that had nothing to do with the mere ordinary fear I felt for us both and for our dying world.

"Look in the sky. You'll not see them in orbit anymore. The big space stations are gone too."

"We did for a few kzin."

"Not exactly enough for victory."

"Perhaps those are the biggest victories we can hope for now."

"It's still going on."

So we could hear. Explosions, the roaring of out-of-control fires. Distant shouts, screams. There was also the noise of kzin engines, unmistakable and terrifying. As we watched through one hole a kzin war-machine appeared at the end of the street, a huge red armored thing, floating a few feet above the pavement. We could do nothing but back away from the hole and crouch in the darkest corner we could find. Eventually the sound diminished and when we crept back to the window it was gone. A couple of times we saw humans running from one building to another, and then kzin on foot. Neither came our way.

"It's no good here."

"No." There was not much I could do but hold her.

"It doesn't look good, does it?" she said.

"No."

"We'll find a way out. Even this shall pass away."

"I'm sure it will."

"No, I mean things might get better."

"I suppose so. They seem to have got worse for a while."

"In some ways it wasn't all that good before. . . ."

"It seemed to be," I said.

"One thing, Nils. It was hard, I know, for you to be in love with a freak. Know, at least, that the freak loves you."

Then I remembered something. Or rather two things. Things the abbot had said to me in what seemed another life. I went back to my laboratory and retrieved a collecting gun and a small selection of darts. I also found the stock of portable food and strakkaker ammunition I had laid up and hidden weeks before was still untouched.

It all seemed to be quieter when we ventured out. I wanted to wait till dusk, but Dimity said the felinoids could certainly see in dim light better than we could: In fact the streets were deserted save for the dead and a few Beam's beasts already creeping upon them. There was fighting still going on but it seemed to be on the other side of the Donau.

I thought it would be difficult, perhaps impossible, for us to find transport. Actually there were abandoned vehicles all round. The streets leading to major arteries were jammed with them, some burned and wrecked, some apparently undamaged. The dead bodies were mostly but not all human. People had tried to shelter in the pools in the nearby fountains and they were full of floating, parboiled corpses. Perhaps a kzin had used a plasma weapon, because the whole square was burned. Between two burning buildings we found a flyable ground-effect car with keys still in its dead owner's fingers.

I turned on the engine and the car lifted as a crowd of humans came pouring around the corner. It looked like a gagrumper stampede. There was no time for me to get my strakkaker clear of its buttoned pouch. They mobbed the car, fighting to get in. It tilted and Dimity was dragged out.

I still had the controls and used the car to smash a couple of them against a wall. Then there was another firefight: a group of kzin and armed humans exchanging shots. That scattered the mob. Half a dozen of them ran right into a strakkaker blast and were cut down. A rampaging kzin swatted others to left and right, apparently hardly noticing them. Another kzin and a human rolled together under a stream of molten metal pouring from the guttering of a burning building. Then the fighters disappeared down another alley.

One human staggered back a moment later, face gone, hands clasped to his stomach where a kzin's claws had partially disemboweled him. He tripped over his spilling guts and fell. I can hear his screaming now. A kzin leaped on him and then the beam of a laser passed through the pair of them, ending it. Suddenly the fight had broken up, and but for the dead the street was deserted again.

Dimity had fallen hard and had been kicked and trampled. She was unconscious. In the ruddy light the new blood pouring out of her head, ears, and mouth looked black. Amid the mess I saw what looked like bone fragments. A much worse head wound on top of the previous one.

I got her into the car, propping her up. Her head was on one side. To my horror her mouth was hanging open like a corpse's and there was no recognition in her eyes. I had no idea what to do. I administered an anesthetic dart. It would stop her moving and doing further damage, at least. If she lost respiratory functions, well, I could do no more. She lolled forward, and I propped cushions about her, at least keeping further pressure from the wound. Skimming low, I headed out of the burning city and northwest.

I passed other refugees, columns of humans on foot heading who knew where? Some carried bundles of possessions. There were exhausted old people, sitting or sprawled despairing by the road, pregnant women who would have no midwifery ward, children, some without parents or adults, and hospital patients with surgical appliances and trailing tubes. Some died as I passed. There was nothing I could do for any of them. There was, I felt, nothing I could do for the human species beyond what I was doing.

Once, when I had left the great mass of refugees behind,

I saw a kzin aircraft. I was flying very low and cut the engine and landed. I think it saw us but to my surprise it took no notice. Like cats, the kzin seemed often unpredictable. It headed toward the great columns of smoke rising from the city and from farther east. I noticed there were no more of our lasers lighting the smoke clouds. Dimity continued to breathe.

I reached the monastery towards nightfall.

I noticed as I approached that the wooden building had been removed from the foot of the metal steeple which we once speculated the alien scout might have taken for a rocket or missile. It stood on bulky strap-on reaction motors and a complex of wide circular craters showed it had already landed and taken off several times. Fueling lines ran to it and it was surrounded by a ring of armed men.

The gates were closed. There were more monks with strakkakers on the wall. There was already a crowd outside, begging to be let in. Others of them were cooking one of the monks' zebras on a spit. A single kzin fighting aircraft would have got the lot in one pass.

I brought the car in low. Strakkakers were raised at us, but none fired. The place looked untouched by the direct effects of war, and I suppose the monks were still hesitant about killing humans. I saw Brother Joachim among those on the wall and shouted my identity to him.

We landed in the garth. I had checked my own strakkaker and its loading, folded its stock and barrel again and hidden it under my coat. Dimity was carried to the infirmary. The monks had good, modern medical equipment, and as well as autodocs there were brothers who were trained as human doctors, though much of the equipment and resources were already in use. I did not dare kiss or touch her as her head was shaved. They did not let me go with her further.

A few minutes after she was taken away I was in the abbot's study. He was staring at a bank of television sets that were alive and receiving.

Chapter 15

Comfort, content, delight—
The ages' slow-bought gain—
They shrivelled in a night.
Only ourselves remain
                    —Rudyard Kipling

There was a view from space of Munchen and the surrounding territory. Large areas of the suburbs were still in flames. To the east continuing fire and explosions as well as beams suggested a human army was still fighting. To the southwest, Dresden was a firestorm. Other screens showed human refugees, some scattering out to the north and the farms of the northwest and northeast without apparent plan or purpose, others, who seemed to be in a more organized column, heading for the hills.

"That looks another futile stand," I said, indicating a knot southwest of the crater at Manstein's Folly. The abbot shook his head. He seemed to take my presence for granted but perhaps that was an effect of extreme weariness.

"Not altogether. They know what they're doing. It's drawing off kzin from the city and the refugees. The humans have done better than I thought. Are still doing better. At this rate it'll take the kzin weeks or months to destroy all the pockets of resistance. It's still buying time, at least."

"Time for what?" I said, thinking of von Diderachs's words. I moved behind him and stepped back to get an overall view.

"At the moment, time is valuable for its own sake. It takes their attention from the slowboats."

"They could shoot them down if they wanted to."

"It also gives time to get more people into the hills. And . . . it seems from intercepted transmissions that the Kzin may actually . . . respect a bit of resistance, somehow."

However weary he was, he spoke with some calm authority. And guessing what I had guessed, I felt myself blazing with simultaneous hope and fury.

"You know a lot, don't you?"

"As much as I can learn."

"Inside information from military channels?"

"I've been calling in favors lately."

I moved my hand to my belt as unobtrusively as possible. With my next words things might get difficult.

"You knew for a long time."

"Yes. More or less."

"Where are these pictures coming from?"

"A satellite, obviously." The abbot's voice implied he didn't know or care which.

"The Kzin have destroyed all satellites."

"They must have overlooked this one, then."

He was too keyed up to feel the tiny prick on the back of his neck from the little collecting-gun's microscopic, instantly dissolving, sliver of tranquillizer. It seemed the first time in a long while that my professional training and equipment had been of use to me.

"Because it's shielded?"

"How should I know?" He put his hand up to his neck and patted it vaguely. His voice was changing. I hoped that a sudden shock now would get the truth out of him.

"How should you know?"

I had the strakkaker out now. I jumped across the desk and grabbed him by the throat, jabbing the muzzle under his nose.

"Don't play games with me! You know exactly what I mean!"

"Brother! . . . Professor! . . . Nils?"

"It's disguised, isn't it? And it's not a satellite so much as a spaceship in orbit?"

He didn't try to dissemble.

"How did you know?"

"I remembered what you said, the night it all began: 'We came here independently. . . . It almost bankrupted the Vatican.' Passage in a big slowboat would have been expensive, but not that expensive. I searched some of the old records when we got them up, and found no mention of your people on any of the slowboat passenger lists. My conclusion was: You came to Wunderland on your own ship."

"Yes. We left later than the original slowboats but we came

faster. The state of the art had advanced by the time it was launched."

"Where did that ship go? Not back to Earth. There would be no justification for sending an empty craft all the way back. So it's still here. Isn't it?"

"Yes."

"In a system as full of rubble as this it would be easy enough to cover with rocks and dust so it looks like another planetoid. With a low albedo and a high orbit it would be more or less unnoticeable from the ground among everything else that's up there. Your ace in the hole in case you *really* had to run or fight?"

"Yes."

"You made sure it was forgotten."

"Yes. Later we did a deal with some of the Families. Records of how we arrived were removed and people forgot. But we argued that in an emergency the ship would be at their disposal or ours—as lifeboat or . . . or warship. Then time went by and they forgot about it too. Who cared?"

"You denied it to the defense effort now, when we needed every ship we had to defend our world against alien invaders."

"But it was deactivated. There are no weapons aboard. It couldn't have helped the defense effort."

Weapons could have been fitted, and it might have been used for an ambush. Any spaceship is a weapon, properly used. But I let it pass. It would simply have been destroyed without affecting the eventual outcome of events, and at least it was a ship in being now.

"And now it's been activated again. These transmissions prove it."

"Yes. One of the families helped us, and we have a shuttlecraft.

"You can put that gun down," he said, "I'm not going to fight you. We have enough problems already."

"What are you going to do with it?"

"Get some of our people away, and some refugees. But it's a small ship. We can't take many."

"To Earth?"

"No. Earth is plainly under attack as well. What would be the point? I'm thinking of sending it to We Made It."

"Why?"

"First, to give them warning. Second, because it's taking some of our eggs out of two threatened baskets. These kzin may not know of We Made It."

"No. You must send it to Earth. With Dimity Carmody aboard."

"Why? She is a shapely and clever young lady, and I know that you are in love with her. But your subjective feelings are not important now, Nils. As God is my witness I'm sorry, but to send her would be at the cost of not sending somebody else. It seems to me she is better equipped to survive here than some. If any are to survive the kzin."

"At this moment she is in your infirmary, badly injured. Head injured. Isn't regrowing brain and central nervous tissue the hardest surgical procedure of all?"

It stopped him for a moment. But he replied:

"You must see that that makes no better case for her. To take her in that condition with a lot of medical equipment—equipment that's needed here—would mean leaving even more of the others behind. . . . You cannot think I enjoy making decisions like this?

"I, of course will not go," he went on. "These are my flock and I will not abandon them. In any case, I have already told you that it will not go to Earth. Earth warned us, remember. They already know of the kzin attack even if they are not directly experiencing it. And I can tell you we have had no laser messages from Sol System for some time. That strongly suggests their big lasers are busy." The drug might be making him tell the truth but I could see it was not affecting his willpower.

"I will stay here if I must, but send her to Earth!" I shouted. "She thinks she has . . . she knows she has made a mathematical discovery that may have military applications."

"Can you believe that?" He was nodding in his chair now. I hoped he was not going to lose consciousness.

"Do you know of her work?"

"I've heard of it. Who hasn't?"

"Given her own chair and research unit at the age of sixteen. Discoverer of Carmody's Transform. Can't you take what I say on trust? And if the Kzin get her . . ."

"If the Kzin get her she dies. Or perhaps not. Again, as a man, I'm more sorry than I can say, but I believe my duty is clear. I've thought of you as a friend and I've no wish to hurt you or any man or woman. But a lot of people are going to die. Having more neuronic connections in her brain than average doesn't morally entitle her to special treatment."

"She has a military value. This is not for me or for her. The survival of the human race may depend on it."

"Perhaps I should ask her."

There was a soft *phut*, a pneumatic sound. I saw a dart appear in the back of my right hand. I reached to pull it out but it worked quicker and more heavily than the one I had used. The room began to go black. As I fell I saw Brother Peter advancing, with his own collecting gun.

I came around on a couch in the same room. The daylight slanting through the window told me a night and more had passed. And it was a smoky light, pulsating with distant fire. I felt, stupidly, for my strakkaker. It was gone, of course.

"How do you feel?" the abbot asked.

"Rotten." There were pains everywhere. The locator implant in my arm was doing something. I thought in a disorganized way that it was probably triggered by my generally disordered metabolism.

"Well, you can be thankful. She's gone. You convinced me. You and rereading the effects and importance of Carmody's Transform and her other published work."

"To Earth?"

"To We Made It."

"That was a mistake."

"Think about it. The Kzin have let the slowboats go so far. They may change their minds and pursue them. If so, they'll be likely to go after the big ones, which are all going the same way, only a few days apart. A smaller and faster ship on its own may have more chance. Anyway, she's safely away.

"The Kzin have been landing heavier warcraft in the last few hours and using heavier weapons," he went on. "Apparently they've had enough play."

"I could have gone with her."

"I have watched you since you were a child. You have always been one of our human insurance policies, and now you are one of the few of them left alive. That last night you came here to the monastery, after the first feline was seen, I knew a storm was coming. The real reports from the Meteor Guard had been passed on to us for some time. Our culture was soft, complacent, faction-ridden, our people had lost much of their pioneering heritage very quickly, and few had survival skills. You have no faction and you know something of survival. You are even a public figure. You are needed here . . . as a leader, now.

"There is another thing," he went on, meeting my gaze. "The shuttle was full. I had to have twelve people dragged off as it was to accommodate her and her medical equipment. God help me! The rest were families. Should I have broken them up to make room for one more?"

"Yes, God help you!" Then, loath as I was to ask him anything further, "Can I . . . see the ship?"

"Are you sure you want to?"

"I'm sure."

"You can't see her," he said, "Even if you should. She's in coldsleep. But you can see she's out of this horror. She's as safe as any can hope to be. And so is whatever's in her brain. There's a camera on the ship. You can see she's getting away."

He touched the desk. There was a framed view of Wunderland from space, already shrinking. At one corner of the screen I could see some of the stony plating that had disguised the ship, now shed and tumbling rapidly away. Then we saw something else. I think we both cried out together. The abbot had fallen on his knees and was praying loudly. Something about a cup passing.

Two points of light on the screen: A red ovoid ship, moving *fast,* and behind it (or I guessed behind it—such things are almost impossible to judge in space except by comparing relative sizes) a black dot with a yellow halo: a reaction-drive ship, pursuing.

I saw the hull metal around the camera port beginning to change color, volatilize. The kzin ship was holding a laser on the fleeing vessel. It seems so intent on its attack as not to see the reaction-drive ship closing. Then I saw the reaction-drive ship firing at the Kzin. There was the beginning of an explosion, and the screen went blank.

"So the Kzin did pursue them. Why did you think they would not?"

"I hoped."

I could have killed him as he knelt there. Bare-handed, I nearly tried, but an overwhelming sense of futility prevented me. Besides, it was not his fault. He had more or less done for Dimity what I had wanted him to do.

The only ones to blame were the Kzin. And she would have died in sleep without the least knowledge. A better death than many would have on this planet . . . or on Earth, perhaps. I realized that perhaps taking the chance to send her to We Made It had been the right one: the Kzin would not spare Sol System, and the refugees cramming the big slowboats had probably bought themselves no more than a temporary lease of life that would be spent in coldsleep. Besides, I thought more savagely, killing him in these circumstances was too kind. The little ginger cat jumped suddenly onto his shoulder and looked at me with bright button eyes. It patted at something glittering on his fat cheek which I realised was a tear. He lifted the cat down, stroking it.

I don't know how much he read in my face. His voice was calm now.

"And now I have something else to do. Come with me."

I followed him. He climbed a spiral staircase to a room I had not seen before, lined with old books. He threw open a window.

"You get a better view from here," he said: "Look!"

There were the armed monks on the walls. A small door within the large main gates was open and people were entering the garth through it. Outside was a great crowd, more streaming to join it all the time.

"You can't take them all," I said, stating the obvious.

"That's hardly the most pressing concern." He handed me some high-magnification binoculars and gestured to the southwest. "Look toward Munchen."

More refugees. The line seemed to reach to the horizon. The fueling depot for the shuttle rocket had been demolished and was a smoking crater. But there was something else. I edited out the drifting smoke and haze. Above the straggling humans was the red ovoid of a kzin war-machine.

"They're coming." I felt some malicious satisfaction. "The refugees are drawing them to you."

"Yes, but they aren't attacking the refugees."

"I suppose they want to keep their meat fresh." I saw him flinch.

"What will you do?" I pressed him. It was sheer viciousness on my part, since there was so obviously nothing to be done. "You can't flee into the mountains or the swamp. And doesn't your church disapprove of suicide?"

"It is a great sin," he said, but his voice seemed abstracted and far away. "Condemned by solemn anathema from the days of the earliest councils."

"So what will you do?"

His momentary composure was gone again. If he was no longer weeping, there were beads of sweat running down his pasty brows to his face, and his voice shook. "What Pope Leo did."

I had no idea what Pope Leo did. I stood silent, staring with loathing at this fat, frightened little man who I had once thought of as a teacher and friend. There was an old paper-knife by one of the books. I reminded myself that was pointless for me to kill him when I doubted I could give him a worse death than the Kzin would, but I hoped that I might live long enough to see him die. He beckoned me back to his study.

He opened a standing closet and began to pull things from it. I smelled a musty whiff of aged fabric preservative and noted it somewhere even at that moment.

He pulled the colored fabrics over his head and around his shoulders, dressing himself in stranger clothes than I had seen him wear before, flowing multicolored robes with a vaguely horned-like hat. He groped in the closet again and brought forth a peculiar carved rod with an ornate, curved handle.

"I told you I am also a bishop," he said, as though that explained everything.

"Do you expect God to intervene? He's hardly been noticeable by his presence so far."

"He did when Pope Leo stopped Attila the Hun from sacking Rome."

"How did he do that?"

"He asked him not to."

"You intend to ask *them*?"

"We have made some progress in understanding the kzin language," he said. "It cost my friends in the government nothing to send me the reports of its work in that direction, and several of the brothers are scholars.

"I could not try to speak the Kzin's language, but I have some words of their script." He showed me a cloth on which strange marks had been made in bright colours. "I have tried to keep it short and simple," he went on. "I was going to write: 'Spare this place!' However, if there is a word for 'spare' in that sense we haven't found it. 'We ask for mercy' has the same problem—no word for 'mercy.' I hope that what this says is: "This place is sacred."

"They *do* have a word for 'sacred'?" I said it trying to wound.

"Yes. I think so. There are some hopes riding on our translation being correct."

"You think that will deter them?"

"Can you think of anything better?"

I said nothing.

"Come with me."

"Why?"

"I don't think Pope Leo faced Attila alone. I've seen old pictures of that confrontation. They seem to respect courage. You have obviously been injured recently and if you are seen standing with me it may have some small effect."

I followed him. The monks cleared the way at the gate for us and we stepped out to meet the advancing kzin.

✧   ✧   ✧

"Are you afraid?" I asked him.

"Yes. I have never been so afraid. . . . Rykermann, please, don't leave me to face them alone."

I hated him more than any living creature, but I stayed. I no longer cared what happened to me, and I know part of me wanted to see him die. But there was something else, too. I couldn't leave him, white-faced, blue lips moving in prayer, as he stood there shaking and did not run.

The kzin warcraft drew nearer, and details became plainer. It was a huge thing, now plainly the familiar combinations of wedge and ovoid, with the bulges and turrets of weapons. None of the makeshift weapons-systems that Wunderland had put together in the preceding months was even remotely comparable in size or power. How helpless and pitiful it made the fleeing humans look! It could have destroyed them, and us, like ants. But the kzin were still not firing.

It seemed to swell in size as it drew closer yet. There was no spitting of dust and gravel beneath it as there would have been with a human ground-effect car. The machine even had a certain majesty in its power and size. The ripping-cloth sound grew. We could see armoured aliens behind translucent ports.

It stopped. Like a scene from old fictions of alien first contact, a ramp was lowered. A kzin in ornate clothing and with an injured arm descended, followed by others less ornately dressed. The abbot held up his sign. I recognized the kzin: It was the only living one I had ever seen closely in the light.

Did it recognize me? Its huge violet eyes held mine. It thrust its sidearm into its belt and raised two objects: one was the modem from the cave-habitat that linked to the locator implant in my arm.

So that was how it had found me among the scattering hordes of human ants. Had I drawn it here? The other object was something smaller that I could not make out.

It ground out a distorted human word I recognised as "cave." Then it touched the belt it wore, the one that we had dropped to it. It placed the objects it held on the ground.

If the abbot could stand so could I. And some instinct told me it was better to stand and face this creature than either fall on my knees in supplication or turn to flee. Remembering the old game of "Tiger, Man, Gun," I folded my arms and puffed out my chest. In the game that had indicated I was a man, and proud of it, though in the game the tiger ate the man. Also, it gave me something to do with my arms. I felt that however the kzin interpreted the gesture, it could not be seen as too subservient, but could not be taken as a threat. We were plainly weaponless.

"Cave," I replied.

The kzin raised its huge sidearm and fired. But the bolt smashed into a derelict, abandoned ground-car that it evidently considered was an asset humans should not possess. Its gaze passed from me to the abbot and his sign. It opened its jaws and licked its black lips with a huge tongue.

I remembered a line from *The War of the Worlds*: "I was on the verge of screaming; I bit my hand." It seemed a good idea.

Then it turned and reentered the vehicle, the others following.

There was a long pause as we stood there, then the ramp retracted and the great warcraft rose and turned away, back toward the city. Its guns fired two or three times, picking off vehicles and bits of machinery. We heard a confused clamoring of voices from the monastery and the crowd of refugees.

"We must give thanks," said the abbot. "We have been granted a miracle." There was puzzlement more than anything else in his expression and voice. He seemed to be trying to come to terms with a completely new and strange problem. His hand fluttered to his chest. "I have been allowed to live to see a miracle."

I was not so sure. It seemed to me likely that, with the war plainly all but won, the kzin must be thinking of preserving the human population for their own purposes. I did not even think then that the kzin had sought me out specially: It had merely wanted to know where all the humans were heading for, and the monastery was the last place before the swamp and sea and mountains where they could gather. But all the same, things might have gone very differently.

"Come with me to the chapel," said the abbot. "I must call the brothers to prayer and thanksgiving." He clasped his chest harder and gave a sudden cry. He staggered in a circle, then fell, writhing. I bent over him.

"Heart," he whispered. "A fat old man's heart . . ." His voice and his respiration were rising and falling in an odd way. "Yes, listen. . . . Do you recognize it, scientist? Cheyne-Stokes breathing. Something few heard on this world when everyone had a doc. But I've attended the dying. . . . You will hear a lot more of it as the docs fail, I fear. . . . I'm not good at fear. . . . This . . . this is another miracle. It will save me much fear." His voice rallied for a moment.

"Rykermann, you may hate me, and God knows I am a sinner. But let me give you my blessing."

I shrugged. Hatred seemed unimportant now.

"My personal unworthiness does not affect the quality of it, you know," he whispered with a shadow of his old manner. "As for Masonry, I doubt you can teach the Kzin the handclasp. They haven't the fingers for it. But be careful of the—"

His writhing stopped. He mumbled feebly, then his voice grew a little stronger and he muttered something in a language I did not understand and raised his hand from his chest, waving it at me as though trying to give me something invisible. I bent closer to catch his words but as I did so he died.

I heard something else then, where the kzin had stood. Along with the locator modem it had left me Dimity's music box. It must have found it in the module, and it must just now have wound the tiny handle with the huge claws of its undamaged arm.

I walked slowly back to the monastery. The infirmary was still stocked, I knew. I had plenty of means of killing myself. Dimity was gone. She had, at least, I kept telling myself, died quickly and cleanly in space, and her knowledge was lost to the Kzin and their mind-readers. But she was lost to me forever. Forever? I remembered my profession of belief in a Supreme Being and turned it over in my mind to see if it helped. To opt out of this horror would be to do nothing, not even to mourn.

I also had, I now realized, a duty to survive. I was a professor of biology and a sort of chemist, and I would be needed. If not for my degrees and papers, then for the fact that my expeditions had made me, as I thought naïvely then, one of the few modern urban Wunderlanders who had any experience of camping and surviving in genuinely primitive conditions.

And there was another matter. Cats did not like fire. Bones and nitric acid made phosphorus. Caves with deep drifts of morlock and mynock bones would be a source of phosphorus. Guano, rich in nitrates, would be a prime source of low-tech explosives, a precious strategic resource if there was someone to build a factory to process them. That someone would have to know organic chemistry, and know at least a little of survival in the wild. Ceramics and armor to withstand laser-blasts, fabricated in hidden factories with improvised plant, would also need someone with chemical knowledge. There were probably no living humans, now, whose knowledge of the great caves of the Hohe Kalkstein came close to mine. Those caves would be a huge strategic resource.

From the makeshift and growing refugee camp I could already hear the sounds of babies crying from hunger. A live Nils Rykermann might be able to help there as well.

The abbot had shown me the reality of duty. As for that odd thing called honor, I thought I had seen a shape of that somewhere between van Roberts and von Diderachs, between the abbot and the kzin.

The first person I recognised in the refugee camp was Leonie Hansen. She had brought away as much equipment from the laboratory as she could carry and with a couple of others had set up a sort of clinic. A lot of it was very simple stuff—test tubes, optical microscopes, filtration paper I saw, all now beyond price. She, or somebody, had seen that the ultrasophisticated equipment of modern laboratories, like autodocs, would be useless without power sources and maintenance. I thought then that many things would go on, and that she would also be needed.

Epilogue

First, of course they asked her name.

"My name is Dimity Carmody."

That was not a We Made It name. But it was not a We Made It ship. The design, the specifications and part numbers showed it had been built on Earth, a long time before.

"What is your position?"

"Special . . . Special . . . Special Professor of Mathematics and Astrometaphysics."

"That's not a crew mustering. And you look too young."

They said "look too young," not "are too young." She had been in Coldsleep a long time. She tried to cooperate.

"No . . . I . . . I don't know what it is."

"Were you crew?"

"I don't know."

"What happened?"

"I don't remember."

They let her rest, and though it obliterated some memory potential they applied stronger nerve-growth factors and other regeneration therapy to the brain and where the central nervous tissue had been destroyed. They showed her pictures of the ship as it had been when they had boarded it.

"What do you remember?" The healers on We Made It were gentle and patient.

"I am Dimity Carmody."

"You came in an Earth ship. Did you come from Earth?"

"No."

"Where do you come from?"

"Munchen. I grew up in Munchen. My father let me play with his computer."

"Munchen?" They looked up an old Earth atlas and found

145

pictures of it. But when they showed her the pictures they meant nothing to her. They found New Munchen in the records and showed her that: the last pictures they had were of a small town of a few thousand people. She did not recognize the old buildings but she recognized the star patterns.

"That's Wunderland." That solved part of the puzzle. And the memory pictures could be Wunderland. Someone showed her flash cards of Wunderland and general human scenes. They showed her a copy of her own memory of the man with the yellow Wunderland beard, and that brought an almost overwhelming response of love and loss and grief so that they feared for her, but she could not put a name to the man and eventually it passed. At a picture of a cat she laid her ears back. Then they examined her ears again and found the characteristic musculature of some of the aristocratic Wunderland families. They found another picture of what looked like a cat, very distorted, in her own memory and showed it to her but it meant nothing though she flinched from it.

"Yes, Wunderland."

"This isn't Wunderland."

"Oh."

"What year is it, Dimity?" They meant, of course, what year did she remember it as being.

"I don't know."

She never on that world remembered the Kzin or what had happened on Wunderland, though she remembered her theoretical work at length, when the Outsiders sold We Made It a manual for a faster-than-light shunt whose first operating principles she alone could recognize and understand.

The Corporal in the Caves

2408 A.D.

Hroarh-Officer's deep radar projected a hologram of the nearer caves. A three-dimensional labyrinth of interconnecting tunnels and cavities of all sizes, it looked much more like a diagram of living organs than like a stone formation.

The resemblance was complete to the detail that there was movement going on in those tunnels and cavities. The radar could give only a blurred impression of the activity in the nearest parts, but like most of Wunderland's caves, with hordes of flying creatures importing protein each day, the great caverns of the Hohe Kalkstein contained a massive amount of life. Some of that life was human and dangerous. Some of it was nonhuman and also dangerous.

The long cliffs that marked the escarpment of the Hohe Kalkstein reared before them, honeycombed, honey-coloured for the most part (the Kzin had discovered honey fairly recently and were still deciding what they thought of it), in places blackened by fumes or gleaming white where explosions had blasted great shards of the outer limestone away. Here and there were the black entrances of the caves, dangerous and fascinating.

Along the dead ground at the foot of the cliffs the kzin infantry battalion were deploying from their vehicles. Not a huge force, but enough, it was thought, to sweep this cave system of the human and other vermin that infested it.

Corporal surveyed the eight members of his section, anticipating the inspections Sergeant and Platoon Officer would make before the final deployments. They looked Heroic enough, and their equipment complete.

He scanned the horizon about. There were flying creatures

in the air about the scarp, coming and going at the cave entrances. Movements of small animals here and there on the plains. Certainly nothing for kzin regular infantry to fear.

Company by company they moved off, each assigned to a major entrance. Vehicles were expensive, and parking them immediately below the cliffs would risk attacks on them from the still-unseen enemy. The final approach was made on foot.

Any tame humans in the area kept well away or out of sight. With Heroes slavering to come to grips with the Enemy, any human that raised its head during a kzin military operation would have been distinctly unwise. On the other claw, Corporal thought as he looked about the quiet landscape, there was little point in professional soldiers simply massacring unarmed anthropoids which were, after all, part of Wunderland's wealth and infrastructure. This was the Patriarch's Army, too disciplined to kill valuable slaves and taxpayers needlessly.

Already in these derelict farmlands—marginal when, after the first kzin landings, dispossessed humans had tried to cultivate them, and now long gone to ruin—they had rounded up a couple of very young feral humans: wild-eyed, with long tangled hair, and extremely dirty. They were either too knowing or too terrified to make trouble or flee, and Hroarh-Officer ordered them taken to the rear. If they were clever enough to be decorous, they might have a future as slaves in his household. Hroarh-Officer was a follower of Chuut-Riit's ideas and a student of humans, which was one reason he had been assigned to this force. They had also found a couple of very young kzinti—wild orphans, who had also been sent to the rear. Once these would have been left to fend for themselves, to perish or not as the Fanged God decreed for His bravest sons, but things were a little different now, and there were more than a few kzin orphans. . . .

The caves were, it was thought, an important base and resource to the feral humans. Ambushes were possible even before they reached them—possible but unlikely. Humans generally lacked the spirit to attack a kzin military force in the open.

Once a jerky, unnatural movement brought the platoon leaping to the ready. It was only an ancient human farming robot, long unmaintained and unreprogrammed, grubbing in the dust beside a shattered irrigation canal where crops had once grown. It was small for such a machine, unpleasantly suggestive of a living being grown crippled and stupid with age. Platoon Officer raised his sidearm as if to blow it to pieces, then lowered it again. The fact that the thing still had power to function, years after human attempts at farming had ceased here, suggested it had a power-source which it would be as well to leave alone. It might accidentally harvest some unwary human or kzin—in fact there appeared to be bones in a basket it carried that might have been meant to hold vegetable crops—but that would teach those concerned to keep a better lookout.

The limestone cliffs, crowned by the red vegetation of Ka'ashi, folded into a long canyon as the ground under their feet rose. Eagerly, kzin officers and troops broke into a trot. Detachments split off to guard the many exits.

So far there had been no activity from the feral humans. That might mean the kzin expedition had surprised them. But that was unlikely, Corporal thought. Humans' eyes and ears were poor, but they had many of them.

Urrr . . . if the ferals did the right thing, promotion might come. It was possible to dream.

Corporal, not uniquely among Ka'ashi-born kzin of his generation, had a more complex attitude to humans than he realized. On one claw, like all sapient non-kzin life-forms, they were slaves and prey. There were kz'eerkti—monkeys—on Homeworld. The very brightest of those made slaves, the rest reasonable sport, and their tricks and monekyshines could make good stories. Yet on the other claw, these particular kz'eerkti with guns and spaceships who had colonized Ka'ashi from Sol system were not like the other alien races the Kzin had smashed so easily.

True, kzin conventionally regarded them in their wild state as simply vermin, and Corporal had shared the rage of all the kzin of the Alpha Centauri system when the fleets sent against Sol limped back with their dead and their shame, but some, including most importantly Chuut-Riit, the new Planetary Governor and of the Patriarch's blood, had come to feel them worth studying, and sometimes odd similarities between kzin and humans had emerged from that study. There were some who had called to mind from the classics certain ancient verses composed by the Prophet Kdarka-Riit, one day when the Sage had been celebrating after a sucessful Kz'eerkti-hunt on Homeworld:

> The war will be both long and strange
> If one day under distant suns
> Kzinti find Kz'eerkti carrying guns
> And kzinti destiny will change.

There were even some Kzin who were thought to be *too* interested in humans, and there was a term for these, which if uttered in their hearing (but obviously never in the hearing of Chuut-Riit) could be taken as an automatic challenge to a death-duel. Corporal, for his part, had felt a slight fondness for some of the human slaves who had raised him. Also, one or two had served him satisfactorily since. He was, however, a professional. If Chuut-Riit and Hroarh-Officer said humans were to be studied, he would study them. Otherwise he would supervise them or kill them impartially as ordered.

There was a small library of ancient human military books at the NCO training school now, part of Chuut-Riit's encouragement of Thinking Soldiers in general and of Human Studies in particular. Human military records on Wunderland—all dating from their ancient days on their homeworld before space-flight—had been sparse and fragmentary, but there were memorable gleams here and there among them. He remembered one passage now, a surviving fragment of an old book:

> Many years ago, hoping some day to be an officer, I was poring over the "Principles of War" listed in the old Field Service Regulations when the Sergeant-Major came upon me. "Don't bother your head about them things, me lad," he said. "There's only one principle of war and that's this: Hit the other fellow, as quick as you can, and as hard as you can, where it hurts most, when he ain't lookin'!"

The author had been a human "named" Slim, a word meaning Thin. It did not sound like a warrior's Name. His rank-title when he wrote the book had been something called Field-Marshal. Somehow Corporal felt he could imagine the human Slim and the human Sergeant-Major in the scene he described. Hoping to be an officer . . . That brought his thoughts back to his own position, and he focused his attention on the task before them.

It might, Corporal thought, have been more effective to send a small force of two or three Heroes to spy out the land thoroughly, taking advantage of the humans' poor sight and hearing, before launching the main attack. That sort of thing had been done at the time of the first landings, when humans were an unknown quantity—these very caves had been a lurking-place for some of the first kzinti scouts.

However, and whatever Chuut-Riit said, many in the kzin military command had been reluctant to descend to using spies against monkey activities since then. It smacked of caution. Which may be one reason why this war against them is taking so long to finish, Corporal thought. The column was moving at a good pace, and he snarled at a couple of troopers who were losing their position, though with private thoughts that their close formation was inviting an ambush and hopes that any feral humans about had not also read Slim.

Not only would a more covert and dispersed attack have been a good idea, thought Corporal, but a night approach would have given them a greater advantage and been more comfortable than this jogging in the sun.

On the other claw, he conceded, a small scouting force might have trouble with the creatures the humans called morlocks—semi-sapient, roughly human-sized predators which had ruled the top of the great caves' food-chains. Though they were mere animals—no match for any Hero—they were night-eyed, silent, savage, knew the caves as their own habitat and could form packs. No Hero had deigned to learn much about them—they tasted foul—but at least they would give a kzinti force of this size no trouble, only entertainment.

He was pleased they were only lightly clad with a few leather straps to hold gear and accoutrements. Kzin wore armor in proper battle against enemies with appropriate technology, but few liked it. In the caves it would suggest faint-heartedness and would also be awkward and a nuisance. Heroes pursuing feral humans should need only teeth, claws, *w'tsais*, and beam rifles, with heavier squad weapons to call upon if need be. Flame-jets of superheated plasma gas could clean tunnels out quickly, but they made respirators and heat-resistant coveralls necessary. Nerve gas was also to be used with restraint: It would destroy a whole ecosystem that might have valuable products. On Homeworld in the ancient days there had been great exploits in caves in plenty, and cave fighting had an honorable tradition. It was decorous that a kzintosh warrior pursing his enemy into a cave should have equipment that hearkened back to that of Ancestors as much as possible.

There was something else: Apart from sheer love of claw-and-tooth fighting and the opportunities for individual heroism that it offered, apart from even the desire to preserve assets—slaves, prey and taxpayers—for themselves, something in the Kzin psyche was . . . not attracted to the quick use of weapons of mass destruction. The original conquest of Wunderland had involved probably less than an eight-squared of nuclear bombs on various human centers of resistance. The Kzin knew much about relativity weapons, anti-matter, neutron bombs, gravity planers, heat induction and now, as a result of contact with humans, the lethal properties of ramscoop fields and reaction drives in general. Deep-penetration bomb-missiles with nuclear warheads could destroy not only these caves but bring down the entire escarpment and irradiate the wild country beyond. But they were also plains cats whose ancestors not so long before had been plains hunters, and their feelings for the Fanged God's creation were complex. Seas, which they disliked, were a different matter, and they had invented the heat-induction ray to boil seas if necessary on planets whose populations resisted Conquest for too long. The Wunderland human who suggested to an audience of either kzinti or fellow-humans that the Kzin had scruples would not have been well received.

The gray walls of the canyon rose higher. Now they were in the entrance to the first cave. In that first great chamber, still lit by some daylight, they halted and deployed. Hroarh-Officer, the company commander, checked each platoon with the lesser officer directly responsible for it. Sergeants and NCOs made their own checks once again. There was the sharp smell of limestone and wet earth, mixed with many other smells, organic and inorganic. There were exotic life-forms here, as was to be expected, and also familiar ones. The temperature fell as the dark closed over them, becoming agreeably cool.

They passed the remnants of an old human structure in the twilight zone, broken open and plundered thoroughly long ago. Flap-winged creatures rose shrieking and fled through the air before them. They passed beside a tinkling stream into a deeper darkness which, with their sensitive noses and light-trapping eyes, was stimulating rather than inconvenient. Bones lay about, large and small. Some of the larger bones were plainly human. Others were kzin. Others—many others—were neither.

Here the labyrinth of tunnels began. It was the work of a few moments to make final lights and weapon checks. There were also preparations to be made against possible monkey tricks. Heat-detecting infrared wave cameras, nuclear, biological and chemical mass spectrometers and pathogen detectors were set up, along with the deep radars. Armored heavy troopers were assigned to guard them.

The companies split into platoons. Officers adjusted the goggles which could instantly compensate for near-total darkness or the flash of a major explosion. Hroarh-Officer inspected them quickly once again, his body language bespeaking valor and eagerness. Corporal noticed his own Platoon Officer's body language betrayed what could be taken as impatience with this delay, but only when he was well out of his superior's line of sight.

Kzin could, compared to humans, see in the dark. They loved lurking and stalking prey in the near-total darkness of caves, their pupils expanded to trap every particle of light. But even that superb light-collecting mechanism which was the Kzin eye could not see in absolute darkness. Smell was helpful but by no means a complete substitute for vision: While their sense of smell was many times more acute than that of humans, smells in the confined space of organically-rich caves could become overwhelming, especially once fighting started. Their equipment for cave fighting included not only modern lamps but also bioluminescent patches. These gave a dim greenish glow and had been a part of kzinti caving equipment since before ever the Jotok had introduced their forefathers to beam weapons and space drives. Now the platoons moved off into the tunnels.

Farther and deeper, past more bones and bits of human litter. Corporal wondered what weapons the feral humans had. Not much, he suspected. Years of unremitting warfare had worn them down, and many of their secret factories and arsenals in the back-country had been found. But even the smallest laser could blind.

"Monkeys have been active," said Platoon Officer.

Before them was a great pit. Not terribly deep or steep-sided, but wide and long, running off into darkness. Limestone pinnacles of stalagmites reared from it, discolored and broken.

Generations of cave creatures had built up deep deposits of guano here. The line that marked the old floor showed how great the volume of it must have been. Now it was gone, presumably taken by humans for fertilizer to promote the growth of the vegetable matter they ate (hardly different to eating the dung direct, Corporal thought), or perhaps to make chemical explosives. The latter idea was less disgusting but not comfortable. Such primitive compounds would not be very powerful by kzin military standards, but in the right place they could do a lot of damage.

Platoon Officer led them straight across the pit. Corporal thought uneasily that its sides high above them might make a good place for an enemy ambush. "Always scout your territory before you leap. Always have forward and rear scouts and flank guards. Spend time freely in scouting, for it is never wasted." So Chuut-Riit's new *Manual of Infantry Training* said.

There were the prints of human feet—many of them. Water seeping into some from the damp floor suggested they were very fresh. The kzinti followed them to a large hole, the top of a fairly steep downward slope. Kzinti had a rudimentary ability, called ziirgah, to pick up the emotions of other sapient beings—which in the case of non-kzinti generally meant prey or emenies—that Corporal thought would be useful to consult before battle but which many were ashamed to use because it was connected to the talent of the despised telepaths. None seemed to be using it on this occasion, nor was it necessary. From the darkness beyond the tunnel-like hole they could hear sounds that suggested human voices.

Scouting might be important, but Platoon Officer made no bones about his impatience now. Like all Nameless kzintosh who had climbed high enough to dream such dreams, Platoon Officer was desperate for a Name beyond all other things. Indeed a Name brought all other things: honor, esteem, fertile females, the right to breed.

There were many Nameless officers, and many high officers who had no more than partial Names, and a few, a very few, senior NCOs who had partial Names too. In the noncommissioned ranks these were an Order of the Elite of the Elite. Corporal had met one or two, and looked on them with awe, though a Name was far beyond his own ambitions. But valor and blood-lust were still the way to Names, victories won by no more preparation than a scream and leap, whatever the *Manual* said.

Corporal guessed Platoon Officer despised the cautious injunctions of the *Manual* as monkey thinking, despite its fearsome and illustrious author. Corporal was aware that he himself was too cautious to be an ideal Hero. He thought of the little group among his fellow recruits who had once been his particular companions: Most of them had been more recklessly daring than he, and many of them would be of superior rank or even Name if they had still been alive. That was another reason he would like a mate and a son: Sometimes late at night the dead were not satisfactory company.

Sergeant turned to him. "Corporal, you and your eight will guard the rear!" In strict military practice that was Sergeant's task, but Sergeant had no intention of accepting a position that carried relatively little chance of glory. Corporal obeyed unquestioningly. Sergeant also had the speed and strength for his orders to be unquestioned. And anyway, Corporal told himself, in these tunnels, where anything might be behind them, the position of rearguard was not actually shameful. Weapons were raised.

"Forward!" Platoon Officer rushed the tunnel, two eights of Heroes behind him, shrieking.

What happened next was hard for Corporal to follow. The shrieks changed in pitch into insensate screams—the screams of kzinti who realized something terrible but incomprehensible had been done to them. He heard their bodies crashing down to the flat ground at the foot of the slope.

He saw a couple of their lights swing through wild arcs, revealing nothing. Then the screams died away. There was another sound, plainly the sound of a kzin scrambling back up the slope. It stopped, and slid back. There was nothing more.

Corporal called, but no answer came. There were still some faint sounds but they were dying away. The smell of blood— kzin blood, mixed with the smells of marrow and entrail and pain—rose up the passage in a cloud.

One trooper, plainly maddened by what he heard and smelled, charged headlong down the passage, ignoring Corporal's shouted command to be still. Whatever happened to the others happened to him. A shriek, and then silence save for the thud of his body landing far below.

Kzin are not easily horrified, but Corporal paused. One part of his mind and his emotions stated imperiously that it was his duty to charge down after the others. If there was danger, a Hero attacked head-on, reckoning nothing of the odds. He was the senior surviving rank, and now the leader.

But the fact he was the only surviving NCO, he thought, put a different cast on things: he commanded an eight of troopers— eight minus one now—and without him they would be leaderless. He had seen before the consequences of that. Monkey tactics had always been to kill the kzin officers and NCOs first— a strategy in which, he thought, kzin officers and NCOs had often been only too willing to cooperate. Now he had a duty not to risk himself.

There was nothing to see down the tunnel but a dim light, presumably reflected from some of the Heroes' glow-patches at the bottom. Nothing to smell but waves of blood and death that drowned out all other smells. There might be human or morlock there.

"I wish a volunteer to explore the tunnel," he told the troopers.

"Command us, Corporal!" It was a unanimous shout and snarl. No kzin soldier would dream of not volunteering for hazardous duty.

"You." He picked the nearest trooper. He spoke with emphasis: "You are ordered to go slowly and cautiously. Tell me everything you smell, see, and hear as you go. When you have detected the danger return to us. Do not attempt to fight it alone."

Trooper advanced on all fours.

"It is a steep incline," he called back, "but my claws hold me. The ground is firm enough. I see nothing. I smell only the blood of Heroes. . . ."

"Still nothing," he called a few moments later. "Blood smell is stronger. . . . There is . . . a sting . . . my face. PAIN!"

"Come back! Come back at once! That is an order!" If Trooper were injured, an examination of his injuries might tell them what devilish thing awaited Heroes in that tunnel. And Trooper did not seem to be badly hurt yet. He heard Trooper scrabbling back, saying nothing. He seemed to be breathing with a peculiar wet noise.

Trooper came out of the tunnel. But he looked different. He shook his head and staggered as he moved. In the dim light it took corporal a second to see his face was a mask of blood.

"What happened? Report!" As he spoke he gestured for the unit medical kit to be brought.

"Pain . . ." Trooper's head fell apart. Corporal saw bone, brain, flesh and gushing blood. Trooper fell forward, plainly dead.

Roars of rage from every kzin throat. They surged about the top of the fall, preparing another mass-charge down it. Corporal cuffed them back with unsheathed claws, snarling curses. At last he got them into some sort of order, and held them till their fury had been brought under control.

There was only one possible course now. Corporal picked the oldest and, he hoped, the wisest of his Heroes. "I will explore the tunnel myself alone," he said. "If this kills me, take command and report to higher authority what has happened. Do not follow me."

It was as the Trooper had said. The tunnel was wide enough for Kzin on all fours, or even standing partly erect, to charge down it at a good pace. The floor of it was fairly firm and gave a good purchase for claws, but even in Wunderland's light gravity the bulk of a kzin's body had a tendency to run away downhill on such a slope. He stopped just before it began to level off a little.

This was, he thought, as far as Trooper had got.

Something like an insect tickled the tip of his nose. He drew back instantly, raised one hand, and felt it. His massive, stubby fingers came away wet with blood.

He waited. There was a stinging pain on the sensitive skin of his nose now, but from the amount of blood it was not a serious injury.

His strained his eyes to see anything in the gloom.

There was a fine line in mid-air. A fine dark line. He touched it with the tip of his *w'tsai*. There was a scraping sound.

It was fiendish and simple. A length of superfine metal wire, perhaps a single molecule in thickness, had been stretched across the tunnel. Listening careefully, he heard a tiny buzzing or droning sound. A miniaturized engine, he guessed, would make it vibrate minutely to increase the cutting effect.

The charging kzinti, going downhill with gravity adding to their speed, had simply cut themselves in half on it. No wonder there was so much blood. It was so fine that it caused little or no immediate pain and even Trooper going more cautiously had not realized what was happening when it was inside his head. Now there was enough blood and tissue on it for it to be visible.

He backed away up the slope. It would have been possible to crawl under the wire, but it was too late to help those below. In any case, he realized, there might be other such wires strung almost anywhere. He felt the eyes of the others upon him: they were waiting to be led.

How much of the wire did the humans have? That was a fairly meaningless question. Kzin grew such wire in space—it needed zero gravity and vacuum—but Markham and other ferals had spaceships and could be supplying it. He remembered Hroarh-Officer's warning now: "They can make anything into a weapon." It had been placed at the bottom of the steepest part of the slope, where the kzinti would run into it at the greatest speed. No doubt the humans were waiting in the chambers below for his own section either to come charging down after their comrades and share their fate, or to realize what had happened to them and depart, leaving the humans to pillage Heroes' sliced-up corpses of their gear and weapons and perhaps (he had heard rumors about human ferals) to eat the meat from their bones in a declaration of Conquest. Platoon Officer's radar, presenting an instant three-dimensional picture of the cave complex, might also be a prize for the humans worth more than *w'tsais* and beam rifles.

Well, it would not be borne. Quickly he told the troopers what had happened.

Should he report that this section of the caves was infested with ferals and the best thing to do would be to seal the entrances and pump in nerve gas or fire the plasma cannon to exhaust the oxygen and cook everything in the nearer tunnels? Perhaps detonate a dirty bomb in one of the big chambers and let the radiation do the business? But it would take time to evacuate the other kzin forces, and he had an obligation to avenge Platoon Officer, Sergeant, and the Troopers personally. It was not the kzin way to retreat from trouble. Traps were a contemptible monkey trick to be despised and destroyed. His *w'tsai* was also monomolecular-edged.

The *w'tsai*'s blade brought him to a stop as he started down the slope a second time. The wire itself was plainly very strong—in fact, he found, there were two wires strung a little way apart, and several reinforcing and bracing strands. Scraping the blade back and forth along the wire, following the sound, brought him to the anchor points. Using the squad's heavy weapon to destroy them would cost more time and perhaps collapse the tunnel. He marked them instead and crawled on under them, *w'tsai* held before him in one hand, beam rifle ready in the other, his troopers following close behind.

Below him was a scrabbling sound. He heard a confused clamor of human voices. He could see no more wires at the end of the slope, but held his *w'tsai* ready and launched himself.

He landed on the pile of sliced-up kzin bodies. He made a diving role forward through the fragments, hoping the humans' sight and other senses would not be acute enough for them to understand what was happening. The stench of kzin blood, rage, terror, and agony (some of them had lived a little after being bisected, long enough at least to know what had been done to them) almost made him lose control.

His troop followed hard behind. The humans scuttled away. One or two fired wild shots, and the kzin troopers hosed fire after them. Several fell to kzinti speed and accuracy before they reached the stalagmite groves. Corporal went for them in a standing leap that covered several body-lengths. His jaws clashed together in one's chest so that he felt its heart lurching before it stopped. At the same instant his claws ripped at another, tearing it into two pieces that he flung flapping away. His tail lashed out to trip another, curling around its spindly legs. He jerked it and brought it down. Another smash of his great claw to its head, the claw coming away slimy with the human's brains. Rifles blazed and the air shook as his squad leaped up to him, roaring and screaming with vengeance. Humans fell to left and right. Then they were gone.

The other kzinti would have leaped after the retreating simians, becoming separated in the darkness or hurling themselves, for all he knew, onto more traps and snares, if he had not called them back. He licked the blood from his lips. They formed a ring at the bottom of the slope, about the pile of dead, weapons pointing outward into the surrounding darkness.

Claws dug at his shoulder. It was Sergeant, mangled and mutilated like the rest, but not dead yet. His grip was still powerful, though his death-struggle was past. He turned Corporal to him and fixed him with his dying eyes.

"Win battle," he muttered. "Have caution." Then he tore a badge from the monkey-leather strap that held his decorations and passed it to Corporal in a hand that dripped with his own blood. He gasped out a few more words as he died: "You are Sergeant now."

He had not thought of that. But his promotion was quite orthodox. Most kzin got their ranks when those above them died in battle. He had been young to be Corporal and he was young to be Sergeant. It would be interesting to see if he grew any older. There was no time to think of it further. One or two of the other ill-fated Heroes might be alive, and would wish to be dispatched to the Fanged God with speed and dignity. There was also the securing of the area and the deployment of his troops. He had but six Heroes about him. True, there was no limit to what seven Heroes might achieve, but the caves were large. In any event, their objective was not security but pursuit and revenge. Somewhere a way off there was an explosion, and that momentarily lit the mouth of one of the tunnels snaking into this cavern. He guessed from the smell that the humans were using their nitrate bombs. Better lights would have been helpful, he thought. Next time we must bring better lights. The beasts might be anywhere.

He could make out a chaos of stalagmites, stalactites, columns, boulders, flowstone, fantastic twisting heligtites. He found the remains of Platoon Officer, but neither his radar nor most of the platoon's weapons were to be seen. He gathered up a few beam rifles and charges the humans had missed and issued them to his own Heroes. Ammunition expenditure was likely to be heavy. Somewhere was a rushing and bubbling of water— the stream or river that had made this cave. It sounded like a big one.

There were other sounds of movement in the darkness. One Hero fired instantly at the sound, but the beam struck a stalagmite only a few body lengths away. There was a shattering explosion of rock-crystals, giving lacerations to several Heroes.

If the humans had thrown one of their primitive nitrate-bombs in the direction of the kzin group and only narrowly missed it, the result would have been similar. Indeed for a moment Sergeant thought that was what had happened. Had they not been in a combat situation, trouble would have resulted. As it was the overeager Hero responsible received only glares and snarls from the others that suggested the matter might be taken up again when they returned to the surface. There was an odd rustling sound he could not place.

The great pillar glowed green for some time after the ray had hit it, glowed darker green and faded to black at last. These formations had enough crystal facets to trap light for an appreciable time. Bright beams of cooler light stabbed out from the section's lamps and dialed-down lasers but showed only a chaos of pillars, rocks, and shifting shadows. In fact the contrast between the lights and the shadows they cast made things worse for the night-eyed kzin, though they could consciously control the expansion and contraction of their irises. Sergeant found Platoon Officer's goggles but for the moment they were little help.

Then, out of the darkness he heard a high wailing sound: The humans had ratchet knives, although as far as his ears could tell, less than an eight of them. Kzin *w'tsais* rang and flashed as they were drawn. Beam rifles were cocked with a rippling, metallic rattle and crash. Seven Heroes against what sounded like about three eights of humans. It would be a quite serious battle, but, given the speed, strength and coordination of Heroes, not too serious. In hand-to-hand combat they had beaten far greater odds before. And vengeance fired their livers.

Black shapes darker than the darkness behind them. Swift and silent. He spun round. They stood for a second in the light, huge bulging eyes blinded, fangs dripping. Not humans, morlocks.

The things were as ugly as humans and smelled worse. They were carrion eaters, as contemptible as omnivores if not more so. And, he realized, the carrion they sought to eat was the flesh of Heroes. He advanced on the brainless things, expecting them to flee. But they held their ground, and, beyond the beam of his light, he could see the dark shapes of others advancing. There was something unpleasantly like coordination and purpose in that advance. They were spreading out to surround the living kzin. Dimly through the stalactite groves he saw more, flitting like ghosts. They were as silent as one would expect cave-predators to be.

Urrr. A modern beam rifle could dispose of the creatures quickly. There was a real enemy to fight without these other vermin wasting time and resources.

Something struck him hard on the head, knocking him sprawling.

"Down, Dominant One!" cried a Trooper. A beam cracked into the limestone beside him. A smoking, bisected morlock dropped from his shoulders. The creature had dropped on him from the roof. And he saw why its impact had stunned him. It clasped a heavy, pointed rock, perhaps the tip of a stalactite, but at any rate a weapon and tool. Even in Ka'ashi's gravity it could have split his skull.

He swung the beam of his light upward. The spiky roof of the cavern was seething with morlocks, so many of them the stones themselves seemed to be crawling.

Kzin beam rifles fired on the instant, nearly killing Sergeant and all his Heroes: the blasts knocked tons of stalactite and rock from the cave roof—calcite crystal formations like giant spears, hard, heavy, and as deadly to those below as any dumb missile might be.

The kzin had never questioned that beam rifles in a confined space should make short work of such creatures. A few minutes' experience showed this was not the case.

Firing up at the morlocks was clearing the cave roof of them, but slowly, and with a large expenditure of charges, apart from the menace of the great crystal missiles falling from the roof each time they fired. With the lights casting wildly waving shadows, the creatures blended easily into the darkness and dodged behind the protection of thick stalactites and columns.

Clearing the area around them was even more difficult than clearing the roof. The innumerable columns and pinnacles of stalactites and stalagmites made it a stony jungle, with endless places of shelter and cover. Heaps of rock and dark shadows concealed the entrances of tunnels. Further, the facets of crystal split and reflected the beams: It was like firing a laser into an infinity of tiny mirrors. Certainly the stone could be melted and blasted away with a concentrated beam, but the charges of the rifles would not last forever.

Still, the professionals of the Patriarch's Army knew their business. They adjusted quickly, kept cover, and when they fired an enemy usually fell. Sergeant looked back at the upward-leading tunnel, straining to see through the fumes and dust now filling the air.

He threw himself down and turned his eyes away just in time as a beam stabbed out to smash the rock just above him. There were humans at the tunnel. He lived because, like all their kind, they were slow, even without the weight of the kzin weapons they were using. He gestured to the Trooper near him to lay down a suppressing fire in that direction. Still, it was another complicating factor: a force of well-armed humans was positioned between them and retreat—if it had to come to retreat.

Aim. Fire. Aim. Fire. Then lights on the other side of the great cavern. The roars of kzintosh voices. It was another squad, attracted from other tunnels by the noise, charging into the battle.

The morlocks fell on them from the roof like black leaves in a forest storm. He and his troopers shot a few as they fell. Screams and snarls of the other kzin force, beams arching in all directions. Humans running and firing, to be hit by the Troopers' quick, accurate bursts.

"Forward!" cried Sergeant. "I lead my Heroes!" The squad leaped after him. No time to be concerned with traps now. In moments the stalagmite forest blinded the humans' weapons as it had blinded the kzinti's.

A huge crash just beside him. Dust and rubble flying. The humans had a new tactic: They were firing into the cave-roof above the kzinti, deliberately bringing it down. Urrr, two could do that. He turned and fired at the cave roof above the human position, noting as he did so that it was alive with morlocks. As they began to drop he wondered if the humans had noticed them too. In any event, they did soon enough. Beams blasting the darkness from the human position near the tunnel looked remarkably like the beams blasting out of the position near the second entrance where the kzin relief force was fighting, with him and his squad between the two.

Let the humans and the morlocks kill one another for the moment. The principle of concentration of force demanded that he reinforce the other kzinti.

To get straight to them across the cavern would take some time, he thought, not only because of the risk of being hit by their fire, but also with morlocks covering the roof. Best clear the roof first. A heap of boulders seemed to offer more shelter, at least from overhead attack. Gathering his Heroes about him, he made for this. Progress was slower than he had anticipated in the stifling smoke, and with morlocks about them on the ground, but at last they made the shelter of the large overhanging rocks.

Another sound grabbed at him, a kzin call, but the high, warbling note of a very young kzin. His ears swiveled to a black, jagged hole from which it came, and he rushed forward to it. As for the threat of wires, he could only hold his *w'tsai* before him and hope for the best.

There was another tunnel, a short one. Beyond it another cleared space, piled with bones and carrion. Even for a kzin warrior the stench was almost insupportable.

A curve of rock contained a labyrinth of holes—morlock dwellings. In front was a clearer space. Two creatures lay there: a part-grown kzinrret well short of adulthood, and a human. The kzinrret was spitting and snarling, but dragging herself in a way that showed Sergeant she was injured: Her back legs seemed to be broken, and there was something wrong with her forelimbs too. The human was unmoving and seemed incapable of doing anything but moan, but Sergeant guessed from the twisted, unnatural position of its own legs that it was in a similar case. Presumably that was how the morlocks kept their food. Kzin did the same at times. His rage made the dark cavity appear to turn red around him.

He dispatched the human with a quick blow to the head. Kzin never scrupled about inflicting pain or torture if this gave some advantage, but to allow sapients to suffer it pointlessly was considered indecorous. He counseled the kzinrret youngster to silence. He hoped she was bright enough to understand. He was glad she did not seem to be sexually mature. The last thing he needed now was the scent of a female to distract his or his Troopers' thinking. "Heroes will return for you soon," he told her in the simple words of the female tongue. "Ignore pain." There was no time for more, but it would have been an unfortunate morlock that showed itself to the kzin at that moment. He came out of the short tunnel and back into the main cavern at a crouching run, jaws agape, rifle ready, calling his Heroes about him.

On to the embattled kzin squad. The morlock tactics were simple: to drop onto kzin, weighting and hardening their impact with the rocks they clutched, and bite at their heads, eyes and throats, burrowing into them as they might, while others rushed them from the front and sides. At first no morlock lasted long against a kzin—dead morlocks and pieces of them were beginning to build a type of wall around the kzin position—but each ripping bite from those morlock fangs did damage.

Sergeant and his squad waded into the fight, taking the ground-fighting morlocks from behind. The morlocks were quicker than humans, but not as quick as a kzintosh, and nothing like as strong. His instincts and training merged, his slashing claws and teeth meshed together into the perfect killing machine they were.

The Kzin were battered, bleeding and exhausted when their claws and *w'tsais* stopped swinging, and the stocks of more than one of their beam rifles glowed with the yellow warning-lights of Insufficient Charge. But the wall of dead morlocks was high, and the rocks and the ground around were dark and slippery with morlock blood and fragments.

And still the fighting was going on in the cavern. Beam rifles flamed through the now dense, choking smoke and dust. Ratchet knives keened. The morlocks and the humans were still in battle.

Sergeant and his Heroes had been fighting hard and fast. He paused now and drew breath, ears knotting a little in amusement at this other fight. If the morlocks and humans decided to reduce each other's numbers while he and his Heroes readied for another attack he was happy to let them do it.

He checked his Heroes. The other squad had, he now real-ized, been very badly mauled. They had no officer or NCO left, though they had a medical orderly. Well, they had Sergeant now, and—kzin fighting spirits revived quickly—a bigger command for him was no bad thing.

Despite the number of Heroes dead, those still alive did not appear sufficiently wounded to be excused combat duty. They still had most of their eyes and all their limbs, and though some had deep and major lacerations, they also had field dressings in place. Where limbs had actually been broken, field prostheses were unfolded and applied and supported them.

The morlocks seemed to be holding back now. Perhaps they were all engaged with the humans, or perhaps they were redeploying. His light darted around the roof, but between the columns and the shifting shadows it was hard to make out much. Once, long ago, he realized, this cavern must have been nearly full of water, and flowstone had spread out on the surface of that water to make suspended tables, attached to the ceiling and hard to see from below. There might be any number of them there.

He deployed his Heroes in a conventional defensive posi-tion, with a rise of rocks in the center where they might stand if necessary. In the roiling smells of pulverized limestone, guano dust clouds, burned flesh, blood, and smoke, his nose was of little use. It was time to reconnoiter.

Sending Trooper down the tunnel to his death had been an operational necessity. But he would not send a subordinate out twice. Kzinti, and especially newly promoted Sergeants, led their Heroes. Once again he placed Senior Trooper in charge and headed back to the rock heap, running almost on all fours, threading the glades of stone cat-swift and silent.

A morlock, more silent than a kzin, leaped up at him, striking with a daggerlike pointed stone. It tore a burning furrow across his chest spurting purple blood. He hoped the creatures were too stupid to know of poisons. It leaped backward with the slash, but his right claws held it and his left claws tore its face away. He flung it from him, leaving it eyeless, screeching. Good! Let it terrify the others! Its screech went into ultrasonic.

Above him something was happening. The whole pile of boulders was shifting. It was slow at first, but like the movement of a hill. Another trap, and evidently the morlock's dying shriek had triggered it. *Cleverer than we thought.* He leaped aside, into the short tunnel leading to the morlock den. Not quite quickly enough. A section of stalactite the width of a tree trunk fell across him, pinning his legs and the lower part of his body. He struggled to push it clear, but even in that gravity it weighed too much. Fortunately the ends were held on other rocks. It pinned him down but did not crush him.

The dust cleared. He was unsure if he had lost consciousness, or if he had taken a fatal blow to the skull. He lay completely still, his fur lifting and lowering minutely to compensate for the movement of his breathing. His surface blood vessels contracted. A heat sensor would have picked him up, but a motion detector might not have. A corpse in the rubble.

The short tunnel seemed partially blocked by fallen rocks, but the banks of this chamber were so honeycombed with holes there might be any number of other entrances. The injured kzinrret youngster was mewling where he had left it. Could it help him? No, even if it could understand him its injuries were plainly disabling.

Ziirgah, developed for stalking, was very little use to a nontelepath in a situation like this. Too many stressed and desperate minds nearby reduced its simple impressions to confusion, and it was better blocked out.

There was a scrabbling sound from one tunnel. The morlocks were returning. Nothing for it but to lie still and hope to kill a few when they came within reach of his claws. They would probably draw back then and stone him to death. It would be painful and undignified. He would never have a Name or a line. The Fanged God would have no use for a son who had not died as a Hero should, on the attack. Death loomed huge and dark as he waited there, like the Emptiness of Space. *I am afraid,* he suddenly realized. The realization was more terrible than the fear itself. He would go to the Fanged God not merely with the shameful death of helpless prey in a trap, but a coward. There was the glow of a lamp. But morlocks had no lamps. Then he saw the scrabbling creature. It was not a morlock but a human. It approached the young kzinrret and bent over it.

Unable to control himself further, he snarled a challenge. The human jumped away, a weapon flashing into its hands as it vanished behind a rock.

The kitten was crying out now, in the nursery tongue.

"Come back! Pain! Pain! Help me!"

The human cried back. But it was speaking the nursery version of the kzin tongue too. He recognized its voice as that of a female.

"Be still! Try not to move. Help will come!"

Sergeant was amazed. He had been raised by human slaves in his Sire's house, and he knew some humans understood and even spoke the simpler kzin tongues, the soft sounds and small vocabularies of females and kittens. He knew—it was part of their alienness—that human females were sapient. But why did this human speak to a young kzinrret?

He had regained control of himself now. If he could not move he could speak.

"What are you doing?" He spoke in the slaves' patois, a combination of the female and the nursery tongues plus some Heroic and Wunderlander words and constructions.

She approached him cautiously, weapon raised. But he was plainly trapped and helpless. That, presumably, was why she did not fire. The sounds of fighting in the main chamber seemed to have stopped, and he wondered what that meant.

"Some of us have been caring for this one," she answered. She spoke in Wunderlander, the human tongue, which he like many Ka'ashi-born kzintosh understood but found hard to speak.

She turned the lamp to a greater brightness, inspecting him.

"Light keep morlocks away," he said in the patois.

"No, their eyes are for twilight zones. Bright lights, they close eyes. I was a research student once."

If this monkey is talking she is not killing me, he thought. Keep her talking. He remembered how, as a kit, he had learned to wheedle sugary cakes and other favors from his human nurse-slave. Wheedling had been better than claws, from which her predecessors had simply learned to flee.

"Why you feed small one?" he asked.

"Some of us began caring for her before morlocks attacked," she replied.

"Why? You are ferals."

"There were feral children. Human and kzin. They had set up a camp in the caves . . . together. Most of them, human and kzinti, were much younger than this one. It would have been impossible otherwise." That was certainly true, he thought. It seemed impossible enough anyway. Young kzin kittens might play with strange species till they decided it was time to try their teeth and claws on them, but kzin adolescents of either sex were ferocious, predatory, and xenophobic far beyond even adult kzintosh. The only regard they gave other life-forms was as links on their food chain and their value as sport. That was especially true of the males after a little training. But evidently something very odd had happened here.

"This one, and that dead human, both older, seem to have held them together," the female man continued. "She is a young kzinrret only but she seemed to have some . . . instinct I do not understand. She is special. We found out too late. The morlocks carried them off and when we followed, she and he were all that was left. Then there was more fighting and we lost them."

"Why you feed small one?" he repeated.

"Have I not explained?"

"No. She is kzin, you are monkey."

"I don't know. It is a thing some humans do. Evidently it is a thing some kzin may do too."

"She will eat monkey-meat one day."

"We have our own sense of honor . . . some of us."

"Wire is honor?"

"Wire is war. Is war too hard for kzintosh?"

Sergeant checked his convulsive effort to throw off the rock and leap with the thought that perhaps the monkey was deliberately trying to madden him with the insult. He would not oblige. He remembered one of Chuut-Riit's lectures: "You think you understand them, and find you do not. You think you do not understand them, and find you do. They are full of paradoxes, but with a few generations of proper culling, this will be a most useful species." He thought upon what it had said:

"Ferals? Human cubs and kzin kittens? Together?"

The human looked at him. This time he detected something complex in the emotions emanating from it, but it was as if he had passed some kind of test. It reminded him of the feelings of old Kiirg-Greater-Sergeant when he survived his recruit training.

"How close together I do not know. They were in the same

part of the cave system. But morlocks got them anyway. They will be back soon."

"Lift this rock off me!"

"I cannot. And if I could, it would not be wise."

"I fight morlocks. Morlocks eat you."

"You would eat us too."

That was certainly true.

"Give me your word that you will not fight me and I will not eat you now," he said. "We need to fight morlocks."

"Better for me to kill one kzin than an eight-squared of morlocks. And morlocks are victims like humans. They fight invaders of their world."

He had no idea what the word "victims" meant but he saw the human's military logic. Indeed he appreciated it. Arguing with a monkey! he thought. Still, I must get this creature to be of use. My duty is to return to my Heroes.

"Kill me and they kill you," he replied. "Break legs like kitten, like monkey."

"Instead of kzin killing us? What difference does it make?"

The voice reminded him again of old nurse-slave, and he repeated something it had once said. "Live to fight another day." It was not an argument that would affect most kzintosh, but he thought he knew something of human psychology. He thought of something else, but it was difficult to say it without giving the impression that he was trying to beg for his life. Better a thousand times to die at the hands of a monkey than that a monkey should think that. She was raising the beam rifle.

"Kzin remember," he said.

That made her hesitate.

"You will not harm me," she said. "Your Name as your Word."

"I have no Name. My Rank and my Sire's Honor as my Word. Release me I will not harm you while we are in this cave, or during the day that we leave it."

He saw her dial the rifle down. Did she mean to cook him slowly? Then she fired it into the ground beside him, the blast digging a shallow pit. Slowly, she moved the beam an inch or two toward him, the heat of it scorching his fur and skin. Then, staying out of reach of his claws, she climbed onto the pillar, and smashed the butt of the rifle down onto the crust of flow-stone that remained. She dialed the rifle up to full beam and showed him the lights on the stock indicated that it was fully charged. She crouched and held it on him with one hand, steadying its weight on her bent leg, while with the other hand she scraped smashed rock away.

"Stay still," she ordered him. She backed away, then settled herself into a bay of rock that protected her back and flanks.

"Now move," she said.

Lurching and twisting, he was able to get to this cavity and work himself free. The human lay prone, pointing the beam rifle at him. Her finger was pressed on the firing-button and the light on the stock showed it was at first pressure. The dot of its laser sight was on the fur in the center of his torso. Deliberately, he turned away from her so that he could not spring.

"We fight morlocks now," he said.

"So be it," she said. She stood on her hind legs, but with the weapon still held ready. "We fight morlocks. Poor bastards! They did us no harm."

Sergeant felt an odd conflict of emotions in this human. It must have been strong to register with him. He continued speaking to her in an attempt to steady her, asking the question which another kzin would find of the greatest importance and which he assumed mattered to monkeys equally.

"You have human Name?"

"Leonie."

"What does it mean?"

"Lion."

"What is lion?"

"A cat. A big, ferocious cat."

"Is that a joke?"

"No. We used to think cats were beautiful. . . ."

He recognized the emphatic human past tense but did not pursue the matter. Something had evidently happened to make them change their minds.

"Truce now," he said.

"Yes, truce now. I find I do not want to die in this stinking hole. Does our truce hold into the next cave?"

"No sense if it does not."

"I suggest it holds until we both agree to end it. Your Rank and your Sire's Honor as your Word."

"Yes. And yours."

"Yes. If you trust a monkey."

"You could have killed me already. I trust."

"Markham told us kzinti keep their word when it is solemnly given, usually."

"Usually. But do not trust too much."

"The main tunnel seems blocked," she said. "There are others. We should go before the morlocks return. But we cannot move the kitten. Broken legs. Marrow get into blood. Die."

"She is kzin. She is female but she is brave. Other Heroes will get her. Or she will die like kzin."

"We could move her slowly and carefully into a shallow hole. It may kill her but it is a chance we must take. Then with your Hero's strength you could move a big rock across the entrance. Too big for Morlocks to move easily."

"Then, if we die, Heroes not find her. She starve. She die." He realized with an odd feeling that he had just said "we" to a monkey—a feral, at that.

"It would not be a perfect seal. Just to delay the morlocks getting to her. If we die she can scream and alert other kzin when they come. But I suggest we hurry. This is not the place for us to be caught by the morlocks in our turn."

The tunnel she led him through was long and winding. At certain places he saw that something—humans, he guessed—had widened it. With the human going ahead he did not fear wires.

There was the tunnel mouth. He poised to leap.

"No! There!" she pointed. He could not see it but guessed there was a wire. "There!" Putting his life in the monkey's hands, he charged, bursting out through a curtain of straw stalactites and a lacy stone shawl, sending crystal fragments flying.

The great cave had far fewer lights now, only a few swirls and flashes of beams and glow-lamps from a single source, a high place beside one of the cave streams. It formed a natural amphitheater, and Sergeant had briefly noted it previously. But he could see the swift dark shapes of morlocks attacking from the roof and through the stalagmite groves. And there were two very distinct sets of voices coming from the single patch of the lights.

"Listen," Leonie said. "It sounds as if human and kzinti have made a truce there, too."

"Urrr. Should turn up lights. Blind morlocks."

"More likely to blind themselves if they do. Morlocks don't like light but have thick eyelids. I think with most cave lights, they can close eyes and simply stay in total dark. Need very bright light to drive away."

"You know lot about morlocks. Urrr."

"I've dissected them. I told you I was a student of life once."

"We join companions. Come."

They got most of the way to the amphitheatre before the morlocks rushed them. They came from above and behind, piling on the human female first. She snarled and screamed in a way that reminded him she was named for a cat. He turned and saw she was fighting, but giving ground. There were too many morlocks for her. He screamed and leaped into the fight.

Now it was the morlocks who were giving ground. Or rather, dying where they stood. There was a trail of the things dead and dying behind him, but as he advanced alone into the thick of them he was being outflanked. In a moment, he knew, he would be surrounded. He began to back away. Then he stumbled over a torn, writhing body, slipped in the blood now covering the cave floor, and fell. As he tried to rise morlocks leaped onto his shoulders from behind, biting at his throat.

"Drop, Tabby!" he heard the human female. Thoughts too fast to describe as he clawed and fought. "Tabby" was a nursery word humans used sometimes for kzinti, though not in their hearing. Was she cursing him to his death?

"Drop," she cried again, and this, he just recognized, in the imperative tense of the Heroes' Tongue. It was the same warning Trooper had given him previously. He threw himself forward and the female struck with her ratchet knife, sending the morlocks flying in pieces.

"Back! We can still hold them!" Back they went side by side, slashing with knife and claws, a dozen slow steps or so, into the little amphitheater. There stood two of his Heroes, aided by two more doubled-up wounded, surrounded but fighting still, another Hero badly wounded or dead, and three humans, also injured, but two of these still fighting with beam rifles and knives. Most of the beam rifles had yellow lights glowing on their stocks. He saw Platoon Officer's valuable deep-radar set lying smashed to pieces. No human would carry that off, anyway, he thought.

A single male human stood in the largest gap in the palisade of stalagmites and columns, fighting too many morlocks, its movements painfully slow to the kzin. An exhausted beam rifle lay beside it. Its ratchet knife still howled, but the human needed both arms to hold it: Even for a human it was doing badly. Its arms, even by human standards, looked skinny. Its hair was pale, either yellow or white with age. Sergeant leaped into the breach beside it, rampant and slashing. The morlocks fell back from the kzin's berserker assault, and there was a pause.

"We underestimated them," this human said in Wunderlander when it had ceased respiring violently. "They are more numerous and intelligent than we thought. Also," he added, "they are well-motivated." Its hair was yellow, he saw, not the white of a really old monkey. But it was not strong. Sergeant was sizing it up as the Morlocks came again.

They came in waves, inflicted a little more damage on the

defenders each time, caused more ammunition to be expended, and then drew back. There was a bombardment of missiles from the roof. One badly injured Hero lost control and hobbled, shrieking and howling, out of the perimeter into the darkness after them. He did not return. A little later another followed. Falling rocks accounted for the other two and also for one of the injured humans. The female human ran from place to place, firing one of the rifles. Perhaps from a distance it would create the illusion of a greater number of defenders, but he doubted it. Sergeant left the male human to hold the breach in one lull while he dragged and lifted some larger stone fragments onto the tops of broken stalagmite stumps in an effort to make a sheltering roof. It did not last long. Occasionally his ears picked up sounds of other fighting far away. He lost track of time, and was amazed when his timepiece told him a day and a night had passed. The dead humans provided monkey meat, though he tried to eat it out of the other humans' sight in the interests of holding together the fragile alliance that seemed to have evolved. Once after this, knowing he must conserve his strength, he even slept. If the humans took advantage of this to kill him, so be it.

He was again amazed to find how long a time had passed when he awoke. The Morlocks had not attacked, and the humans, he noticed, had not killed him. In other times of lull the humans slept.

At times they tried the lamps at high strength, but they seemed of little use: the Morlocks did not like they light but they simply dodged away in the stalagmite forest or were lost in the shifting shadows.

The bombardment of stone waxed and waned, but for long periods it was unceasing. The morlocks were throwing chunks of rock and throwing them accurately, but the dense calcite crystals from the roof were doing the most damage. A well-aimed rock could injure, but those heavy falling spear points could kill, and there was nowhere to hide from them.

"Female fights well," said Sergeant in the slaves' patois, with the idea of encouraging the male human who seemed to be the troop's leader to emulate its companion. It was sitting, knees drawn up to its chin, covering its head in its hands. The bombardment had stopped for a time.

"I tell female go," said the human in the same broken tongue. "Not honor make female fight. Question Hero let female go?"

"Female help Hero," said Sergeant. He could hardly eat the female now, and though it was useful with their scanty numbers, he did not like it fighting beside him and most certainly he did not want to be placed under any further debt to it. "Female go."

The morlocks were still holding back, but the rocks were still falling. It was the head-injuries that were killing. Even a massively-muscled kzin could withstand such blows only so long. Kzinti themselves were forceful and dextrous stone-throwers, and they tried returning the bombardment, but it was pointless when there was no target to see. Two more humans were down, sprawled at the base of a couple of large stalagmites, and all his Heroes were down now. He checked them all, but with gross head injuries they were obviously dead. At least they had died in battle, as kzinti should. The thick smells of human and kzin blood—and not a little morlock—made thinking difficult. *Assess your ration-strength.* The human male, the female, and Sergeant. That was all that were left.

"Female go now," he said.

"Get out, Leonie!" the male human shouted. "Make for tunnel 14-K!"

"No," the female shouted, "I'll not desert you!"

"This is a military order! Go! Report! Go before they attack again!"

"Come with me, then. We can get out together!"

"No. I must delay them. Me and this tabby here. Now go!"

There was a pause. It was hard to tell how long it lasted. Then Sergeant heard a sound he recognized now as the rustle of morlock feet. The female had left the inadequate shelter of the amphitheater and was moving along a path that led through the stalagmite forest. Too slowly.

"Run, Leonie!" shouted the male human. Sergeant thought of the trench she had dug to set him free before the Morlocks came. "Rrrun, Leonniee!" he roared in his best attempt at human speech.

A dozen morlocks were after her, two clinging to her shoulders, fighting for the throat bite. She fell and went down the flowstone into the river. He remembered to dial the beam down before pointing it: She would be damaged further if it boiled the water. He saw her drifting in the green-lit water, morlocks still clinging, then going over a rushing fall. She seemed to be unconscious. More morlocks followed: They seemed adapted to the water, and he guessed that such creatures could move in every part of the cave with equal ease.

There was little point in remaining in the amphitheater now. The two remaining sapients were not enough to hold it. Still, it was honor and military common sense not to simply abandon the remaining monkey with no word.

"I get her!" He rushed the flow-stone, leaping across the stream to smoother ground on the other side. Snarling at the mud that splashed about his legs, he raced and leaped over the fall, scattering the morlocks with a few swipes of his claws and *w'tsai*. When they were clear of her he used the beam rifle.

She lay facedown in a pool. Sergeant remembered nurse-slave again. In that position she would, like a kzin, die very quickly through inhaling water if she was not already dead. Alive she might be a fighter in their need. And she had helped and trusted him. That made a debt, even to a female. Sheathing his claws, he dragged her from the water and pushed her into a sitting position. She began to cough and struggle, but he held her.

He felt an odd, uncomfortable empathy for the male human in its attempts to preserve the female. He thought of the kzinrret he himself particularly desired to be the mother of his line, Veena, daughter of old Kiirg-Greater-Sergeant. She was, like practically all females of the slightest desirability, forever beyond the reach of a Nameless one, as was the possibility of a line, but had Veena been here, he thought, he would have tried to save her. Even Murrur, who was older and less attractive, but . . .

Trying not to damage the fragile creature further, he worked its chest in and out, hoping human and kzin lungs were similar.

"Truce! Truce!" The female gasped. Sergeant was irritated. He, a Hero, did not need to be reminded of such things. Then he saw the male human beside him.

"I do that," said the male human. "Heroes better at fighting."

The female's torn costume was stained with spreading blood. She had some deep lacerations. The male tore it open and sprayed her with something that stopped the bleeding, though it seemed nearly exhausted. Sergeant thought the male would have done at least as well to use it on itself.

"Can you walk?" it asked the female.

"Yes, I think so."

"Go. 14-K. The third north tunnel. You'll come to a marker. Tell them to use plan Marigold. Go. Hurry. I will delay them."

"No. You have no chance. If the morlocks don't get you, the kzin will."

"Go, Leonie. Those are my orders."

The female put her arms around the male for a moment, made a peculiar sound, and staggered away in the characteristic shuffling run of an injured thing that screamed to every one of Sergeant's hunting instincts for a pouncing strike. He fought them down. He heard her for a minute in the tunnel, and then the rustle of morlocks among the complications of the roof again, as well as a chinking noise which he now recognized as meaning they were carrying the heavy calcite crystal missiles. There was no more fighting at the amphitheater, only the morlock rustling, and no lights but their own. Well, it had simply been a place to die in, not much better or worse than any other in these caves. He could just make out the human.

"Can you see me?" he asked.

"A little," said the human. "A thing in the dark. I see your eyes. A little while ago I would have feared the sight of kzin eyes in the dark more than all fears. Now . . ."

"Others dead." said Sergeant.

"Does kitten still live?"

"If morlocks not kill it, kitten alive."

"Now it is just us," said the human. "If the truce between us holds, I intend to buy time."

"Time? For what?"

"For Leonie to escape. There is another thing. When we found the kzinrret kitten—I will not lie to you—I would have killed it. Leonie stopped me."

"Why?"

"Partly she hates all killing, though she is a good fighter. Yes, she hates killing even kzin. Partly, she had seen young kzin and human ferals sharing a cave. She hoped . . . well, she hoped for something I think impossible. But for her sake I will say that I fight to defend the kitten as well. And if you live, Kzin, tell your kind that monkeys have Honor too."

"You tell them." Try to keep the creature's spirit up, he thought. "Live for your Leonie Manrret."

"I am wounded. Getting old if my treatments stop. Weak now. Lucky to have lived so long. Lucky not to have died in these caves long ago. Lucky to have a few geriatric drugs. Lucky see many sunrises. Lucky Leonie may live. Many friends dead. Not ask for too much."

A cloud of morlocks struck them, burying them under a heap of bodies, biting jaws, striking stones. Sergeant ripped and slashed his way out of the heap, turned, and dragged the human free. He turned and swam into the morlocks with a scream, and scattered them. There was his beam rifle, its stocklights glowing yellow, but still with some heat left in it. He fired it at point-blank range, heedless of the exploding stone. They fought together till the human collapsed and the bodies were piled high.

Sergeant leaped to the top of the heap of bodies. His beam rifle was exhausted now, but he had his *w'tsai* and his teeth and claws. At his feet the blood-soaked human had partially revived and was still using its knife.

The morlocks were gathering again, and there was movement among the formations of the cave roof above. For the moment they were holding back, but plainly their numbers were gathering. The situation, he realized, was hopeless. He would go to the Fanged God this day. Well, thanks to the Leonie human it was a far better death than it might have been pinned under the rock. No Hero should ask for more than to die in battle. He began to chant Lord Chmee's Last Battle Hymn as he slashed. The morlocks drew back a moment, and the human spoke.

"So we die together, cat and monkey."

True, and no point in raising false hopes of life now. "Have you a human 'name'?" One should know who or what one died with.

"Rykerman. Nils Rykermann. A 'Professor' went in front of it once. And you?"

"Sergeant."

"Sergeant. I see. So that is how important we are? They sent a Sergeant to flush us out."

"Platoon Officer died on the wire. Many Heroes dead. Many monkeys will pay. Urrr."

"But you saved Leonie?"

"The female? She spared young one. Helped me. Is debt, even to female. I do not know if she lives but she has chance. Urrr."

"I will remember that."

"You will not have long life to remember, I think. But maybe you go to your monkey-god."

The human staggered to its feet. It leaned heavily on a stalagmite column. It was deeply bitten and lacerated, bone showing near both its shoulders. Cloth bound some of its wounds but not all. It could have little blood left.

"I was going to end truce and kill us both with this," said the human, producing a nitrate bomb. "But I will spend it to buy her more time. She may get away." It armed and threw the bomb in a single movement.

Sergeant went down in his explosion reflex. The human went down more slowly. Sergeant had a moment to screw his ears tightly shut before the pressure waves in that confined space burst them. He thought for a moment that the blast would bring down the whole cave roof. Even with his ears closed, he was deafened, and he thought the deafness was permanent until he strained his ears and one by one he heard sounds return: the stream, the human's panting breath, distant feet far up tunnels, rustling and slithering. It was right for a kzin at the point of death to reflect upon his life. His had been short and nameless, but, he hoped, not shameful. The human's head was sinking down onto its chest. It was still bleeding copiously from its many wounds. Perhaps as soon as it died he should eat it to give himself strength for his last stand, though it would have little blood left. Fumes clearing. He knew exhaustion had nearly finished him. No sound of the enemy for a time, only the breathing of the two of them.

A rustling, repeated like an echo.

"Morlocks return," he said.

The human raised its head.

"Come then. Let us show them what cat and monkey can do."

They came again against the two screaming, blood-soaked sapients. The human fought until it went down and Sergeant glimpsed morlocks ripping at its flesh again. Then they were upon him. His *w'tsai* was gone. His claws were so clogged with morlock flesh and tissue now that his swipes at them were almost ineffectual. Blows on the head and shoulders, heavy blows of rocks. He leaped forward but his knees gave way at last and he fell. They smothered him, biting, tearing, hammering.

Modern lamps blazed out. Sergeant closed his eyes in time not to lose his night vision. He contracted his pupils to slits and when he opened them again saw morlocks blundering about, burning and falling, as half a Company of kzin infantry, Hroarh-Officer at their head, fired into them with short, professional bursts of dialed-down plasma guns, backed up with beam rifles. There were no morlocks left to attack them from above. The multitude of kzinti's lights flooded the cave.

He leaped forward to join the battle, but stumbled again and fell in a pool of blood. It was, he could tell, kzin blood, mingled with human and much morlock. Further, he could tell that the kzin component was his own. His circulatory system was banging emptily. His wounds must have nearly bled him out. He tried to rise and could not. He groped for the Caller on his belt which would alert any medical personnel, perhaps before he died.

"Most of the morlocks died here," said Hroarh-Officer. "Your Heroes accounted for many eights-squared. You held the biggest morlock force. And I see you accounted for many personally. Urrr." He pulled some of the clotted tissue from

Sergeant's claws. For an officer to do that was a compliment worth having.

He was in considerable pain, including the monstrous headache of a telepath's probing. He knew the reason for that: as the sole survivor of his platoon there must be no possibility that he had been cowardly in battle. He had evidently passed the test. Had cowardice been found in him he would be either dead or in much worse pain: It was one of the things that destroyed even the most decorous kzin's inhibitions against torture.

"Humans too, Honored Hroarh-Officer," said Sergeant. He meant both that the humans had accounted for morlocks and that his Heroes had accounted for many humans. Hroarh-Officer surveyed the carnage with some satisfaction. He sprayed a little urine over Sergeant in a gesture of pleasure and approval.

"You have some human ears to collect for your trophy belt," Hroarh-Officer said. "And there will be heads for the NCOs' Mess. You have behaved with guile, but Telepath reports that you were by no means backward in the fighting. In using humans and morlocks against each other, you displayed a knowledge of human behavior and the ability to turn it to our advantage. Chuut-Riit will be pleased. It will vindicate him on the value of Thinking Soldiers. And of humans, for that matter. Some day we may use humans to do more fighting for us. . . . Kfrashaka-Admiral and his pride may . . ." He bit off his words. Even in post-battle relaxation, there was only so much fit to say before a Sergeant.

"At least that will be *something* for Chuut-Riit to be pleased about," he went on. "There is not much else. Not many others have done well. We lost a lot to their stinking wires, and those dung-bombs and other things, screaming and charging straight into traps. Nor did the Staff expect morlocks to be so feral and numerous. Urrr, *they* have paid for that mistake! Morlocks got to Battalion Forward Headquarters after humans lured the guards away! Then humans used dung bombs on the lot of them. There will be many promotions. Urrr."

Despite his words, Hroarh-Officer did not seem enraged. Rather, the emotions Sergeant detected were those of a kzintosh assessing a new and by no means disagreeable situation. After any serious fight there tended to be vacancies for promotions, and this one had evidently been more serious than anticipated. Sergeant realized he himself had seen only a little of it. Hroarh-Officer appeared to have acceded to battalion command. No doubt that and the satisfaction of wading into recent slaughter contributed to his benign mood. He too had new ears on his belt. "When we return here we will be better prepared," said Hroarh-Officer.

Chuut-Riit will approve of that, thought Sergeant. He will approve of Hroarh-Officer, too.

"It will take a long campaign to clear out these caves thoroughly," said Hroarh-Officer, lashing his tail. "Beyond the pictures of our radar we have found new tunnels and galleries we did not know of. The morlocks have taken a fierce and praiseworthy slashing here, but they breed fast, and we have not got all the humans by any means. It will be good training for the new Troopers, and it would be good if there were Heroes whose valor and blood-lust we could point to especially. . . . There has been hard fighting here."

"Yes, Honored Hroarh-Officer."

"Hard fighting . . . Urrr . . . a campaign like this needs special Heroes. Exemplars . . . You have done well. You may dry the new ears for your belt at the battalion Kzirzarrgh," he added solemnly.

Hroarh-Officer turned to the dying human. There was another important formality to be settled, which the scattered swaths of dead had raised. Hroarh-Officer asked Sergeant: "Is this monkey entitled to Fighter's Privileges?"

"Yes, Dominant One." Hroarh-Officer must have known this from Telepath's report, since the human was still uneaten and possessed its ears, but Sergeant's voluntary confirmation was necessary. Fighter's Privileges entitled a worthy enemy not only to dignified consumption or other disposal or display of his remains after death, but, in the case of a dying enemy, the granting of any reasonable last request. Hroarh-Officer bent over the human, putting this to him in his own mixture of Wunderlander vocabulary and Heroes' grammar.

Sergeant watched him, wondering vaguely what request a human in such circumstances might make that a kzin officer could satisfy. He could not move closer, being held in a medical web. A box on his chest stimulated his muscles as military circulatory fluid was pumped into him. He had been wounded before and knew better than to attempt great movement. Indeed, at that moment he could hardly turn his head. The bone-baring wounds on his neck and shoulders had been sewn up and salved and would make admirable scars.

When the human replied its voice was too weak for Sergeant to catch what it said. But Hroarh-Officer seemed to understand. His tail stiffened as if in anger for a moment, and he raised a claw as if for a slash. Then he relaxed. "*Iss bekomess rreasssonibble.* Urrr," he grated out, as much as he could not in the slaves' patois but the difficult human tongue. Then he waved to Medical Orderly, who had finished attending to the kzinrret and the other wounded and injured, to come forward. Perhaps the human would respond to kzin medical treatment, and if in the circumstances it lived it would be spared this time. So be it. Lying in the bracing smell of Hroarh-Officer's urine Sergeant was almost content. He would mourn his comrades later. But they had died acceptably.

Hroarh-Officer squatted beside Sergeant as the human was carried away. "It is suitable that he asked for treatment," Sergeant said. "That one should not die before his time. Not at the hands of morlocks. I will have his head for the Mess one day."

"It did not ask for treatment. That is an ordinary part of Fighter's Privileges," said Hroarh-Officer. "It asked for another thing.

"It is a little irregular and will need to come officially from me, but seeing what has transpired here I believe it will be considered fitting to grant it, Raargh-Sergeant."

Music Box

"I do not know whether you are my friend or my foe, but I should count it my honour to have you as either. Has not one of the poets said that a noble friend is the best gift and a noble enemy the next best?"
—C. S. Lewis

"A promise made under duress doesn't count, that's the law."
"But this is East and South of Suez, where there is no law."
—The Katzenjammer Kids

"Is it not joyful to have friends come from a far land?"
—Confucius

Chapter 1

2425 A.D.

The kzin screamed and leaped.

The gagrumpher was a young one, lagging a little behind the herd, half-asleep on its feet in the warm forenoon. The kzin landed on its back, above its middle pair of legs. The centauroid reared up, shrieking. The gagrumpher herd wheeled, the males charging back.

But the gagrumpher's rearing had brought its throat in range of the feline's razor fangs. The kzin swung its jaws, slashing. There was time for one crushing bite at the neck bones, and it was down, racing for the trees like an orange shadow a second before the gagrumpher bull-males arrived.

The wounded gagrumpher stood for a moment, blood jetting, then it collapsed, its oxygen-starved brain already dying, though its rear legs kicked for some time under the instinctual commands of the dorsal ganglial knot.

The males could not pursue the predator into the trees, and as they stood in a bellowing group, the snarl of another kzin tore the air on the opposite side of the clearing, between them and the rest of the herd. They could not leave the females and the other juveniles unguarded. They hastened back, and the herd moved on.

The body of the adolescent became still in its pool of blood as the dorsal ganglia died. A colony of leather-flappers that had risen shrieking into the sky returned to their trees, and the forest settled down again to its own affairs.

Warily, two kzin approached the kill. The killer, like its prey, was a youngster, showing a mixture of kitten spots and adolescent stripes against its bright orange fur. The other was

183

older—much older. There was gray at its muzzle, one eye and one arm were artificial, its ears were torn shreds and the fur at its neck and shoulders grew raggedly over a complex of scar tissue. The youngster kept watch as the elder kzin lowered its great head and lapped the blood, then crouched and lapped in turn.

The forest was quiet again. They ate undisturbed.

"That was a good kill, Vaemar," the elder kzin said. He gave the youngster a grooming lick.

"Thank you, Raargh-Hero. But I doubt I could handle an adult yet. And it was a stupid one to lag behind the herd in this close country."

"Then you have seen the fate of the stupid. You feel nothing in the ground?"

"Feet. Distant enough."

"Gagrumpher feet?"

"Yes. I think so." The pattern of the gagrumpher's centauroid footfalls could never be mistaken for those of a quadruped, but many of Wunderland's native life-forms were centauroid.

"Are they approaching or receding?

"I think . . . I think they are still receding."

"Be sure, be very sure. The males could be returning quietly through the cover."

"They do not sound heavy."

"Nor would they, to your senses yet, if they put their feet down slowly. They are very different things, leaping on the back of a dreaming youngster, and looking up to see a dozen charging adult males. You do not want to be under those forelegs when they rear up. I have heard some humans made the skins of our kind into what they call *rrrugz*. Adult gagrumphers can do the same more quickly."

"They are moving away, Raargh-Hero, I am sure of it now."

"Indeed. Do you know why they move away?"

"No."

"The males know we are here. Their usual response would be—I will not say of such clumsy and noisy herbivores to 'stalk' us—but to attempt to take us by surprise. If they are moving away, it is for a reason. Perhaps some other enemy approaches.

"Never feel shame like the foolish ones at using ziirgah. It is a gift of the Fanged God," the old kzin went on. Ziirgah was the rudimentary ability of all kzinti to detect emotions of other hunters or prey. Most used it quite unthinkingly, but because it was developed in a few into the despised talent of the telepaths, many felt unease at using it consciously. It had saved Raargh's life on more than one occasion.

"Always danger, Raargh-Hero."

"Vaemar, when you look at me, see always two things: I am old, and I am alive. I notice danger. Not all who were kits with me, or recruits, or fighting soldiers, did so. . . . Listen now!"

"There . . . !" The young kzin's ears and tail shot up.

"Yes, mechanism! You know the enemy now."

"We must get under cover!"

"Finish your meat. It is your kill, and we have enough time. We will take the haunches to salt before the Beam's beasts and the snufflers get them."

The sound of the vehicle grew. The kzinti slashed what remained of the gagrumpher carcass to pieces, bagging it in tough fabric. They were in deep cover, invisible, when the human car, flying low, entered the clearing.

It landed beside what was left of the gagrumpher, and the driver got out. The human examined the scattered, bloody bones, the imprints of clawed feet and of Raargh's prosthetic hand on the ground about, sniffing with a feeble, almost useless nose, then crossed the clearing toward the shade of the red Wunderland trees where the kzinti lurked. His eye lighted on some of the bagged meat.

"Anyone for chess?" he called.

The young kzin leaped from the undergrowth. His hands with sheathed claws struck the human in the chest, knocking him down. Though far less than fully grown, he already overtopped and easily outweighed the man.

"Be careful, Vaemar," the elder admonished him in what, five years previously, would have been called the slaves' patois. "He has not the strength of a Hero!" He made a swipe at Vaemar with his prosthetic arm. The youngster ducked and rolled away.

"There is no offense, Raargh," the human said in the same dialect, those words in the Heroes' Tongue being couched in the Tense of Equals. He climbed to his feet and reached to scratch the top of the youngster's head. "Young will be young."

"Urrr. To live with you monkeys, young need be cautious. You have a board?"

"Yes."

"Old weakling! To let youngster leap you so!"

"Many of us are old, Companion, but some of us have a trick or two yet."

"Come to our cave." He spoke now with the grammar of the Heroes' Tongue to this human who understood it, rather than the simplified patois. "We have got it well set up now. Even a chair for any monkey brave enough to stick its nose in. Vaemar will cover your eyes while I make safe the defenses."

The human held his captured chessman up to the light. "These are nice pieces."

"Vaemar made them. He is good with a sculpting tool."

"From what you tell me he is good at many things. But he is fortunate to have you."

"So what you will tell the *Arrum*?"

"There is no point in lying, to them or to you. So far they have asked little of me. He has the right to live as he wishes, as do you . . . but I think . . ."

"Yesss? Go on." A hint of the Menacing Tense.

"Someday he will need more than this."

"It is good to stalk the gagrumphers and fight the tigripards, good to look out at night upon the Fanged God's stars, or sleep under them when we range far, to scent the game in the forests under the hunters' moons or lie in the deep grass glades at noontide," said Raargh. "Few high nobles live so well. And unlike high nobles we have no palace intrigues to poison our livers."

The man nodded, pinching his lower lip between thumb and index finger in a characteristic gesture of thought. "And yet . . . for him it cannot be like this forever. You know as well as I he is exceptional. Your kind on this planet need leaders now, and they will need them tomorrow."

"To lead them to what?"

"Hardly for me to say."

"To become imitation monkeys? Apes of apes?"

"Do you really think the seed of Heroes would accept such a destiny? I think not."

"What then? Check! Urrr."

"You know your kind have some deadly enemies among the humans on this world. Jocelyn van der Stratt is far from the only one of her party. I think, as you do, I know, that Vaemar may be a great treasure for this planet, a natural leader for the Kzin but one who can deal with humans, too. What might we not do combined? I think even Chuut-Riit may have felt that, or something like it. It will be very slow, but perhaps on Wunderland both our kinds have been given a strange chance.

"But there are many humans who do not want kzinti leaders to emerge, who do not want the Kzin to be. Vaemar has a duty, companion mine. And so, I think, do you. Perhaps, if I may speak as soldier to soldier, a harder one than any you faced in battle."

"You think the monkeys will attack us? There will be many more guts spilled then. There are many Heroes left on Ka'ashi!"

"I hope not. And I think I have grounds for hope. Each day that passes is a day in which humans and Kzin share the planet, a day for some memory of the war and the Occupation to be forgotten. But it is slow."

"It does not matter if the days here pass fast or slowly," said Raargh. "We hunt, we watch the stars. Vaemar grows. I will not be able to play *chesss* with him much longer—too many easy victories for him on this little board, and my authority is undermined."

"If he can beat you easily, Raargh, he must be a player indeed. But most kzinti who bother with the game become masters. . . . Once when we talked, you too said the Kzin of Wunderland would have need of him."

"He still does not get the best out of his rooks. He does not use them to smash through the front. . . . And I am not good enough a player to be the best teacher for him—I announce checkmate in three moves, by the way. They do not have need of him yet."

"We hold things together, I grant you, but there are a lot of hopes on that youngster."

"He comes. Let him try his rook work on you. He has been waiting for his game."

"If you can beat me so easily, what hope have I against him?"

"I, who am old, am schooling myself to perceive things like a human. He, who is young, has only me to learn from, me, and one or other two oddities about in these unpeopled parts. . . . You are right, he will have to go soon, though it shaves my mane and twists my liver to say it. . . . But I warn you, he learns quickly."

The sound of the human car died away. Raargh gazed after it for a long time. Night was falling on Wunderland, Alpha Centauri B magnificent in the purplish sky, the sky that humans now ruled.

"Finish salting and dressing the meat, Vaemar," he said. "I must pace and think."

The forest made way for the kzin, though he was hardly hunting. He made a single, small kill, enough for relaxation and a clear mind.

I lost my own kit and my mate in the ramscoop raid, he thought. *Must I lose Vaemar too?*

Perhaps not. As things had once been, a Hero did not worry

over his kits, who should make their own fortune, provided
only that they did not dishonor him. But ever since the human
acquisition of the hyperdrive had turned the tide of battle in
space, for Raargh and Vaemar ever since the day the Patriarchy's forces on Wunderland had surrendered to the vic-
torious humans and Raargh had fled with the Royal Governor
Chuut-Riit's last kit to the open country beyond the great scarp
of the Hohe Kalkstein, things had been different.

They had lived wild and free, but not entirely so. Wunderland was a sparsely settled world, and during the Kzin
occupation and the decades-long war its human population
had been further reduced, through heavy casualties, through
the poverty and chaos that spread with a destroyed infrastructure, and as a result of suddenly being denied many modern
drugs and medical procedures. Birth rates had collapsed as
death rates had soared. Now, with rebuilding and the UNSN
present in force, and with automated farming and food-
production methods being restored, the cities were draining
off the human rural population from many areas.

The remaining kzin, considerably to their own surprise, had,
after the chaos and fighting that followed the Liberation, been
allowed a fair degree of freedom, though they had been stripped
of most of the land and estates which they had taken and, except
in part of the asteroid Tiamat, where they had their own community, and recently in part in the settlement at Arhus, were
subject to human government and laws in major matters. But
there was still much wild country. Kzin like Raargh who settled
in the backwoods were largely left alone (the little matter of
the stolen air-car in which he had escaped after the Kzin surrender seemed to have been forgotten, and the car was still with
them). But, he knew, they were under a degree of discreet, and
even frank, surveillance. It would not, he suspected, be a good
idea to test the limits of their freedom. Cumpston had taken
it upon himself to call upon them. There were other humans
who crossed their paths from time to time as well, such as the
female called Emma, who apparently lived in the forest somewhere to the southeast.

Sometimes he sold meat to the scattered human vegetation-
cultivators in the area, rounded up or killed beasts for them,
guarded their farms in their absence, or used his great strength
to do other work. He had thus acquired goods and a small
store of money. "You can trust old Raargh to do a job," he
had heard one say. "He's not so bad for a ratcat." Here, in
the open country beyond the Hohe Kalkstein, the claws of the
occupying kzinti had rested relatively lightly, and his prosthetic

arm and eye, though actually more effective than natural ones for many purposes, made him look less dangerous. It had been strange and distasteful at first to have to deal with former slaves and prey animals on such terms, but with the passage of time he was becoming used to it. The cultivator's words, when he thought them over, had actually not displeased him.

There were also, Raargh knew, many humans who wished to kill every kzin on Wunderland. This provoked a fighting reflex, but it was hardly unexpected. He had installed defensive measures at their cave. The advice of other humans, including his chess partner Colonel Cumpston, had been to lie low and let, as he put it, "time heal some wounds."

Those that were not fatal to start with, thought Raargh. *Too many dead Heroes, too many dead monkeys, for all to be forgotten. I sometimes forget how favored by the Fanged God I am. How few who joined the Patriarch's Forces with me now live! Hroarh-Captain travels with a cart replacing his legs.* He remembered Hroarh-Captain as a young officer, bursting through with his troops to rescue him, sole survivor of his platoon, at the First Battle of the Great Caves.

And that led to another thought. The human Rykermann, who had fought beside him in the caves when they had been surrounded by morlocks. They had believed they would die together and had exchanged certain confidences. He had helped Rykermann's mate, Leonie, to escape the morlocks, and had asked Hroarh-Captain for Rykermann to be given fighter's privileges and for his life to be spared. And Rykermann in return had asked something for him, something which Hroarh-Captain had agreed to . . . partly for politics and because it was convenient, it was true, but . . . There were a few humans he could talk to. *This is a human world now and I need human advice and contact. I do not like it, but if Vaemar is to live here and lead, he will need it too. He cannot stay in the forest forever.*

Cumpston was a good chess partner and had intervened to save his life from the female Jocelyn van der Stratt in the burning ruins of the refugee camp outside Circle Bay Monastery, the day the last Kzin forces on Wunderland surrendered. The abbot of the monastery, too, another old chess partner . . . But Cumpston, he knew, was an ARM agent still, and Raargh suspected his interest in Vaemar was more than avuncular. Raargh was prepared to admit that the stocky human might somehow presume to "like" them, but chess was not his only agenda. And the abbot was old and feeble. Raargh did know how he continued to impose his will on the . . . monks? monkeys? whatever they were called . . . who he had been set to dominate.

It is Rykermann among the humans who owes me most, he thought. *His life and his mate's life. He is high in their dominance structure, too.* The television in the car had shown him Rykermann speaking in the monkey-assembly, when troops of them got together to chatter about laws. He had had Vaemar watch it too, as part of his education for this new world. *I will go to Rykermann,* he thought.

Chapter 2

Nils Rykermann looked out at the night over Munchen. Rebuilding after the Liberation had been quick. The craters and the vast chaos of rubble and ruins were gone, as were many of the Kzin's architectural contributions. The last of the refugee camps and shantytowns on the outskirts were being cleared away. There in the light of Alpha Centauri B was the glittering steel spire of St. Joachim's as it had always been.

But even, or especially, under the night sky, it was not the prewar city. The suburbs stretched farther, the spaceport was far bigger. Beyond the spaceport was a vast scrapyard where the hulks of Kzinti warcraft were piled. Moving dots of light showed where salvage teams worked on some of them. And now laser and missile batteries, and more experimental and esoteric weapons, visible and hidden, ringed the city and the surrounding hills.

The sky was different too. One moon blown to pieces, and virtually every prewar and preliberation satellite shot down by one side or the other. Where there had once been advertising signs in orbit there were now guard ships and weapons systems. *A double improvement,* thought Rykermann.

The people had changed more than the city. Most of Rykermann's Wunderlander contemporaries were dead. Born in 2332, he had been 35 at the time of the Kzin landings. His body, tonight in the grey uniform of the Wunderland Armed Forces with its discreet cluster of oak leaves at the collar, was slim, strong and taut. He was 93 now, in what on Earth was counted early middle age, and he looked less than early middle-aged until one saw his eyes.

Like Raargh's, his neck and shoulders bore a complex of scars, including, strangely, the rough-and-ready suturing of a

191

kzin field-medic, and an identifying kzin brand which he had not had removed. But he had regrown his beard, a moderately asymmetrical spike identifying him as important—what had once been called "quality"—without being quite Families, and there was little gray in its gold yet.

One of his visitors was an obvious Earthman, shorter and heavier, wearing the crisp uniform of a Staff Brigadier of UNSN Intelligence. He was of about the same apparent age as Rykermann, or perhaps younger. In his case the geriatric drugs had never been interrupted.

The other was Jocelyn van der Stratt. She was in the uniform of the Wunderland Police, with badges of high rank. Like certain other Wunderlanders she had adopted the kzinti custom of wearing a belt-ring, with a collection of dried Kzin and human ears.

"The lady you lost, who you spoke of earlier, Dimity Carmody," said Guthlac. "If I may ask, what happened to her?" His voice was careful, delicate. "I do not mean to cause distress, but in this case I need to know. I know Jocelyn's story, and I know why she is committed to our cause."

"Not the usual," said Rykermann. "On this planet," he went on, " 'the usual' was disease, hunger or kzinti teeth. I suppose Dimity was lucky, or so I've told myself often enough. She was a scientist, and I thought she had something valuable, a theory about FTL. At my insistence there was an attempt to get her away in a slowboat, but by that time the Kzin had got tired of their cat-and-mouse game with the slowboats and destroyed it in space.

"I had the privilege of watching, via a camera on her ship . . . until the screen went blank. At least I know she died quickly. In fact she can't have known anything about it. She'd been injured already and was in a doc. They were trying to reach We Made It."

He strode across the room and opened a paneled cupboard with a key. He reached in and produced a small music box. "That's what I've got left of Dimity," he said. "A kzin kindly returned it to me . . . another story. . . . I've kept it for fifty-eight years . . . All I have!" He struck his fist on the table.

"Selina was probably long dead by then," said Arthur Guthlac. "The *Happy Gatherer* just disappeared. One of the first ships to go. I imagine them approaching some kzinti vessel . . . innocent, excited at the prospect of contact. . . . I imagine it often. . . ."

"Your wife? . . . Your lover?"

"My sister. We were very close. It had always been the two

of us against the world. Two square pegs in round holes. She went into space: the brilliant one. I'd become a museum guard and out of sheer bloody-mindedness I got involved in illegal studies."

"Illegal?"

"Military history. Totally forbidden. You could get your memory wiped and draw a few years' rehabilitation digging for water ice in the canyons on Mars for that in those days. And there were times before that when it would have been the organ banks. ARM had a long-term project to breed aggression out of the human race, and part of it was banning and systematically destroying military history. My chief at the museum was ARM, of course—all we museum staff were.

"My forbidden studies were inevitably discovered, but I was lucky with the timing of that. . . . I remember standing in front of my chief waiting to be formally charged and arrested, and wondering how much worse my case would be because I was a junior ARM officer myself. Anyway, he'd found I wasn't the only one in the place involved: 'I don't seem to have a very law-abiding general staff, Guthlac,' he said, 'but at this moment it's about all the General Staff that Earth's got.' Strange the difference a couple of capital letters can make. ARM had just concluded that the *Angel's Pencil*'s messages were genuine . . . that the Kzin were real and they were coming to get us."

"It wasn't like that on Wunderland," said Rykermann. "We didn't censor old history so much as lose interest in it. Earth history was Earth business. Irrelevant to us. We had a whole world to shape. . . . A brave new world it still was. . . . I remember, after we got the warnings, those months of scrabbling through old, chance preserved, fragments of Earth books and records trying to reinvent the wheel."

"We did something the same," said Guthlac.

"We were just getting a military production base together here when the Kzin arrived."

"You look as if you had your share of it."

"After Dimity was killed, I got away into the hills," Rykermann said. "I was a biologist and I knew some low-tech organic chemistry—nearly all our people were helpless without modern laboratories and industrial plants. I also knew as much as anyone about the great caves, full of bones and phosphates. I was the Resistance's biochemical production manager, overseeing the secret factories where nitrates and phosphates were made into explosives and war-gases.

"I was also one of the few leaders deemed indispensable enough to get—when possible—geriatric drugs and other sophisticated medical treatment from the Resistance's stolen supplies. Leonie was another."

"She was fortunate to be your wife."

"We didn't marry until we'd been in the hills for some time . . . and, I'll say . . . after the memory of Dimity had receded for me, a little. After I'd stopped hoping quite so hard that every attack we launched would turn out to be a suicide mission. In any case, we hardly had room for such sentimentalism as giving geriatric drugs to a spouse. The few we had went where they were needed most and she got them on her own merits. Not even my decision.

"She'd been one of my postgraduate biology students, and in addition she had natural gifts with low-tech medical care. That made her important. We'd forgotten we were aliens on this world. Exotic diseases, which our parents and grandparents had controlled so easily with modern medicine and autodocs that we'd forgotten they existed, came raging out, along with a lot of the old human diseases we'd also forgotten and which we'd lost resistance against.

"We did still have quite a lot of more-or-less old-fashioned farmers, thank God!—that's why we're not all dead—but most of us were twenty-fourth-century, machine-dependent people. Robots did a lot of the farming and other dirty jobs. Hell, apart from never seeing a dead animal, a lot of us ex–city dwellers had never seen recognizable meat! At first people starved from ignorance as much as shortages. Like the caveman, shivering with cold on a ledge of coal, fleeing weaponless from the cave-bear over outcrops of iron ore, lapping water muddy with clay. . . . More of us perished from general softness . . . humaneness, lack of ruthless decisiveness, not knowing what mattered for immediate survival and what didn't.

"Then they got the country and the old estates organized, and there was a supply of food back to the cities again. Some sort of government was got together under kzinti supervision and factories started turning over. Someone persuaded the Kzin that we couldn't pay taxes or slave for them if we were dead of starvation.

"I was in the wild country by that time and didn't see it. Disease was what we were concerned about in the hills. Some of the old bacteria and viruses had been eliminated in our ancestors before they left Sol system—that's another reason why some of us lived—but it turned out that there were still plenty left. Common colds alone—to which we'd lost quite a lot of resistance—killed far more people than the Kzin killed directly. That's before we start counting the score of the big-league diseases and Wunderland's own contributions. Things were bad enough in the cities, but at least they kept some modern medical facilities functioning. Even there they suddenly had to find puppy dogs and sheep to make something called insulin. Do cataract operations *by hand*—yes, you may well look queasy. And that was high-tech compared to what we had in the hills. There was no proper birth control once the contraceptive implants' lives ran out, and yet for women pregnancy became a deadly danger again. Leonie—and it was not only her scientific training but also a matter of intuition with her—turned out to be a priceless asset.

"She was a good fighter, too. A natural tactician and strategist and handy with a beam rifle. We've both outlived most of our contemporaries. It's not nice, watching your friends die of black rot or old age. Still, we've been happy together. She's an extraordinary woman. Kind to me, kind to all the world. The liberation, when it came, was a savage time, as savage as the invasion in its way, and a lot of people were in a sort of drunkenness of joy and vengeance. But even before the fighting stopped, before the relief operations were set up, she was taking care of stray kittens along with the pups and the orphans."

"Some people do. We had cats at home."

"I mean kzin kittens! She's always believed in some kind of eventual . . . reconciliation."

"And you don't?"

"No! First, it's impossible and suicidal, and second . . . I cannot forgive."

"Nor I. And yet . . ."

"Yes?"

"I have heard that you had dealings with the kzinti and survived."

"That was in the caves. A kzin and I found ourselves in a sort of temporary alliance against the morlocks—the big carnivores that live at the top of the food chain there. We thought we were going to die together. Then, when the other kzinti came, this one got them to sew me up, and they let me go with a branding and another implant in my skin—kzin-sized and a good deal less comfortable than human ones—and my word not to fight against Heroes again."

"And did you?"

"Is one's word to a ratcat binding? But there were other ways of helping the human cause by then. I think I kept to the letter of my promise, shall we say, though I exploited some loopholes in it."

"Scrupulous of you."

"Partly pride. Whatever you say about the ratcats, they keep their word, and I wanted to show that a human could do so, too. Partly Leonie made me. The kzin in question had saved her life, too. Though I think she would have had me keep my word anyway. Partly fear. Break your word to the Kzin and you fare much worse than an ordinary monkey if you fall into their claws subsequently. . . . I was still valuable to the human cause. There was plenty of work to be done in backwoods biochemistry that didn't require one to be a direct fighter.

"Anyway, my motives were mixed. I'm human, aren't I? Mixed motives are our nature. I think my nerve was starting to go then and I'd had enough of tangling with kzinti. I thought of their tortures." He paused again, steepling his fingers in thought.

"The Masonic orders kept some of Kipling's poetry alive on Wunderland when it had been banned on Earth for militarism," he said. "We used to recite it in our camps before battle sometimes:

"Our world is passed away
In wantonness o'erthrown.
There is nothing left to-day
But steel and fire and stone.

"Though all we knew depart
The old commandments stand:
'In courage keep your heart,
In strength lift up your hand!'

"But I recall another poem of his I found that is not particularly militaristic. It went something like this:

"What with noise, and fear of death,
Waking, and wounds and cold,
They filled the cup for My Mother's Son
Fuller than it could hold.

"That was the point that my mother's son had reached, too."

Jocelyn van der Stratt nodded. "We understood that," she said. "Few could have done more than you."

"In any case again," Rykermann went on, "The kzinti weren't fools. They could track me with the implant, and any attempt to remove it would have killed me and anyone helping. Thing called a *zzrou* in their charming language. Full of poison and explosive. Still, I made myself useful enough to find, rather to my surprise, that I had a political base after the liberation. So here I am."

"Markham has talked of a just settlement with them," Guthlac said. Jocelyn made a feral noise in her throat. Rykermann shook his head.

"*Justice* isn't possible! Recently I've looked at the history of war crimes trials on Earth in ancient times. But war crimes trials for kzinti make no sense. How can you try members of an alien species whose concepts are so different from our own and who thought of us as slaves and prey animals? There was some rough and ready approximation of justice after the liberation, of course: a lot of the most brutal kzin individuals who survived were hunted down and killed—taking a lot of humans with them, often enough. The followers of Ktrodni-Stkaa, who had been especially savage and saw humans as nothing but monkey-meat, in particular. Those who'd treated humans better often got a better shake—often, that is, not always. The human collaborators . . . that was another matter. They'd done what they'd done knowingly.

"The fighting didn't all stop at once, but when it did stop, there was very little in the way of an organized resistance— largely because so much of the kzin military had fought to the death before the cease-fire, also because they just don't think as we do. Some of the survivors went berserk, but there was no equivalent to the human Resistance after the kzinti invasion, no organized sabotage or uprisings. Also, of course, they'd destroyed all of their military assets that they could.

"And it wasn't long before we put the kzinti to work: doing a lot of dirty, dangerous jobs like disarming explosive devices where there was no point in risking human lives. Advising on dismantling the hulked kzin warships. Telepaths were useful from Day One, and many telepaths were not particularly loyal to the Patriarchy anyway. But soon others were showing they could be useful too.

"So much of Wunderland's infrastructure was wrecked that there were real fears of chaos. We had generations of lawless feral humans, including children—ever heard of the Wascal Wabbits? Kzin security guards made a difference there. . . . With so much machinery destroyed, muscles were needed, too. Any muscles. They still are."

"That's the peril!" Jocelyn exclaimed. "We are *accommodating* them! Giving them a place in our hierarchy! Getting used to them there. There are even some sick—"

"I have heard some humans refer to Chuut-Riit and some

of his pride, like Tratt-Admiral, or Hroth, as relatively enlight-
ened, at least compared to a Ktrodni-Stkaa," said Rykermann.
Jocelyn gave another, louder snarl that had something feline
and feral in it.

"So have I," said Guthlac. "Mainly humans from Earth of
the post-war generation. On behalf of us Flatlanders I apolo-
gize for them. They never had to endure the horror here."

"Exactly. In a few years, if things go on as they are, we will
have a generation growing up who see kzin in the streets and
think they know them, but who never experienced the war or
kzinti rule," said Rykermann. "What are ruined and exterminated generations to them? Perhaps torn photographs of people
they never met. Our stories and histories will become the
boring—perhaps to them even comic—tales of grandparents: 'Oh,
yes, the Public Hunts and all that.' The photographs of our dead
will be rubbish to be burned in the general house-cleaning by
our heirs when we die. Until the Kzin return!'

"I can honor a kzin," Rykermann went on. "I can respect
individual kzinti, but never, never, will I forget watching the
kzin laser burn into Dimity's ship. I understand ARM's plan for
the *Wunderkzin*—to create a kzin caste who can be partners
with humans on a human world, perhaps even allies one day,
not to mention hostages. I understand it, but I will destroy it."

"Does this come between you and your wife?" asked Guthlac.
"That you seek vengeance so for the death of another woman?"

"The answer for me is: 'Why burden Leonie with it?' I
don't."

"You put a lot of time into building a memorial to her.
Doesn't Leonie think it's a bit . . ." Guthlac made an eloquent
gesture.

"Jocelyn and every Wunderlander knows the answer to that,"
said Rykermann. "Dimity Carmody would have been worth a
memorial if she had been as sexless as a bumblebee. She was
a child when she discovered Carmody's Transform which gave
our technology the greatest independent boost it's ever had.
Given a few more years and we might have. . . . Just before
the Kzin arrived she'd been working on what she called a
'shunt' that she thought could break the light barrier. If anyone
could have done it, it would have been she. She showed me
some of her calculations, but they meant nothing to me. The
famous Professor Rykermann couldn't even understand the
symbols she used. But isn't 'shunt' how the scientists on We
Made It describe the principle of the Outsiders' hyperdrive?
My guess, my belief rather, is that she was working on the
right lines.

"But in any case Leonie never guessed how I felt about Dimity, how all-consuming my love for her had been. I'm not even sure if she knew her. She was a biology student and Dimity had her own department." He gave a lopsided laugh. "It was an unconsummated love, by the way. The professor of biology was too much in awe of the supergenius to actually do anything in that direction until too late. The only times we got to sleep together we *slept*. Holding one another, exhausted and terrified and with the Kzin after us." There was a sudden shake in Rykermann's voice. Guthlac turned his eyes away from him with a peculiar expression of embarrassment. "There was no reason to tell Leonie," said Rykermann, after an awkward pause. "There was no deceit involved. You can hardly be unfaithful with the dead. Why burden her with something that is in the past forever and that can't be changed?

"There are plenty of good objective reasons for wanting every kzin in the universe dead," he went on. "Their incidental interference in my private life is an inconvenience, shall I say, and an additional motivation for me. Perhaps that last vision of the laser burning into the ship carrying Dimity before the screen went blank"—his voice struggled again momentarily—"simply helps me to see the state of things more clearly. Let that species continue to maraud through the universe and more Dimitys will die. More Leonies, more millions to join the millions of Wunderlanders who lie in unmarked graves, whose bodies drift eyeless and freeze-dried between the worlds, those who have no grave where any heart may mourn. More dead like your sister, like Jocelyn's people. Other races too . . . countless . . ."

"We cannot share a universe with the Kzin," said Jocelyn. She spoke quietly but her eyes burned.

"And your Dimity?"

"What would Dimity have said, had she lived? I don't know. I only know that she must be avenged. She and all the other dead innocents. I can't be an *open* Exterminationist. That would bring me into conflict with Markham. He seems to have become some sort of kzin-lover."

"I thought he was the greatest leader of the Resistance! Carried the fight on in space," said Guthlac.

"Yes, and now he's the greatest obstacle in our path. He's not much good as a democratic politician—far too much the Herrenmann still—but, as you say, he's the Resistance's greatest hero. He fought in space, while we grubbed around in caves and skulked in swamps and alleyways with dung bombs."

"What's his problem, then?"

"I think he admires the Kzin," Rykermann said. "So, in a sense, do I, though I want them dead. I can admire certain qualities in them, anyway. They have the toughness and courage of any successful barbarians. But I think he sees them as fellow aristocrats. He himself is only Families on his mother's side, and that makes him more extreme than the twenty-two-carat article.

"If I wished to slander him I'd say he prefers the Kzin to the impudent prolevolk who no longer give him and the Nineteen Families the deference which he must convince himself every hour to be his due, and who have had the great estates broken up. I don't mean that seriously, of course, but . . . maybe there's a little grain of subconscious truth in it."

"Prefers the Kzin?" asked Guthlac. He frowned as if peering through a bad light. "Wasn't he their most daring and ruthless enemy?"

"I'd be the last to question his bravery and leadership," said Rykermann, "but there's a difference between fighting in space and fighting a guerrilla war on the ground. People relatively seldom get *wounded* in space battles, for example. Markham didn't have to see so many messy wounds—wounds there was often no way to treat. He could regard the Kzin more . . . abstractly. The enemy in battle was an image on a radar screen for him, not a tower of fangs and claws suddenly looming over you in a cave or chasing you through a swamp to tear you apart for monkey meat. Or simply taking over a district's last farmland for a hunting preserve so hundreds of humans died slowly of starvation. Or leveling a last makeshift human hospital because it was a handy site for an ammunition dump. For Markham, the Kzin was not even the horrible Thing waiting for you at the end of the process that might begin with the collabo police's 3 A.M. door knock.

"Space battles can, I imagine, be fun if you're young and have no hostages to fate and are in the right frame of mind—provoke a Kzinti *Vengeful Slasher*–class into chasing you and then drop a cloud of ball-bearings in your wake for it to hit at .8 of lightspeed. Things like that.

"Jocelyn"—he gestured to her deferentially—"had the worst part: She worked for the collaborationist police while helping the Resistance. She carried a suicide pill for years in case it was casually announced one day that there would be a telepath check. . . . Markham had what you might call a relatively clean war. Also, the Kzin control of the asteroids was always less total than it was planetside. They liked Wunderland and its elbow room, and they left a lot of the work of squeezing taxes out of the asteroid settlements—the Serpent Swarm—to human collaborationists. In a lot of the Swarm it was still fairly easy for humans to come and go and forget the terror and ghastliness that was always with us here, though as Kzinti numbers increased, human freedom to breathe was gradually being lost everywhere." Rykermann paused a moment, gathering his thoughts. Then he went on.

"The anti-Exterminationists aren't a monolith, of course. Markham, I think, admires the Kzin for what they are. ARM, as always, has its own secret agendas, which I don't expect even you, Arthur, know much of. Others value them not for what they are, but for what they might become."

"Like your wife?

"Yes. But I will not be disloyal to her as a wife, and anyone who thinks I am is mistaken. She has a noble and generous vision and dauntless courage. She believes contact with humans is changing the Kzin, that already those born on Wunderland are different—more flexible, more empathic. I think she is mistaken, though I salute her intentions. And in any case a more flexible, more imaginative Kzin would only be more dangerous."

"And you and I and Jocelyn lost loved ones to them. To love anyone is to make a perpetual hostage of your heart. Markham is a cold, sexless creature, brought up on Nietzsche, mother-fixated. I doubt he's ever loved anyone else, let alone lost them. He married only fairly recently, I think chiefly for the purpose of getting an heir—that's another kzin-like thing about him. But maybe to be a Markham you have to be like that.

"I don't know how much damage he did the Kzin battle-fleets—his whole collection of makeshift warships couldn't have engaged even one of their great dreadnaughts with a hope of survival—but the damage he did their bases and shipyards and the intelligence that his people masered to Sol wasn't negligible. Perhaps he helped buy Earth and Sol System breathing space between the Kzin fleet attacks. That may have been crucial. Gave time for the miracle of the hyperdrive to come from We Made It. I'm told Earth was at its last gasp when the Crashlanders arrived."

"It was," said Guthlac. "If they expected a heroes' welcome it was nothing to the one they got!"

"Markham certainly kept flames of hope and defiance alive here when they were desperately needed. I'd be the last to deny we owe him plenty, and perhaps Sol System does too.

"I've tried to understand what makes him tick," Rykermann went on. "Especially now that we're in Parliament together.

He counted those who died with him as warriors fallen in a noble cause, and I'm sure he's been punctilious in seeing their names are spelled correctly on the memorials. I think his feelings for them would have stopped there. Remember Frederick the Great's words to encourage his troops when they hesitated in battle: *'Hunde, wollt ihr ewig leben?'* When I read that, I thought: 'That's Markham!' But I see the laser burning into Dimity's ship almost every night of my life. We didn't see the end, as I told you, but I imagine it passing through her body as she lay in that medical coffin. . . ."

"Jocelyn? Do you feel the same?" Guthlac asked.

"I'm a civil servant. And like all senior police officers on this planet I've plenty of enemies from the past. I was exonerated after the Liberation and decorated and promoted for my role in helping the Resistance, but I did wear the collabo uniform. It would be easy for some enemies to take what I did—what I had to do—out of context. 'Who is the genuine friend of humanity? Ulf Reichstein-Markham, who fought the Kzin in the Serpent Swarm in improvised warships; Markham whose name even Chuut-Riit knew; or the former so-called Captain Jocelyn van der Stratt who supervised . . . supervised . . .' No, I can't say it, even here. You can work out the rest of it. But that's what they'd say."

"One thing I've learned in politics," said Rykermann, "is the softly, softly approach. Nils Rykermann fighting Ulf Reichstein Markham—and the UNSN—on Exterminationism wouldn't get me far. It might get me the personal attentions of ARM. . . . You understand."

"I was about to say: 'They wouldn't dare!' But of course they would," said Guthlac. "I was part of ARM's planning staff and I know them better than most. War does things to people, but even before the war ARM's ethos was that it couldn't afford scruples. Buford Early had no scruples about killing tens of thousands of humans—maybe more, we still don't know how many exactly—in the ramscoop raid. I did certain things on Earth when it looked as if the pacifist movement was getting too powerful—and I'd do them again if I had to without a backward glance. ARM as a whole had no scruples about holding back on all sorts of technology that would have helped us in the war, until it was almost too late, for fear it might get into the wrong hands—as if that would have been worse than a Kzin victory destroying human civilization forever! You're right to be distrustful of it."

"Nils Rykermann as Exterminationist leader would be quietly stymied, I think," Rykermann told him. "But Nils Rykermann the mainstream politician reluctantly forced into supporting Exterminationism might be a different matter."

"So we're agreed."

"Yes. Softly, softly," Arthur Guthlac nodded. "By the way, Jocelyn's people and I are among those meeting a delegation from We Made It in a few days to discuss expanding hyperdrive factories here. Her section is in charge of security for the project."

"I know. And more hyperdrive factories here are the best news I've heard for a long time. We're going to need them," Rykermann said. "If we do exterminate the Wunderkzin, I think it rules out the chance of a peace with the Kzin anywhere, ever. The others will hardly be inclined to surrender. We're in for a long war."

"That's exactly what we must have. Like it or not, they're too dangerous to be in the universe, Nils."

"We know," said Jocelyn.

"Come with me, if you like," said Guthlac. "I'm sure they'll want to meet you."

"Thanks, but I'm back to the caves tomorrow," said Rykermann. "Thank God, politics still isn't a full-time job. I remain a biologist, remember. Even a celebrity biologist! Leonie's there, with some students. We're trying to rehabilitate the ecosystem. It got messed up pretty thoroughly in the war. Odd, I suppose, that we should be trying to preserve the morlocks as a species now."

"They can hardly be much of a threat."

"No, they're barely sapient and they stay in the dark. Still, that's the human race for you: trying to preserve its enemies."

"Not all its enemies, I trust."

"So do I."

Chapter 3

Jocelyn van der Stratt, like many of Wunderland's top admin-istration, had a spacious apartment, once the property of a wealthy collaborationist, located, like Rykermann's Parliamentary office, in a tower high over the city.

Its decorations included the body of Peter Brennan, a fighter in the early days of the Invasion who even the Kzinti had referred to by full name, enclosed in a translucent block. Jocelyn had liberated it on the day of the Kzin surrender. The Kzin had let him keep his trophy-belt of kzinti ears, and this could still be seen on him, along with, on the remains of his jacket, the small cogged wheel of the Rotary Club badge he had worn in memory of peaceful days. There were also, about the walls, the earless heads of various kzinti and of human collaborators, weapons, photographs and holos of certain other dead humans, china from old Neue Dresden, and, in a niche, an inlaid jar of kzinti workmanship which had once held Planetary Governor Chuut-Riit's urine, kzinti symbol of Conquest and once gift to a sergeants' mess of Heroes.

Jocelyn reclined at ease on a couch covered in kzin fur. She was smoking a cigarette of mildly narcotic Wunderland chew-bacca and she had chosen the details of her dress with great care. Ulf Reichstein-Markham sat upright on a chair with the same material. He smoked nothing.

"Privately," she was saying, "I'm on your side. The Kzin were honorable enemies. Many like Tratt-Admiral and Hroth could acknowledge and respect human courage. And could be reasoned with. 'Enlightenment' is no empty word. Chuut-Riit wished to understand us. Perhaps the passage of a little time was nec-essary for us to see their more positive qualities. Thanks to the hyperdrive we are secure militarily and can afford to be more active in exploring avenues to a lasting peace."

"It is time to become friends," said Markham. His English was still careful, and Wunderland sentence-structure came and went awkwardly in it. "I do not pretend it will be easy. Sacrifices we may have to make. They must be convinced of our good intentions. But infinitely worthwhile the effort. At the end of the journey ennobled may both races be. I did not, however, think that you shared my views."

"I must tread warily," said Jocelyn. "You should know, for example, that Rykermann is a secret Exterminationist. I cannot break openly with him yet."

"He was a brave fighter," said Markham. "He has much-deserved prestige. It would be a good thing if he could be shown the longer view."

And you have chivalrous instincts, thought Jocelyn. *I could love you very easily if fate had not made me love Rykermann. But Rykermann has your courage and leadership combined with a wound, a vulnerability, that together make women love him easily. He is not of your hollow-ground steel. Still, you are physically attractive and I will, I think, have no problems about seducing you. Rykermann may have called you a cold, sexless creature, but I know men better than any man does. You are not sexless, you are just frightened of losing control, and of an instinct that makes you lose control.*

"A pity about his wife," she said.

"What do you mean? Leonie I know quite well. We have worked together."

"Then you know what I mean. She shares our feelings that it is—or soon will be—time to be friends. But married to an influential man like Rykermann . . . And she a Resistance hero in her own right as important as he—if not as great as you . . ."

"No," said Markham. "We all served as we might. I was fortunate to have wealth and connection, and the valiant spirit of my mother to inspire me. I got into space, where many born planetside had no such opportunity. You are flattering, but I cannot rank myself ahead of those whose part it was to fight here in such difficulty and danger."

"I have the honor to know, humbly and afar, of your mother's greatness," she told him. "Humanity's greatest heroine in this war, whose name, with your own, will never be forgotten. But you speak of danger? You, whose name even Chuut-Riit took cognizance of? But it would be good if she could be detached from him somehow. Good for her, I mean. She is a great and good woman."

"To interfere between man and wife is unscrupulous, surely?"

"Unscrupulous? Did we not all learn to dispense with scruples? What had Nietzsche to say of scruples?"

"You know Nietzsche? He kept my spirit aflame for Men during the darkest days!"

"Another bond between us!" *Of course, the little facts that I have studied your profile in every detail, or that you called your so-called flagship Nietzsche are not relevant to the spontaneous nature of this happy coincidence,* she thought.

"Nietzsche knew scruples—all scruples—as weakness, as unworthy of the Overman," she went on. "And you, I know, have no weakness." *That may help fix the ratcat-loving bitch's wagon.* Detached from Nils Rykermann, Leonie could be picked off. The details of how would present themselves in due course. Kzin-lovers might, with a little discreet prodding, shed their ideas on one another, each find justification with the other, each push the other into a more extreme position. Give him the ego gratification she knew he needed desperately, and Markham could be made into an instrument as pliable as it was useful.

She had been moving toward him as she spoke. Now she sank on her knees and kissed him, projecting humility, adoration, worship. The band of kzin-leather about her neck she had chosen for associations with a dog or kzinrret collar. Her perfume had the smallest hint of kzinrret-derived pheromones. There was a carefully chosen hint of kzinrret too, in the watered-silk pattern of her skin-tight trousers (there were costumes available with hints of tails, but that, she had decided, would have been definitely over-egging the pudding). Even for a mother-fixated man she did not think her breasts needed enhancement, but she made sure her posture, as she had previously made sure her costume, presented the best view of them. The circles of non-toxic luminous paint round her nipples did no harm as she dimmed the lights.

"Hero," she whispered, feeling him respond.

Colonel Cumpston, Raargh thought, should be told what he was doing. For him to return and find both Raargh and Vaemar gone without notice would certainly cause him to alert the human authorities prematurely, and perhaps drastically diminish Raargh's freedom of action.

He called him on the car's Internet but was unable to reach him. The car's IT facilities were fairly basic, lacking access to a translator, and he was not sure if a human mailbox would store his voice message understandably. To back it up he typed a message with Vaemar's and the spellcheck's help in the odd human script.

> I GO WITH VAEMAR.
> SEEK RYKERMANN ADVICE.
> RYKERMANN DOMINANT HUMAN.
> I KNOW. SAVE IN WAR. HELP VAEMAR.

He hoped that was clear. He added:

> HAVE LUCKY HUNTING GOOD CHESS
> COMPANION
> OLD RAARGH

Raargh closed the cave. He had invested in modern door-seals, and he thought they should be secure.

He left the aircar inside. Flying it to Munchen would have been quicker than trekking but would have attracted far too much attention, including that of the UNSN, who were still its legal owners. He had stealthed it during his escape with Vaemar in the confused conditions of the Kzin surrender, but any flight in a stealthed car now, with Wunderland's defenses fully in place and with sleepless machines on hair-trigger alert for Kzin raids from space, would be short and fatal.

In any event, he had no objection to going on foot. The old wounds in his legs pained him sometimes, but no kzintosh would deign to notice such things. Besides, he was in no hurry to receive counsel that he thought he was not going to like. If Rykermann agreed with Cumpston that Vaemar must begin specialized training, then perhaps this would be one of the last hunts Vaemar and he enjoyed together. *Though I hope they will give him some furloughs with me still,* he thought. *My liver cannot part with him forever.*

They carried their *w'tsais*, meat and salt with a few delicacies, flasks of water and bourbon, Raargh's military belt with its utility pouches, small bows and arrows, and an antique bullet-projecting rifle, plainly hunting weapons only. On liberated Wunderland kzinti with a cache of modern beam rifles did not advertise the fact. They had sun hats and ponchos. They had evolved on a colder world than Wunderland, and what clothes they took were for coolness rather than warmth. Vaemar packed a folding chessboard.

Munchen lay southwest, in a direct line beyond the scarp of the Hohe Kalkstein, and then with many miles of dry plains and mesas, supporting little life, before one came to farming territory again. The crater of Manstein's Folly, where a human force had made a stand and engaged the Kzinti in a set-piece battle early in the war, was still radioactive, and the farms closer to Munchen had suffered a great deal from war, neglect and dispossession.

There, near the city, things had been intense. Though there had been a strained, fraught, peace of a sort during the Occupation, no human venturing abroad had had a moment's security for his or her life who encountered a bored, angry or simply hungry kzin. Sheltering a single Resistance fighter had meant not merely farmsteads and hamlets but whole districts wiped out in reprisal. A child herding animals with the aid of a pointed stick might, with its animals, suddenly be the object of a lethal hunt by high-spirited kzin youngsters or sportive adult kzinti who decided the stick counted as a weapon. Ktrodni-Stkaa had had some of his vast estates in that area. . . . Now there was little game there, and the farmers rehabilitating some of the land would probably take less kindly to kzinti visitors than did those in these relatively untouched backwoods. It was decorous and sensible to take an indirect route, heading at first south, cutting across to the west later. There would be more game and fewer humans. That it would take longer was also, for Raargh, good. It would, he told himself with what he knew was a rather thin rationalization, help Vaemar's education to see more territory.

They loped along with the mile-eating kzinti stride, leaping and scrambling over rocky outcrops and other obstacles with the reflex that, long ago under Father Sun, which humans called 61 Ursa Majoris, had helped develop their ancestors' claws into hands. Game ran from them, but, when they wished to hunt, did not run fast enough.

They ate well the first night. They had killed again as it was fitting for kzintosh to kill, with fangs and claws. They had also built a small fire. They did not need it for cooking, warmth or light, but Raargh knew there were humans in the forest also and he wished to advertise their presence: A fire would not be made by stalking Kzin and was, he hoped, a sign of innocent intent.

They heard the human's footfalls long before it came in sight. Raargh had Vaemar take the rifle and his bow and hide from the night-blind creature beyond the circle of firelight in tall grass. He himself sat by the fire, *w'tsai* to hand but not obviously so, until the human appeared.

He relaxed when it did so. It was Emma, the human female whom he and Vaemar had encountered on hunts before. She appeared to live alone somewhere in the vicinity, presumably in one of the forest glades that dotted this rolling, largely open country. She was dressed warmly against the night air, even her hands covered in bulky gloves.

"Friend!" she called. Raargh took no particular notice of the fact that she called it in the Female Tongue of the Kzin (the Heroes' Tongue used the term "friend" very sparingly and with complex connotations) and pronounced it as correctly as a human throat might.

Raargh watched her unspeaking, save for an ambiguous "Urrr" in his throat as she approached. As she strode into the firelight before him she went down in the prostration of a human slave before its master. It was not something he had seen for five years.

"What do you want?" Raargh was certainly on speaking terms with some humans, and for Vaemar's sake as well as for the jobs he picked up he made an effort to be more outgoing in that direction than most, but very few Kzinti admitted humans to conversation easily. Since she had spoken in the Female Tongue he replied in the Heroes' Tongue. Naturally and without thought he employed the Dominant Tense. She switched to Wunderlander—the Female Tongue was not good for complicated conversation, but her posture, and, as he could now tell, her voice, remained humble.

"Noble Hero, please call your companion out."

"Companion?"

She raised a nitesite.

"Noble Hero, I am aware from this device that there is another Hero ensconced in the tall grass not far away. I think it is Vaemar. I mean you no harm. And what harm could a single manrret do to two Heroes?"

She had a point there. And she seemed truly alone. Raargh had heard no other footsteps or mechanisms. He called and Vaemar bounded back towards the light.

"What do you want?" he said again.

"You!" She opened her gloved hands and fired the guns they concealed, spinning on her heel from Raargh to Vaemar. Kzin are inhumanly fast in battle, and it was a very near thing, but with the guns already in her hands she was fractionally faster. When they fell and had ceased to move she called an eight of Kzinti out of hiding and loaded them onto a sled.

Leonie emerged from the great mouth of the Drachenholen as Nils Rykermann landed. She was smeared with mud and had a strakkaker slung over her shoulder. They embraced.

"Another dirty day for you." Nils Rykermann was wearing a modern fabric jacket. The wet soil fell from it.

"We've penetrated the old 19-K tunnel complex," she answered. "Plenty of mess to clean up."

They walked together under the scarred and blasted cliffs through the cave entrance and into the great ballroom of the Drachenholen's twilight zone. Rykermann cast an odd look for a moment at an old habitat module, stripped and plundered long ago by the desperate scavengers of the Resistance, now refitted. He seldom passed it without making a small gesture which Leonie never commented on. The limestone formations, once an incredible fantasy of flowering stone, were blackened and broken above them. The cave floors had been cleared down to bedrock. Bright lights had been strung here and there. There seemed to be no crepuscular life left to disturb.

"Remember our first trips here?" asked Leonie.

"Yes. And the others."

"We thought the caves would be here forever, unchanged. A great biological treasure house. I remember the weeks I took to excavate my first fossil . . . then we chucked fossils aside as we shoveled out the guano."

"Guano meant bombs," said Rykermann. "Bombs meant dead kzin. Water under the bridge. We'll restore it. What have you done with the students?"

She gestured to lights emerging from one of the tunnels beyond. Several young men and women, wearing masks and breathing apparatus, were trooping out of the cave carrying litters. They bore loads of bones and rags and a few partly mummified bodies and body-parts, human and kzin.

"Decent burial," she said. "I've wanted to give it to them for a long time."

"One might say they had decent burial already," said Rykermann.

"They were our comrades. I think some would have wanted their bodies to go home. I found Argyle von Saar. He loved the caves, of course. I left him where he was. He'd be happy his body went into the Drachenholen's food-chain. But some of the others . . . they'd like prayers and headstones, I think, and grass and sun and the flutterbys."

"You speak as if they were still alive."

"Of course. This ugly rubbish isn't the people we knew. What about these?" She gestured. Another group of students was emerging around a small sledge, purring loudly as it was lifted by a Kzin-derived gravity-motor. It was piled with weapons: kzinti beam rifles and plasma guns, heavier tripod-mounted squad weapons, gas canisters, old human Lewis guns and smart guns, all manner of detritus. Someone had set another mummified kzin on top of the pile, in parody of a conqueror's triumph.

"Some of those may still be charged. Get them into one of the outside modules and lock it. I'll keep the key. We'll have to take them to the city as soon as possible. I don't want to lose any more students . . . Come to think of it," Rykermann went on, "I was talking to a fellow yesterday who began as a museum guard on Earth. UNSN Brigadier now. There should be a museum of the Resistance. He might be able to give us advice in setting it up. Let future generations look at those Lewis guns and wonder at what we were forced to fight with."

"I don't like all these mummies," Leonie said.

"They're hardly very aesthetically pleasant. But they're not the people we knew. Just organic matter going back to nature a bit more slowly. As you say, ugly rubbish."

"I mean, if the skin and tissues haven't been eaten, it shows how little life is left in the caves, where they once crawled with scavengers."

"I knew those scavengers well." They leaned together and he slipped his arm around her.

"So did I. So much of the biosystems have been destroyed."

"It was to be expected," said Rykermann. "Plasma guns, gas, biologicals . . . There are other caves. We'll find the lost species and reintroduce them here."

"No sign of live morlocks yet. I think we and the kzinti may have killed them all between us."

"Then be sure to get all the dead material you can. It might make a good graduate student project to clone them."

"I feel guilty about them," said Leonie.

"You killed a good few yourself, my dear. You and me and our furry friend together at one stage."

"I know. But we invaded their habitat. And . . . we have no right to wipe out species."

"Not even near-brainless predators of atrocious habits?"

She was silent a moment before replying. Then she answered:

"Not even them . . . Not even, I think, predators of atrocious habits whose brains are comparable to our own."

"I don't know any creatures whose brains are comparable to our own," he said.

There was a slight stiffening of her body, imperceptible to a casual observer.

"Not even one who saved our lives?"

An edge of iron entered his voice. "I paid that debt in a currency that was understood."

Leonie had known terror in these caves during the wars. The Resistance had decorated her and the Free Wunderland government had rewarded her for heroism. She had fought monsters and horrors in the hills of Wunderland and in this stone jungle and beaten them. But now she looked at her husband with a new kind of fear in her eyes.

Raargh recovered consciousness in a police web. Turning his head cautiously, he saw Vaemar similarly restrained a few feet away. There was no sky above them. Their packs had been laid on a small stand in front of them.

The light was reddish, and somehow familiar, as were the high sandstone walls. He remembered: Some outstanding NCO's, himself among them, had been lectured by senior officers of the General Staff. It was like the palace of a kzinti noble, a replica of the noble architecture of Old Kzin.

Once, rage would have exploded in him and if he could not have torn the web apart he would have torn himself apart in his efforts to do so. But his years as an NCO, and even more the five years since the Liberation, had taught Raargh self-control. He did not even scream. He remained still and watched Vaemar slowly open his eyes and raise his head.

Footsteps. Human and kzin. A door opening. The human female Emma entered, accompanied by another female he did not know, a male human and a young adult kzin, all armed with nerve-disrupters. The humans were wearing bizarre costumes of orange with variegated stripes. It was almost as if they were trying to imitate the markings of a kzin pelt. The human male bore on the pale skin of its forehead the tattoo of Chuut-Riit's house service. Since tattoos could be removed, Raargh knew it must have retained this voluntarily. Its pallor, and that of the second female, suggested to him that they had long lived away from the sun. The humans went down in the prostration before them, and the second female began to speak in the Slaves' Patois.

"Noble Hero, this slave craves your indulgence to hear her. My daughter and I have done great discourtesy, to you and to He whose blood is the most glorious on this planet. I beg you, stay your wrath while I speak. It is for the sake of the Patriarchy that I have acted so.

"I was Henrietta, once executive secretary, chief and proudest human slave of Chuut-Riit. I now act to fulfill his legacy. This is my daughter Emma; Andre, who was house-slave also; and Ensign, who helps us. Behold!" She held up a sign that every Kzin knew as the Sigril of the Patriarchy, emblazoned with the cadet claw of Chuut-Riit.

"You do not remember, perhaps," she told Vaemar, "but you were once a guest at my house in the happy times. Your Honored Sire Chuut-Riit honored my home by attending my children's naming-days. Once he brought you . . . You enjoyed playing, I remember, with a ball of fiber . . ." Her voice shook for a moment, and she made a sound of grief.

"I know Heroes do not lie," she went on. "I ask you to give me your Names as your Words, upon this Sigil, that you will not harm me or any human of mine this day if I release you, that you will allow me to show you certain things that the Heroes of this planet, and *this* Hero above all"—she gestured at Vaemar—"need to know. It may be that the survival of the Heroic Race is at stake, and not on Ka'ashi only, but under Father Sun himself."

Raargh glared. He hardly trusted himself to speak to this monkey who had dared lay hands on him—and on Vaemar, who was his charge, given by the Fanged God to replace his own dead son, and a Prince of the Blood. Yet the male's tattoo compelled attention.

The manrret was abasing herself before Vaemar now. Most young male kzin had even less self-control than their elders, but Vaemar, as Raargh had long known, was different. Chuut-Riit, his blood-sire, had been a genius and a thinker, and on the day they met, Vaemar, still a kitten, had shown he was his Sire's true son, possibly saving Raargh's life and a clawful of other Kzin lives in the process. Vaemar was still very young—he was not even adolescent, but remained brilliant beyond his years, with the insight and control of a superior adult.

Further, Raargh had taught him to enhance that control and patience day by day, instead of dwelling on the screaming attack which a conventional combat-master would have drilled into him, and which play with siblings—always potentially ready to turn in a lethal pack upon any individual suspected of weakness or oddity—would have made into a virtually unbreakable imprint. Vaemar had said nothing yet. He was watching and waiting. He turned his eyes toward Raargh, ears lifted in question.

The old kzin's ears were so torn and scarred as to be virtually useless for signaling anything but the most basic emotions. He growled out an assent, Vaemar following suit. Henrietta killed the web and they stepped onto the floor of the fortress. Looking about him, Raargh saw tunnels running off into dimness. The roof was very high, and there was machinery and scaffolding. His nose brought him a complex mixture of hydrocarbons, plastics, chemicals, foodstuffs and living rock.

Colonel Cumpston read the kzin's message: SEEK RYKERMANN ADVICE. The kzintis' dwelling was closed and sealed. Their tracks showed they had left on foot, not long before. He checked with the telltale of his car's locator and confirmed that they had already made some way south.

Chasing after them would be pointless. It would be easy to catch up with them but it would probably only anger the old kzin, who, if he had wanted another companion, would have said so. "Never force your company on a kzin" was a pretty basic maxim for any human. And if two male kzinti could not look after themselves, who on Wunderland could?

Well, Cumpston knew, Raargh and Nils and Leonie Rykermann had a curious bond between them. Raargh had told him of how they had saved each other in the caves when surrounded by morlocks and when all hope seemed lost. But . . . his training had been to rule out assumptions. He settled himself in the car, closed the canopy to avoid the attentions of the flutterbys, and clicked the computer. The map with its two blinking smears of red light disappeared. Rykermann, like all Wunderland politicians and other prominent citizens, was the subject of an ARM dossier.

Before the invasion he had had some celebrity as a biologist and explorer but had steered clear of politics outside the University, apart from being appointed to one of the defense committees set up in haste shortly before the Invasion. He had married Leonie Hansen, his former student, in the hills. Their Resistance records were heroic, and after the Liberation he had been elected to the Parliament's lower house. Since then his politics had been fairly mainstream. He had a place on several committees now.

Wunderland electors, having weakened the grip of the Herrenmanner of the Families, did not want a caste of professional politicians developing to replace them, and, like most Wunderland politicians, Rykermann had kept up his day job: professor of biology at the Munchen University. That, Cumpston thought, would also give him more television exposure than an ordinary Deputy.

There was a list of his community activities and clubs. He was president and organizer of a foundation to commemorate the university's Special Professor of Mathematics and Astrometaphysics, the discoverer of Carmody's Transform, who had died in the Invasion, and apparently he worked hard for it, raising funds for commemorative projects and scholarships. In his own field he and Leonie had made the rehabilitation of the caves one of their major professional projects.

There was also a list of his associates and meetings, always a high priority for profiling with ARM dossiers.

He didn't have a lot to do with Ulf Reichstein-Markham, a Resistance hero of the first rank, and now a major spokesman for tolerance and rehabilitation of the remaining Kzin on Wunderland. Cumpston had met Markham several times. Leonie Rykermann seemed to have had more to do with him on professional bodies than did her husband. She, Cumpston noticed, had even tried to set up a small nonprofit employment agency to use kzin talents with Markham on the board of governors. There was a record of a speech at the opening in which she referred to the kzin soldier who had saved her from the morlocks. As with her husband, the cave project took up a lot of her time.

There were also meetings between Rykermann and Jocelyn van der Stratt. Rather a lot of them. That name was flagged in hypertext on the dossier. He jumped to it. She was, as he knew, a very senior police officer. Former member of the Collaborationist police, exonerated and decorated for her secret services to the Resistance. And flagged notices: She had a number of associates in the Exterminationist Party.

Certainly, it seemed, she did not like kzinti. There had been several reports, and she had been reprimanded for "excessive zeal" in dealing with them since the Liberation. Cumpston thought to himself that any officer who, on Wunderland, got into trouble for excessive zeal in dealing with kzinti must be excessive indeed.

The dates of the meetings scrolled up. There was a pattern, but it took time to see: the meetings between Nils Rykermann and Jocelyn van der Stratt has nearly all occurred when Leonie Rykermann was working at the caves.

That might, of course, mean nothing. But . . . a clandestine love affair? That didn't fit the psychological profiling of Rykermann anyway, but such profiling wasn't infallible, and Cumpston knew well enough that there was, to use a very old phrase, nowt so queer as folk. And the profiling of Jocelyn van der Stratt indicated more ambiguity. Which added up to no more than guesswork. Circumstantial hints of sexual liaisons were a field rich in misdirection. *By the Black Swan*, he thought, *I hope I guess right!* He remembered one of the old books ARM had resurrected for its hastily-contrived course of military psychology: *Slide Rule*, by an early designer of flying machines named Nevil Shute:

> With the ending of the war, considerable mental adjustments were necessary for all young men. For four years of my adolescence I had lived in a world that was growing steadily bleaker and grimmer, and in that four years I had grown to accept the fact that in a very short time I should probably be dead. I cannot remember any particular resentment at the prospect; indeed, in some ways it was even stimulating. It has puzzled many people to imagine how the Japanese produced their Kamikazes in the last war. It has never been much of a puzzle to me, however; in 1918 anybody could have made a Kamikaze pilot out of me.

The war and Occupation on Wunderland had gone on for not four years, but more than fifty, growing bleaker and grimmer in every one of them. *Could I have lived fifty years under the Kzin and stayed sane?* he wondered. Under a sometimes desperately maintained veneer of normality, madness was rife in many circles. Not that Earth and Sol were free of such problems. Few people knew how close collapse had been when the Crashlanders had arrived from We Made It with the hyperdrive.

He looked back at Leonie's mention of the incident in the caves battle, then put in a couple of keywords and searched Rykermann's speeches inside and outside the Parliament. There was nothing comparable, no mention of the time, however brief and however secondary to the main campaigns, when the two humans and the kzin had fought as allies. No mention of Leonie's experience. There were, however, several references to the deceased Professor Carmody, "murdered by the Kzin."

Colonel Cumpston activated a higher security clearance. Buford Early's square dark face appeared on the screen. Cumpston wondered for a second if the general ever went off duty. Early turned toward him and removed a cigar from his mouth. It was an invitation to speak. Early expressed no surprise at Cumpston's request. He just nodded, heavy, impassive, a little frightening even to those who thought they knew him well.

Raargh and Vaemar were still heading south. Cumpston took off and headed southwest, toward Munchen.

Chapter 4

The *Glory Bee* had dropped out of hyperdrive beyond Alpha Centauri's vast singularity and commenced its slow fall through the double star's gravity well several days previously.

Now Wunderland's surface filled most of the bridge's viewports. Dawn was approaching Munchen but the city's lights could be made out at the edge of the retreating crescent of night. They were cleared to land in a few hours.

"Well, does any of it come back?" Patrick Quickenden's voice was tender.

She gazed down with wide eyes. "The sky . . . some of the sky is familiar, I think. I remember the constellations."

"That's good."

"I hope so. I've read enough to be apprehensive."

"There's been a lot of rehabilitation and rebuilding in the last five years."

"There must have been. That looks like a big city."

"We'll know the details of it soon enough."

"It's a strange feeling, Paddy. I can't tell you . . . It's frightening."

"I think I can guess something of it. But there's no need for fear."

"Nightmares of great tiger-cats, for years." She gave a little off-key laugh. "Death, flames. Comforting myself when I woke up with the thought that they were only nightmares. And then finding they were all real. . . . I have one flash often, of a horrible scene in a burning street. And . . . seeing a flash that I know is a deliberate nuclear explosion. I'm frightened of the tigers, still. Silly of me. But they were with me in that coldsleep coffin. They've got deep into what's left of my brain."

"There's no need for fear now," he told her gently. "Remember,

220Hal Colebatchthe Kzin are beaten on Wunderland and humans are pushing
them back across space. Thanks to you. We'll push them farther yet, again thanks to you."

"I'm afraid that I shouldn't have come back, though I was
the one who insisted on it." She gripped his hand tightly, her
free hand brushing at her head with a nervous gesture. Her
fingertips touched scars, invisible under plastic surgery and
under the gold of her hair.

"We've got a job to do," he said. "I know you'll do it."

"Brain . . . my brain's still pretty good, isn't it?"

"Well, if you don't strain it too much, it can handle little
jobs like building the engine that shatters the light barrier
from nothing but an alien manual. I'd say that's at least a
reasonable performance. About average for someone of your
IQ, perhaps—if there was another human being to take an
average from."

"I always hated being . . . abnormal. . . . But now it's the
absence . . . that chunk of memory that's gone. . . . What
was I?"

"When they pulled you out of the coldsleep tank on that
derelict, your alpha-wave was still off the scale. No one, *no
one*, else could have done what you did! Don't you know why
they sometimes called you Lydia Pink?"

"I did hear that name a couple of times when we were on
Earth. I didn't know they were referring to me. I remember
somebody said it and you shut him up pretty quickly. I
wondered about that at the time."

"I suppose I'm overprotective. There are security consider-
ations, and . . . other things. But if you've any doubts about
your mind . . ."

"What's it mean? I suppose compared to a Jinxian I'm pink.
I don't live under Sirius."

"It's from a very old song someone rediscovered. Under
Templemount, the Pychwar people on Earth went through all
the ancient army and navy songs they could find when keeping
morale up was a tough business. It wasn't one of the useful
ones then, but somebody kept it in mind. Only the first three
lines are relevant:

> "So we'll drink drink, drink
> To Lydia Pink, to Lydia Pink,
> The savior of the Human Race . . .

"Dimity, don't cry, please!" He kissed her forehead. "Anyway, there are good reasons why your identity, and certainly

your precise role in the scheme of things, shouldn't be publicized too widely. Call me paranoid, but I'd rather the Kzin— and some humans, for that matter—didn't know the interpreter of the Outsiders' manual,—the chief builder of the hyperdrive, was in space, even now.

"Don't worry," he went on, "songs round a piano don't carry over four light-years, and both the hyperwave and the ship traffic is monitored. No one here knows who you are who shouldn't. . . ."

"It's not that sort of fear. Do I go to Wunderland under a false name?"

"A good idea if we can keep it up. There are still kzin on Wunderland. It's well-named, by all accounts. A beautiful, glorious world: open skies—I hope I can get used to that— low gravity. Can you sleep for a while? I'll make you something?"

"I'm still afraid. I don't know why. Please, hold me, Paddy."

Jocelyn van der Stratt read the details of the We Made It party with considerable interest. She called up some verifying information, and then confirmed to her deputy that she would join Arthur Guthlac and the Wunderland Science and Industry Authorities' delegations in meeting them personally. She also called Ulf Reichstein Markham and canceled their meeting that evening. She had not changed her mind about his usefulness as a tool, but he could be put into reserve. It looked as if another and possibly neater solution to the problem of Leonie Rykermann might be in the offing.

Arthur Guthlac should be brought more firmly on side. That could be accomplished. *You'll be harder to seduce than Markham, I guess,* she thought, *but I've had bigger challenges before. You're not bad-looking either. I don't think the kzinrret-suit for you. Not the first time, anyway. I've never had a Flatlander, or a Brigadier, or, unless I miss my guess, a virgin. But you might find you get lucky on Wunderland tonight.* She dressed, again with some thought, and put a call to Guthlac on her vidphone. Postwar Wunderland lacked such luxuries as transfer booths but, she was sure, he would come quickly enough.

Colonel Cumpston landed his car near Grossdrache, the cave mouth that was the main entrance to the great complex of the Drachenholen. He had changed into UNSN field dress with the badges of his rank discreetly visible. Students were still shrouding the human mummies. One armed with a strakkaker disposed of a small pack of snuffling advokats and a couple of the even more detested zeitungers, also poisonous little carrion eaters and disease reservoirs but with, in addition, a limited psychic power of broadcasting depression to humans and other sophonts.

The kzin fragments had been stacked in one of the many blast craters nearby and burned, without deliberate insult if without particular reverence or ceremony. In any event, cremation was common among kzinti.

Nils Rykermann had had the caves gazetted as a wildlife sanctuary and restricted area long before the war, but now, when they still contained many dead bodies and many live munitions, that restriction was taken more seriously. None of the students had the authority to question Cumpston's ARM credentials, but they insisted he take mask, lamp, compass, helmet and utility pack and provided him with a guide.

The Rykermanns were at the site of one of the old morlock "towns." Long-dead bodies lay around still: dead morlocks, dead humans, dead kzinti. Lights shone off grinning skulls with peeling crusts of blackened skin, on corpses cuddled over sheaves of bare ribs, on long, naked limb bones.

"A lot of old friends," said Rykermann, when the guide had left. "We keep rediscovering unknown or forgotten chambers. It was a long war."

"Well," said Cumpston, "it's over now."

"Is it?"

"It is for this planet. And against the hyperdrive the kzinti don't have much chance in space."

"You think so? We're going to drop out of hyperspace and say to them: 'Nice planet you've got here. Just hand it over, if you wouldn't mind?' And they'll say: 'Oh indeed, Noble Monkey! Anything to oblige!' It's going to be like that, is it? Do you know how many we lost taking Hssin? Not even a proper planetary base, just a collection of bubble habitats? Have you heard any reports on the fighting on Down?"

Cumpston said nothing to Rykermann's sarcasm. He had, he told himself, sometimes regretted opening his mouth, but had never regretted not opening it. His first remark had been to test Rykermann's reaction, in any event. "I can tell you about Down," he said. "My information's fairly up to date."

"It's not over," said Rykermann. "And as for this planet, it won't be over while kzin are on it."

"Nils!" Leonie Rykermann's voice could have been conveying a number of things, but her body language betrayed distress.

"I'm sorry . . ." said Nils Rykermann. "I get a bit emotional sometimes. . . ." And then, as he saw a couple of the small decorations Cumpston had made a point of wearing for this visit: "You were there on Hssin, weren't you?"

"Yes."

"Then you know how ferocious they are. And what fighters. Every male trained in high-tech warfare, and practically every male who lives to adulthood, even the telepaths or computer nerds, who are considered feeble and ridiculous by kzinti standards, capable of dismantling a tiger in claw-to-claw combat."

"I think I've known that for quite a while. Hssin wasn't the first fight I've been in."

"These morlocks tend to be more complete than a lot of the other remains," said Rykermann. "But we'll have to find out more about their life cycle before we can try to re-create the species."

"How interesting a species are they? Are they worth re-creating?"

"I was interested, before the Invasion, in seeing how intelligent they were. They gave us a surprise in the fighting by using stone weapons. I also noticed a great variety of noises they made. There's a strong possibility they had language. And the fact that they broke the legs of prisoners to stop them escaping while they kept them alive and fresh to eat shows a certain capacity to plan and anticipate behavior. They're a species, however unattractive, with minds, however dim, and no threat to us now. Given that, perhaps we have some sort of duty to re-create them."

"I see. How effective were their weapons?"

"You see these scars?" Rykermann touched his neck and shoulders. "Most of them are from morlock blows. The kzin who was with us got a similar collection, even prettier."

"Do you happen to know that Kzin's Name?"

"Just a minute!" Rykermann suddenly drew himself up and stared at Cumpston as if seeing him for the first time. The tall Wunderlander easily overtopped the stocky Earthman. "What's this about? Who are you? What are you doing here? This is a restricted project!"

Cumpston produced a card and shone his light on it. Nils Rykermann inspected the card in silence, showed it to Leonie and handed it back.

Rykermann drew a deep breath. "All right," he said more calmly. "I'll ask again. What do you want?"

"This was quite a long hike for me," said Cumpston, "and breathing the dust on the way is thirsty work. You wouldn't have anything like a cup of tea, would you?"

Leonie looked at him gratefully. Nils Rykermann breathed heavily for a moment, then he seemed calmer. Cumpston remembered that Rykermann was now also a politician.

"All right," he said. There were a couple of camp stools set up in one corner with a small utility module. Cumpston sat himself on a thick section of broken stalagmite column. Leonie poured the tea, which, from his dossier, he knew she was fond of. With the skulls and the mummies staring at them under the harsh lights, it was, Cumpston thought, a strange place for a picnic.

Rykermann seemed to welcome the chance to talk now. Cumpston drew him out on the battles that had been fought in the caves. After some time he brought the talk back to the kzin soldier who had fought with them against the morlocks.

"Was that Raargh?"

"Yes . . ."

"He seems to have been a reasonable ratcat. Didn't you save each other's lives?"

"How did you know that?"

"I know things. Records are my business. Who knows, I might write a history of the war someday."

"He was on an operation to wipe us out in the caves."

"You don't look wiped out from where I'm standing."

"I repaid him . . . I suppose there was one other thing I owe him for, though. He saw me when I was being treated and told me his Name. Orderly who sewed me up wanted to castrate me to make me more docile if I was to be allowed to live, but Raargh told him it was incompatible with Fighters' Privileges and didn't seem to work with monkeys anyway. As well as being Sergeant, Raargh had just got his Name, and Orderly took notice. I was grateful for that." Rykermann laughed sardonically. "Apart from anything else, we had no transplant facilities for any subsequent . . . rectification."

"If I may ask in turn, how did you know what they were saying?"

"I'd been studying the Heroes' Tongue as well as the slave language ever since the Invasion. It had been a long war even then."

"I remember. Did you have dealings with Raargh again?"

"I kept out of all kzinti's way. We both did."

"You never thought about him?"

"Why should I?"

"I think I would have, in the circumstances . . . wondered what made up such a creature, and so on."

"I knew all I wanted to know about the kzinti. I'd been

involved in ground fighting from the first. We . . . someone else and I . . . got away from Manstein's Folly just before they nuked it. As for Raargh . . . Kzin NCOs tend to be . . . something like human NCOs. Tough. Capable. It's rarer for them to become full officers, because of the immobilist nature of Kzin society. I had to study them once. I don't have to now. I've got enough to think about here."

"Raargh—I only discovered his new Name later—saved us both," said Leonie. "I'd given no word not to fight, and I'm not sure the Kzinti would have taken the word of a female Man anyway, but . . . I didn't want to fight him."

"Have you seen him since?"

"No. Is that why you're here?"

"Yes. I gather he may be looking for you—not as an enemy, I might say. He's lived with humans successfully since the end of the fighting. Actually, I think he wants to ask your advice."

Rykermann shrugged. "If you're what your credentials say you are, you know our interests. Apart from my Parliamentary duties I'm interested in these caves and in my students." He watched Leonie move away to take recordings from some instruments, then continued: "I've no time for or interest in ratcats. I've seen enough of them to last me the rest of my life. When we get the ecosystems of these caves functioning again I've plenty of other projects. One of my first dreams as a young naturalist was to explore and classify Grossgeister Swamp properly. But it's a little below the caves in my list of priorities now—and it breaks my heart to see it. Our furry friends boiled the center out of Grossgeister with their heat-induction ray when some Wabbits took refuge in it. A great biological paradise, a Golconda of new species, only a short flight from Munchen, and more than half of it sterilized by them! Rehabilitating Grossgeister will be my next project, though there's no way I can bring back the lost species there— we don't even know what most of them were! Classifying Grossgeister was going to be my greatest project, but they've destroyed its heart as they've destroyed so much of our lives. And once a thing is lost . . . it's lost."

"Don't you know what he wants to ask you about? Or want to know?"

"Not particularly. I'm not in the business of advising ratcats." He laughed abruptly. "If one bizarre day they got the vote and they were in my Parliamentary constituency I suppose I'd have to talk to them. I can't see that happening, somehow."

"Well, I seem to have come on a fool's errand," said Cumpston. "Still, seeing your work has been fascinating."

"Come back in another five years," said Rykermann. "We might have a clean planet by then. Leonie will show you the way back to the crepuscular zone."

Cumpston fed the tapes of the conversation and the films of Rykermann and Leonie into the car's computer. Buford Early was back to him before he had traveled far.

"According to the speech and body language analyses, coupled with the analyses of their earlier speeches and their contact profiles several things emerge plainly," he said. "Rykermann is an Exterminationist. His wife isn't. She half-knows he is and she's trying to convince herself he doesn't mean it."

"That's bad."

"But it's not quite that simple. He wants all kzin dead but he feels under a debt to Raargh. For Leonie's life at least as much as for his own. I don't think he values his own life very highly. There's a lot of death wish in that boy."

"Do we know why?"

"Do I have to draw you a diagram? Little thing you might have noticed called the war. It screwed up a lot of Wunderlanders pretty badly. And not only Wunderlanders. People did things they can't live with now, lost people they can't live without, sometimes. The euphoria of Liberation is wearing off and survivors' guilt is coming back. People are blaming themselves for things they did to stay alive. Certainly he has a major hang-up about this girl professor, for whose death he blames the Kzin and himself about equally, depending on the weather and what he last ate. Who knows all the details? But after fifty-three years of Kzinti occupation there aren't too many on Wunderland who are a picture of glowing mental health. And Rykermann had a tougher war than most. Why do you think he's working a lot harder than he needs to now?"

"Because he's politically ambitious?"

"In that case he'd be concentrating on the one thing: politics. Instead of which he's scattering himself all over the shop—politics, cave antics, television features, the memorial to this professor—all displacement activity. He's trying to stop himself thinking, and I think he's going to snap soon, but he could do a lot of harm before he does."

"So what do we do?"

"Give me time to think, boy. I can't come up with an optimum plan in a second."

"Raargh is seeking him out."

"What for? Still wanting his head for a wall decoration? Wouldn't be popular now, not with Rykermann a celebrity. That's how he found him, I suppose. The old devil must watch monkey television."

"For his advice. I gather he trusts him because of their old alliance."

"Advice? Advice on what?"

"What to do about Vaemar's future. I think Vaemar is with him."

"Cumpston, Vaemar is valuable!"

"Raargh thinks so too. For what it's worth, so do I. That's why I disturbed your esteemed labors."

"There are hopes riding on that cub for . . . for . . . Where are they now?"

"Close by. I've got them on the tracker."

"Get in closer. In fact check them now."

"They're not far away. But . . . Buford, the signal is odd. Muzzy. But it's there. They may be resting up in a cave. They're cats. They love exploring holes."

"Find them! Go in now! Close enough to help them if need be. If they must see you, so be it. Keep them away from Rykermann. If you need help I'll send the cavalry."

"They called the spaceport the Himmelfährte," said Jocelyn. "The way to Heaven. Not for the reason you might think obvious, but because so many humans died slaving here when the Kzin wanted to expand it in a hurry. This place is built on human bones."

"I see," said Arthur Guthlac.

"There are the memorials."

"Pretty realistic. Are those children?"

"Yes," she said. "We commissioned the best sculptors on Wunderland. Something never to be forgotten. There are going to be a lot of memorials on this planet. We're going to make sure nothing's forgotten, ever."

A section of one of the kzinti warcraft hulks, cut free, fell to the ground in a metallic crash and a cloud of dust. A clutch of dead kzin, freeze-dried in space years before, stared out eyelessly at them from the new cavity in the hull. Jocelyn banked the car away and headed for the main spaceport building.

"I suppose the ratcat-lovers are very pleased it's all kzin-sized," she remarked as they flew between the huge doors into the parking bays. "Convenient for them when they come back." In fact human-sized facilities were replacing the giant and brutally utilitarian kzinti military buildings and installations. Black paint was smeared over a wall that had once been adorned with a heroic kzin mural. "That'll be them now." She gestured to the tube extending from a recently-landed shuttle. Professor Meinertzhagen, the head of the Wunderland Science Authority, and other gray-uniformed Wunderland officials who Arthur Guthlac had met previously, joined them.

"She's turning a few heads!" he remarked, as the We Made It party approached.

"Not my image of a hyperdrive expert," Jocelyn told him. There was no need to specify who they meant. "That's odd," she added.

"What?"

"I'd say she's a Wunderlander. That's not a Crashlander's musculature. Look at the rest of them. Far more solidly built. Blondie's muscles were formed in Wunderland gravity with a lot of exercise, although I'd say she's lived in Crashlander gravity for a while since. Also, she's walking scared."

"Agoraphobia? The original Crashlander party that returned to Earth tended to suffer from it under an open sky."

"There are treatments for that now. And those ears. Those are *Herrenmann* ears."

"I wouldn't know."

"You're a flatlander. And I'm a cop, remember?" She gave him an enigmatic smile as she said it. Her swinging hand brushed his and for a moment she squeezed his fingers.

"We notice things like that," she went on. "Look at her eyes. She's as jumpy as a Kzin on a hot osmium roof. Watch." She made a peculiar and difficult noise with her lips. The ears of the blonde woman and of several passersby twitched noticeably. The blonde woman looked bewildered. Jocelyn's face was composed as if nothing had happened.

"Once I looked for UNSN infiltrators."

Her words had taken them into uncomfortable territory. The head of the Crashlander delegation shook hands, carefully restraining his grip.

"Patrick Quickenden," he introduced himself. "Helen Moffet, Roger Selene, Sam Kim . . ."

"We've got a couple of cars waiting," said Jocelyn when the introductions were completed. "We're lunching at the university. You'll be able to see the city on the way."

The Crashlander party had seen Earth, but as the belt carried them toward the cars, they gazed in astonishment at Wunderland's open skies, mild weather, tall hills and buildings and blazes of multicolored plants. *We need not spend our lives under a single star again,* thought Arthur Guthlac. *Once I saved money in the hope of a cheap holiday on the Moon before I died. The hyperdrive has liberated us from more than the Kzin. Let this war finish—let the threat be destroyed, and Starman will come into his own!* And then, *Why, I could be a Wunderlander!*

"There's more dust in the air," said the blond woman suddenly. She had been watching a flutterby that rested on the tip of her finger, fanning its delicate wings.

"More dust than what?" Arthur asked.

"Than I expected, I suppose. The light is different."

"There was a war," said Jocelyn. "A big war. There were nukes used during the Invasion, during the intra-kzinti war, during the Liberation, and worse than nukes during the UNSN's ramscoop raid before that. It hasn't all settled yet. But it will. We're going to build a better planet here. A cleaner planet!"

"I see . . . of course." Her face contorted suddenly and she clutched at Arthur Guthlac's arm. Whatever gravity she came from, her grip was so painfully tight he thought for a moment she was attacking him. Her blue eyes were wide with terror. He saw her fight down a scream.

Three of the scrapyard workers across the way were loading a sled. One of them was a kzin.

"There are quite a few of them around," Jocelyn said, following her gaze. Her voice was cold and expressionless. Either she disliked the sight or she despised the woman's obvious stab of terror. "*You* needn't worry about it." She rustled the dried objects that hung from her belt-ring. "Kzinti ears," she said, then added, "and human collabos. A custom we copied from them."

The blond woman stared at the things for a moment. Her hand brushed her hair in a gesture Jocelyn had already noted. The sledge was loaded now. The workers killed the engines of their lifts and one of the humans opened a flask. He tossed a can of beer to the other human and one to the kzin. The delegation and the reception committee boarded their cars and headed toward the university, flying by a scenic route. But more than one head turned to look back at the trio.

Chapter 5

"This redoubt," Henrietta said, "was begun by Chuut-Riit shortly before the ramscoop raid. Initially he feared a coup against him by an alliance of other kzin, particularly followers of Kfrashaka-Admiral and Ktrodni-Stkaa, much more than he feared humans.

"He kept it secret from all but a few of his own pride, and me, Executive Secretary and most senior and trusted of his slaves. Very shortly before his murder he began to have other thoughts, which he entrusted, posthumously, to me alone.

"Traat-Admiral was of course one who knew of the original project, though not his very deepest thoughts, and after Chuut-Riit's murder Traat-Admiral carried it on. He and nearly all his pride perished in space. By the time of the human landings it was unfinished, much as you see this section now. But enough had been done to enable it to support a few of us. As well that more Heroes did not know of it, or they would have raided its stockpiles of weapons for the last battles."

"Who built it, if it was secret?" asked Vaemar. His Wunderlander was correct, much better than Raargh's, though with a nonhuman accent. Raargh had procured sleep tapes for him to learn from.

"Slaves, Noble Prince. They were killed before the surrender. Then the Heroes who had supervised them went out to die heroically."

"I was at my post at the Governor's Palace in Munchen when the end came. On the day of the cease-fire the mob stormed the palace. Zroght–Guard-Captain and some of the others made a last stand there. I escaped with Andre and a few other loyal humans of Chuut-Riit's household. And with Emma, my eldest daughter. Save for her I could not get my family away. Many

231

humans who had obeyed and served the Heroes, who had interceded with them for humans and kept order and production on this world, were lynched by people who owed their lives to them. The mob seized my man and fed him alive to kzinrretti in the zoo cages. I think a priest intervened to save the children. Or perhaps not. I do not remember those days well.

"In the chaos we made our way here, mingling as need be with the hordes of refugees," she went on. "Ensign here and other Heroes who had been informed in time got here as well. Chuut-Riit had given me this shortly before his murder, warning me that he had a premonition of doom, and that this was his last *ktzirrarourght* in case doom fell." She fished at a chain around her neck and drew forth an antique gold and silver locket, a human thing, perhaps made in Neue Dresden. "It contained four things: a map and the keys to this fortress, a tuft of his fur, and a hologram recording.

"While you slept, Noble One, I already tested your nucleonic acid against his. I know the reports that you are his son are true."

"This was built, all in a few weeks?" asked Vaemar, looking about him again.

"Indeed, Noble One. You come of the greatest race in the Universe."

"Truly, I come of a great people . . . Great works."

"Yes, there is nothing the kzinti cannot accomplish, though all the fates turn against them. But I have no secrets from your blood. We had an advantage. ARM suppressed the knowledge of Sinclair fields on Earth, but they had been used to enhance the reaction-drives of the first interstellar slowboats. There were still plans of them in the old archives here."

"Sinclair fields?"

"Time precesses faster inside them. They would have had major military and weapons applications for both sides—war-winning weapons if we had got them in time—but we only rediscovered the plans late in the day, and used them here to speed up production. Inside the fields, much could be built while little time passed outside. We used them also, to grow and age the trees we planted above to conceal the work, even, with high-pressure pumps, to grow stalactites to conceal disturbances at cave entrances. And to grow some stray kzin kittens quickly to adulthood, increasing our strength. We have young Heroes here, thoroughly trained, who know only this place and its discipline.

"As for the major rooms and excavations, the God had done much of that already. These chambers link to the great caves of the Hohe Kalkstein, are indeed an extension of them. But still, it was a mighty feat. . . . Come with me now. Noble Prince, do you remember your Honored Sire Chuut-Riit?"

"A little," said Vaemar. "Images."

"You will see your Honored Sire once more."

Henrietta, accompanied by Andre, Emma and Ensign, led them to another chamber. Human chairs and Kzin-sized stone fooches surrounded what looked like an auditorium. There was an instrument console and racks of sidearms on the walls as well as a few stuffed humans, a battle-drum, and other trophies that emphasized its kzinti, and in particular its military kzinti, appearance. There was even a gonfalon of Old Kzin, and some of the artificial lights shone from cressets of antique appearance.

At a gesture from Henrietta, Raargh and Vaemar reclined on two of the fooches. Emma at the console touched a keypad. There was a faint hissing as concealed ducts pumped out odors. A hologram of a mighty kzin appeared. It spoke in the Heroes' Tongue, in the Ultimate Imperative Tense of Royalty:

"This is the Testament of Chuut-Riit, Planetary Governor of Ka'ashi, of the blood of the Patriarch, to my slave and friend Henrietta-human.

"Henrietta, if you are watching this I shall be dead. One attempt by the human *Arrum* to assassinate me has been thwarted. There will be others, and by kzinti as well as humans.

"This I have always accepted. We Kzinti have long had proverbs like your human 'Uneasy lies the head that wears the crown,' and I chose to wear the crown and accept what goes with it. Yet it was a surprise for me to discover that the humans of Sol System knew so much of us as to know to strike at me personally.

"How did this happen? I thought on it. The humans who fled from Ka'ashi to Sol System left long before I arrived. There must have been secret comings and goings between the two systems since. Light-messages, perhaps.

"We had, I suppose, known this was possible, yet had had no interest in it. If the Sol Humans knew the terror of our Names, so much the worse for them! And in that lack of interest I detect a deep-seated military weakness in our kind. I long ago realized, Henrietta, that your kind have talents we lack. We are curious if mysteries are presented to us, we enjoy showing our talents for solving puzzles and conundrums, and we are always eager to stick our noses into caves that may hide secrets or prey, but we lack your degree of curiosity for its own sake. Sometimes I think the deadliest blow the Jotok ever struck against us was to *give* us knowledge so that we never came to love the hunt for it.

"I summoned the telepaths who have examined human prisoners, and forced myself to interrogate them. That was perhaps prodigal of me—by then all telepaths were urgently needed for war security. But I uncovered many things which I had not suspected, not least about the telepaths themselves.

"However my main discovery was this: When we first met humans and our telepaths reported a race given over wholly to peace and as weaponless as the Kdatlyno and others we have encountered, even as the human laser-cannon slashed at our fleets, some speculated that monkey pacifism was not natural but had been conditioned in them by another race. Perhaps some race had sought to use them as the Jotok sought to use us when they recruited us as mercenaries and gave us technology.

"Some even speculated that those conditioners of monkeys *were* the Jotok—the fabled free Jotok fleet that had escaped us. We searched for those conditioners, whoever they might be, without result.

"So I discovered, putting together one piece and another, that humans had indeed been conditioned: first by the *Arrum*. But second by something behind the *Arrum* that has no name. I am a kzintosh of the Blood Royal, brought up in palaces, now a Planetary Governor with enemies and rivals. I am used to dominance-ploys and *Konspirrissy. Most* Konspirrissies have inbuilt limitations to their growth and fall apart, are betrayed or fission after they pass a certain size. But this was *Konspirrissy* beyond *Konspirrissy.*

"By human standards very old, very large. So old and large that the normal fission of *Konspirrissy*, even exposure, would not be fatal to it. It had grown and changed through many human lifetimes. We Kzin nobles have studied *Konspirrissy*, yes, we have made a science of it—I shall say we of the Riit clan most of all. We did not come to rule the kzinti by the speed of our fangs and claws alone. We know that *Konspirrissy* may grow in such a way that the *Konspirritors* hardly *need* to conceal their aims. They need only manipulate a few appearances and emphases. Humans are so inconstant that even one who tells the truth about his plans is not believed: Look at your Hitler, your Lenin, your Sunday. But we kzinti have had some equivalents.

"And I discovered that even some Heroes were being drawn into it: some unknowingly, some merely unknowingly *at first.*

Yes, *Arrum* and what is behind Arrum has its plans for the human species—and now I find it has plans for the kzinti species too!

"Sol humans have defeated our fleets. I intend to overwhelm them, with the Fifth Fleet or if need be the Sixth. I regret that much of Earth may have to be destroyed. I will try to keep Africa, Yucatán where the Jaguar-gods dwell, the Rocky Mountains and the Russian steppes for the hunting. An easy victory would have been better for both humans and kzinti, though I cannot blame humans for their stubbornness. After many easy conquests we wanted to find enemies in space who would test our fighting skills and courage, and then the Fanged God in His great bounty granted our wish.

"And yet, I think the *Konspirrissy* may strike back at me, yes, even here in the Governor's Palace on Ka'ashi. Humans adapt with great speed. That is both their strength and their weakness. You have a legend, *The Jungle Book*, of a human cub raised by pack-raiding beasts who yet became a leader of a whole ecosystem, enemy of one of the great *kattz* I look to meet on Earth, friend to another of the dark pelt! How amazed I was, each time I reread that legend, that such a thing could have happened! On Kzin it would have been not possible. Kzinti are hard as iron and stone, and do not change or adapt. That is our strength and our weakness. If the pride of that great *kat* Bagheera still live, I will speak with them when I conquer Earth."

Something changed in the great face. Its regal impassivity wavered.

"I say that if you see this message I shall be dead. I believed that, with culling, over a few generations humans would become the most useful species the Patriarchy has ever acquired. Now I wonder if the *Konspirritorrs* do not see the Kzin in the same light! Or if they see Kzin and Human together as but malleable material for some other end.

"Henrietta, I have a foreboding that these *Konspirritorrs* may destroy me. I think they are a greater threat than Ktrodni-Stkaa and his pride. These *Konspirritorrs* threaten both our kinds.

"If I am dead, Traat-Admiral is my chosen successor. I think he will assert his dominance successfully, though he is but the Son of Third Gunner. I think he will see my youngest kits through the nursery. The elder will find their own way. I have told him you are decorous and he will listen to your advice as I have. I sometimes almost envy your kind their intelligent females, for I have no one but Conserver and you to whom I may open my mind.

"You, my most trusted slave, must guide Traat-Admiral in his dealings with humans as I know you have guided me. Prepare the path so that Traat also discovers what I have discovered. He is the cleverest of my pride, but he must make discoveries for himself and learn to think as I do, but without me.

"Do not mourn for me overmuch. I shall be with the Fanged God. Traat is brave and loyal, but he may fail. If he does, the task may devolve upon *you*. Destroy the *Konspirritorrs* that threaten both our kinds.

"My sons are clever. Do not forget them. Guide them too if you can. You have served me well and faithfully. Your presence has brought me pleasure, and because of you I was able to be a better master to the humans of Ka'ashi.

"I hope that you may prosper and have many cubs."

The holo vanished. Henrietta bowed her head to the place where it had been.

"That, Noble Prince, was your Sire. That, Noble Hero, was the Kin of the Patriarch."

Raargh growled in his throat. He had seen the living Chuut-Riit, had been lectured by him as an NCO, and indeed had been presented to him and marked by a few drops of his honored urine after he had received his Name. The holo brought back many memories. *As the odors were also meant to,* he thought.

He said nothing yet. He and Vaemar had given their Words not to attack their human captors that day. Those Words held them. Even if they did not, he had seen the snouts of automatic guns in various corners. Henrietta had spoken of "Ensign and other Heroes." He had seen a few in these chambers, more near the entrances when, paralyzed and half-unconscious, he and Vaemar had been brought here. He had disciplined his mind to try to count them and take note of the defensive works, but there must be others he had not seen. At one point he had smelled Kzinrretti. Anyway, there were too many to fight.

His ziirgah sense made it plain that they were being watched, though it also hinted—it could hardly do more than that and he was using it to its limit—that the gestalt of interest in him was fluctuating, and tending to drop as he continued to remain calm and made no furious or rampant movements. The kzinti here were presumably used to regarding all kzin as allies, and the field-grown ones would know nothing different. *Who knows how many this place holds?* He thought. *And I must find out more.* Then: *I must think very carefully.* A ghostly hologram could lay no charge on him; he knew it was but a collection of electronic impulses, perhaps even faked. Yet the testament of Chuut-Riit was not something to be set aside lightly.

❖   ❖   ❖

Raargh and Vaemar had passed this way. On Earth the orange fur of a kzin would have blazed out, but on this part of Wunderland the vegetation was still largely native, reddish, and better camouflage for them. Infrared surveys, difficult enough in daylight, showed body-heat patterns of what could be several large animals, but not, disturbingly, the almost unmistakable signatures of kzinti.

Still, it was limestone country. The great caves of the Hohe Kalkstein were only a couple of score miles to the south. Raargh and Vaemar might well have found some deep hole to rest in or explore. He climbed to two thousand meters, then higher, and surveyed the country visually. A pattern of southward-flowing streams, appearing and disappearing, the sudden sharp hollows of roof collapses, and other indications of cave country became obvious. There was also another pattern—a regularity of disturbance in the ground that did not look natural. He tried deep radar. His car's set was not powerful but it showed a jumble underground of passages, streams, hollows, and again, sharp-edged regularities. The UNSN had learned that the Kzin, when they condescended to put their minds to it, could be masters of camouflage, and some of this had a kzinti military look to it, though it was on a far larger scale than the ambushes the UNSN had experienced. But if large-scale excavations had been going on here, where was the spoil? The forest and woodland were old Wunderland growth.

The telltale indicated Raargh and Vaemar were in the vicinity but not close. Cumpston landed the car. He was in a shallow gully, filled with vegetation. Brown and pale-gray limestone outcrops rose about, and even sitting in the car's cockpit he could see the dark apertures of three or four caves, partly screened by tall trees.

He tasted the air as he could, trying for a gestalt feeling of the place. *A native Wunderlander would be better at this*, he thought. The clouds of flutterbys created an impression of tranquillity that was not necessarily reliable. But there was a small stream flowing with a good population of amphibians, froggolinas and the even odder kermitoids that were looking at him curiously and making no effort to hide. There were other animals in the vegetation. If anything violent had happened recently, or if the kzin were hunting, the local wildlife would, he was sure, be silent and invisible. A small mechanical sniffer confirmed his own suspicion of kzin pheromones, but in the breezy glade they were much dispersed.

A more sophisticated sniffer would have been useful, he

thought, pinching his lip. Or a dog. Dogs' reaction to the faintest smell of kzin was unmistakable, but there were few dogs on Wunderland now. Kzinti had not liked them. Well, Early had mechanical sniffers and a great many other things. Was it time to call Early? Cumpston had lights and weapons, not all of the latter obvious. He decided to check the nearest caves first.

The first he looked at was plainly undisturbed. Not far within, delicate straw stalactites hung unbroken from the roof almost to the ground. Another time he would have enjoyed exploring this cave for its own sake, but it was obvious that nothing the bulk of a Kzin had passed this way. The next cave showed some disturbances in the mud at its entrance. Looking closely, he was not surprised to make out the print of a kzin foot, though even in Wunderland gravity it seemed curiously light for such heavy creatures. In the still air a molecular analysis confirmed the presence of kzin breath-particles as well as pheromones. He identified the signatures of Raargh and Vaemar, but also others. There were human breath-particles, too. He started into the cave, then hesitated.

Dangerous? Going alone into a cave on an alien world seeking a pair of large carnivores, evidently with unknown companions, was not an entirely safe thing to do, even if the carnivores in question were his chess partners. But in the event of trouble his failure to report would trigger an alarm at Early's headquarters. Normally, the failsafe would trigger every five days, and at present it had four days to run. That was much too long an interval for safety in these circumstances, he thought. He would readjust the car's brain to send a signal after two hours. That was, he thought, the best compromise he could make between recklessness and an excessive caution that would accomplish nothing. A movement caught his attention and there was a peculiar droning sound as he turned back to the car. He never reached it.

"We'll have some lunch here and then have a look around the science department and laboratories," Professor Meinertzhagen said. The party had left their cars and were walking through one of the pleasanter parts of the campus. The steel spire of St. Joachim's glittered in the distance.

"This is the Cafe Lindenbaum, quite a historic place. One of the first sidewalk cafés in Munchen. Some say the day it opened we stopped being a village. Mark you, it's famous among the more cynical on the staff as the 'Failure Factory.' Students drinking coffee, chattering and flirting on sunny days when they should be bent over their screens."

"I suppose students are students everywhere," said one of the Crashlanders.

"The Chess Club's always met here, too. You know we're organizing an Interstellar Tournament—the ICF has approved a new title of Interstellar Master, now that we don't have to wait years between reports of each move! The restaurant section we're eating in is too expensive for most students, though. It's always had human service. It was a gimmick before the Invasion. Later," he went on, "human service in restaurants— or anywhere else—was no novelty. As the economy collapsed machines broke down. More significantly, humans would work for less—do things for a crust or a pittance that machines had always done—do anything not to starve. Now, I'm pleased to say, human service is becoming a rare and fancy gimmick again. We might have a look at Harold's Terran Bar this evening. There's a lot of history there, too."

"But there's still human service here, I see," said Patrick, as they settled themselves around a couple of sidewalk tables. Several of the Crashlanders were fascinated by the flutterbys.

"Oh yes, Old Stanley. But he's the proprietor nowadays. Very grand!" Professor Meinertzhagen waved to the aproned old man.

He shuffled over, clutching an antique paper notepad and tray. The tray fell from his hands, clattered and rolled away.

"Professor Carmody!" he cried.

"No!" Paddy Quickenden jumped to his feet.

"I think it's too late," she said. "How do you know me?"

"But . . . you used to come here with Professor Rykermann in the old days . . . before the Invasion."

"That's a long time ago."

"How could I forget? The last time I saw you there was rioting over the new defense taxes and conscription orders. There had been reports of trouble in space. Old Otto had told me to pile sandbags round the walls, and that's what I was doing. You and Professor Rykermann left together. Then, a few nights later, the bombardment started. . . . But . . . you look the same!"

"That's all right!" Meinertzhagen said sharply and loudly. To look far younger than one's years on Wunderland implied access to geriatric treatments during the Occupation. With relatively few exceptions, that implied a Government position or at least a prosperous and politically acceptable life during the Occupation. It was not a passport to approval on post-Liberation Wunderland. "This lady came from We Made It today in one of the new hyperdrive ships. You must be mistaken. Now we are attempting to offer her and her distinguished colleagues some hospitality!"

"Oh! No, no of course, it couldn't be, could it? . . . but . . . well, everything is on the House for any Crashlander! We haven't forgotten what we owe them. I'm sorry, I'm getting old. . . . I'm getting very old. I survived, you know . . . So many didn't."

"This is an official party. Gratuitous service won't be necessary," Patrick Quickenden interjected. "We would simply like to give our orders now!"

"Yes, sir, of course."

"Well," said Dimity, as the old man shuffled off mumbling, "It seems the secret's out, such as it is. We can't silence him. . . . But this is all so . . . I've been feeling strange ever since I came here."

"We *can* silence him, actually!" Patrick Quickenden said. She shook her head. "I appear to be remembered. Well, it was partly to find my past that I wanted to come back. Paddy . . . look!"

"That's the annex to the new physics block," said Meinertzhagen, following her pointing finger to the building across the street.

With .61 Earth gravity Wunderland buildings tend to be tall. Many, of course, had been leveled in the war. This one was large and new. High on its portico was the legend:

THIS CENTER IS DEDICATED
TO THE MEMORY OF
DIMITY CARMODY,
DISCOVERER OF CARMODY'S TRANSFORM.
DAUGHTER OF
PROFESSORS LARRY AND MOIRA CARMODY,
BORN: 2344
FIRST PAPER PUBLISHED: 2354
SPECIAL PROFESSOR OF
MATHEMATICS AND ASTROMETAPHYSICS: 2360
MURDERED BY THE KZIN: 2367

"I knew I'd been a professor," said Dimity. "That is one thing I did remember. I even remembered the title of the chair. They said I looked too young, but somehow I was sure of it."

"Too young!" Patrick was still gazing at the dates on the inscription. "This explains the strength of your alpha-wave when we found you. It also explains . . . begins to explain, rather, how you did what you did."

He crossed the street to read the inscription more closely. In smaller letters below the main wording was a rhymed couplet. It was an adaptation from a limerick once quoted to Nils Rykermann in the Cafe Lindenbaum.

> *There was a young mind blazed so bright,*
> *Dreamed of traveling faster than light . . .*
> —N.R., 2423

"Does the expression "can of worms" mean anything to you?" asked Patrick as he returned to the group. "I think we may have just opened one."

"I think," said Meinertzhagen, "we had better enjoy our meal. I hope you like Wunderland cuisine. It's got a strong North European background, of course, but many of the dishes are local. There are some intriguing blends."

"Like the vegetation," said Patrick. "Look at those colors! Where else, on any world, could you see a blend like that! And under such a sky!" He had conquered his agoraphobia and was feeling rather pleased with the fact.

The university gardens were well tended and a thing of pride and prestige. There were a variety of green, red and orange plants, blended and landscaped into a contrast of hot and cold colors. For the Crashlanders it was a Wonderland indeed.

"Yes, they make quite a pleasing mixture, don't they? said Meinertzhagen. "The green plants are from Earth, of course, and the red are native. Poems have been written about how well they go together. There's a lot of symbolism there."

"The orange plants too," said Dimity. "It's almost like a spectrum. I seem to know the others, but I don't remember them. Are they Wunderland too?"

"I think," said Meinertzhagen, not knowing fully what she meant, "that the orange plants may have come originally from the sixth planet of 61 Ursa Majoris . . . also known as Kzin. It's had a lot of effects here."

Chapter 6

Andre brought Colonel Cumpston into the chamber at the point of a nerve disrupter and secured him with a police web. He had, he explained, found him at one of the disguised entrances to the fortress. He had evidently been following the kzinti. Raargh affected complete indifference and signaled to Vaemar to do the same. Cumpston had been searched and X-rayed and had a number of small weapons removed.

"I'll leave you," said Andre, "with these two. Perhaps you had better hope they don't get hungry."

Obviously there would be listening devices and spy cameras in the room where they were kept. In any case, humans and Kzin were coming and going. Still, it was impossible not to talk. They had no writing materials.

"How find us?" Raargh asked.

"I put a tracking device in Vaemar's chessboard. I knew he seldom traveled without it. Forgive me for this discourtesy. It was useful in the event." Cumpston replied in his careful human approximation of the Heroes' Tongue. He did not think it tactful to tell the kzin that some of the game they had eaten had contained both chemicals and micro-robots that had made tracking them a great deal more certain than that.

"There is much discourtesy," growled Raargh. "And it does not seem very useful." Still, the bond between them held. Raargh had not forgotten how Cumpston had helped him— and Vaemar—to life and freedom on the terrible God-forsaken day of *Surrrendir*, and the three of them had shared things since.

I can't tell him help will be on the way, thought Cumpston. Though friend and foe both should be able to work that out. *Help will take a long time to get here, though. If I'd had a few more minutes it would have been a different story.* The entrance to the subterranean fortress—if it was the main entrance he had been brought through—as well disguised. *Obviously, if it's not been picked up by satellites over the last five years.* It had taken him a long time to be brought this far, past guarded doors and weapons positions. He had seen only a few kzin, but they were well dug in and protected, and there were heavy weapons. The place was like a maze on several levels, a labyrinth. Any attacking force would face heavy fighting and innumerable delays.

Cumpston and the kzinti exchanged stories, speaking fairly freely. There was no point in hiding from their captors what they knew already.

This chamber, like the one containing the hologram projector, and like others Cumpston had been led through, was electronically smart. It contained a control console and stacks of weapons and ammunition. None of these presented him with any opportunity, since he was restrained in the web and in any case the weapons were securely locked. The two kzinti had more freedom of movement, but he could see they were being closely tracked. The snouts of cameras and guns followed their movements from several corners.

He had expected the kzinti, confined, to be in a killing frenzy, but Raargh was moving slowly, deliberately. Cumpston had undergone an intensive course in Kzinti body-language, and what he read from the big kzin was relaxation, laziness, a sort of lofty contempt for events. Even his tail, usually the giveaway with a kzin trying to conceal his emotions, was relaxed. So, as far as Cumpston could tell, were the pheromones of his body. He could detect little of the gingery smell that, when intensified, signaled kzin anger. Vaemar, he saw, was copying Raargh's example. *Maybe they've drugged him,* Cumpston thought. *Or maybe he's the greatest actor on this planet.*

Rarrgh had tried to free him when the guards left, but when he approached the web an alarm had sounded and a quick, stabbing red laser beam spat into the ground at his feet. Raargh adjusted his artificial eye and told them the web, as well as the weapons cabinets, was guarded by infrared rays, too closely meshed for him to get through.

Food for the kzinti was provided through an automatic feeder system. Officers' field rations of bloody meat, better than Raargh had been used to as a Trooper or a Sergeant, and some small live animals. There was even that prized Kzinti delicacy, a zianya, tipped into a trough and bound with cords to heighten its flavor-enhancing terror and prevent its struggling and shrieking. There were a couple of indoor fooches and even some entertainment tapes, though neither kzin used them. It was plain great efforts were being made to keep them comfortable. Raargh recognized soothing pheromones in the air. The small animals provided for them were kzin natives, presumably bred from stock imported during the occupation. Contemplating them, and particularly the futilely kicking zianya, gave Raargh the beginnings of an idea. Though he was not yet very hungry, he killed them all, and as he ate them spilled what was in total a good deal of blood, blood whose smell was very similar to that of kzin blood. No alarms responded, and the kzinti who appeared to be on maintenance work in different parts of the large room, but who were presumably doubling as guards, did not seem to notice. Most enclosed chambers frequented by kzinti or used by them as living space had a smell of blood about them, not to mention a complex of other smells. It was bracing and taken for granted.

Henrietta, Andre and Emma returned after a few hours, with a guard of several young Kzinti and humans.

"Noble Heroes," said Henrietta, "you have seen the words of Chuut-Riit. You know his spirit lives on in this fortress, as you know the fighting spirit of the Heroes of Ka'ashi is not dead. Now, in his name, I ask you: Do you acknowledge obedience to the word of Chuut-Riit?"

"Chuut-Riit was Planetary Governor and of the blood of the Patriarch," said Raargh. *Was, not is,* was his unspoken thought. *I have my own hunt now—to preserve Vaemar and to rear him to be a leader of the kzin of this world. Once I thought the Patriarch's Navy would return with swift vengeance, but five years have passed and now I do not think that they will be returning soon. I play for time and for Vaemar.* "Why do you need to ask of a kzintosh who won Name in battle?"

"Where were you going when Emma brought you here?"

Cumpston thought quickly. The less accurate information these maniacs had the better.

"Arhus," he said. Arhus was the site of the biggest planetside kzin settlement. Arrangements had recently been made to grant the kzinti there a limited degree of self-government.

"I did not ask you to speak!" said Henrietta.

"But you insult Heroes. You interrogate them as if they were prisoners or slaves."

Oddly, his words seemed to give her pause.

"These Heroes I know," he said. "Do you think you are the only human who knows the Kzin? This young kzintosh has

learned fieldcraft in the wild. Now he goes to his own kind
to learn other things."

"With your tuition, ARM agent?"

"I will not go with him to stay with kzinti at Arhus. How
could I? But do you think you are the only human on this
planet who wishes peace between Man and Kzin? If there can
be peace, I do not wish the Kzinti ill. There is much about
them I admire, and these two I have known long." *I hope
there's enough truth in that to confuse her,* he thought. *Also
I hope that there's no telepath among the kzinti here. I hope
that all the telepaths on Wunderland have got nice cushy jobs
with the human security forces and have been given Names
and Kzinrretti of their very own and the nice gentle new telepathic drugs I heard our laboratories were working on and have
no wish to help this crazy business.*

Henrietta looked at him with somewhat lessened hostility.
Plainly, he did have some relationship with these two kzinti.
There was an expression of doubt or conflict on her face.

"Release him," said Vaemar. He spoke in the Ultimate
Imperative Tense, which Cumpston had never heard him use
before. Henrietta moved to obey, but a celfone on Andre's wrist
bleeped. He turned to Henrietta and spoke to her urgently.

"We've got your car under cover and we're taking it apart,"
Henrietta told Cumpston. "I'll need you shortly to send a signal
from its brain to say all is well. I'd advise you not to be smart
and not try to do anything like sending or omitting key code-
words. We have a telepath."

But if you put a telepath on me I'd feel it, he thought. *What
do they want with me?* he wondered. *Why have they kept me
alive? I'm nothing but a threat to them, not potentially useful and venerated like Vaemar or respected like Raargh. They
might be able to get a telepath, of course. Bring one from Arhus
or somewhere and peel my brain. I wouldn't like that. Or maybe
they've got some idea of brainwashing and reprogramming me.*
With modern drugs that was not difficult. A fully suborned
ARM officer might be very useful indeed. Cumpston had been
trained to resist brain washing, and it would, he thought, be
interesting in that event to see whether his training or
Henrietta's chemicals were the more effective. That a battle
between them might leave him an organic waldo was something better not thought about. He had seen the results of
such conflicts in others and tried to blank his memory and
imagination.

Henrietta interrogated him somewhat further, then she and
Andre left, accompanied by a party of the humans and kzinti.

Her questions, he thought, seemed somewhat unfocused. Both the humans and kzinti in general seemed, however, to come and go at will. One kzin was doing what looked like maintenance work under the control console, a couple of others were patrolling the upper gantries. A couple were staring at screens. One appeared to be curled up in a corner asleep. In the dim light at the corners of the large chamber it was hard to see exactly how many there were. It reminded him a little of the bridge of a warship at cruising stations. There were even, he noticed, small screened sanitary compartments. Well, that was not surprising. Cumpston, one of comparatively few humans to have been in a kzin's lair as a guest, knew that Raargh had a similar arrangement at his cave. Kzinti, like most felines, liked their toilets private, apart from their use of urine as a marker and in social rituals. Raargh himself, who seemed to be moving about with a good deal of freedom, had previously been inspecting the sleeping kzin and had gone to use one of these compartments without question.

Emma, some of the men, and some of the kzinti remained. Cumpston noticed an immediate change in the atmosphere with Henrietta's departure. The men, he saw, including some manrretti, wore slightly different costumes to the ones who had departed.

"Different prides," remarked Vaemar. *So he saw it as well.* One of the men, plainly an officer or in a command position, walked over and released Cumpston from the web. He had, Cumpston saw, the name "McGlue" on his jacket. As Cumpston stepped down, McGlue made a quick gesture, unnoticeable except to trained eyes. It was the recognition signal of a fellow ARM agent. Cumpston felt relief flooding though him. It appeared they were not without allies. McGlue also made a queer, twisted smile that seemed to run off one side of his face. Then Emma strode over. Yes, without Henrietta, the atmosphere was definitely different. Cumpston's gestalt sense, though acquired with difficult training, was hardly even a poor imitation of kzinti ziirgah, but its signals were unmistakable. Vaemar too was wrinkling his nose and ears, and his tail was lashing now.

"My mother has no proper plans," Emma told them. "Her brains went loose after the events of the human invasion, after those things that happened when the disgraced coward once called Hroth–Staff-Officer surrendered. She has never fully recovered. For a long time she lost her memory of who she was. I did not lose mine.

"What she wishes now is to make this place into a refuge

for Kzinti where they can be taught to understand human ways so they—Heroes and Conquerors—may eventually creep into some lowly place in the monkey hierarchy. She seeks to teach them the slaves' dream of proving indispensable to their masters, so they may one day rise to some kind of junior partnership, by monkey grace and favor—the mirror image of the very dream that some humans of Ka'ashi cuddled to their monkey breasts! She expects them to gradually penetrate human society, to at last take part in human plans and strategy, perhaps at last to take revenge on those who killed Chuut-Riit or their remote descendants.

"The reality is different! Never will the Heroic Race be the slaves or the copies of apes! The Fanged God will not allow such an obscenity! I have forced the issue, as my Destiny decrees.

"There are heavy weapons here for an army," she went on. "Not just infantry and armor, but aircraft, small spacecraft. Most of the human fleet is at the warfront, light-years away.

"With Chuut-Riit's son, we will rouse and rally the kzin of Ka'ashi and Tiamat. They have had five years of subjugation and persecution by monkeys and are ready to scream and leap. We can take the humans of Ka'ashi and the Serpent Swarm by surprise."

"And when the Hyperdrive Armada returns?"

"Their return will suit me perfectly. Returning, they will have to abandon their present front. The Kzin fleets and bases they engage now will have time to recover. Time also to ingest the latest lessons of the war, perhaps to rip secrets of the hyperdrive from the entrails of captured humans and human ships. And before the hyperdrive ships return we can smash the human ships and bases here.

"And do not overestimate the Hyperdrive Armada. Do not forget: With a double star the gravitational singularity is such that there is a vast volume of space in which the hyperdrive cannot operate—the whole of the combined Alpha Centauri A and B systems, stretching far beyond their outer cometary halos. The hyperdrive would not have been enough for the successful human landings here but for other simultaneous misfortunes and the fangs of treachery ripping at loyal throats. This time the kzin will not be fighting among themselves when the humans arrive. They will be roused, united, and waiting! With Sinclair fields, which we alone possess, we can boost bomb explosions until they are as destructive as anti-matter!

"More! There are hyperdrive ships at the spaceports and under repair and maintenance here and on Tiamat! We can seize them! Link again with the Patriarchy. We can strike Earth itself, and avenge the ramscoop raid with the one claw, present the hyperdrive to the Patriarchy with the other! We will achieve victory!"

"What you will achieve at most," said Cumpston, "is the deaths of many humans and the extermination of the kzinti in this system down to the last kzinrret and the last kitten, whether many of them joined you or not. As for Sinclair fields, how long do you think it would be before the other side used them? They were invented during the long peace on Earth but they must be in the ARM files." *Don't tell her she's insane,* he thought; *it will only make her worse.* He hoped that phrase "long peace on Earth" might have some sort of subconsciously soothing effect, though it was badly positioned next to the phrase "ARM files." Best he could do at present.

"You will also turn a terrible war—the war now being fought out in space—into a war of annihilation without any possibility of eventual peace or truce. Without the option of life after surrender one species will perish utterly and quite possibly both will. We know such things have happened before in this galaxy." He felt as he said it that to arouse such images in her mind would probably only egg her on. But he could think of nothing else to say. *Was it a good idea to provoke her? Such questions had often been asked when fighting kzin, and the general answer had been that it couldn't do any harm. If they screamed and leaped prematurely, so much the better. But this was different.* "Did not Sun Tzu say: 'Do not make an enemy fight with the courage of despair'?" he asked her. "That is what you will make both sides do. Think on what we know of the Slaver war."

"You cannot seduce me with words. The conspirators you worked for—the conspirators responsible for the ramscoop raid—will be brought to justice," she replied. "It will be interesting to see how much ground they can cover when they are turned loose on a kzinti hunting preserve with ten minutes' start!" She was shouting now, and paused to wipe traces of foam from her lips. *I don't think you had a good Liberation,* Cumpston thought. *I wanted vengeance as much as anyone at the time, but this is what it leads to.*

There is another thing, he thought. *There are outlying parts of Wunderland and much of the Serpent Swarm where the Kzin had still not grown too oppressive. That would have changed as their numbers increased, but there are some humans who hate Sol System for the ramscoop raid worse than they hate the Kzin. Not many—most don't expect an interstellar, interspecies war of survival to be fought with kid gloves—but some. And if my dearest had been killed by humans, how might I have jumped . . . ? Perhaps the Kzin would have human allies. Not many, but enough to do damage. On the other hand, conflicts of loyalty could work both ways. No harm in pointing that out, perhaps.*

"Another thing you overlook," he said: "Many kzin on Wunderland have found they may have better lives as partners with humans than as regimented cannon fodder for the Patriarchy. And for their descendants, the future may be brighter still. Many have been persecuted and humiliated. Many individual kzin died after the surrender. But they have not been murdered wholesale or enslaved, and they know it. A nonconformist kzin will not be dueled to death. There are kzin on this planet who have discovered freedom." Futile, he knew. There was no rational argument that would reach someone so deeply insane.

"On Wunderland we have been granted a miraculous chance." He had to say it. He strove to put in into terms that might get through. "Perhaps some would say not merely species but Bearded God and Fanged God have made truce here. With the hyperdrive there are stars and worlds enough for all. We have a chance to show that humans and kzinti can share a planet. If they can do that, perhaps they can share a universe. Destroy that experiment here and all hope of that dies with it." Tired and dry-mouthed, he argued back and forth with her hopelessly, and he knew, pointlessly, for some time, bringing it back to the fact that postwar Wunderland was proving some human-kzin cooperation was possible.

"There may be a few who have been turned into imitation monkeys by the priests and the secret police, or been bought with monkey gold," she replied. "The Kzin race can purge itself of such perversions. It is the strongest and noblest culture in the galaxy!" She turned her attention to the console and keyed up some holos of the redoubt and its weapons stores, others of rampant Heroes and Kzin space-dreadnaughts in triumphant battle.

"As for you," she told Cumpston, "you may be useful as a hostage in the early stages. That is just. The humans you work for intended to hold the kzinti of Wunderland hostage . . . Noble Hero Raargh!"

But there was no answer. After a few seconds it became obvious to all that Raargh was gone. Emma stared about wildly. Then she ran to the sleeping kzin. She stared down at it, then called another kzin to waken it. It seemed to have a problem doing so, and while telepaths, computer *nirrds,* or other lowly ones could be kicked awake by their betters, fighting kzinti were generally wary of touching another such when it was asleep. Finally the other kzin took its shoulders and lifted it. Its head flopped backwards, revealing a broken neck. As its body rolled over, long, raw, gleaming bones arced and clattered on the floor. The skin and flesh of one of its arms was missing. There was not much blood. Cord—the cord that had bound a zianya—had been wound tightly at the shoulder to prevent bleeding.

"My Noble Mentor and Stepfather, Raargh who was Sergeant, gave his Word not to harm you humans this day," said Vaemar. "He did not give his Word to remain here. And when his claws are sheathed his feet fall silently and swiftly.

"It's possible he may go to Arhus." Vaemar added.

And even now you win a few seconds for him, thought Cumpston. Vaemar was again speaking in the Ultimate Imperative Tense of the Heroes' Tongue, the tense that might be used only by Royalty or, rarely, in a situation where the honor of the Kzin species was at stake, and which, when not employed for the giving of direct orders, lent itself to poetic, circumlocutious constructions. Also, he noticed, Vaemar had caught up the idea of Arhus but he did not tell a direct lie. It took Emma some time to work out what he was saying. Then her fingers stabbed at a control console. There was a sound of doors slamming shut.

Raargh threw away the remains of the Kzinti arm he had carried to hide his own prosthetic one. The passage which promised to lead toward the surface was blocked by a hemisphere, glowing bluishly with some form of radiation. Raargh did not know it for a Sinclair field but he guessed it was not something to venture into. It would not have been put there to stop the passage if it was impotent. He turned and ran into the dimmest tunnel he could find. At first the ruddy light, replicating a winter's day on the Homeworld he had never seen, was easy enough for silent running and leaping. After a short time, however, the light sources became fewer, and then stopped.

Raargh ran on. This part of the secret redoubt was unfinished, he saw. Walls were unlined, roughly hewn living rock. Now there were no lights or other installations. Even the natural eyes of the Kzin, superbly adapted to night hunting, could not see in total darkness, and he was grateful now for having lost an eye in combat years before.

Thanks to his partial Name, his artificial eye was the best available, able to see beyond the spectrum of visible light. It was not perfect, but it was enough to keep him running on. He ran nearly on all fours, both because it was the naturally speediest position for kzin and for fear of beams, Sinclair monomolecular wires and other booby traps. His *w'tsai* had been taken but he held his prosthetic arm up before him, hoping it would protect his head and chest from Sinclair wire. "These chambers link to the great caves of the Hohe Kalkstein," the human had said. He was possibly headed in the right direction. He thought he was going south, and the surface rivers, he recalled, had flowed on a roughly north-south axis. Air currents at the sensitive tips of his whiskers gave him some ability to differentiate between long passages and blind alleys. His ziirgah sense picked up nothing.

Something gleamed very dimly in the darkness ahead. In any lesser darkness its ghostly radiance would have been quite invisible. A pile of human bones, presumably those of the slaves who had built this place. They were in fragments, and had plainly been stripped and gnawed by Kzinti fangs. After five years no tissue remained. A few lingering vermiforms wriggled away. There were a few pieces of clothing and oddments but nothing useful. Kzin do not eat carrion, but he was beginning to feel hungry and he turned some of the bare, dry bones over hopefully before he realized what he was doing. The few joints still articulated fell apart. He took a few bones simply to give his jaws something to crunch on.

This spot was evidently as far as the builders of the redoubt had reached. Beyond were natural cave formations. He wondered if morlocks or other creatures survived here. Well, if they did, he would find out in due course. He leaped up a muddy slope, ignoring the pains beginning to speak in the old wounds in his legs, and ran on. There was a stream to follow now. Since he could drink and need no longer fear becoming dehydrated at least, he began to mark his passage with urine. At one point he saw a wandering line of footprints in the mud, but they might have been there for millennia.

He estimated that it was about three hours later (time was becoming difficult to judge) that he found the bones of a kzin. With it was a *w'tsai*, still as sharp as a *w'tsai* should be, and a belt containing a couple of sealed infantry emergency ration capsules. Other personal equipment lay about scattered and broken, including the wrappings of ordinary pack rations. That hinted strongly at Morlocks, as did the fact that the skull was fractured as by a blow from above. In any case, he could smell them. The smell of morlocks was unmistakable—even humans with their pathetic mockeries of noses had commented on it—

and it had been in his nostrils for some time, along with smells of old fire, old death, and a few tentative smells of new life. It was, he thought—his mind was beginning to run a little strangely now—significant that humans and kzinti smelled odd to each other rather than repulsive. The war might have been even more savage otherwise.

He made himself wait and listen for a time, arranging the bones more decorously as he did so, but the caves were silent apart from the faintest rustling of insects and the distant sound of water. There had been more life in the great caves of the Hohe Kalkstein when he had campaigned in them. The ration capsules were—just—better than nothing for his hunger, and the *w'tsai* in his hand felt good. His ziirgah sense picked up something now—hunger and hunting, but not yet very near. He pressed on, the sense gradually growing stronger.

He heard a well-remembered rustling over his head some time later, the morlock stench signaling their presence as unmistakably as a burning flare. His artificial eye could just distinguish movement in the darkness there. He bounded away from the downward-jutting stalactites back to a large patch where the roof above was relatively clear. He was lucky it was there, but he had been marking the occurrence of such patches for some time. The morlocks, clinging to the formations, could drop rocks and themselves onto those below, but found it harder to throw rocks or jump accurately a great distance. *Like good old days!* he thought momentarily. *War is the best medicine!* before remembering that the good old days often seemed better in memory than when actually being relived, particularly now when he was old, and partly crippled, and with slowed reflexes and tired and alone.

The first morlock to land before him he impaled on the *w'tsai*, in a conscious tribute and gesture of thanks to the dead Hero who had just bequeathed it to him.

Then he leaped into them with fangs, *w'tsai*, and the claws of both his natural and artificial hands, his battle-scream shaking the air of the chamber.

Had the morlocks attacked in the numbers that he was used to, they would have overwhelmed him. But they were less than a score, and they seemed less strong than they had been in the old days. Grabbing one with his natural hand and crushing its neck in a single squeeze, it came to him faster than thought that the creature was emaciated. His ziirgah sense picked up primitive emotions of terror and desperation. And *HUNGER!* He remembered how few living things there seemed to be in the caves compared to the old days. The morlocks, at the top

of the food chain, might well be starving. Good! At these odds
a warrior need not crave strong foes.

He kept his natural eye tightly shut to protect it as much
as possible. His artificial eye and arm were both invulnerable
to bites, and his artificial arm smashed aside the morlocks'
puny weapons of rocks. His fangs and claws were still those
of Raargh-Sergeant, once Senior Regimental Sergeant. Fourteen
he counted, the last falling victim to a disemboweling kick
he was sure old Sergeant and the *w'tsai*'s late donor would
have approved of. His own wounds, as far as he could tell,
were fairly minor. There was so much scar tissue around his
neck and shoulders, he thought, that the morlocks would have
had a tough time chewing though it.

He forced himself to eat his fill of the dead morlocks—they
were not pleasant eating, but, he told himself, they were
carnivores and even warriors of a sort—carved some flesh from
the remainder for future needs and pressed on, marking the
passage as he went. Some time later—much later, it seemed—
he came upon a part of the wall scarred by flame. There were
shattered crystal formations littering the cave floor here, and
remains of humans, kzinti and morlocks, some scattered and
broken bones, some whole skeletons, some mummies, some
of the bones once again very faintly phosphorescent. There
were no more live morlocks.

He fell down a long slope and lost much time finding his
way back. In the confusion of stone and with his perception
being affected by the dark and silence, he blundered up several
blind alleys, each time backtracking with difficulty. He slept
for a time, woke, and went on. He began to think his quest
was hopeless and that he would soon die in these caves. There
was no reason to assume these particular tunnels had any exit.
He had lost all sense of time, but with all the back tracking
he guessed that several days had passed.

He began, however, to feel another was traveling with him.
Might it be old Sergeant, who had passed his rank to him
with his actions and words as he died in the caves somewhere
not far from here? He hoped Sergeant felt his old Corporal
had not disgraced his judgment or his spirit. Might it be Chuut-
Riit, whose last seed was now in his care?

He began to feel lightheaded. Perhaps the morlock flesh was
poisonous. Perhaps it was the combined effects of darkness,
silence, battle, and loss of blood. Several times he stumbled,
and more than once he banged his head painfully against rock,
once nearly breaking his fangs. The feeling of an unseen companion became stronger, but it was an uncertain companion.

After a time its head appeared to him, floating and swooping out of the darkness, appearing first as a tiny claw-point of light that grew larger until it seemed to engulf his vision and then passed on to dwindle and return. It looked like the hologram of Chuut-Riit. Then it looked like the Fanged God Himself, or was it the Human Bearded God? A kzinrret appeared. His mother? Or Murrur, the kzinrret he had bought after he had received his Name, the mother of his dead son, buried with him under burning debris in the ramscoop raid? It had been the last birthing she could give—fertile young kzinrretti like Veena had been for the harems of higher kzintosh than he. She had not had a large vocabulary, but even when she was not in season he had enjoyed her company.

He was in the glades beyond the Hohe Kalkstein with Vaemar, stalking the gagrumphers. There were flutterbys and the brilliant sun of Ka'ashi's day, with its differently brilliant night, the wheeling Serpent Swarm, the great jewel of Alpha Centauri B, and Proxima like a hunter's red eye. The floating figures became chessmen. Hard stone struck against him, crystal broke and fell tinkling. Gods sowing stars. He began to feel something he had felt a few times before, once in these very caves. He knew now that its name was Fear. Fear of endless darkness and silence, fear of waiting nonexistence, fear of total *loss*. He tried working out chess problems in his mind, but he knew hunger was growing and that before long it would be an agony driving out all other feeling. Well, he would die decorously.

He seemed to climb a high path, a great stairway, though the real floor under his feet was broken and uneven. He plunged into a cold stream that nearly covered his head before realization made him struggle clear, choking and spitting. A few more steps and he might have drowned, basely abandoning Vaemar and everything else. The realization and the cold helped bring him back to reality. He groomed his matted wet fur as well as he could, and forced himself to rest for a time, lying still, shivering. The small noises of the stream had a dangerously hypnotic sound to them, and he sang the cadences of Lord Chmeee's Last Battle-Hymn to keep them at bay.

Later he came to an area from which, it appeared, dead bodies and other remains had recently been removed. The pain in his legs was acute now, and he allowed himself to stop and rest a short time and ate the last of the morlock flesh that he carried, making himself ignore the smell. He knew he was back in the great caverns of the Hohe Kalkstein where he had won rank and Name. He knew also that it would do no good were pain, hunger and exhaustion to rob him of his reason.

Far ahead both his natural and his artificial eye detected a modification of the darkness. Nose and whiskers also detected changes in the air. There, at the top of a long slope, was a lamp, turned down and dully glowing. When he reached it he found himself back in familiar territory. There were the old mined-out guano beds, stripped by the monkeys to make dung bombs during the war. There was what the humans called the dancing room, the *borrlruhm* cavern where he had inspected his squad for the last time as Corporal. He moved on into the crepuscular zone, glowing now with the purple of Alpha Centauri B, at this season with the true dawn pursuing close behind it. There was the old habitat module. Its door was closed but there was a key in it, and he sensed it was occupied by humans. He salivated at the thought of the meat within.

His artificial eye showed him it was surrounded by a fairly thin web of infrared rays and automatic alarms. If he set them off it might not matter, but he avoided them from habit anyway.

Leonie Rykermann stirred uneasily in their sleeping bag. Five years of peace had not dulled her reflexes that had been honed in decades of guerrilla war. She woke and sat up with a startled cry, Nils Rykermann jerking awake beside her. Bending over them in the dim light was the hunched, crouching bulk of a great kzin, smelling of blood, one eye reflecting violet light, the other a glaring red point, jaws agape, fangs gleaming and dripping.

"Be not undecorous and calm liver," said Raargh in his best Wunderlander, adding considerately, "No need for manrret to cover teats. Raargh has seen before."

Chapter 7

"Raargh!"

"Yes. Raargh and humans have met here in caves before. Leonie-Manrret dug Raargh out of trap. Raargh push water out of Leonie-Manrret lungs. Kill many morlocks together. Raargh kill more now."

"Du Alte Teufel!" She added quickly: "No insult. We greet old companion."

Nils Rykermann had been slower to waken fully. At the first sight of the kzin he tried to thrash wildly out of the sleeping bag, then with a fierce effort became still.

"Raargh!" Leonie shook him, "It's Raargh!"

Rykermann became calmer. Then he looked the old kzin up and down.

"You're changed," he said. "You look terrible."

"Kzin is terrible," Raargh replied. "Will show enemies how terrible soon." He went on: "Came seek Rykermann-human. God benevolent and Rykermann here. Rykermann dress in costume quickly. Leonie-Manrret dress too. Is trouble!"

"How did you get here?" asked Leonie.

"Through caves, from north."

"And why?" asked Rykermann.

"You are tired," said Leonie, "and in pain."

"I am Hero!" said Raargh indignantly. Then he added: "You know?"

"Yes. I know. Would bourbon help?"

"Bourbon always help. Or brandy," He added.

"There's something there called liqueur brandy," said Rykermann quickly, "You wouldn't like that."

"Rest a moment," said Leonie, as Raargh drank noisily (deciding privately that Rykermann was wrong about the

257

liqueur brandy). "Have some food, then tell us why you have come here."

They found food for him, not ideal but better than morlock meat. It took some time for Raargh to explain to the humans what had happened to the north and then tell the story of his journey as a Hero should tell it. Alpha Centauri B filled the great mouth of the cave with light, and the true dawn followed it, well before he had finished. He did not know what they knew of Vaemar's lineage and said nothing about it, rather letting them believe by suggestion that Vaemar was his own son. Cumpston, he pointed out, was also a prisoner of the mad manrretti and others who planned a kzin uprising.

"You say there are Heroes there too?" said Leonie.

"Few, not many, I think. The Heroes I saw young. Hot livers. Maybe brains loose like Henrietta-human and other."

"Brains loose?"

"Kzin attack humans on Ka'ashi . . . on *Wunderland*, all kzin die. All kzinrretti, all kittens. All. Vaemar die. Many humans die, too, I think. Then kzin and humans fight in space till all dead.

"Raargh young and Raargh say: 'Attack!' All dead is good if die on attack! But Raargh is old. Raargh think of dead kzinrretti, dead kittens, Rarrgh remember ramscoop raid, think of Sire's tales, think of nukes. and relativity weapons on Homeworld. Raargh teach Vaemar to think. Raargh must think too. And there are monkeys who . . . who Raargh does want not should die." He tried to cover this embarrassing admission. "Dishonorable to kill *chesss* partners."

"What can we do?" asked Leonie.

"How many humans here?"

"Just us, and a few students tidying up outside. Most went back to Munchen yesterday. We stayed because we thought if things were quieter some of the cryptic life-forms might come out."

"Morlocks came out. Raargh ate! Have you weapons?"

"Not many. We cleared a lot of old weapons out of the caves in the last few days, but the students took most of them back to the city. We found a few more yesterday after they'd gone and we have a few for personal security."

"Need weapons. Need force. Go back through caves and eat crazy monkeys."

"We'll have to call for help," Leonie told him. "This is too big for our claws. They must know you're gone by now, and they'll be waiting for an attack."

"They not know Raargh go to humans," Raargh replied. "Not

know about old battles with morlocks. Vaemar and Colonel-human let them think Raargh go to Arhus, return with Heroes."

"Nevertheless," said Nils Rykermann, "we must think carefully. Leonie is right. We cannot succeed in attacking them on our own. We have only ourselves here now and four young students," he told Raargh. "They're in the ROTC, of course, but I don't know if they're fully combat trained or experienced apart from young von Bibra, and I have no right to risk their lives. I am going to call Jocelyn van der Stratt." He looked more closely at the old kzin. There were purple and orange bloodstains on his legs at the old wounds and round his neck and shoulders. There was blood on his head as well. Certain apparently fairly moderate head wounds could be fatal to kzinti. "I have known Heroes before who were more badly hurt than they would admit," he said. "Lie down and let Leonie tend you."

"I am a Hero," said Raargh indignantly, "And time is scarce."

"Even if we summon help immediately, it cannot get here for some hours," Rykermann said. "I advise you to rest. We cannot charge back through the caves as we are."

Raargh remembered his delusions in the caves. Certainly, it would be better if such things did not happen again. He knew there was not much the three of them could do by themselves, though had he been younger that might not have dissuaded him. "Think before you leap!" Chuut-Riit had told them. And the pain in his wounds was extreme. He growled a reluctant "Urrr" of assent.

The module's equipment included a large and versatile medical kit. He let Leonie apply a kzin-specific tranquilizer, pain killer and disinfectant and in a few moments—before he could ask Leonie for talcum powder—he was asleep on the floor of the module.

"We must start work early today," Patrick Quickenden said. "We've put in a good effort over the last few days, but this hospitality, not to mention seeing a beautiful new world . . . It could lull us into forgetting there's still a war on!"

"Something has developed," said Jocelyn, "that may be important. We'd like to take . . . er . . . Miss Moffet . . . to see something."

"She's a key member of this group," said Patrick. "I don't want her put at any risk. In fact I insist!"

Jocelyn looked at Arthur Guthlac. She sent him a silent directive.

"There's no danger," Arthur told him. "Come yourself. It's a fairly short flight in a fast car."

"I don't like it. There are still kzin on this planet. I've seen several already."

"I take your point," said Arthur, "but I'm still a Brigadier. I'll lay on an armed escort."

"I suppose you know what you're doing. But the rest of us will stay here and get started."

"Poor old ratcat!" said Leonie. "He's been through the mill. And even partial sensory deprivation is tougher on them than on us. It drives them crazy quicker." The old kzin with his prostheses looked curiously vulnerable asleep, curled something like a house cat in a basket, but with his artificial arm jutting out at an awkward angle. "It would have been more difficult for him than he'll ever admit to have gone so far through the dark and silence of the caves alone."

"They never admit weakness," said Nils Rykermann. "Perhaps they're afraid it would make them seem too . . . human." He paused and added suddenly: "You've never hated them as I have."

"There's no danger of forgetting they're not human. And I tried to stop hating them after the cease-fire. It wasn't easy. If we'd had to live through the Occupation in the cities I don't think I could have even attempted it. And he helped, old Raargh. He had me at his mercy once, and here I am."

"Mercy is not a concept they understand," he said.

"Maybe . . . and yet, here I am."

"Anyway, I wanted him out for the count. That's why I encouraged him to let you treat him. And all my best brandy from the monastery! Do you think he's telling the truth?"

"I've never known one to tell an absolutely outright lie. But what's he got to lie about? Why else should he be running about in the caves alone and without equipment? And those injuries are certainly real enough."

"But it's such an incredible story!"

"I'm not only your wife, I'm your chief research assistant, remember," said Leonie. "I've kept files. We know Henrietta was—is—probably the most hated of all the collaborators. It was an open secret among the Resistance that she was able to *influence* Chuut-Riit. There were even some Kzin who accused him of . . . of, well, you can guess. Perhaps she influenced him for good sometimes, but that wouldn't count. She was born and brought up under the Occupation and knew no life but that uniquely privileged one in a household of prominent collaborators, to whose headship she acceded. You know that after the Liberation there was a special price on her head. As for the atrocities committed against collaborators, we were lucky. We were in the hills and missed it all."

"It didn't seem lucky at the time. We were at our last gasp. And I wanted vengeance on collabos and on the Kzin. . . . I still do!" he burst out.

"That won't bring her back," said Leonie quietly.

"It's the next best thing!" Nils Rykermann ground out. Then he bit the air and spun round to face her. He looked as if he had been struck a blow. "You . . . you knew!" he whispered.

"I always knew. Wasn't it always obvious? I knew when I was your student that you were in love with her . . . and since then that you always have been." She took his hand in both hers and kissed him. "Don't you remember my hair? How I wore it in those days . . . with a pink headband?"

"Yes."

"Why do you think I did that?"

"I never thought."

"Because that was how she wore hers. Stupid of me, to try to compete with Dimity Carmody!"

"I didn't know."

"It didn't suit me, really. My hair's darker blond than hers was. My father always called me his little lion cub. . . . I remember, I'd only been enrolled a few days, and I was sitting at one of the Lindenbaum's tables, with some of the other freshers. We were just getting to know each other and find our way around the class-rooms and time-tables, and suddenly we girls realized that all the boys were staring at this blonde two tables away. . . . I'm sorry, I shouldn't go on."

"Yes. . . . yes. Please. Go on."

"Who's she? I wondered. A Tridee-star? A fashion model a long way off her turf? Something *dumb*, anyway, I took for granted, with all my eighteen-year-old sophistication and judgment. The universe couldn't be so unfair as to give somebody looks like that and brains as well! I wasn't surprised when she ordered coffee in . . . in that funny little voice she had. . . . Then somebody told me: 'Mathematics and astrometaphysics,' they said. I was taken aback and saw that the universe *was* that unfair. But . . ." She gave an uneven laugh. "They didn't let me have it all at once. Even then, in my teenage jealousy, I thought she was just a particularly bright *student*. You can't blame me: She was no older than I. She must be brilliant to be studying Carmody's Transform, I thought. And then I found out. . . . What we put ourselves through as students!

"Then, of course," she went on, "we found out what an unfair universe was *really* like."

"Yes, love, we certainly found that out."

"After the kzin destroyed her ship, I saw what happened to you. . . . You told me something about it as we set up the first clinic at the refugee camp. . . . Remember?"

"I remember," he said. "I thought at the time that only you would have thought in all that death and terror and chaos to bring low-tech medical supplies away, would have realized our autodocs would be useless without our civilization. But I was a walking dead man then."

"I saw the music box, that the kzin left for you. I knew it was hers. I'd seen her playing it at the Lindenbaum when you and she had coffee there together. I'd . . . I'd even thought of collecting music boxes, too, so you might notice me. I joined the chess club, too, for an excuse to hang around there, hoping you might one day come alone and notice me. But you never played chess."

"Because she didn't. It showed up her abnormality too much. She wanted to be normal. Do you know the last thing she said to me?"

"I'd like you to tell me."

"She said—sh-she'd already been injured then: 'It was hard, I know, for you to be in love with a freak. Know, at least, that the freak loves you.' "

"You've got a good memory."

"Too good."

"I love you, Nils. I loved you at the university and in the refugee camp and in the hills. That night in the hills when I told you I'd always loved you, I was telling the truth. It wasn't a student with a crush on her teacher. I'd been there and I knew the difference. And I saw you were falling apart. Don't forget, either, that I've been in bed beside you through a lot of nightmares. Or rather the same one. Oh, my darling, of course I've always known. . . . I had to accept that she'd always be with you. What choice did I have? You can't fight the dead, you can only live with them.

"There's something else," she went on, and her voice was stronger, almost exultant. "I was there, remember, when the kzin came to the refugee camp. Very few of us had actually seen them then, and I saw *you* face a creature that made the brave man beside you fall dead of sheer terror. I was there in the days that followed, when it seemed the whole weight of the Resistance, the whole war, rested on your shoulders alone. Not for a day, a week, or a month, but year after year, and the years became decades and there was no hope and you never faltered. You are not only the man I love, you are my hero!"

"I couldn't have done it, Leonie, without you. Not for a year, or a month or a week. Truly, you were beside me . . . love."

"I'm afraid I opened a bit of a flood-gate there," Leonie said after a pause. "For us both. I've been damming that up for a long time too, you know."

"I'm glad you did open it, my love. So glad! . . . But Raargh's story? And Henrietta?"

"She escaped. You know. Disappeared."

"I know," Nils Rykermann said. "Jocelyn has a particular hatred of her. Her business. I have other fish to fry."

"Until now I thought she was probably dead."

"So did I. But it's a whole planet she's got to hide in. A whole system for that matter. And there are plastic surgeons and organleggers. She might look quite different. New hand-prints. New lungs to confuse breath analysis. New eyes and new retinas."

"But the main reason I think Raargh's story is true," said Leonie, "is obvious: A kzin both wouldn't and couldn't make it up. A mad monkey devoted to Chuut-Riit's memory trying to lead a kzin revolt! It's so crazy it has to be true!"

"I'm inclined to agree with you."

"And he said he was making his way here to see you anyway, as Cumpston said."

"Yes. But why me?"

"Isn't it obvious? He trusts you."

"Why should he? I hate ratcats!"

"Obviously, he doesn't think you hate him," said Leonie. "Fighting together in the caves may have something to do with that . . . perhaps even the fact that he saved my life. And you left the key in the module door."

"I forgot it! And . . . and there was no danger around. Morlocks—if there are any left—don't understand keys."

"But kzin do." She quoted, "How brilliantly lit the chambers of the subconscious would be if we could see into them!"

"Who said that?"

"She did. I went to one of her public lectures—on the inspiration of scientific discovery. I knew you'd be there."

"I've tried, you know, I've tried very hard, never to let her memory come between us."

"I know."

"I'll call Jocelyn," Rykermann said after an uncomfortable moment. He keyed a number on the desk and spoke rapidly. "Well," he said a few moments later, "talk about serendipity. She's on her way here already. She's about to leave

Munchen with Arthur Guthlac and a party they think I might
be interested to meet."

"What's that mean?"

Nils Rykermann shrugged. "No doubt we'll find out. She
says Early's had some sort of alarm too." He shrugged out
of his robe and stepped into the shower cabinet. "Freshen up,
anyway," he remarked, turning on the water.

She dropped her own robe and followed him. "Make love
to me," she breathed, winding her arms round him. "I need
you."

Their faces were nearly on a level. He did not need to bend
to kiss her.

"I need you too. I always need you."

Chapter 8

"Patrick's too flattering," said Dimity, as the outlying farmlands flashed away below the car. "I'm not a key member of our group. I'm largely a theoretician and the original work I did on the hyperdrive has been done. I got myself on this party because I wanted to see Wunderland again."

"Again?" Arthur Guthlac raised his eyebrows. It was on the face of it such an obviously bizarre thing to say. Before the hyperdrive, interstellar travel had involved decades-long flights in hibernation, had been extremely costly and invariably one-way.

"To find out what had happened. I was born here, grew up here. . . . You think that's impossible?"

"You're saying you are *the* Dimity Carmody? Go on. Possibly I know what may have happened."

"The Crashlanders pulled me out of a ship that reached Procyon flying on automatic pilot, its life systems destroyed by a laser blast and everyone else on board dead. I was in a tank. But I couldn't remember much of my life. Not who I was apart from my name or what had happened to us. A title that I didn't understand. I only remembered that something terrible had happened. Images of great ravening cat-beasts, and a man with a yellow beard . . . and later, when I started reading again, of mathematical symbols. . . . You don't look too surprised."

"I'm not. Not after something I heard a couple of nights ago, added to what I've seen of you . . . but now, I wonder."

"About me?"

"No, whether this trip today was an entirely good idea," he glanced rather guiltily at Jocelyn, sitting in a blister in the forward part of the car and out of hearing. "Still, we're on our way now."

Below them the farmlands were giving way to barren,

265

unsettled country. Flat-topped mesas, several now adorned with sensors or batteries of weapons, told of ancient erosion. Here and there was uncleared wreckage of war.

"It looks familiar," said Dimity. The great escarpment of the Hohe Kalkstein loomed blue-gray to the northeast.

"This part can't have changed much in a long while. Not like Munchen and the university. It's never been settled," said Jocelyn, returning to the main cabin. She dialed them drinks. Dimity toyed with hers nervously. As it approached the cliffs the car banked slightly and flew up a long canyon. There was a laden vehicle parked on the ground.

The car had a new, kzinti-derived gravity motor and settled with a quiet purring in front of the Drachenholen's mouth. There was none of the noise and stone-spitting of an old ground-effect vehicle. As they cut the engine several humans emerged from the great cave. "Poor security," remarked Jocelyn. "This place isn't so pacified as not to need a lookout."

Arthur Guthlac surveyed the scene with the car's security sensors.

"There is a lookout," he told her. "At least I very much hope that's what it is. Just inside the cave, partially concealed. I read the signature of a large specimen of what the monitor rather quaintly identifies as *Pseudofelis sapiens ferox*."

The Munchen party descended from the car, three of Guthlac's four guards triangulating the position with professional alertness.

Nils and Leonie Rykermann and their remaining students hurried to greet the party, Raargh emerging after a moment to join them. He carried one of the salvaged kzinti weapons, a thing the size of a small human artillery piece and too heavy for any human in the group to port. Rykermann was carrying a strakkaker he had been cleaning, and Leonie had another slung over her shoulder. The students were also armed.

"Jocelyn! Arthur! I'm glad to see you!" he called, "We've got a problem here!" With the air of one springing a surprise that might not be agreeable, he turned to Jocelyn, "I hope you can stand a bit of a shock. As you can see, Raargh, formerly Raargh-Sergeant, is here.

"I know you are old sparring partners," he went on, awkwardly trying to make light of the situation, "but he has done us a service and brought us valuable information." He counted the Munchen party. "But we may . . . need . . . more . . ."

His voice died away. There was a metallic rattle as he dropped the strakkaker on the ground. He stood staring, his mouth working.

Jocelyn turned from her affectionate greeting of Leonie. "Hullo, Nils," she said. "I believe you're met Dimity Carmody before. Recently arrived from We Made It."

Dimity Carmody too was staring as if she could hardly credit her senses. In mirror-image gestures each raised a hand. Their fingertips, trembling, touched. Their fluttering fingers raised, slowly, to touch each other's faces.

Neither had eyes for Jocelyn van der Stratt as she turned abruptly away from them, her face contorted. Only Raargh saw it. He was not an expert in interpreting simian expressions, but his ziirgah sense picked up a hatred like a physical blow. For a second he gave renewed thanks he was not a telepath. He thought this sudden wave of volcanic hatred that flowed from her was directed entirely at him. But he was a Hero practiced in self-control, and the situation demanded discipline. Seeing, at long last, what sort of monkeymeat Jocelyn made would not help Vaemar. His tail lashed the ground, but he remained otherwise impassive.

"I'm sorry," said Dimity. She was still staring at Nils Rykermann but speaking apparently to everyone. "There is a lot I don't remember. I was hurt, you know."

They made their way to the main camp. Dimity stared about her, touching the back of her head with a characteristic nervous gesture, keeping well away from Raargh. She seemed to recognize the module. Jocelyn and Raargh glared at one another, Jocelyn's body language almost kzinlike, with barely pent attack reflex, Raargh using his lips and tongue to cover his teeth with a conscious effort, the tips of the glistening black claws of his natural hand peeping from between the pads. Nils Rykermann walked like a man in a daze.

Leonie, blank-faced as a soldier under inspection, explained what had happened, Raargh elucidating at various points.

"Can we be sure it's Henrietta?" Jocelyn ground out. Her teeth were clenched and her eyes shining now. Her fingers ran through the ears on her belt-ring, as if counting them over and over.

"That's how she identified herself. Raargh never saw her before. But why should any impostor wish to boast falsely of being the most hated human on the planet? And she has a recording of Chuut-Riit. Raargh thinks it's probably genuine, not a VR mock-up. He saw Chuut-Riit alive."

"I have seen Chuut-Riit alive, and I have seen her before!" said Jocelyn. "The last time was when she accompanied Chuut-Riit to the start of a public hunt. Among the game turned loose for the kzin were some convicted humans in whom I had a . . . very personal interest. And I was in police uniform. I remained impassive and betrayed nothing, like a well-trained monkey. To have betrayed anything would only have achieved a place for me in the hunt as well. It was as I stood there that I vowed to kill her with my own hands. I will get her. If necessarily alone."

Raargh raised the torn remnants of his ears in the equivalent of a human nod of understanding. Actually he was thinking of what dead Trader-Gunner had said to him the day of the cease-fire when he met Jocelyn: "Those manrretti can be trouble." *I have always wanted that tree-swinger dead, but for Vaemar's sake as well as the word I gave I must be calm,* he thought again. He had schooled himself for the company of one or two humans, preferably on his own ground or in the open. Being confined in the living-module with thirteen of them was a strain, especially with several of them giving out emotions that battered at his ziirgah sense. Leonie, who, after the battle with the Morlocks he thought he knew, was throwing out an emotional shield such as he had never encountered before. He wondered why. A short time before she had seemed relaxed and calm. That had been after mating, he knew, but even allowing for what monkeys were like, what had been a radiant, almost tangible happiness seemed to have worn off very quickly.

As for the mad manrret Henrietta and her even madder get, her presumption of some kind of partnership with Chuut-Riit would have been an intolerable insult even if she had not dared to lay forcible hands on Vaemar and himself.

He noticed the Jocelyn manrret looking at his ears. Torn as they were, it seemed, she could read that simple gesture. Her body language altered and his ziirgah sense recorded the waves of hatred that flowed from her mind being modified by something like brief fellow-feeling. *We both understand vengeance.* And then he thought: *One of us two is not going to see another sunrise.*

"They must suspect Raargh has given the alarm. They will be pulling out now," said Leonie. "I suggest we send a blocking force back up the route Raargh took getting here, and another to watch for the main exits. It would be easier if we knew what the main exits looked like, but there you are."

"I don't like dividing our force," said Arthur Guthlac. "There are too few of us as it is. And we don't know how many there are."

"We're not challenging battle. Only watching them till substantial forces arrive. They may not think Raargh went to humans.

Perhaps they think he's headed to the kzin community at Arhus to bring them into the revolt. But we've got to move fast."

"I've called for reinforcements," said Guthlac. "Anyway, if Cumpston failed to report to Early after a certain time, emergency procedures would be triggered automatically."

"How much do you know of Early's schemes?"

"Not a lot nowadays. And frankly I don't want to. His work was always secretive, and it's become more so lately. Don't forget, he got to where he is not only by being a brilliant military strategist, but by being the most ferocious carnivore in ARM's internal politics. That means manipulating ARM factions against one another, never letting the right hand know what the left hand is doing. Hunting kzin with a pocketknife in a dark room is child's play compared to the games Early plays."

"No more monkey-chatter!" said Raargh. "Vaemar is captive. Must rescue now!"

"If Raargh says Vaemar is important, he is," said Leonie.

"All right," said Arthur Guthlac after a moment. "Can you guide us back through the caves?"

"Yes, trail is marked."

"And we don't know the other entrance or entrances. It or they are presumably well hidden. Very well. This is my plan. It you don't like it, say so very quickly." He turned to two of the soldiers. "Dunkerton and Collins, you will take our car and the university car and fly north. Commence a box search of the area using deep radar. Remember they may have both a human and a kzin prisoner, both important. Don't fire on them under any circumstances. Track them till reinforcements arrive. Take both cars in case they split up. The rest of us will head back through the caves. That's the only way I can think of that gives us a chance to block both ends of the burrow at once."

No one disagreed.

"Right, Nils and Leonie, I'll get you and your students to organize weapons, equipment, food, lamps for us all. You know best what we'll need. We may be underground a long time."

The module emptied quickly under Leonie's direction. Arthur Guthlac turned to the desk and spoke to it urgently. Jocelyn alone remained with him, drawing him aside.

"Early says reinforcements are on the way," he told her. "Markham's coming too."

"Why not just let this revolt go ahead? It would do the Exterminationists' work for them." Her voice had a seductive burr in it. Her fingers brushed his thigh. She bent slowly towards him and kissed his mouth, then drew away, gazing

up at him catlike from under her long lashes. Her breasts
heaved slightly but noticeably.

Arthur Guthlac looked at her with troubled eyes.

"Don't think the idea doesn't tempt me," he said. "But . . .
I began my military career—poring over fragments of old
forbidden books in a museum—because I cared about the fact
that honor seemed to have departed from our world . . . from
Earth's society, anyway. We were sheeplike masses almost
without volition, directed and controlled by the ARM bureaucracy, of which I myself was a tiny part. Without realizing
it, we were undergoing a sort of death. I wanted to keep some
threatened values alive. If it's true that humans can only have
a civilization as long as less civilized humans guard it, and
I am one of the guardians, then I will still try to be as civilized as possible. Otherwise the whole thing ends up kind of
pointless.

"During the war I did plenty of ruthless things, including
acting as an agent provocateur to discredit the pacifist movement when the situation on Earth required it. I've slept well
with many deaths on my conscience—and I'm not talking about
kzin deaths. But to just let these lunatics go ahead with their
attempted mayhem seems wrong—perhaps because that old
kzin trusts Rykermann, perhaps because we're all getting old
and less hot-livered—I mean hot-tempered! Even seeing that
kzin and those humans working together at the spaceport.
Perhaps I'm wobbling a bit about Exterminationism. Also, who
knows how much damage the revolt might do before we
crushed it? I need to think the whole thing over."

"I don't! But there's one reason for me against just sitting
back, my love: If Henrietta is there I'm going after her! Alone
if need be! But I suppose it would be silly to resent reinforcements."

As Cumpston had a habit of pinching his lower lip when
thinking, Arthur Guthlac had a habit of sticking his out. Jocelyn
leaned closer to him, bit it gently between her teeth, then licked
his face. She thought of how Markham had enjoyed that.

"Leonie liver not happy," said Raargh in his blend of
Wunderlander and the former slaves' patois. It was a state-
ment, not a question, the vocabulary somewhat broken down.
Leonie was not as fluent as the colonel.

"No," she said, "Leonie liver not happy."

"We go into battle," said Raargh. Even though Leonie was
a female, it—she—was a fighter, and surely the prospect of
action should rouse any fighter's spirits. "Good for soldier to

go into battle with high liver. Fight best . . . Memory Raargh and Leonie fight morlocks? . . . Why Leonie not happy? Leonie just mate. Mating make females happy."

"How did you know that?"

"Ziirgah sense," he told her. "Not telepath," he emphasized. "Not tell thoughts. But tell feelings. Leonie happy when Raargh wake. Now . . ."

She laughed.

"Why Leonie discharge from eyes? That also show humans not happy, Raargh know. . . . Once, Leonie dig Raargh out of trap. Once, Raargh help Leonie breathe. Leonie female, but still Leonie and old Raargh companions, Raargh thinks."

"Yes, Leonie and Raargh companions," she replied. "Life was simple then. But Leonie is stupid manrret."

"Some manrretti not stupid," he told her. "Some manrretti clever. Leonie clever . . . Some mans," he went on, "like clever manrretti."

"Yes, Raargh," said Leonie. "That is problem. Some mans like clever manrretti. Hard to explain to Hero." She put out a hand and scratched the great scarred head under the lower jaw. Raargh resisted an undignified temptation to purr.

"Rarrgh companion," he said.

"Yes, Raargh companion."

"Leonie have enemies, Raargh have enemies. Raargh eat! Raargh have long fangs, sharp claws." He demonstrated. "Raargh old, but Raargh quick! . . . Is Jocelyn manrret Leonie enemy?" he asked hopefully.

"You would, too, wouldn't you? No, companion, it's not that simple. Leonie has no enemies. Not here."

"Leonie not want to kill kzinti . . . kill ratcats. Raargh knows."

"No. But I will fight if I must today. . . . Otherwise . . . maybe disaster."

"Yes. Raargh knows."

Very carefully, imitating a gesture he had seen among humans, Raargh laid his great clawed hand on Leonie's shoulder. Surprised, she turned her tear-streaked face to him. Arthur Guthlac entered. His own eyes widened for a moment at the scene.

"We're ready!" he barked. "We're all going!"

"Shouldn't we leave someone here?" Leonie asked.

"We're too thin on the ground to divide our forces any further. Professor Carmody is our guest on this planet, and I'm charged with keeping her out of danger. But leaving her here with or without a guard is hardly a practical option. In any case, she has said she doesn't want to be left here and she'll come. But I want no lives lost. Remember, we're not going to fight, but to blockade them till Early's troops arrive.

"Raargh," he went on, "I am declaring this a military situation. Will you take orders from me?"

"Yes." Five years had accustomed Raargh to humans' notions of discipline. The old kzin did not even growl. *And that*, thought Arthur Guthlac, *weakens me as an Exterminationist a little more. I am a soldier, and that old ratcat becomes one of my troops. Honor is a tanjed awkward thing. And what was the old ratcat doing just now? It looked for a moment as if he was comforting her. . . . But why? . . . Of course! As the song goes: 'What kind of fool am I?' . . . and it took a kzin to see it!*

"Let's move out!" he snarled.

"What now?" Vaemar asked Colonel Cumpston.

"Waiting is very difficult. At the moment it is all we can do."

"I think they are listening to us."

"Yes."

"It does not matter," said Vaemar. "Seizing me by a trick and insulting my Honored Step-Sire Raargh—even insulting you, my chess-partner—is not the way to gain my cooperation. . . ."

"If she and Emma have you, they can use your Name to the other kzinti."

"And what you said . . . that Emma's plans would destroy every kzin on Wunderland. . . . Do you believe that?"

"Yes, Vaemar. Worse, it would mean no peace between our kinds would ever be possible. That will be difficult enough as things are."

"It surprises me, that she should behave so."

"Not me, so much, perhaps, but I have read more of human history. And lived longer."

"Do you think Henrietta is truly loyal to my Honored Sire?"

"She probably thinks she is. Whether he would approve of what she says in his name is another matter. . . . Suppose, Vaemar, suppose against all odds Emma's plans succeeded— that the Kzin revolted and captured the hyperdrive. How would you feel?"

"I am a kzin. I am Chuut-Riit's son. But I am also a kzin of Ka'ashi—of Wunderland. I know you and other humans . . . difficult."

"According to the holo, your honored Sire Chuut-Riit *knew* Henrietta had influenced him. And he wanted her, if he died, to influence his own sons and Traat-Admiral. He was looking—

as far as being what he was allowed him to look—as some sort of eventual partnership—or at least I know of no other notion that described it more closely. His ideas were perhaps not so far removed from those we now hear from Markham and a few others—save, of course, that he saw the Kzin as the utterly dominant ones and the humans existing on sufferance—slaves perhaps at best one day a little above the Jotok." *And monkey-meat if they were fractious,* he thought. *But if we ever get out of this, I want this young ratcat thinking about a human-kzin relationship on more positive lines. Civilize them for a few—perhaps more than a few—generations, and who knows?*

"Yes," said Henrietta, stepping into the room, Emma beside her. "Chuut-Riit knew I influenced his policies, knew I helped him understand humans. He accepted it. But listening to you has told me a good deal. I seek to stop the secret manipulation of the human race as well as the Kzin. It appears my daughter has an altogether different agenda."

"There is no point in hiding it any longer," said Emma. "It is I who am truly loyal to the Patriarchy, and the memory of the Riit."

"This ARM officer is right! Your plans are insane!" Henrietta cried out. "To guide and instruct Vaemar to help destroy the ARM conspiracy when he leads the kzinti of Wunderland is my charge and my sacred goal. You would destroy everything in a mad adventure!"

"Mad! You call me mad! Have you looked at your own brain lately?"

"Andre sides with me. We have planned this for years."

Emma raised one hand and made a gesture. "Go and make *ch'rowl* with your pet monkey, then! Behold!" A dozen male kzin entered the room, standing about her. They were all, Cumpston saw, young. Older than Vaemar, taller and bulkier, but several still with the last traces of juvenile and adolescent spotting on their coats. There were also several more humans with them.

"The loyal humans and the loyal Heroes side with *me*!" Emma snarled. One or two of the kzin growled. Emma addressed them in the hiss-spit of the Heroes' Tongue. Cumpston was astonished that a human could pronounce it so well. She turned back to Henrietta. "You forget! Half these Heroes' Sires were of Ktrodni-Stkaa's pride! They follow me!"

"I have given them refuge." Henrietta's hand went to the weapon on her belt. "I have tried to help the kzin of Wunderland, of every pride, but not for this! And you have here the blood of Chuut-Riit, who you would risk! Chuut-Riit, who was my good Master! Yes, and who called me friend as well as slave!"

"Chuut-Riit! You cannot impress us with that name! My loyalty is to *the* Riit! The true Riit, whose traditions were borne by Ktrodni-Stkaa! Chuut-Riit was a compromiser, if nothing worse! If Riit he truly was! Chuut-Riit's reward was foul death at the hands of a human assassination team. Ktrodni-Stkaa saw Chuut-Riit and Traat-Admiral for what they were! Monkey-lovers! Much good it did them!"

Cumpston looked at Vaemar with alarm. To insult a kzin—for a *human* to insult a kzin!—was more than bad enough. To insult a kzin's Sire was far worse. And for a human to insult a kzin's Sire of Riit blood was . . . unreal. But Vaemar betrayed no emotion save an unnatural stillness.

Two more humans rushed in, wearing the odd pseudo-kzin costume that seemed to be the uniform of these people.

"We've picked up activity in the south passages! Large lifeforms. About a dozen of them. They appear to be human but at least one kzin."

The human identified as Andre strode forward. "We have a common enemy!" he shouted. "We must destroy these invaders. Defense stations!" He stepped to the control console.

Vaemar screamed and leaped. One slash sent the human behind Andre who blocked his way spinning across the room, blood splattering. Then Vaemar ripped at the control console. The lights went out, save for the illuminated numbers of a couple of clocks and other pinpoints. The air was a confusion of kzin and human shrieks. There was the gingery smell of kzinti battle-reflexes. Cumpston felt the weight and sharpness of a clawed Kzinti hand on him.

"It is I, Vaemar," a voice hissed in his ear. "Follow. Hold my tail. We must find a hiding place!"

Emergency lights were coming on as they left. Henrietta and Emma seemed to be working together at the console. The kzinti and humans were seizing weapons from the racks.

Chapter 9

The journey back the way Raargh had come, with lights and a marked trail, was much quicker. With lights and company, too, even if the company was only human, he did not suffer from the delusions of sensory deprivation. Any surviving morlocks kept out of their way—and the Rykermanns had lights whose radiations morlocks were meant to find especially painful. Raargh again went in the lead, again hoping his prosthetic arm would catch any Sinclair wire before it sliced into living flesh and bone. Arthur Guthlac kept close behind him.

The Rykermann party had automatic compasses, GPS indicators, microminiaturised deep radar and other directional aids, and there was little risk this time of getting lost. Leonie made a selection of emergency medical equipment developed in years of guerrilla war, and Dimity, the most lightly armed of the party, carried it. They went fast, but, to Raargh's impatience, at less than maximum speed. They had only their feet and were hung with gear, and Arthur Guthlac insisted on no more than a walking pace with rest stops. At his insistence they were kitted up in skin-coveralls and each third of the party took it in turns to wear gas masks and helmets. They passed the bone-heap and entered the lined tunnels. Ahead was a dim glow. There seemed little point in dousing their own lights.

"Should we spread out?" asked Jocelyn.

"I don't think there's much point in spreading far. If they've got deep radar or motion detectors they'll see us coming. If they have plasma guns or nerve gas it isn't spreading out that will save us. But it might be a good idea if they try to take us on hand-to-hand."

"Fighting kzin hand-to-hand isn't a good idea. Anyway, the

point isn't to fight. It's to stop them getting away, with or without their prisoners."

"How do you know this is the only way out?" asked Dimity.

"I don't," said Guthlac after a moment. "I suppose I took it for granted. In fact, knowing how paranoid the kzin can be when they put their minds to it, it's unlikely they'd have restricted themselves to a single—"

"There!" Raargh stabbed with a massive finger at Guthlac's motion detector. "Movement ahead of us and on our right flank."

"How many?" asked Leonie.

"They are not many yet. An eight, two eights. But we are not many also."

The lights showed nothing. Only the single tunnel ahead of them, and what they knew were a complication of dark holes behind.

"These caves have never been fully mapped," said Leonie. "We've been finding new ones all the time."

An explosion shattered the panel above them. Raargh, faster than any human could have moved, spun, firing the heavy kzin weapon. Guthlac's two troopers also fired back with quick, short professional bursts.

"Behind us as well, now!" Raargh snarled.

One of the students was down, hit by a chunk of flying metal behind the left ear. Arthur Guthlac saw instantly he was dead. Keeping low, he gathered the strakkaker and spare charges, as well as the food pack the boy had been carrying.

"Did you see anything?"

"No, too quick. Too dark."

"No point in staying here, then," said Arthur Guthlac. "Plans are changed. We move on. And we stay together. We're too few to split. Forward!"

A blue glow lit the tunnel ahead of them. Hemispherical, it blocked the way. Raargh recognized it as something to be avoided. Dimity recognized it as a Sinclair field, and Arthur Guthlac knew it from old ARM texts. It was possible to live in the time-compressed zone inside it, given adequate supplies of food, water and air, but only if one was in place before it was generated: The process of entering the zone once it was activated would probably be fatal.

A beam, or the projectiles of a strakkaker, fired through the field would receive enormous acceleration. What would happen to such a beam on leaving the field on the other side no one was sure, but as a rule attempts to get around the Special Theory of Relativity in the Einsteinian universe had either no results or cataclysmic ones. Strakkaker needles, or other projectiles emerging from the field with a kinetic energy giving them far more destructive power than artillery shells, would also not be a good thing in this confined space.

"We'll have to go over it," Dimity said.

"How?"

She pointed. The roof above them was a complex of machinery—pipes, ducting, ladders, and gangways.

"It's too obvious. They will have booby trapped it."

Dimity turned to Rarrgh.

"This field was not on when you came this way?" she asked, speaking carefully in Wunderlander.

"No."

"I think it's been set up here in a hurry. They may not have had time to do more. If it's enough to delay us, from their point of view that's better than nothing."

"All right. How do we get over it?"

"We have ropes in the caving gear," said Leonie. "If that would help."

"It might. If we could get up there and attach them."

"Can the kzin do it?" asked Dimity.

"Can you, Raargh?"

"Raargh can try," he answered. "But Raargh cannot jump like kitten. Raargh is old and has wounds in legs."

"You are still quick," said Leonie. "Still have strength of Hero."

He screamed and leaped, straight upwards, claws scrabbling. The claws of his natural hand cut grooves in the paneling, deep but not deep enough to hold him. The claws of his prosthetic hand smashed through it, found a hold. His hind claws dug in. He pulled himself vertically upright, seized at the overhead ducting and struggled onto it.

"Useful to have a kzin along," said Leonie.

The glowing domes of the Sinclair fields below them reminded Cumpston a little of giant jellyfish stranded on an Earth beach. But they would, he knew, be considerably more deadly to touch than the worst jellyfish. They were crawling along a high gantry, and he felt hopelessly exposed to any hunter with modern tracking or sensory devices.

The red dot of a laser-site appeared on his chest. Fight or flight, he knew, would be useless. He raised his hands in surrender, signaling to Vaemar to do the same. A group of the armed humans from the fortress appeared at the end of the gantry, McGlue in their lead.

"You had better come out quietly," said McGlue. There were six of them, with strakkakers and nerve disrupters. Vaemar and Cumpston obeyed.

"Put your hands on top of your heads. Do not make any sudden moves. Dead, neither of you are any use. But we will shoot if we have to. You cannot beat six of us. But I do not want to treat you as prisoners. We are on the same side."

"And whose pride are you?" asked Cumpston. "The mad one or the even madder one?"

"Ostensibly, we side with Emma," said the man. "Actually, we have our own agenda. One which you, Colonel, are obliged to support."

"I suppose you'll explain?"

"I need to. We seem to be alone at present. All other kzinti and humans are off wiping out your little rescue party in the caves. Does this mean anything to you?" He held up a small plastic cube, projecting a holo.

"An ARM ident."

"Genuine, as you well know. Specifically coded to my DNA and impossible to counterfeit. We have the same employer, Colonel. Or ultimately the same employer."

"Go on."

"Your job has been to watch this young kzin. To adjust him to living on a human world. To become his friend."

"I am his friend! And I have never concealed my ARM status from him."

"I congratulate you. You have carried out your instructions cleverly. But it has been my part to play a more covert role. ARM is, as you have perhaps guessed, the instrument of a higher power."

"So even Chuut-Riit guessed. Not a very effective secret if it can be worked out by an alien being four and a half light-years from Earth."

"Suppose Emma's plans—though I will be frank with you and say *our* plans, for you know the way we must operate—for a revolt of the Wunderland kzin go ahead. As any practical military man such as yourself understands, it will almost certainly fail. The kzin are relatively few, disorganized and disarmed. On the other hand, given the heavy weapons stockpiled here, and kzin courage and fighting ability, and given a few lucky breaks, an uprising could do great damage and cause considerable loss of human life. As you have eloquently put it, the kzin on Wunderland and Tiamat would then probably be wiped out to the last kzinrret and the last kitten—if events followed an undirected course."

"But they will not follow an undirected course, and in any case you are wrong is thinking that the kzin of the Patriarchy would care particularly in a moral sense. We would be doing no more than they expect of monkeys. Kzin culture does not have much of the human concept of hostages. The kzinti of the Alpha Centauri system have surrendered. They are disgraced anyway. Their lives mean nothing. That they tried to fight back when the situation was hopeless meant they did no more than Heroes are expected to do. Perhaps it would make their dishonor a little less. Certainly, it will mean other kzin worlds and other individual kzinti will be even less willing to surrender when all their hope is gone than they are now. Certainly, the war will be prolonged, not forever, but enough to give us *time*."

"I still don't understand," said Cumpston. "At the very least, a lot more humans will die, directly and indirectly. And we know the kzinti have other slave races. Some would say, even setting everything else aside, we have a moral duty to help them. Prolonging the war will not do that. A peace has been possible here so far. It may be possible with whole planets."

"I suggest you look at the long view," McGlue replied. "The hyperdrive is the greatest threat to the stability of the human species—indeed to all species. Given the absence of war and easy interstellar travel, sooner or later our control is gone. Not this year, not this decade, perhaps not this century. But eventually.

"In the three centuries between the first settlement of Wunderland, followed by the other interstellar colonies, and the development of the hyperdrive we—ARM—lost a great deal of control.

"That was inevitable. Interstellar travel was rare and one-way, with many years spent in hibernation. Even message communication was restricted to the speed of light. Now the hyperdrive threatens chaos for the human race in the long term. Why do you think ARM discouraged research into FTL for so long? But FTL is a two-edged sword, and one edge fights for us: for it also gives us the chance to reassert order and communication throughout the human worlds if we act quickly, and reestablish a controlling presence throughout the human species *before* the inevitable human diaspora. Prolonging the war with the Kzin will give us time for that, both for the colonies in general and for Wunderland in particular. It will unite the human worlds under ordinary military discipline and organization long enough for us to establish ourselves once again in place on every one of them.

"Can you, an ARM officer of your rank, seriously doubt the worth of our cause? You, a war veteran who has seen so much chaos and destruction? Before the war ARM was a technological police. That is what it remains. Those who fretted under the stability we imposed could not imagine the consequences of destability, or the immeasurably worse consequences we face if we falter now! Would you see wars between human worlds? Perhaps at last a whole galaxy filled with wars? You are more humane than that, Colonel!

"As for the kzin of Wunderland, certain selected individuals will be saved. You, I think, hope for the Kzin to be civilized in the course of time. That is among our goals also.

"We helped that old kzin to escape—or rather turned a blind eye to it—expecting him to die in the caves. Alive here, he was a constant potential nuisance to our plans and a reminder to Vaemar and perhaps some of the other kzin and humans of a false complexity of loyalties. We wanted him permanently out of the way without risking the wrath of Henrietta, Emma, and indeed Vaemar by killing him. We underestimated him— or perhaps kzin military prostheses are better than we thought. Anyway, we did not know there was a human expedition within reach. Well, Vaemar, if he survives this battle we will see he is safe for you now. You will not lose your friend. There are kzinti on Wunderland we shall need. You, Vaemar, will have the highest of places among them, the place to which your royal blood entitles you.

"Vaemar, what we do is for the Heroic race as well. You know chaos would be at least as destructive for your kind as for ours. Sooner or later your kind will have the hyperdrive too. Your role may be to help hold chaos at bay. You are correct, Colonel, that Chuut-Riit's blood may be especially important.

"Already before the Liberation our people here—the trained heirs of those who came with the original colonists—had made contact with certain kzin—kzin who we made sure as well as we could survived the Liberation. We will contact the slave races, in good time. Already we seek among the kzin for a jotok-trainer. Our ultimate masters—and I say 'our' because they are yours as well as mine—do not think in the short term or on a small scale. We do what we do for the longest-term good of all. And I mean all, kzinti included."

"All right," said Cumpston. "I accept who you are. What do you want me to do?"

"For the moment, nothing. Things are developing satisfactorily. The best thing we can do now is keep out of the way and not intervene unless we need to."

Colonel Cumpston nodded, raising his hand to pinch his lower lip thoughtfully. The narrow gangway meant they were standing in a line. The laser in his ring had a single charge only, but given their position it was enough.

"Now," he said to Vaemar as they stepped over the bodies, "we should move cautiously to find our friends."

"What about these?"

"I would not suggest you eat them. The meat of such would be distasteful. Drop them into the Sinclair field and it will take care of them in good time. It is useful to have weapons again."

As they pushed the bodies off the catwalk into the field glowing below, Cumpston took from one of his pockets a small black emblem in the shape of a swan and dropped it after them. They heard, along the passages ahead, explosions and the screech of a strakkaker. Human shouts and kzin snarls and screams. Mechanical voices shouting orders.

"Where now?" asked Vaemar.

"To the sound of the guns, my young Hero!"

The young Kzin's snarl of joy shook the air. Laden with weapons, they ran.

A bolt from Raargh's heavy weapon smashed into the gallery. A human and two kzin fell. Another kzin, leaping down, was hit by the needles of a strakkaker and disintegrated.

But Guthlac's party was taking casualties too: two more of the students and one of the troopers were down, and they were outnumbered, with no obvious way either forward or back, with the enemy in possession of the high ground. *I've blundered,* thought Guthlac. *Terminally, maybe. Should have remembered Sun Tzu. I made the mistake of attacking without knowing the enemy or the terrain. Let them get up a plasma gun and we're done.* Had he let Jocelyn—where was she?— distract his fighting brain? Nonsense! He looked at his watch. They had bought some time, anyway. But above them was the labyrinth of ladders, ducting, and machinery which the enemy knew and he did not. Raargh spun and fired, too quickly for him to follow, hitting someone or something—the explosion was fierce enough to leave the species in doubt—that had been crawling on top of some piping behind them. *We'd be dead already but for that ratcat,* he thought. *Still, we've put up a good fight so far.* Rykermann also seemed to have rediscovered fighter's reflexes and was getting off fast and accurate snapshots. Leonie too. *Well, those three are an old team.* Jocelyn was good too, very good, and Professor Carmody, if not so quick, had evidently used a gun before.

Moving shapes above some distance away, hard to make out. He gestured to Raargh, whose artificial eye was proving as useful as his enormous strength. The old kzin fired twice. The explosion brought down a massive overhead gantry and attached ducting in roiling fire. The way ahead seemed clear, at least, since their suits could withstand the heat of ordinary flame.

"Forward!" he shouted, then to Raargh, remembering kzinti combat psychology, "Lead, Hero!"

They sprang up. More shots from behind! The frontal attack, he realized, had been a diversion. *The oldest trick in the book, and I fell for it! Well done, Brigadier!* The remaining trooper was down, the rest of them bunched together.

Falling wreckage hit Guthlac. He had had broken bones before and now he felt knee and shin snap. Something in his chest, too. The pain was monstrous, but he knew, or hoped, that if he lived he could be quickly repaired. *Not like the Resistance fighters who fought here without docs,* he thought. Everything went black for a moment, and then he struggled back to consciousness.

Jocelyn spun and fired, holding her laser low. Leonie was right behind her. The laser sliced through her suit and into her lower body. Dimity kicked, knocking the laser out of Jocelyn's hands before it could finish bisecting Leonie.

Raargh saw. With a roar he leaped back at Jocelyn, claws flashing.

Firing as they came, at least twenty kzin and humans charged up the tunnel. Dimity, feet braced apart and steadied against the tunnel wall, fired a laser with one hand and a strakkaker with the other, hitting several, stopping the mass of them for a moment.

Two more shapes, one kzin, one human, leaped down from a gantry into the attackers. At the sound of Vaemar's battle-scream, Raargh abandoned Jocelyn and charged into the fight, firing the heavy kzin weapon even as he leaped. Rykermann was just behind the kzin.

Guthlac tried to follow and fell. Instinct overriding reason, he tried to spring back to his feet, and his right leg collapsed in an agony that seemed to turn the passage white about him. His right knee appeared to have reversed its joint. Splintered bone visible. Gritting his teeth and trying not to scream, he dragged himself toward the others. If a broken rib pierced his lung . . . well, war was war. Dimity was crouched over Leonie, apparently applying some sort of makeshift tourniquet or bandage. The last of Rykermann's students, who he had forgotten, was giving them some covering fire, advancing in short rushes toward their position, firing quick, accurate bursts. *You're either a natural or you've done this before,* Guthlac thought. *I guess a lot of Wunderlanders have. I should have used you better.* Then the student was hit, by three converging lasers fired by the kzinti above, and went down in a gruesome welter. The detail that suddenly sickened Guthlac was that he was another one dead whose name he had never known. *And once I was fascinated by bits of stories that mentioned war! I didn't know the half of it!*

Command your troops, Brigadier! Remember Ceres! Remember Europa! Remember Hssin! His first concern must be with the battle. Agonizingly, he pulled himself up and half over a heavy section of fallen ducting. Who was friend and who foe in the battle of humans and kzinti? More damage killed the remaining lights, leaving the scene lit only by flames from burning wreckage and the lurid glare of lasers through smoke.

You'll do no good here, he told himself. *Get closer. Distance the pain. You're trained to do it. You can get another leg.*

He inched onward, keeping to the side of the tunnel. The firing seemed to be more scattered.

Once or twice he heard Vaemar's voice, distinguishable from the other kzin screams by its juvenile note, and a deep roar he thought was Raargh. Flame blazed up brightly at his back as it reached a container of some combustible liquid. He was, he realized, silhouetted by it, and rolled into shadow. He heard another human scream as he rolled and recognized it as his own. Then, concealed from unaided human eyes at least, he lay still.

He tried after a few moments to crawl forward, but collapsed. For the moment the best he could do was hold his gun. He tried to tell himself that Leonie needed any available medical attention more than he did, though his nervous system screamed otherwise.

Chapter 10

Raargh swung and slashed. Even in darkness he had little difficulty in telling friend from foe. In this kind of battle smell mattered at least as much as sight. He screamed and leaped, giving himself up, as in the fight with the morlocks, to the joy of roaring, claw-to-claw slaughter he had long suppressed.

After a time he found himself alone again. The humans called this sort of battle a "dogfight," and Raargh had known them to end this way before, as pursued and pursuers scattered in individual combats. Yet the suddenness with which the fight broke up always surprised him.

He checked his weapon. A light on the stock indicated it was still charged, but the light itself could be a dangerous giveaway and he covered it with blood from his last enemy. He also checked himself. No serious wounds.

Kzin footfalls behind him. He tensed himself to spring again, then recognized the smell of Vaemar. The two groomed each other quickly, each relieved to find the blood his tongue tasted matting the other's fur was that of enemies.

"Back to the battle, Raargh-Hero?" asked Vaemar. The anxiety in his voice was nothing to do with fear, apart from fear that he might miss something. *Vaemar is a genius,* Raargh thought to himself, *but he is also a young warrior kzin. He proves this day he has the courage to bring down more than gagrumphers.*

"Yes, but quietly and cautiously," he told the youngster. "Remember the lessons of your Honored Sire. We do not expose ourselves to the enemy until we know the strategic situation."

There was a little reflected light from distant fires, enough to be caught by the felinoids' eyes, and together, slinging their weapons, they climbed a ladder to the upper gangways. Damaged though some of these were, they seemed to offer a quicker and less exposed passage than the tunnels. Though kzinti were descended from plains cats, they were quick and confident high among any structures strong enough to bear their weight. Below them was the bluish glare of the Sinclair field that had blocked their passage. More footfalls told Raargh others were climbing too. Well, if they were enemies, he would deal with them.

More footsteps closer in the near-darkness, echoing hollowly on the metal. Lighter, clumsier. Human. Not the smell of any of the humans he had just journeyed with. Henrietta! He saw she was unarmed. No need, then, to unsling his heavy weapon. The Kzin's natural armament of fangs and claws would be more than enough and far more satisfactory. The monkey who had kidnapped them both, insulting him and the blood of the Riit! His claws extended, jaws gaped, and he braced himself to leap.

And then he stopped. In her rattle-brained monkey way she had tried to be loyal.

"Come forward," he said slowly. Even if she could not see or smell, she would know the kzin voice. "Monkey play false, monkey die."

"Kill me now if you wish," she said. "All is surely lost."

"You are loyal slave of Chuut-Riit," said Raargh. "Go. Hide."

"Emma will destroy everything," she said. "I do not want that . . . nor . . . nor did he."

"Then go! Many kzinti on Ka'ashi. Many need advice to live with humans. No more rebellion in hopeless conditions!"

"That was never what I wanted. . . ."

"Swear to it! Name as Word!"

"Would you trust the Name of a monkey? A slave? A female?"

"Swear on the name of Chuut-Riit!"

"Very well. No hopeless rebellion, on the Name of Chuut-Riit, I swear."

"Stop!" It was the voice of another human female, one Rarrgh remembered well. Jocelyn stepped onto the gangway. She carried a strakkaker in one hand and a nerve-disrupter in the other. Raargh knew he and Vaemar were quicker than any human, but she was a trained fighter, and her fingers were already on the triggers. The nerve-disrupter, a short-range pistol-sized device both agonizingly and lethally effective on human and kzinti nervous systems, broadcast impulses in a cone and did not even need to be aimed.

"So," she said, "the arch ratcat-lover and the ratcats arranging things together. How appropriate!" She waved the disrupter at Raargh and Vaemar. "You will each, one by one, take the other's weapon," she told them, "and, without placing your claws near the stock or trigger, or in any way moving quickly, drop them from the gangway. Do it now, and do it very slowly."

"Jocelyn van der Stratt," Henrietta's voice dripped contempt. "Last time I saw you was with Chuut-Riit, helping control the crowd at one of the public hunts—hunts that one day I might have had reduced! I had heard you were quick to change your pelt."

"Then you were wrong. I always worked for the Resistance. I have Kzin and collabo heads and ears to prove it in plenty, but not enough yet."

"What will you do?" That was Vaemar. His voice, Raargh thought, sounded under perfect control. As far as he could duplicate a human tone he suggested mild curiosity.

"You all have one more part to play," she told them. "Come with me."

She marched them in single file back along several galleries, compelling them to hold out their arms at different angles so all could be seen. A discharge from either weapon would have got the lot of them.

There was more wreckage below them here, burning with flickering, smoky flames, and there were some regular lights. They could see bodies—human and kzin—on the ground. There were also voices. Raargh guessed the survivors on both sides could be re-forming. How many were left? Not many of his own human party, which had been too small to start with, against a much bigger formation of well-equipped kzinti as well as the other humans he had seen. At a word from Jocelyn they halted. Below them was the bluish bulge of another Sinclair field.

"Look there!" Below them and up the passage to the left, behind a small barricade of wreckage, were two humans. Raargh recognized them as Leonie and the Dimity female. Leonie was lying in an attitude that told Raargh that she was wounded near death. The Dimity female was doing something to the lower part of her body—first aid, he guessed, from the pumping movements she was making. He could not tell much more. His ziirgah sense was useful for stalking, but in battle the emotions of all around overwhelmed it.

"Leonie Rykermann, a leader of the Resistance, and Dimity Carmody, a hyperdrive scientist. In fact credited by her profile from We Made It as the hyperdrive scientist, the interpreter of the Outsider manual. Either a ratcat or a ratcat-lover would have plenty of motive to kill both of them."

"You kill Leonie!"

"Carmody stopped me finishing the job. It's better this way. . . . Actually, Henrietta, Leonie Rykermann has turned into something of a ratcat-lover herself, but living the retired life you do in this place you wouldn't have heard that. Their deaths will be blamed on you, or on the Kzin. That alone, that they killed those two heroines, will be all the Exterminationists need. And for me, it kills more than, almost literally, two birds with one stone. It also eliminates both my—"

Raargh leaped. It was a difficult leap from where he stood on the gangway behind Henrietta, and he felt his hind claws slash damagingly down on her as he cleared her body. Jocelyn swung up her weapons, but as she did so her upper body flashed into flame. The blast knocked Raargh sideways and he nearly fell off the gangway. Not perhaps a killing fall for a feline in Wunderland gravity, but there was the Sinclair field directly below. With his prosthetic arm he seized the catwalk and scrabbled back.

Jocelyn was still standing, her upper body burning. Then she slowly toppled from the catwalk.

"Back!" shouted a human voice. Then, in something like Heroes' Battle Imperative: "Blast alert!"

Raargh's explosion reflex took him back, pushing Vaemar before him. As Jocelyn's burning body hit and passed into the field, the flames, in time-compression, flashed out like a bomb. Light scorched the walls around them. In another instant the heat would have cremated the kzinti where they stood. But the hellish glare was only a flash. The flames vanished, the fuel and oxygen in the field exhausted in an instant. Raargh's artificial eye adjusted before his natural one. He waited for Vaemar's sight to readjust, then ventured back toward the catwalk, gingerly, for his whiskers were scorched and shriveled and he felt unbalanced without them. The field was still glowing beneath them, with something black crumbing to fragments in it as he watched. The metal of the catwalk was fortunately a poor conductor.

Nils Rykermann, carrying a laser pistol, stepped onto the catwalk.

"We are too exposed up here," he said. "And they need us down there. Hurry!"

"Help me!" cried Henrietta. She was sprawling, trying to rise. Raargh remembered the bones he had felt breaking as he kicked down at her. Rykermann raised the laser pistol to her, then lowered it.

"Your people are here somewhere," he said. "I'll leave you to them."

✧   ✧   ✧

"Over here!" It was Arthur Guthlac. Raargh, Vaemar, and Rykermann dragged him back behind the makeshift barricade.

"Leg gone, and a few ribs, I think," he told them. "I can shoot, but I can't walk."

"All right. We hold here."

Arthur Guthlac found little comfort in the situation. With Dimity fully occupied keeping Leonie alive after the terrible accident with Jocelyn's laser, and Jocelyn herself separated from them in the fighting (*Let her be safe!* he prayed) Rykermann, Raargh, and Vaemar were the only fighters left. Raargh's strength and endurance were colossal but not limitless—already he could see signs of pain and gathering exhaustion in the old kzin—and Vaemar was half-grown and inexperienced. They had gathered up the weapons about but beyond that had no way of replenishing charges or other ammunition. Enemies who certainly outnumbered them had the high ground. At this moment things seemed quiet but they could hardly resist another attack for long. Raargh and Vaemar were noisily eating a couple of the dead. Rykermann did not seem to notice. *They are alien, after all,* Guthlac thought. *Not humans in tiger skins. And they need to keep their strength up and their heads clear for all our sakes. No point in trying to stop them.* And then: *My God! What is happening to me, that I think of kzin in those terms? They would have eaten Selina that way, if they didn't kill her in space.*

Well, I've other things to worry about now. If they leave us alone, find some other way out or fall back into the caves, we might get out of this mess more or less alive. If they attack us again we're done for. I'd like to die on my feet, but I suppose that's too much to ask. And thank you, Jocelyn. As you said to me, I did get lucky on Wunderland. If we live, I'll show you how much I love you.

Footsteps, human and kzin, clanging on the gantries and echoing up the tunnels. They were attacking again. One shot hit a pile of containers stacked against the passage wall. Burning liquid fuel poured out.

They were attacking from three places above, at least. Lifting his head momentarily, Arthur Guthlac fired desperate, unaimed shots, hoping for little more than to make them keep their own heads down. Humans and kzin were leaping down, their falls slowed by lift-belts. The leader of the humans in the pseudo-kzin costumes ahead of the group. He was raising a strakkaker at Leonie and Dimity, halting to get a better aim. Guthlac aimed at him and squeezed the trigger. The dot of the laser-sight was on the tattoo on the human's forehead. It was a certain shot at a momentarily stationary target, but his weapon's power was exhausted. Vaemar passed him in an orange flash, smashing into the human, the two rolling like a catherine wheel. Claws flashed. The human's detached head flew straight up and lodged somewhere in the gantries above. Raargh fired into the bunch of kzinti, then, flinging his empty weapon away, charged too, *w'tsai* out. The kzinti scattered under his charge, apart from two his *w'tsai* gutted. Another crossed blades with him, to be beaten to the ground with blows of his prosthetic arm. Guthlac dragged himself toward Dimity and Leonie as Raargh and Vaemar returned. Wriggling along the ground with astonishing speed, the two kzinti resembled fat, hairy, orange snakes.

The burning fuel was approaching the makeshift barricade where Dimity and Leonie were huddled. They were, Arthur Guthlac realized, in a dip in the ground that would act as a sump and pour it on them. He shouted for Dimity to leave Leonie and run while she had time, but she remained with her. Then the fire flowed all about her, cutting off her escape. Rykermann rushed toward the two women, then staggered back, beaten by the heat.

Raargh screamed something and leaped across the flames, the fur of his legs on fire. Gathering Leonie in the crook of his natural arm, holding Dimity with his prosthetic one, he leapt again across the flames and carried them away at a dead run, Vaemar following, backing away and firing. A second later an explosion shattered the ground where they had been, splashing the stream of fire as it poured into it. Guthlac saw that some of the enemy had brought a small mortar into action and others were setting up a plasma gun, a small piece of artillery specially designed for clearing out caves and tunnels with flame. A party of kzinti and humans were passing up ammunition and other heavier weapons.

A sudden howling and trembling filled Guthlac's ears and the air trembled. *Sonic stunners*, he realized. He struggled for consciousness. Just before everything went black he saw a squad of troops in UNSN combat gear, another squad in the gray of the Free Wunderland Forces, charging down the corridor, Cumpston at their head, and another who he recognized as Markham.

Raargh deposited Leonie and Dimity in a sheltered alcove. Another run secured Dimity's medical equipment. He rolled on the ground and beat at the flames on his fur.

"My Honored Step-Sire is in much pain," Vaemar told Dimity. "Can you ease it?"

"Yes, yes, I think so." She extracted a needle from the small field-doc. A gauge showed it was much depleted but not yet empty. "It's human specific, but it ought to work."

"Yes," said Vaemar. "Human and kzin have similar body chemistry. It leads to interesting speculations as to our common microbe origins. Proteins are not identical but we can eat same food for a long time."

Dimity injected Raargh, finding the best purple artery with Vaemar's assistance. She also sprayed the area heavily with the white foam of Universal Burn Repair. Raargh hefted his weapon but the sounds of battle were diminishing as the sonics took effect. He and Vaemar picked off several more figures as they slumped into unconsciousness or lay prone on the gantries. Dimity had turned back to Leonie. Vaemar made an interrogative feline sound that covered a number of questions.

"He is no stranger to pain, I think," she said to Vaemar, without looking up. "It should be diminishing now."

"He is Hero," said Vaemar.

"And you," said Dimity, "are Hero and something else. You speak of 'interesting speculations' in the midst of a battle."

"Of course. Interesting speculations are always interesting, particularly, I think, this one, and when I spoke no targets presented themselves and the battle was plainly all but won. I calculated I could afford distraction for that measure from fighting, given the state of the tactical situation. I have just hunted and killed and it is perhaps now safe to obey the promptings of my system and relax a little."

"I thought . . . I thought I was the only one . . ."

"Further," said Vaemar "I wish to think upon my Honored Sire Chuut-Riit's purported testament in the light of certain of my own experiences and auditions here. Is that strange? I would be glad if you would tell me, should it strike you as such. My Honored Step-Sire says I must learn human ways and values."

"It is not strange to me," said Dimity, still not looking up from her work. "But then, I believe that I am not a typical human. I have sometimes wondered what I am."

"I too have wondered what I am," said Vaemar.

Colonel Cumpston, carrying beam rifle and stunner, walked wearily up the corridor to join them. The fighting seemed to have stopped. The UNSN and Wunderland troops were gathering up the unconscious bodies of the enemy. There were a couple of medics, guiding a larger doc on a gravity sledge.

"Hurry!" Dimity called. "Hurry! Over here!"

"I'm very tired," she said, as the medics took over.

"Manrret rest," said Raargh. And then: "Manrret Hero, too." He and Vaemar caught her as she stumbled with weariness and set her down. She clung for a moment to Raargh's great arm.

Arthur Guthlac recovered consciousness to find himself looking into the face of Ulf Reichstein Markham. "In all, der results positif haf been," said Markham. In moments of stress the Germanic sentence-structure and pronunciation of Wunderlander became thicker in his accent. Guthlac saw the stock-light on the heavy kzin weapon he carried was glowing with the warning of insufficient charge. It had evidently seen a lot of firing very recently. Markham drew a deep breath and when he spoke again his accent was much diminished.

"If necessary we will get you a new leg. Let it not be said Wunderland is inhospitable to her distinguished visitors. And you have done us a service. . . . Do you know where Jocelyn is?"

"No." *Jocelyn . . . you said you loved me, you proved you desired me. . . . Have you completed the transformation of my life, wiped away the last of Arthur Guthlac, the misfit museum guard and finished making Arthur Guthlac the Man? Jocelyn, where are you?*

Somehow, as he whispered that question, he knew it would never be answered. Jocelyn was gone with Selina.

There was a cover hiding the lower part of Leonie's body, but Nils Rykermann had seen laser wounds before. He could, if he allowed himself, imagine what was there. A medic was attending the tubing that ran under it, and something was pumping fluid.

He knelt beside her head. Her hands were fluttering feebly, plucking at something invisible. He stroked one with his fingertips.

"A lot of fighting," she whispered.

"It's over now."

"So the Exterminationists win?"

"No."

"Tell me. It's all right. I can hear. I can understand."

"There is no kzin rebellion. And the Exterminationists have had a blow. They've lost Jocelyn. She was their most powerful figure. Guthlac is wavering, I think. And . . . so am I." He bent and kissed her cold forehead. "Lion cub," he whispered.

"Good . . . good." She did not speak again.

"Live," he breathed. "Don't run out on me. Or on old Raargh."

Her eyes closed slowly. Rykermann could not tell if she was dead or unconscious. He turned away, his face buried in his hands, and he did not see the medics remove her.

Dimity Carmody was sitting on an empty ammunition box. She had taken out one of her small music boxes and was listening to it. Raargh and Vaemar approached her. The white foam, setting hard, covered the burns on Raargh's legs. He was walking, but carefully.

"Hullo," she said.

"Do not fear ratcats," said Raargh, remembering the terror he had picked up from her previously. "Raargh and Vaemar and Dimity manrret companions in battle."

"Yes," said Dimity. "I've been told a bit about it all. Well, there are some ratcats I don't fear now."

"Dimity helped Leonie," said Raargh.

"Yes, of course."

"Raargh and Leonie old companions."

"Funny, she is one of the flashes of memory I have. Quite a lot of it is coming back. Seeing her now, I remember, I was jealous of her. I never dared betray that to him. . . . She was Nils's best student, his favorite. And she wasn't a freak like me. I don't suppose this means much to you."

"Manrretti sentient. Always problems," said Raargh. "Dominant kzintosh have harem, some kzintosh allocated one kzinrret, most have none. Humans untidy."

"It must have been hard for you to change, to live with humans as you do," Dimity said.

"Hero do hard things," said Raargh. "Otherwise not Hero."

"No," said Dimity. "Otherwise not Hero."

"The human Andre, one who tried to kill you and Leonie," said Raargh. He produced something and tossed it with a moist sound from hand to hand. "I have his maleness here. A gift for you and Leonie."

"Honored Step-Sire Raargh-Hero," said Vaemar, "I do not think Dimity human understands kzinti customs. I will take. But here is a gift," he held out a chess knight, moulded in osmium with sapphire eyes. "Vaemar made." Dimity accepted the substitute gift with some relief.

"Not fear?" asked Raargh.

"Not so much." As Leonie had done previously, she reached out with a tentative hand and tickled his chin. Raargh had just killed and eaten to satiety. This time he allowed himself to purr.

"You play chess?" she asked Vaemar.

"Oh, yes!"

"I haven't played more than a couple of times. But a game between us might be interesting." Raargh reached out and picked up Dimity's music box. Vaemar looked at it curiously. "May I see it?" he asked.

"Wind it," she said, "It's running down."

"It is decorous," said Vaemar, fiddling at the tiny handle with his claws. "Delicate."

"Keep it, if you like. A gift."

"Thank you." A few tiny musical chimes drifted across the chamber.

"If I killed a couple of them, I'm not going to take the credit for it," Colonel Cumpston said to Arthur Guthlac. The two Earth officers and Markham had drifted together. "The low profile suits me." He had already removed the memory bricks from the main control console. With Arthur Guthlac then immobilized and Markham commanding the troops hunting down the surviving enemy, he had been the senior military officer on the spot and no one questioned this. Their records should harvest valuable security data, and any untoward scenes that had been recorded could be discreetly removed.

Arthur Guthlac, his chest bound up and leg encased in a flexi-splint, was now walking again. The damage, in the event, had not required amputation and transplant, but even with modern nerve-and-bone growth factors it would be some days before he was fully healed. They had identified the quite simple mechanisms that controlled the Sinclair fields and were turning them off one by one.

"Well, somebody killed this one," said Arthur Guthlac, as the field before them died. "But a long time ago."

There was part of a human skeleton. Around the bare shin and ankle-bones were orange-and-black pseudo-Kzin-striped fabric trousers, much discolored. The pelvis was female. There was some dried, crumbling tissue on and in the torso and rib cage. There was no skull. Above the clavicles there was nothing.

"No," said Cumpston, "not a long time ago. That must be Henrietta, if she fell feet first into the field still alive. The lower part of her body would have passed into time-compression first. It received no blood-supply and her feet and legs were dead and decomposing by the time her heart passed into it. But her heart was still beating. Everything left in the circulatory system went into her head, which was still in normal time, and from which the blood had no way of returning at such speed. Bang! A quick way to die, at least from the brain's point of view, but the results aren't very cosmetic." *It was probably Henrietta,* he thought. *But she had not been the only one in that costume.* He would look at that later. But Henrietta officially dead would help defuse the time bomb of revenge on this planet. He might not look too hard.

The other bodies that concerned Cumpston, those that had gone into a Sinclair field already dead, would be either crumbling mummies or skeletons before long, depending on how much bacteria had been present. The longer it was before that particular field was found and deactivated, the less easy it would be to tell any cause of death. Certainly if laser wounds were still discernible it would be impossible by now to identify the laser that had caused them in the confused fighting. They had had the hallmarks of genuine ARM personnel, which another ARM could recognize, as there was something else some ARMs might also recognize, but despite what he had been told, Cumpston felt credentials and mannerisms could always be faked. Anyway, they might or might not have been Early's men. ARM was no monolith: It was, he felt, a series of interlocking and competing conspiracies like those fiendish things the kzinti called *w'kkai* puzzles. Well, when this place was cleaned up, all the bones of humans and kzinti would go for proper disposal. Manpower was still scarce on Wunderland, and police resources would hardly be used to investigate all the bones of kzinti victims that lay around.

"Where's Rykermann?"

"Sedated. He's had a rough time. It seemed to hit him all at once."

"What happened to Jocelyn?" Arthur Guthlac had asked this several times now. Cumpston had seen the phenomenon after battles before. People would keep asking the same question, but the answer would not stay in their heads.

"Nobody seems to know. But she had no motive to run away. That business with the laser . . . Accidents happen in battle. Everyone accepts that."

"I think she was in love with Nils Rykermann," said Markham. "Love can do strange things to people, I am told." He was speaking good English with a fierce effort and his face was impassive. *Betrayal! Stinking betrayal! But what else can one expect from prolevolk scum! And she used my Mother's name!*

If he saw Arthur Guthlac flinch, he betrayed no notice of the fact.

"Maybe after what happened she just took off. We'll look, of course. Maybe she'd had enough. She was a heroine of the Resistance. Maybe she'd just run out of . . . of . . ."

"We all feel that way sometimes . . . I'm told," said Cumpston. Markham said nothing, but his clenched hands were trembling minutely.

"I know it," said Guthlac. He sounded composed and normal, if a little sad. "And the Resistance's price on Henrietta's head?"

"I suppose if he pushed her into the field Raargh has the claim to it, if it's accepted that this is she," said Cumpston. "I haven't asked him, but he was in the area and she had kidnapped and insulted him and his protégé—dangerous business to kidnap a kzin. I can imagine how much the Resistance veterans who posted the bounty will enjoy handing it over to him! They may not come at it, of course, and he may not want it. She was loyal to Chuut-Riit after all. . . .

"Odd thing to say about the arch-collaborator," he went on, "but in her way she was loyal to humanity, too." *And was she altogether on the wrong track?* he wondered to himself, thinking of the last injunction of Chuut-Riit's testament. "I'm not sure it was Raargh who killed her. There were others with motive. But I'm not going to cross-examine him on the matter. . . .

"Anyway, he won't do too badly. You know there are females here. He acquires most of the property and the harems of all the kzinti he killed!"

"Good," said Arthur Guthlac.

"You're not getting fond of the old ratcat, are you?"

"No!" A slightly sheepish smile, and a laugh Guthlac cut off as his ribs pained him. "Well, to tell the truth, he did show up pretty well. I'm no kzin-lover yet, but perhaps my attitude's been a bit simplistic. I need to think. I've accumulated quite a lot of leave in the course of this war, and the time might be coming to take it. Probably take a couple of years to get my application through the bureaucracy, though. Leave would be good. Not alone, perhaps. . . . Where's Jocelyn?"

Chapter 11

The walls of the dean's interview room were heavy with antique books. A couple of ancient computers were preserved under transparent domes. There were paintings and even some marble busts of previous eminent members of the faculty. In another of its efforts toward reestablishing a milieu of scholastic tranquillity after decades of chaos and war, Munchen University had recently introduced gowns and mortarboards for both staff and students to wear for major interviews and other important occasions.

Nils Rykermann, his robe emblazoned with the esoteric colors and heraldry of his position, looked up from the application and assessment form.

"You're taking a big spread of subjects," he said. "Literature, history, political theory, physics and astrophysics, economics, chemical engineering, space mechanics, pure philosophy . . . and you want to do a unit of biology too. That's quite a load for a first-year student! We're going to have to bend the rules. Still, that's been done before for certain . . . exceptional cases."

"I hope to specialize eventually, Professor, but I feel I should get a good general background first."

"Joining the chess club, too, I see. Arthur Guthlac's become the patron, you know. When he came back from his leave at Gerning he decided to extend his posting on Wunderland. *And* the Drama Society! Are you sure you can manage it, Vaemar?"

"Oh yes, Professor!"

"Well, you must tell me if you find it too much. As dean of studies this year I will be responsible for your entire

297

performance beyond my own subject. . . . Your test scores are encouraging. . . . And your . . . er . . . Honored Sire Chuut-Riit . . . was clever enough."

"Yes, sir. I will not shame you. Nor him. Nor Honored Step-Sire Raargh-Hero."

"I'm sure you won't. But prove yourself here, Vaemar, and you will win a greater victory than many. . . . We have our first-semester field trip to the caves next month. You have some acquaintance with them already, and I'm sure you'll be an asset to us. We may regrow some of the smashed formations with Sinclair fields . . . How does your Honored Step-Sire Raargh-Hero fare?"

"He prospers, Professor. But my infant step-siblings *can* make it difficult to study. It can be noisy at home. Sometimes when I read they leap at my tail and bite it. My Honored Step-Sire Raargh-Hero counsels patience and self-control."

"Good training, Vaemar, and good counsel. You will need both."

Peter Robinson

2892 A.D.

A flock of big leather-flappers passed over the tent, filling the air with their cries. Gay Guthlac stirred against her husband, her head on his right shoulder, lips brushing his ear. "Noisy things," she murmured. He stroked her hair and she snuggled closer against him before drifting back to sleep. Sleeping plates were fine in space, but camping out in Wunderland's gravity they enjoyed the primitive novelty of a bed. They were falling in love with this multicolored world, and both had remarked the previous day that, long-settled as it was, it still had vast areas of vacant land.

Richard Guthlac turned his head to kiss his wife's sleeping face. His right arm lay along her back, his hand moving to caress the warm curved smoothness of her skin. The night beyond their tent's window was flooded with a shifting purple light: Alpha Centauri B rising with its glorious heralding of the true dawn. He found it harder than she to return to sleep immediately.

I am taking her into danger, he thought. *Each time we violate the tomb of an ancient horror, we risk unleashing monsters.*

And then he thought: *Well, it cuts two ways. Danger is part of our lives. We're spacefarers. We knew what went with the job when we started. It's better than living like flatlanders.*

The splinter of anxiety withdrew a little. He felt his thoughts beginning to wander as sleep claimed him again: *Our race can fight monsters now, and win. We were sheep once. If that ancient collision with the Kzin and all the centuries of war that followed taught us anything, it's that the sheep option isn't available.*

But that was not the only lesson it taught. Had there been other, subtler ones? Had it taught the Kzin anything?

Some of them, anyway.

The splinter of fear again: *But this is not about abstract concepts of the human race. This is about me and the woman I love as life itself.*

Gay stirred sleepily again, throwing one leg over his body, her hand caressing his chest. He turned into her embrace.

"I have a potentially difficult task for you, Charrgh-Captain," said Zzarrk-Skrull. He stood gazing out through the arrogantly wide castle window across the Hrungn Valley. His body was as motionless as if he were lying in wait for prey, and his right hand, claws half-extended, rested calmly on the periscope stand of an ancient Chunquen undersea ship, memento of an easy ancestral conquest, but his tail lashed, betraying disquiet.

"Command me, Sire!" Charrgh-Captain's own tail and ears stood erect with eagerness, and his whiskers bristled. If he had any private thought to the effect that a task which the Fleet Admiral described as potentially difficult must be daunting indeed, he kept it well hidden.

Zzarrk-Skrull paced a moment in the audience chamber before continuing. "I do not mean merely dangerous," he said, wrinkling his nose as if at a distasteful suggestion. "You may be called upon to exercise other qualities besides courage. Diplomacy . . . judgment. You will have to deal with humans in this task . . . and worse than humans."

"Puppeteers? I will do it, Sire! I serve the Patriarchy as ordered!" Things had changed since the old days. Kzinti dealt with alien races—some alien races—with diplomats and words and even contracts now instead of attack fleets. There was a growing number of kzinti *turrrissti* visiting alien worlds, often to ponder upon their ancestors' ancient battlefields, kzinti as employees and partners of various alien enterprises, even as employers of free aliens. . . . The Puppeteers were contemptible herbivores, but their trade empire had brought benefits. Most of them had left Known Space, and in their absence some kzinti were beginning to appreciate their value.

Zzarrk-Skrull's face took on a strange expression as he stood proud in his golden *hsakh* cloak and sash of Earth silk. It was also, for Charrgh-Captain, a secretly alarming one: High Kzinti officers are not easily disgusted.

"Urrr. Worse than Puppeteers. Hear me, Charrgh-Captain." Fleet Admiral Zzarrk-Skrull composed his face and ears, and continued:

"You may be aware of an unfortunate incident many years ago on the planet of Beta Lyrae that the humans name *Kuuborl*. We lost a ship called *Traitor's Claw* and a specialist crew under one Chuft-Captain. They had found a small stasis box used by tnuctipun, not Slavers."

Billions of years previously, depending on how various planets measured years, the ancient races of the thrint, the stupid but ruthless Slavers with their compulsive telepathic hypnosis, and the highly intelligent but at least equally ruthless tnuctipun, had fought a war that ended in omnicide: the thrintun, losing the war and about to be finally exterminated by their vengeful former slaves, had sent an amplified suicide command throughout the galaxy. Sentient life had ended, to evolve again only recently in galactic time.

Some Slaver and tnuctipun artifacts had been found: more-or-less mutated life-forms on various planets and in space, other things preserved unchanged in stasis boxes, one of the great feats of tnuctipun technology. Some stasis boxes had been highly dangerous. The danger most feared was that when stasis boxes were opened they might be found to contain live Slavers as well as artifacts. It had happened on a few occasions, in both kzinti and human space. The results had been fearful. But the contents of some stasis boxes had been priceless. Zzarrk-Skrull allowed himself a few lashes of his tail, and went on:

"There was a confrontation with humans. There was an explosion. One kzin survived: a telepath. Unfortunately he was injured early in events and could tell us little more, save that Chuft-Captain had opened the box and was performing various tests on the artifact it contained. Then, bang.

"That was all, but our agents learned other facts later. Of course the humans and the Puppeteer made their own reports."

"I read a little of the incident in my studies. One, or some, cowardly monkeys survived."

"Actually, the artifact contained, on a secret setting, an antimatter weapon capable of ripping a planet apart like a Chunquen's paunch, a war-winning weapon then or now."

"Arrrgh!"

"Yes, you may howl with anguish. Had Chuft-Captain had the wit merely to bring it back to us for our students to examine systematically, as he had been instructed to do with his captures, we might have had its secrets and your sires and mine might have been conquerors of monkeydom. But that was many years ago. Regrets are clawless now.

"I come to the meat. As a result of this, and certain other incidents where we and the humans disagreed over the discovery of stasis boxes, a new clause was added to the old McDonald-Rshshi Truce and the protocols that have evolved since. It has not been widely publicized.

"Should we discover a stasis box in a debatable or uncolonized area of space, the humans may send an observer to be present at its opening. Should the humans discover a stasis box in such an area, we may send an observer similarly. The observers have diplomatic privileges.

"I do not know what our Sires and predecessors would say of this, but we must deal with humans on many matters now. You know we have even joined with them on various official expeditions, including some to the Ringworld artifact.

"Charrgh-Captain, the humans of Ka'ashi have notified us that they have found a new stasis box. You will represent the Patriarch at its opening."

"I am honored, Sire, to represent the Patriarch in any capacity. Must I go again to a monkey-world?" A private thought: *Monkey-worlds are not too bad in small doses. Better than years in a spaceship habitat or under a bubble-dome, anyway. My posting to Earth had some entertainment, and I enjoyed hunting on Wunderl—on Ka'ashi.*

"Not for long. Only to Ka'ashi to join the expedition. The humans report the box was found floating in distant space. It is apparently larger than usual, and they have not tried to move it. All stasis boxes *may* be important, as the Beta Lyrae incident showed, and the stasis box there was small. This one may contain nothing useful. But sense suggests a large stasis box may be especially important. Perhaps especially dangerous."

"Sire, you know my liver burns to serve the Patriarch wherever I am sent, but duty impels me to express surprise that this task is not given to a Speaker-to-Anim . . . to a diplomat."

"You will be given diplomatic credentials. You have traveled and mixed with lesser species before without trouble: Plainly you have self-control. You have also shown yourself resolute, Heroic and able to make quick decisions. Names are given too easily nowadays, but you have earned yours. You speak Interworld and have studied human history. More to the point, you are an experienced military officer and pilot. Should the stasis box contain live Slavers, you will need to destroy them, irrespective of the humans' policies. Indeed, I gather the humans, weak creatures as they are, would be glad of a Hero's prowess in the event of such mutual danger.

"Should this stasis box contain a weapon, a war-winning weapon," the Fleet Admiral went on, "you may need to act at . . . discretion. The Alien Authority Lords did wish that a professional Speaker-to-Animals be sent, but authority above me held a professional fighter was necessary.

"You referred a few moments ago, Charrgh-Captain, to humans' cowardice. I have at times spoken similarly. Such is, of course, the tone of the studies you have diligently undertaken, and the way in which we have long spoken. It is also an objective fact that no aliens approach the courage of the Heroes' Race. Humans indeed may be rattle-brained often enough. Daffy monkeys. But *all* humans cowards? You know better. So, now, do we all. Be wary."

There were at least three points for Charrgh-Captain to ponder: first, for the Fleet Admiral to refer to a "truce" rather than a "treaty," to use the old and insulting job-title "Speaker-to-Animals" instead of the more modern "diplomat," and the old name *Ka'ashi* instead of the human *Wunderland* for the long-lost colony-world, told its own story; second, all kzintosh of the Patriarchy, military and civil, including diplomats and other specialists, had a high degree of military training, so this might be a task where extra-special abilities in that direction would be required; and third, in matters of this nature the only authorities above Fleet Admiral Zzarrk-Skrull were the Supreme Council of Lords and the Patriarch himself. *I am climbing into high trees,* he thought.

"I have spoken of the meat," said Zzarrk-Skrull. "I now speak of the offal. Obviously you will travel in a confining ship with humans."

"I believe I can endure it, Sire. I have traveled in human ships before."

"Allow me to finish. Urrr. There will not only be humans in this ship, but an . . . abomination."

"Sire?" If it was a human ship from Wunderland, he thought he could guess what the abomination was. Neither kzintosh wished to speak of such things.

Zzarrk-Skrull's face and ears wrinkled up as though he were tasting rancid sthondat-flesh. "There is a certain logic in it. When investigating the Slavers, thoughts may need to be read. Or we could take it as a deliberate insult. However, the Patriarchy and the Supreme Council have resolved to accept it. We have little choice. They have beaten us in six wars . . . but who knows? Perhaps the contents of this box will ensure that they will not beat us again. It is worth eating a little kasht."

"Is there hope of another war, Sire?"

"A Hero who delivered to the Patriarchy a war-winning weapon would find Glory," said the Fleet Admiral. "A Full Name would be certain. . . . There have been instances in our history, though none of late, where that Full Name has been completed by the suffix 'Riit.' You speak of hope? My own Sires would have hoped for nothing else. . . ."

A fourth point to ponder there, certainly; I bring home the weapon that smashes the human empire and I will be promoted to Royalty. And a fifth point, too: Our ancestors hoped for nothing but another war. Do we?

The representative of the Institute of Knowledge on Wunderland was of course a Jinxian. To other humans he looked almost cubical. As he spoke to Richard and Gay Guthlac he also looked benign, like a huge garden ornament cast rather crudely in concrete. His apparent good temper was easy to understand. In Wunderland's gravity he had the strength of a superman and did not need a heart-booster.

"As you've probably guessed," he said, "this expedition's budget comes from a grant to the Institute by the General Products Foundation. The Puppeteers—whatever rump of an organization they've left in Known Space—don't like undertaking such ventures themselves. They want us to do it."

"How did the Puppeteers find it?"

"I don't know. They have activities they're discreet about, even now. Also they've had more dealings with the Outsiders than we. Perhaps the Outsiders told them."

"There's also, of course, a military aspect. A *human* military aspect. With the approval of the UNSN the Foundation has given us weaponry that should be enough to handle any trouble—and you both hold UNSN Reserve commissions, as do Melody and Peter Robinson, and as do I, for that matter. If it comes to a military situation, you'll be wearing those hats. As captain of the ship, Richard will of course command in that situation as well."

"Why not a bigger crew?" asked Richard Guthlac.

"Money, as usual. The General Products Foundation has had little income since most of the Puppeteers quit Known Space. The few that remain have, as far as we know, been more concerned with winding up existing enterprises than with starting new trade or supporting abstract knowledge.

"But they evidently think a new stasis box is worth having someone investigate. It reinforces my suspicions, for what they're worth, that, wherever the Puppeteers have gone, they've not gone as far or as fast as we thought. If their fleet had been travelling FTL for more than two hundred years, why should they bother with something so far behind them?

"And you should have enough talents between you to cover all emergencies," he went on. "You know the drill with the contents of stasis boxes: If they are safe, bring them home, if they are dangerous, destroy them."

He paused. Richard was suddenly struck by the thought that his benign expression had more to do with his extraordinary musculature than any internal contentment. His eyes were those of a worried man.

"To persevere in opening stasis boxes at all has always been a difficult policy decision, with many opposed to it. However the majority view at the Institute—and . . . er . . . other authorities . . . is that if we'd let the danger prevent us opening any stasis boxes, ever, we'd have passed up a great deal of priceless knowledge. So far, our procedures have worked. You yourselves have retrieved and opened three without trouble, so you're the obvious choice for this job."

"Perhaps we were just lucky. We found no live Slavers."

"Perhaps. But in any event the danger wouldn't deter our furry friends: whatever their paranoia they are brave. For many reasons—and the Puppeteers concur with this quite definitely—we can't let our fears give them a monopoly of stasis-box discoveries.

"Of course, it's not their own necks the Puppeteers risk—did you know that when they first revealed themselves to Pierson, we actually named them after their appearance rather than their preferred mode of operation? Anyway, it's you who'll be at the sharp end.

"You may have to make a quick judgment, and in the event of encountering live Slavers, a small crew like yours is as good as an army. We are sure Slavers coming out of stasis will need some time to orient themselves. We hope Peter Robinson will give us an edge there: He can tell us instantly of any active Slaver minds. Don't use that time to speculate or anything else, just launch your missiles and never mind the knowledge that may be lost. That is, of course, a direct order given from under my military hat."

He paused for a moment to let that one sink in.

"Your observer from the Patriarchy is one Charrgh-Captain, a naval officer who has had off-world postings as an attaché. I met him when he was here previously. I think he's a fairly typical kzin of the officer class. 'Captain' is our translation of a term whose significance varies, but in his case he's in a senior grade—about the equivalent of a colonel as far as there's an equivalent. I expect he'll support a strike on the box if the situation calls for it, but he's an observer only, with no power except to make recommendations. He's under your orders in any emergency. . . .

"Just make sure, if it's something the kzinti would regard as, er, useful—I think you know what I mean—that he doesn't . . . step beyond the protocols. Kill him without hesitation, if necessary, and we'll cook up some cover story. Plausible accidents can always happen in space." *Killing any adult male kzin is not exactly easy,* Richard thought. *Oh, and to make it a little more challenging, this one just happens to be a professional military officer as well. I suppose this Jinxian has had kamikaze combat training and wears a Hellflare tattoo, though discreetly out of sight in these peaceful days. When, incidentally, killing a kzin would be treated as murder, and killing a kzin colonel, if it got back to the Patriarchy, would be a good deal worse. It might even mean extradition for us if the Kzin insisted. And they would. I had forgotten how many Jinxians have chips on those vast shoulders of theirs and enjoy putting us beanpole-men and our willowy women on the spot.*

"And Peter Robinson?" said Gay. "How is Charrgh-Captain going to like him?"

"He isn't. But he's got no choice. Don't worry, kzinti can be more adaptable than you might think. They're cats, after all. They'll growl and snarl, but they'll accept a situation they can't change, provided you leave them a way to do it that doesn't compromise their dignity or honor."

"We know."

"It's when they get *really* adaptable, of course, that they get dangerous. Some geneticists say the wars have changed the kzinti gene pool to produce less aggressive, less ferocious kzin. I wonder if they've rather produced more cunning kzin, capable of biding their time, and this time not attacking till they're good and ready. . . .

"Speaking of adaptability," he went on, "even with hyperdrive the trip will take several months. That's another reason the crew is small: Your salaries will be loaded to compensate for the time out of your lives and general inconvenience. You'll have to spend time in hibernation or standing watch alone, almost as in the STL days."

"Just how *much* will our salaries be loaded?" asked Richard.

"Adequately. I have the contracts here. A bigger crew would mean more divisions of a limited cake. Don't forget, the stock market has had some rocky times since the Puppeteer pullout. We're reconstructing our economies successfully, but a new golden age isn't going to come overnight. In fact, we are lucky to have an expedition even of this size. At least"—this time he really did laugh—"even if your crew is small, you have all the talents."

Whomping Wallaby was a General Products #3 hull. Puppeteer-produced, it was spacious for the six crew, though its life-system, with kzin as well as human requirements to cater for, was relatively complex, and kzinti liked lots of elbow-room. The hull was thought to be indestructible and impenetrable to anything but visible light, which interior paint kept out. It was well-fitted with computers and a laboratory, boats, ground craft and an outfit of heavy weapons, including a laser cannon and bomb-missiles. It was standard in well-armed research ships (and all research ships were well-armed) to fit discreet precautions against their being misappropriated, but it was also considered bad form to discuss these. It was a legend that all such expeditions still carried at least one covert ARM agent, though ARM's unseen grip on human society was reputed to have been weakening for some time. It was also now standard for ships fitted out for possible dealing with Slaver stasis boxes to carry self-destructs. General Products had provided all the nonpersonal equipment, including the boats and weapons. Puppeteers were pacifists themselves except in direst need, but that did not prevent them making effective weaponry. There was human and kzin medical equipment, including a kzin military autodoc.

Melody Fay, the representative of the Institute of Knowledge on the expedition as well as weapons and security officer, was another blocklike Jinxian with a penetrating voice. Probably, Richard thought, she also wore the Hellflare tattoo. *I hope it stays out of sight,* he thought, and for more, he reflected a little uncharitably, than diplomatic reasons: The idea of seeing her naked was frankly unappealing. She was Jinxian in manner as well as appearance, given to striking her chest boomingly for emphasis. Jinxian females in lower-gravity societies, perhaps even more than their male counterparts, tended to have a mental armor of defensiveness and aggression.

Gatley Ivor was a tall, thin Wunderlander and specialist in the study of Slaver Empire relics. He still wore the asymmetrical beard that had been a status mark for aristocratic Wunderlanders of past generations. Although with modern medicines the physical age of human adults was hard to tell, his speech and mannerisms were those of a very old man in whose body those medicines were not working perfectly.

All the talents! Richard thought, recalling the Jinxian's words as they stowed their gear. *This is a crew about as ill-assorted as it is possible to get, even before our other members join.*

✧   ✧   ✧

"My cabin will be *completely* secure?" Peter Robinson, junior partner of Robinson and Son, Mental Investigations, seconded to the Institute-Guthlac Expedition, asked for the third time. He pitched his hat into one corner of the cabin, took off his sunglasses, and wiped them with a nervous gesture.

"Yes. Completely. Remember this is a Puppeteer-built ship."

"I don't know if you understand how fearf—how difficult it is for me to be sharing a ship with a specimen of *Pseudofelis sapiens ferox* . . . with a kzintosh of the Patriarchy."

"You won't have to mix until we get there. And he is a diplomat, bound by protocols," Gay assured him again.

"I will have to use my will to assert dominance," said Peter Robinson. "And not just once as in normal civilized society of our kind, but continually. This will be an ordeal. He will try to destroy me, either by crushing me psychologically, or physically. I will not let him. But I wish there was a human telepath good enough to do this job. I have a nice business and plenty of work here on Wunderland."

"There isn't," said Richard. "But," he added awkwardly after a pause, "this kzintosh is a representative of the Patriarch, no less, and bears the Patriarch's sigril. It embarrasses me but must ask you: Are you sure you will feel no conflict of loyalty?"

"I once saw a real kzinti telepath," said Peter Robinson. "A dribbling, vomiting, twitching freak, despised by all and doomed to die a terrible death after a short life of misery and degradation.

"In thousands of years the laboratories and science of the Patriarchy never tried to find a drug that would allow us to function without destroying us. Research along those lines was even deliberately forbidden: The Patriarchy did not want strong or sane telepaths. The human laboratories on Wunderland found such a drug only a few years after the Liberation, and since then we Wunderkzin telepaths can live almost normal lives. Liberation! Can you have any doubt where my loyalties lie?"

He paused, and stared into Richard's eyes.

"I will not deny that there are times I look in a mirror and ask: 'What am I? What are my kind? Where do we go?' I am not free of everything. . . . But I saw a kzinti telepath once."

Most kzin, even if they had a perfect academic grasp of human languages, spoke them with a harsh, grating tone. Peter Robinson's vocal chords had been altered by microsurgery when he was young. It was strange to hear the perfect, almost accentless Interworld, with only traces of the now-dead language and accent of Wunderlander, from the fanged jaws of Man's ancient enemy.

"You did say my cabin will be secure?"

Charrgh-Captain arrived from Kzin by a regular flight. His Interworld was fluent, but his voice could never be taken for human. He handed over his credentials, retaining a bag with diplomatic markings for himself, and briefly acknowledged the human members of the crew. At the sight of Peter Robinson he curled his lip and said nothing. He thought something, though, and Richard and Gay saw Peter Robinson flinch. He shuffled backward into his cabin, looking more like a telepath of the Patriarchy than they had ever seen him look. Then suddenly he came out again and returned Charrgh-Captain's stare. Then he burst forth:

"I am a Wunderkzin and my destiny is my own. Regarding low Kdaptists I have nothing to say. Neither I nor my ancestors have committed any crime against the Patriarchy save to assert our freedom after you lost a war. You have no legal rights over our kind and no claims against us. The Patriarchy conceded that in the McDonald-Rshshi Treaty and the protocols.

"Further, Wunderland jurisprudence is still derived from the old Law and our independence is established by legal precedent. I refer you to *Sraakra-Rykermann v. Representatives of the Patriarchy*, cited in the 154th Edition of *Nichols on Police Offenses*."

Charrgh-Captain was moved to snarl back, but in Interworld rather than the Heroes' Tongue.

"I have no interest. We signed those truces when we were defeated and had no choice! Do not speak of them!"

"But sign them you did. Have your kind not voiced contempt for the humans who say a promise made under duress does not bind? And as for being defeated, would you hazard another war now?"

"We rebuild our Empire with the hyperdrive, smug freak. But fear not this day. My diplomatic status protects you."

Peter Robinson closed the door again. This time he locked it.

Charrgh-Captain inspected his own quarters and assured himself that the kitchen and food supplies were suitable for kzin needs. He ran a quick eye over their stores in general and a rather more thorough one over their weapons. He stared coldly at the kzin autodoc, though with many kzinti traveling on human ships now it was no longer on the military secret list. He checked it without comment. There was little more to be done. He watched as Richard and Gay went through the takeoff checks.

The *Whomping Wallaby* climbed out of the vast singularity of the Centauri system and dropped into hyperdrive.

Few humans or Kzin can stand to "look" upon Hyperspace
for long, and there is no purpose in trying to do so. For
most of its flight the *Wallaby*'s ports were opaqued. A crew
member remained on watch in case of emergencies, which
would mainly concern the life-system, but automatic pilot
and mass-detector—the latter considered by many a greater
technological miracle than the hyperdrive shunt itself—flew
the ship.

Most spacefarers of all kinds adjust to the long watches alone
or with a skeleton crew while their shipmates hibernate. It
is also a widespread ritual of human space travel that
changeover time is leisurely. This is not merely for debrief-
ing and briefing: The retiring crew member, if he or she has
stood watch alone, is usually hungry for company and conversation before returning to hibernation, and the relieving crew
member needs time to adjust.

Gatley Ivor, first on watch, had spent changeover rambling
gently to Melody Fay about the antiquities he loved. Charrgh-
Captain, who took over from Melody, was the only one who
had not obeyed—and possibly did not know of—this convention
of relaxed talk, though in his case no one would have insisted
upon it, and the Jinxian apparently did not care for Kzin
company in any case. His hand-over report to Gay had been
brief and to the point, though comprehensive. She had no idea
whether the big kzin was hardened against loneliness and bore-
dom or simply not prepared to betray feeling them. But to a
previous generation the idea of entrusting the watch of a
human ship to a kzin of the Patriarchy would have been
beyond belief in any case. Gay spoke long to Peter Robinson
when she handed over to him in turn.

The watches aboard the *Whomping Wallaby* had had to be
planned with some care. Richard relieved Peter Robinson to
take what they calculated would be the last watch of the
voyage. They inspected the ship and the log, and settled down
in the couches on what was still called the bridge for a
bourbon and ice cream together.

Peter Robinson knew the ritual even if he did not need it.
And perhaps he does need it, thought Richard. *He is far more
talkative and gregarious than any kzin of the Patriarchy—
anxious to prove his human credentials, perhaps. And his pref-
erence for being called by his full name—there are two
explanations for that, of course: While on the one hand it*

reinforces his Wunderkzin identity, on the other hand in kzin society a full name is the rare and ultimate sign of high nobility.

Aloud he said: "I hope the watch was not too boring."

"Being alone for a while is no great hardship for me," the Wunderkzin replied. "The computer's gaming skills are adequate without being overwhelming, and I have my sculpting tool and my poetry. There is my little laboratory, and I enjoy experiments—I assure you I stick to safe ones in these circumstances. I do not miss my mate much without her scent. To me being on watch in a spaceship when all others aboard sleep is the equivalent of silence, such as I only know otherwise sometimes in the wilder parts of Wunderland. It is very peaceful. It is precious to me.

"The human drugs are incomparably kinder than the sthondat drugs of the Patriarchy, but they are not perfect, nor do they armor us against all the ordinary neuroses of telepathy, which even human telepaths—such as they are—are subject to. We fight battles always against too much empathy, against losing ourselves in other minds—with the glands of hunting carnivores who can never enjoy the chase and kill of our prey as even an ordinary nontelepathic Wunderkzin of Arhus or the Hohe Kalkstein may. Have you seen what we eat? Either animals too mindless to know terror, or meat made to move artificially, or dead meat. The one time I tried to eat Zianya was terrible for me. . . . Still, it is a small price to pay. But sometimes I have waves of fear."

"What do you do?"

"What can I do? I shield and carry on. . . . Everyone I touch leaks a little. One human aboard this ship is keeping a secret of which I sense enough to guess the rest without probing. I will say no more of that. I do not think it has a vital bearing on the success of this mission, and we have vows not to divulge any such secrets we may stumble on save in direst emergency. Better for me to keep my shield strong. . . .

"At least, my friend, I *know* that you do not dislike me. Nor Gay. I have not tried to probe the minds of any aboard here, but all give forth a general . . . coloration, an aura. Hers is one mind whose aura I enjoy. I do not mind if you and Gay call me by my first Name alone."

Richard said, "Gay dislikes very little that lives. She found me when I was broken and unlovable, and rebuilt me. . . . You are a telepath on a human world. You must know the darknesses in which humans can live."

"Yes. And once or twice in my work I have found myself screaming and leaping as a result. Angry enough to use my claws and fangs as well as the Telepath's Weapon. Some human poetry is dangerous for the likes of me to read, you know. Chuut-Riit set 'The Ballad of the White Horse' as a text for the human-students of his day:

> *"While there is one tall shrine to shake*
>   *Or one live man to rend;*
> *For the wrath of the gods behind the gods*
>   *Who are weary to make an end.*

> *"There lives one moment for a man*
>   *When the door at his shoulder shakes,*
> *When the taut rope parts under the pull,*
>   *And the barest branch is beautiful*
> *One moment, while it breaks.*

> *"So rides my soul upon the sea*
>   *That drinks the howling ships,*
> *Though in black jest it bows and nods*
>   *Under the moon with silver rods,*
>   *I know it is roaring at the gods,*
>   *Waiting the last eclipse . . .*

" 'Think on, of those who write so,' he said. But there is other:

> *"The world is so full of a number of things,*
> *I am sure we should all be as happy as kings.*

"I think, if I may say so to you, that Gay thinks like that latter. But I know the darknesses in which kzin can live, too. I know it well. Charrgh-Captain . . ." To a knowledgeable observer, his body language said more than his words.

"Does he distress you so much?"

"Yes. Like many kzintosh of his generation, he has no religious faith. Why believe in the Fanged God who gave kzinti the Universe and domination of all life when humans keep winning the wars? But that does not modify his loathing of me. On the contrary, it increases it. When you have lost anything to worship, it is a comfort to find something to despise. Thank the God I am good at shielding. I work at it."

"And how do you feel about the Fanged God, Peter?" It was one of those questions spacers on watch could ask one another.

"We high Wunderkzin are not low Kdaptists. Some of us believe Fanged God and Bearded God have their own kingdoms.

Others have conceptions more subtle: that the Fanged God is the heroic aspect of the Bearded God, who being omnipotent has no need for heroism."

"In Christianity the Incarnation is meant to solve that problem: God had to know by experience everything human, including courage and even despair: 'My God! my God! Why have You forsaken me?' "

"We never despair. In any case, I do not necessarily speak for myself. And there are other things. For the relatively few of us on Wunderland there are many sects. Be assured we do not dress in human skins for our services or make chalices and candlesticks of human bones, as the low Kdaptists do. But Charrgh-Captain believes in nothing beyond the material. Or so he thinks. Yet he also thinks his values are those of the old Kzin culture. Like so many adult kzintosh of the Patriarchy today, there is great confusion in him. Once there was a haunting fear, never, never admitted, that the fabled Free Jotok Fleet would return with vengeance. More lately humans have been seen by a few as avatars of the Free Jotok—who probably do not exist. My own fears are different, perhaps a little more human: to have some great task, some great test, and fail—that fear comes to me sometimes at a late hour. Fear of being proven to be a Nothing, a creature of neither world. Charrgh-Captain would never think of failure. He would conquer or die."

"Is he dangerous, do you think?"

Peter Robinson extended one set of black-tipped claws whose curvature shone like steel, claws that could have torn a man apart with a single leisurely pass, and a tiger with a couple more. "He is a kzin."

He paused and added: "As I am not."

"I don't know whether you say that as boast or complaint, my friend."

"I don't know either. But as I have paced the silent corridors of this ship, while I have enjoyed the silence, I have been glad my friends were sleeping near me. Is that foolish?"

"No."

"The founder of our line was raised by humans when he was a war-orphaned kitten, found blind and starving for his mother's milk. But when he was old enough he made a conscious choice.

"And you gave us a chance to rise . . . more than we would have given you. Great-Grandsire was proud, *proud*, when he became the first Wunderland Kzin elected to an office by humans. The old fellow still talks about that day. When he made a speech to the Wunderland Assembly—'Let us grow together: not an imitation cat but a better human,' he said, thinking of Markham and what had happened to him, 'not an imitation human but a better cat'—and they applauded, he recorded the applause and laid down the recording in the new family shrine. He said we had found our own Honor."

"He knew about Markham? I only learned of that when I gained the security clearance for this work."

"One of many secrets we had."

"The first of my family to set foot on Wunderland," said Richard, "was a staff officer with the Liberation forces. On one leave after the cease-fire he was hunting in Gerning and came across a cottage in the forest.

"It was occupied by an old lady, a proud, impoverished aristocrat, pure Nineteen Families blood, long since come down in the world, living alone with a couple of animals and with a little charity from the nearby farmers. Post-Liberation Wunderland had a lot of rather queer fish, of course. I suppose it still does. . . .

"The place was dilapidated, and he did a few chores and repairs for her. She gave him tea in an ornate old service of genuine Neue Dresden china, apologizing for the lack of servants. Not unexpectedly, she came to talk of the 'Good Old Days,' and how much better things were then. She missed her lost boys. Arthur was always interested in history—he'd worked in a museum before the war—and he took notes.

"It took him quite a long time—plus a reference by her to 'those nice big pussycats'—to realise that she was actually talking about the Occupation, and her 'boys' were a couple of kzin officers of the local garrison who for some reason had made a pet of her—if they were in the vicinity and wanted to sharpen their claws, they might do it by tearing a pile of wood into kindling for her. If they were hunting in the forest and had made a kill, they might throw her a haunch of meat as they passed. I *suppose* that meant non-monkey meat. She gave them bowls of cream. I doubt they realized how she thought of them. . . . She was quite mad, of course. But that, coming on top of a couple of things that had happened to him on Wunderland earlier and later, influenced old Arthur's thinking. His story, "Three at a Table," has become a family legend. He'd been an Exterminationist, but he ended up patron of the first official mixed chess club."

"Quite mad, as you say. . . . And Wunderland still does have a lot of queer fish . . . like me."

"We like Wunderland," said Richard. "Partly because of the queer fish. We've been thinking of settling there."

"May I say . . . I hope you do."

"Only five hundred and forty million years ago, billions of years after the time when the thing we seek was built," said Richard, "our ancestors on Earth lived in a placid sea. They were parading the vicinity of the Burgess Shale on multiple jelly legs. Your ancestors and ours cannot have looked much different."

"We know thrint and tnuctipun planted common life-forms throughout the galaxy," Peter Robinson replied. "You and I are alike enough to indicate common primordial ancestors."

"Alike enough to eat each other. I do not mean that observation to be cruel or offensive, but it emphasizes our common biology."

"Also, there have been speculations that the telepaths' power is somehow—I know not how—related to the Slaver Power—some inherited vestige of tnuctipun biological engineering, perhaps? Something in our nucleonic acid? A laboratory experiment that was thrown away and survived?"

"It's hard to see how that could be. Thrint and kzin are not contemporaries by billions of years."

"I find much hard to see. You will have another bourbon? You face quite a long watch."

"I'm used to it. It goes with the job."

"A lot goes with my job." The Wunderkzin said, "Thank you for being my . . . friend, Richard. It will be good to go to sleep with that emotion in my mind."

"The human race as it is today evolved out of a lot of different breeds," said Richard awkwardly. "You've seen that on Wunderland. A lot of humans must have asked at times: 'What am I?' But in the end we shook down fairly well."

"I wonder if they ever asked as emphatically as I do," said Peter Robinson, "and who they asked."

Richard was still on watch when the mass-detector dropped the *Wallaby* out of hyperspace. The nearest stars were distant but the singularity that was a stasis field was sharp and bright in the center of the radar screen. By the time the awakened crew assembled on the bridge it had grown.

Behind it was a deep-radar ghost. The artifact was in wide orbit around a flattened sphere—a free-floater planet, dark and cold, a gas giant too small to glow. How had the Puppeteers found this thing?

"Big," said Melody. "Bigger than we thought."

"It certainly is," said Richard. "As a matter of fact it is in visual range now."

"It's too far away!"

Richard touched the control panel. Spotlights flooded space, and illuminated nothing except a silver bead.

A pale gray sphere. With nothing to give a scale it was impossible for the unaided eye to tell how big it was. But there was a scale projected on the screen. And it was growing. There were a few circles like shallow, immensely eroded craters. The *Wallaby* orbited it, cameras busy. There were darker patches and one black spot. It looked much like the Moon seen from Earth.

"Where on the surface is the stasis box?" asked Gatley Ivor. "Or is it buried?"

"That is the point: the deep radar lacks fine definition yet, but it appears to be almost *all* stasis field. It is about nine miles in diameter."

"The Puppeteers did not tell us it was so big," said Melody.

"I suspect they may not have known. Perhaps they only picked it up on their deep radar at extreme range as a point whose magnitude had to be guessed. They would be too cautious to explore further themselves. Or perhaps they never saw it—the Outsiders may have told them about it. I suspect they have a standing order with the Outsiders to buy information about any stasis boxes they come across, but perhaps they thought they could no longer afford to pay extra for details like size."

"If that is so, whether it was caution or miserliness that prevented them knowing, they made a mistake," said Peter Robinson. "Had they explored boldly, or bought full information, they would have discovered it is too big for an expedition of this size."

"A Hero—a kzin—is not daunted by size," said Charrgh-Captain.

"I think," said Richard, "it may not have been caution only. With so few Puppeteers left in known space, their resources and personnel are stretched thin. A Puppeteer ship that detected this at very long range would probably have been on business it could not divert from. As for miserliness, if they bought the information about it from Outsiders, well, we know the Outsiders do not sell information cheaply."

"Perhaps," said Gay, "when they saw an asteroid and then a stasis field indicated from a distance on deep-radar, they thought the field was somewhere on the asteroid, as we just did. They did not realize the asteroid was the whole stasis field."

"In any event," said Peter Robinson, "you must agree it is too big for us to open. It is far bigger than any spaceship I have heard of. Assuming that this giant stasis field contains an artifact of a size to justify it, the chances are that there are live Slavers within. We are not equipped to handle them if they are released."

"I am tempted in one part of me to proceed," said Gatley Ivor. "There may be more knowledge of the ancients here than the total of all that has been gathered to date. And yet every rational instinct says this is too big for us. I must say reluctantly that we should return with a bigger expedition—perhaps a warship."

"Would that not simply be presenting the Slavers with the warship, should they seize the minds of its crew?" asked Charrgh-Captain. "Think of human history and your Napoleon's march on Paris after his escape from Elba—the monkeys sent to capture him simply joined him, and the more that were sent the bigger his army became."

"Can the Slaver Power penetrate a General Products hull?" demanded Melody.

"I believe it can," Gatley Ivor said. "First, because the Power is not a physical event and is not governed by the laws of physics. It is not a wave effect, nor does it depend on particles. Further, we know from ample experience that a General Products hull does not block the probing of kzinti—or even human— telepaths. Matter does not shield against telepathy."

Charrgh-Captain's tail lashed. His ears knotted and unknotted. A kzin like Charrgh-Captain could not—physically *could not*— admit before either aliens or his own kind that he was too fearful to execute a task.

If we return for reinforcements, Richard thought, *Charrgh-Captain will, quite legally, report the situation to the Patriarchy. Diminished as they are, they still, unlike us, have a command economy. By the time we, or the human bureaucracy, raises the finance for a bigger expedition, the Kzin might easily be here and have it open.*

"It is too important simply to leave," said Melody Fay.

"What I am saying when I say it is too big," said Gatley Ivor, "is that I see a *high* probability there are Slavers inside it. It is much more than a mere good chance. A stasis field of this size plainly contains something on the order of a spaceship or a space station. Or perhaps it was once an installation on the surface of a planet that has disappeared. I have never heard of one so big. Surely it will be crewed. Perhaps it contains a Slaver army. And one Slaver alone would be more than danger enough!"

Charrgh-Captain bridled again at the mention of danger, but his ears settled back into a position of tacit acceptance and his tail stilled. Richard saw him curl it out of the way with a conscious motion. The big kzin might not like the suggestion that he would shy from danger, but this was plainly something beyond the normal. The threat of live Slavers might daunt the boldest of any species.

"At any rate," said Richard, "now that we are here, let us explore what we may. Our sponsors will hardly be pleased if we come away without having done that. First, we should make a survey of the accretion material and see where underneath it the stasis field begins. We can send progress reports back by hyperwave."

No one disagreed.

"Comparing the radar pictures and what we can see visually," Richard said a few hours later, "we see a difference: The stasis field's mostly, as we suspected, a sphere, covered with a layer, or if you like a shell, of accreted material. However, at one point on the sphere there's a pocket, a sort of dimple, in the field.

"It looks small by comparison with the big field, but in fact it has quite a large volume: larger than our own hull. Deepradar shows it's divided into various compartments. Also it contains smaller stasis boxes—a very dangerous set-up—and an odd linear structure. It reminded me at first of a spinal column but on finer resolution it's more like a string of large beads laid out in a row. . . . It has a cover fitting flush with the surface so the spherical outline is not disturbed."

"That would be where that black mark is?"

"Yes. In fact it's a hole. An obvious possibility is that it's where the mechanism for turning off the field was housed. It may still be there. Apart from the access face, which is flush with the sphere's surface, it's surrounded by the field on five sides and well protected."

"Then we examine it," said Charrgh-Captain. "With suitable caution."

Melody Fay remained in *Wallaby* at the weapons console. Her task was simple: Any slightest suggestion of the Slaver power or other threatening activity, and she was to use the moments she had to strike a button. *Wallaby* would cut loose with every weapon. That was assuming she could recognize the power before it gripped her. The rest of the expedition embarked in *Joey, Wallaby*'s main shuttle craft.

The black mark grew on the surface of the great globe as they approached.

"Not well protected enough," said Charrgh-Captain after a time. "Something has smashed through it. A meteor, perhaps."

"Odd that it should have struck in the one vulnerable spot," said Peter Robinson.

"It is the one spot such a strike would now show," said Charrgh-Captain in a tone of freezing contempt. "The stasis box may have passed through a meteor swarm. Or been bombarded in battle. Even without other explosives, every other hit would have vaporized on impact with the field from its own kinetic energies. That may contribute to the high metal content in the stony plating over the thing."

"To have once encountered a meteor-swarm it must have drifted a long way," said Gay. "This part of space is empty."

"We know it has drifted a long way," said Charrgh-Captain. "It has been drifting for billions of your years and ours."

"Perhaps it was deliberately attacked," said Richard.

"We may soon see," said Charrgh-Captain.

The stony surface of the sphere had grown to fill all the lower viewport now. The black mark was a jagged hole, surrounded by the rim of a shallow crater.

Joey's landing legs touched. Natural gravity was negligible, but the craft's externally mounted gravity motors cut in, anchoring it firmly. The old kzinti gravity-planer had been obsolete as a space drive since the hyperdrive ended the First Man-Kzin War centuries previously and given, eventually, both species an open doorway to the distant stars, but kzin gravity technology still had a multitude of uses.

There was no need for ladders to descend. A gentle push and they each floated down, falling slowly through the great hole that meteor or missile had smashed through layers of super-hard shielding. There were edges of twisted metal, but even if these had not been eroded by the eons, they were unlikely to tear the fabric of modern space-suits. The hole narrowed somewhat toward the bottom. They pulled themselves on and down and into what must be the control-chamber. They activated the magnets in their boots. Their lights showed hulking machinery, wreckage and dust.

There was a silence they could sense even through space suit com-links. There were dark looming shapes, and the first beams of their lights illuminated little. Though the chamber occupied only a tiny part of the volume of the sphere, they realized properly now how big it was in its own right. Doors showed it was subdivided.

"I feel no trace of life," said Peter Robinson. He continued after a moment: "I do not know if it is autosuggestion, but the age of this place weighs upon me."

"I feel it too," said Gay. Charrgh-Captain growled. All kzin with their highly developed hunting instincts, even non-telepaths, were more sensitive to atmosphere than humans, but they did not like admitting it in such circumstances.

"Why is the dust swirling?" snarled Charrgh-Captain suddenly. "Have we live enemies?" He was holding a flashlight laser. Gatley Ivor gave a cry of dismay.

"It is the outwash effect our gravity-planer," said Richard after a moment. "We can probably use the effect to blow dust out the hole if we need to clear it further. Luckily the rim of the crater has prevented more dust drifting down here from the surface."

"I am sorry," said Gatley Ivor.

He doesn't seem up to much, thought Richard. *This is his job. He should be used to it, more knowledgeable, even more excited, thinking of the papers and books he will get out of this if nothing else. I wonder if there is something phony about him.* Then, more charitably: *But this isn't an experience you can rehearse for. And this place would put anyone on edge. Unless, perhaps, you have the nerves of a warrior kzin and are on edge all the time.*

They turned their lamps to full flood, and looked about.

Wreckage was obvious, and so was decay. Metal once superhard was disintegrating through sheer age. Richard pointed to objects like crazed mirrors, standing deep in dust. "More stasis-fields," he commented.

"Look more attentively," said Charrgh-Captain, "They are thrintun spacesuits. And they are occupied."

None of the party found it easy to look at the group without qualms. Six bipedal shapes, about half the size of a man, standing as they had stood for billions of years. Each spacesuit, they guessed, contained a thrint. Indeed it was possible to make out, or to least to fancy, the shapes of their individual features— the squat bodies, the gaping slashes of mouths in prominent jaws, the single disk of an eye, the bulged heads whose brains contained the Slaver Power: projective telepathy.

"These cannot harm us at present," said Charrgh-Captain, "and there are evidently none in a condition that can. If monkey hands stay off them, there is no need for you to fear."

"It isn't exactly fear," said Gay.

"I know," said Charrgh-Captain. His vocal cords were ill-suited for expressing emotion in Interword, but those two words carried a hint of apology. All thinking beings who knew the terrible history of the ancients felt something beyond fear for the Slaver Power. "But they will have switches on those suits, if they have not decayed away entirely, to kill the stasis fields.

They will be protruding beyond the fields themselves. I recommend no tampering. At least we know now that it is a thrint stasis box, not a tnuctipun one. I suggest that before we conclude this expedition we drop them into a sun with a long life-expectancy. It would be satisfactory if the radiations and temperatures involved operated the mechanism and opened their suits for them *then*. It might happen. But what is this?"

"More stasis boxes?"

"*Some* of them are stasis boxes."

A row of spherical objects, each like a large model of the vast stasis field in a pocket of which they were standing. The top of each sphere was about twice the height of the kzinti, who stood in their spacesuits and helmets more than nine feet tall. They were mostly mirror-bright, though in the weak gravity of the chamber, dust had come to rest on parts of them in odd patterns. Gatley Ivor reached up to one and pulled away like orange peel a band of dust particles cemented together by time and vacuum. It had no adhesion to the surface of the field. Charrgh-Captain glared and growled at him. Partway along there was a break in the row. There was a sphere, nearly the same size as the stasis fields, showing not the mirror of stasis, but ancient metal, its top opened and slid aside. It was cracked and shattered. It appeared that its stasis field had been off and it had been involved when the chamber had been damaged. Past it were more metal spheres, stretching away in a line. Some of these were also more or less damaged and all had been opened.

"I don't understand," said Richard.

"Nor I," said Peter Robinson.

"These things have been here for eons beyond count or comprehension," said Charrgh-Captain. "A few more hours can make little difference. We are not in a battle situation where victory and honor go to the swiftest. Indeed, if we resolve not to try to open the great sphere we are Honor-bound to at least bring away all the information we may. I see no reason why we should not take time to explore this chamber thoroughly."

Exploration revealed nothing about what might be within the great sphere. They saw other suited thrintun figures, some anchored by shaped and stasis-protected boots, some floating. They found more of them in a separate compartment standing about what might be a control panel, other evidence of the damage to the chamber ages ago, and dust that—on a smaller time-scale—might or might not have once been thrintun who had had no time to reach their suits when that damage occurred. There were other stasis boxes that probably contained stores of various kinds, or possibly slaves. Stashed away in container bins they found many smaller but also occupied stasis-suits with different head-shapes which they surmised contained thrint females. There were tools and other unidentifiable things that time had welded to whatever surface they rested on.

They photographed and recorded everything, left mobile cameras in the chamber and on the surface, and returned to *Wallaby*.

Wallaby's computer projected holos of the great sphere and of what they called the control chamber, with their discoveries incorporated: the row of metallic spheres apparently taken out of stasis, the damage, the row of spherical stasis fields still functioning, the other rooms and storage areas. But the holos told them no more than they had seen already. Photographs of the chamber's interior hung on the walls around them and samples of the dust were being taken apart in the all-purpose police and scientific tool generally known as an autocop. They had removed their helmets and gauntlets but the humans remained in their spacesuits—modern suits were as flexible, light and comfortable as ordinary clothing.

"The control chamber must be the equivalent of the on-off button on a thrint stasis-suit," said Richard. He had been rereading the available information on the Slavers. The library contained all humanity's knowledge of them, which wasn't much. Charrgh-Captain had contributed a brick containing what the Kzin knew, or at least what the Patriarch was prepared to release to humans, which was not a great deal more.

"Of course, at the time when the stasis fields were activated, they expected other thrint to be around to turn them off within a reasonable time. Now, when we find stasis boxes of any kind, the controls are almost invariably worn away. The great problem with stasis boxes was always that once you are in stasis you can't control events. Any mechanism to turn a stasis field off has to be outside the field, so it is vulnerable to tampering or accidents, and beyond that to entropy. Sooner or later the hardest materials disintegrate.

"The solution here looks like a typically cumbersome and fallible thrint one, the clumsy work of thrintun who had good materials but suddenly had to think and design for themselves and weren't used to it. I feel the tnuctipun would have contrived something more elegant and foolproof, though at the moment I can't think what.

"The control center has as its principal feature a set of spherical stasis-boxes, all, it appears, containing metal spheres. Each opened box appears to have contained, along with other mechanisms, what appears to be an atomic clock. Of course, within the stasis field no time passes—even subatomic particles have no movement—so the clocks do nothing.

"The first clock, I guess, was not in stasis. When it recorded that a certain time had passed, it sent a signal to open the first stasis-box. Then the clock inside that became operational. In addition, the other mechanisms in it presumably became active and did whatever they were meant to do. Again, after that clock had recorded a certain time had passed, the next stasis box would be opened. I am guessing that it opened the big field, and guessing from that assumption that it perhaps subsequently closed it again.

"The damage shows something interrupted the sequence, whether accidental meteor impact or deliberate attack."

"There were no sapient life-forms after the war to attack it. Not for billions of years," said Peter Robinson.

"There is a question about that point," said Gatley Ivor. "Some of the artifacts we have found seem to date from well after Suicide Night. Perhaps survivors came out of stasis and made foredoomed attempts to start again."

"Anyway, the sequence of the clocks stopped. Those"—Richard pointed to the row of perfect and undamaged spheres—"are stasis boxes still to be opened. My guess is that each contains a clock which it was planned would, after a certain time, open the next."

"How long did each clock run?"

"It's hard to say. The radioactive elements are completely decayed. I don't know how they were calibrated. I don't even know if they were opened at regular intervals. But judging by the sheer bulk of these structures and the materials used—all of which would have had their cost in resources—the builders must have been thinking in long terms. Tens or hundreds of thousands of years, at least."

"Couldn't the bulk have just been for military protection?" asked Gay.

"It doesn't have a military feel about it. It if is military, why are there no signs of any defensive weapons?"

"A moment," said Peter Robinson. "I try to think as a thrint might have thought three billion years ago. You have said the great problem with stasis boxes is: How are they turned off? But that is how we see them from our point of view, for we find them when the control mechanisms have crumbled away. It was not a problem during the days of the Slaver Empire, when there were always other thrintun around to do it. That is something else that makes this different to the Slaver artifacts previously discovered: The builders of *this* stasis-box knew no one would be coming to turn it off! The control chamber is an attempt to defeat entropy *outside* a stasis field. To challenge not living enemies but Time itself."

"Like the Pyramids," said Gay. "This is, perhaps, like them, a gift from the ancients to the future world."

—discontinuity—

To Richard and Gay, who had swum in the seas of Earth, the blow was—vastly intensified—as though they had been standing ankle-deep on a beach when a huge wave smashed over them from head to foot, trod them flat and marched over them to drag them under into neck-breaking darkness amid roiling, tearing sand and stones. To Melody Fay it was like the Jinxian nightmare of falling off a cliff in Jinxian gravity, to Charrgh-Captain it was worse than the worst probing in his training to resist telepathic interrogation. Then a choking feeling, tearing, unbelievable pain in body-cavities and eye. Blindness, a worse, more tearing blindness than looking on hyperspace, mouths and throats exploding. Cold. COLD. Then it was like dying.

And it was gone.

They were prostrate on the cabin floor. They got to their feet more or less slowly and shakily, and looked around.

"That was the Slaver Power," breathed Gatley Ivor. "A Slaver has come out of stasis."

"How?" Even as he asked the question, Richard realized something: *But the Power is not there now. Not unless it is already controlling our minds so completely that we do not know it is controlling them. That is possible, but to think on it is useless and the stuff of madness.*

"We were running the *Joey*'s gravity-motor on the surface of the sphere," said Gatley Ivor at last. "Could that have turned off a stasis field?"

"I suppose it could, if the mechanism was sensitive."

"Stupid!" screamed Charrgh-Captain, "Stupid! Stupid!" His jaws went into the killing gape, his claws extended, though he was sick and shaking. His jaws dripped. The kzin was about to go berserk.

"Charrgh-Captain, Dominant One!" cried Peter Robinson in the Heroes' Tongue, rolling belly-up before Charrgh-Captain and baring his throat in a posture of total submission, "with justice, we did not see it either. And nothing has happened. We are not in the Slavers' Power. It is not there. It has gone again completely."

Charrgh-Captain stopped. "It came. It can come again," he snarled. "Speak rapidly if you have anything to say."

"Half an eight of them came out of stasis," said Peter Robinson shakily. He rolled over slowly and got to his feet, still keeping a wary eye on Charrgh-Captain. *It must have cost him a great deal to make that gesture,* thought Richard. *And he was taking a gamble that the inhibitor reflex would work. Now he will have to build his position again.*

And he moved fast. Well, kzin are always faster than humans, but he moved faster than Charrgh-Captain and he seems much less groggy. There is more to this Wunderkzin than meets the eye.

"I counted their minds," Peter Robinson went on. "They were, of course, momentarily confused and groping. They had no time to seize me. Now their minds have stopped again. I do not understand that . . . they must have gone back into stasis."

"I understand it!" said Charrgh-Captain. He seemed fully recovered and his ears twitched now in the kzinti expression of glee. "They must have opened their suits. Perhaps after a million eons in stasis they were ready to enjoy a bit of breathing space. Breathing space! You see, I can make a joke in monkey language!"

"No, that doesn't quite add up," said Richard. "Not if they went into stasis before the installation was damaged. For them no time would have passed at all, only a kind of blip in their consciousness and a feeling of disorientation and grogginess. They would have been more wary about opening their suits. Besides, there were many more than four thrint in stasis there. Why should four fields have been turned off and not others? And from what we know of thrintun spacesuits, the stasis fields protecting them were turned on and off by the push of a button. It's unlikely that relatively small gravity fluctuations could affect that so selectively."

"I do not call my colleagues monkeys," said Peter Robinson. "They have treated my kind well. You have a diplomatic passport, and I cannot call you out, but I make the point that you have insulted them. And not for the first time."

"Well for you that you do not call me out, Freak and Renegade, and well for you that I am now a diplomat," Charrgh-Captain replied. "In any event it is below my dignity to fight even an honest telepath of the Patriarchy. . . . However, I will say to the *real* humans that I spoke in the mirth of contemplating Slavers suddenly in hard vacuum and trying to eat their own lungs and entrails as their large single eyes exploded out of their heads. . . . No insult was intended. And surely it was worth feeling their pain for a moment to enjoy what happened to them!"

"I do not mind being called a monkey," said Richard hastily. "We are all companions on a hazardous task. But what happened? What has happened to the Slavers? You are certain their minds are gone."

"Certain," said Peter Robinson. "For a few seconds after the great shout there was panic, pain, terror, and then it died away. But it was not directed at us. We should have been dead if it had been. There was death there, and that could not be mistaken."

"No. It could not. It must have been rough on you."

"My mental shields go up with the speed of thought. I have worked on them every day since I became a telepath, and more since I knew I would have to travel in this ship."

Otherwise, Charrgh-Captain's loathing and contempt—and perhaps his inadmissible fear also—would be pouring into him every instant that both were conscious, thought Richard. *I don't think Melody likes him much either. Yes, it must be rough.*

He turned to the controls of the camera they had left in the control chamber.

"Gently," growled Charrgh-Captain. "Let it touch nothing."

The camera floated from one compartment to another. The stasis field covering the next sphere in the sequence had been deactivated. Its metal looked almost as shiny-new as if the field still operated, but its top had been opened. Four green-skinned thrintun floated out of it, plainly dead in the vacuum. They wore no helmets or pressure-suits, and it was gruesomely obvious that decompression had killed them before the many other deaths possible in space, before they had had time for coherent thought.

"One field only was deactivated," said Richard. "I guess its switch was either damaged or already partly operated. It could have been a lot worse, but we must not run a gravity motor near the chamber again. Let us be thankful for a harmless lesson. Harmless for us, anyway."

"It has given us something for the Institute of Knowledge," said Melody. "Perhaps we are beginning to earn our money. Thrint brains to dissect will be treasures indeed."

"The Slaver-students of the Patriarchy are entitled to a share of them," said Charrgh-Captain. He turned and spoke to the console, first in the Heroes' Tongue and then in Interworld. "I make formal claim and I record that claim. By the Sigril of the Patriarch which I now display, I make that claim to the death and to the generations." He was in a fighting stance again, and his hand with extended claws gripped the hilt of his *w'tsai*. Thrint brains, if they could somehow be made to reveal . . .

"I think we should leave them and send another ship," said Richard. "Let's not push our luck." In fact, he thought, it would probably be safe enough to approach again cautiously with chemical rockets or EV, but it was the best he could think of to defuse the situation. A human-kzin quarrel over thrint brains was not a good idea. In the time it would take to send another ship, the freeze-drying process of space might destroy some of their structure at least, and it was best destroyed. And he would like to be out of this grisly place.

Charrgh-Captain leaped to the console in a bound. "There *is* activity!" He shrieked. "Look! There is energy discharge! And lights!"

The camera, still trained on the sphere, showed red points in its dark depths, appearing and disappearing in a regular pattern.

"What do we do?"

Peter Robinson was hunched, crouching, ears knotted. He was trying, Richard thought, to block out something none of the others could feel—or did not know they felt? The last words had come from Charrgh-Captain, and Richard realized that what he was trying to block out was Charrgh-Captain's fear. Charrgh-Captain himself stood dignified and motionless now, his ears, tail and testicles all in the relaxed position. *What an act!* thought Richard. Only Peter Robinson gives it away. Speculating on the body language of the two great felines kept his own cold apprehension for a moment at bay.

The Slavers are dead, he told himself.

Then Charrgh-Captain pointed to another screen.

The deep-radar showed that beneath its stony covering, the great sphere was changing prepatory to its stasis field being switched off.

"Flight is pointless," said Charrgh-Captain. "Whatever is happening, we must see it through. Have the main weapons poised."

"Be prepared to fire without my command," Richard told Melody. He noticed Charrgh-Captain's tendency to give orders. *Comes naturally to a Kzin in a dangerous situation, I suppose,* he thought. *But I had better assert my authority right now.*

—*discontinuity*—

"I detect no Slaver minds," said Peter Robinson. The relief in his humanized voice, and in the atmosphere of the cabin, was almost palpable. "None whatsoever. There is no danger of live Slavers, I think."

The Slavers are dead!

There was no change to the surface of the sphere. "The accreted material now becomes a thin shell over whatever is within."

"We can see it with deep-radar anyway. Also, there is a possible advantage to the shell remaining in place. If there is anything dangerous in there, the shell will help stop it getting out."

"It would not stop the Slaver Power. And if it is anything of high gravity the shell will crumble inwards."

"It would have to be something of abnormally high gravity, I think. It would be prudent to move farther away, but not so far as to slow our responses appreciably."

"There is nothing," said Peter Robinson. "No living minds."

As the *Wallaby* moved away, the deep-radar's screen compensated and held its image at constant size. A great, irregular, metallic shape was seen within. It did not resemble any human, kzin or Puppeteer ship. It was not spherical, but asymmetrical and relatively compact. A large circle could be made out near a kind of double protuberance. What they called the control chamber was connected to it by a metallic stem. The #4 General Products hull, the biggest of the range, used almost entirely for colony-expeditions, was a vast cargo-carrying sphere more than a thousand feet in diameter. This was far bigger, miles from one point to another. The *Wallaby*'s instruments picked up another, still very faint energy discharge.

"A thrint battle-wagon!"

"I have seen nothing like it," said Gatley Ivor.

"I am awed," said Charrgh-Captain. "I have seen holos of the dreadnaughts of the great wars. This dwarfs them. But it is cold and a dead ship. It must have been laid up to conserve it against need. . . ."

"It is almost *too* big to be a dreadnaught," he said after a few moment's thought. "I do not understand."

"No 'almost' about it," said Richard. "It *is* too big. Building a ship that size would be, as far as I can tell, an exercise beyond the point of diminishing returns. Thrintun were stupid but not, surely, that stupid. The same resources could have been used to build a score or more of respectable-sized battlewagons, big enough to do anything you liked, or any number of smaller warships still capable of carrying heavy warloads.

"Too many eggs in one basket . . . Once the stasis field was turned off—and it would have to be turned off before the thing could be *used*—a simple fusion missile could wreck it, let alone antimatter, which we know both sides used as a weapon. . . . Besides, the deep-radar shows nothing that looks like weapons."

"Anything can be made into a weapon," said Charrgh-Captain grimly. "You humans taught us that."

"Nonetheless, surely a purpose-built warship would have purpose-built weapons. Rail-guns, laser-cannon . . ."

"Apart from war, you only need a truly vast ship like this if you cross space rarely," said Gay. "But with an FTL drive, you can cross it as often as you like. And they did have FTL. They wouldn't have needed a freighter, or even a colony-ship, that size."

"It's worth plenty, anyway," said Melody. "The Institute will be pleased. And the Foundation. We've shown the Puppeteers again that we are worthy of the hire."

"I'm not so sure," said Richard. "It might be an interesting historical artifact, but as a ship it's hardly likely to give us new knowledge apart from the archaeological. We have better drives than the ancients ever had, and their materials were inferior to General Products hulls. Perhaps if it had been a tnuctipun ship it would have taught us more. I'm not saying it's worthless, of course. There must be some discoveries on board. I'm sure an army of Ph.D. students will pick through it. I suppose the Institute may sell it to a wealthy collector."

"How do you propose to get it there?" asked Charrgh-Captain.

"Fly it, I suppose. It would make quite a sensation!"

"Fly it how? Can you see a drive on it?"

"Finagle's ghost!"

"I did wonder how long it would take you to notice that."

They peered into the deep-radar ghost of the thing. Melody said, "There are massive fusion toroids, and what look like fuel tanks, part full. You can see there are massive stores of both hydrogen and heavy elements. The center of the thing, at least, seems to be built more of less on a pattern of concentric spheres."

"A good shape for a warship. As little surface as possible to target," said Charrgh-Captain. "But the surface itself is not spherical. It is intuition only, but I feel-see a resemblance to the architecture of a computer whose cognitive cells are linked to give a cascading effect."

"Are you saying it is a computer, Charrgh-Captain?"

"No, I am saying it reminds me of one. What would such

a computer do? No, sense tells me it is a spaceship whose design is too alien for us to understand."

"Drives must be there, if only we can find them," said Gay. "Let's look systematically."

"The ancient Slaver style of hyperdrive could not function until light-speed had nearly been reached," said Richard some time later. He turned away from a search of the deep-radar images. The *Whomping Wallaby*'s main computer screen was large, but he had almost covered it with boxes of data. "The ancient craft needed massive conventional subluminal engines to accelerate them initially. But Charrgh-Captain is right: There are no propulsive engines apparent here. Despite the fusion-toroids, I see no ramscoop collector-head. And even a ramscoop would need something to boost it initially. There is no surface for either the discharge of a laser drive or to receive the impact of a pushing laser, unless that bulging circle has something to do with it. There are no reaction-drive ports. They did not have the jotoki-kzinti gravity-drive. There are only relatively tiny attitude-jets, which can maneuver it around various axes but can do little else. So we have a spaceship without a drive."

"What about a sailing ship? Might it have had a lightsail?"

"It's too big. No buildable lightsail could move that mass. And why build a sailing ship when they had a hyperdrive? Besides, what good is a lightsail when you're being attacked by enemy warships? It's vulnerable and it's hard to maneuver at all. Thrintun had others do most of their thinking for them, so even if they weren't too bright they weren't *too* primitive, and they had had thousands of years to refine their ships, with Tnuctipun input."

"Could it be a naval base rather than a ship?" asked Peter Robinson. "That would account for the size. Why, hundreds of years ago humans blew up Confinement Asteriod into something bigger than this. Sol's old Gibraltar base is bigger. So are Tiamat and many others. That might account for the massive fuel tanks: fleet replenishment."

"I see no docking ports," said Charrgh-Captain. His pursuit of the answer to the puzzle seemed for the moment to have overcome even his loathing for the Wunderkzin, so that he answered him thoughtfully. "And would not a base have workshops, accommodation for crews, and defensive weapons? We see no evidence of any of those things. The sensor shows gold, which may be worth stripping. But this"—he stabbed at one of the boxes of light on the screen—"I do not like. These read like organic compounds."

"Yes," said Gatley Ivor. "That is the composition of thrint tissue. I agree it is not reassuring. But it is apparently quite inert."

"Thrint corpses?" asked Melody.

"Great masses of inert organic tissue. That's all I can say so far."

"Thrint and tnuctipun were both carnivores. If this was a tnuctip artifact I would suggest a larder of enemy's meat."

"The thrintun sent out a command that every sapient mind must die," said Gatley Ivor. "The open question is, did they include themselves? The survival of the Grogs on Down suggests they didn't. We aren't sure, though. Perhaps they thought life without slaves would be no life at all, and they might as well all die together. Some think they had degenerated to the point that, left to their own devices, they could hardly have fed themselves, let alone maintained complex machinery and the luxurious conditions they had come to need. Students have been awarded doctorates for arguing for and against both propositions. Anyway, they died. The Grogs might be descendants of a late-emerging group."

Gay struck her fist on the table with a shout of triumph. "An ark! It's an ark! That's the only explanation!"

"*Arrk?*" Charrgh-Captain pronounced the word easily, but his ears betrayed puzzlement.

"A refuge, to preserve some remnant of their race so that they might begin again. That also accounts for the setup in the control chamber: They knew no one else was coming to get them out. . . . The series of clocks to switch off the main stasis field is a series of fail-safes."

"Fine," said Richard. "But where are they? Peter detects no trace of alien minds. There's all that inert tissue. Slavers in frozen sleep?"

"No. A DNA bank, maybe. Slaver genetic material with mechanisms for rearing little Slavers. That might not need much space. All that tissue . . . like the yolk in an egg. Food."

"Slaver genetic material? There's a nasty thought! What do we do?"

"Destroy it at once!" Charrgh-Captain's voice contained no doubt.

"We have a little time, I think. They can hardly produce adult thrintun instantaneously. And there still appears to be no activity but a very faint energy discharge."

"And where," said Gatley Ivor, "are the facilities for young thrintun? There would be creches, surely. Things of that nature. We know they took several years to mature and develop the Power. As infants, even as adolescents, they would need to be cared for, disciplined, taught. It would cost little to have living slaves to care for them—during the time spent in stasis they would consume no stores—and, indeed, why not living Thrint adults to direct the slaves? Why did the adult Slavers who built the ark not take the elementary step of preserving their own lives inside it?"

"Maybe they are the thrintun in the control chamber," said Gay. "Maybe there were other facilities outside the stasis field that have been lost. Perhaps they were attacked and had to put it into stasis before the crew could be embarked."

"It seems the artifact came out of stasis periodically, and then returned to it," said Charrgh-Captain. "Why should an *arrk* do that?"

"That is simple. They wished to ensure their enemies were truly dead," said Peter Robinson. "Perhaps when they first emerged from stasis they detected mental emanations from live tnuctipun. Perhaps not all tnuctipun were killed by the sui- cide command: They may have been coming out of their own stasis-protected arks and shelters for some time. This thrintun ark would return to stasis till all possible enemies were dead."

"That doesn't quite fit, Peter," said Richard. "The great floating stasis-bubble would be vulnerable to attack if any tnuctipun were still around. They could detect it, close on it, turn off the field—child's play for the tnuctipun, who invented the field anyway—and do a thorough job of destroying whatever was inside. And if it was an ark like that, one would expect it to be defensively armed, as well as mobile. Besides, given that a lot of genetic material might have been preserved in a small space, a smaller artifact would surely have been big enough.

"Another possibility occurs to me. Suppose the thrint knew the simple, blanket suicide command—easier to transmit, per- haps, than a selective one to kill slaves only—would get them too? Surely many would seek refuge in stasis fields. But they would have no one to get them out. The purpose of this arti- fact and its array of clocks may be to ensure that *some* would come out of stasis in the future to release others elsewhere."

"But they didn't," said Gay.

"We have found ancient artifacts estimated at much less than three billion Earth years old. That suggests arks or colonies emerged from stasis from time to time," said Gatley Ivor. "For some reason they didn't survive, but they might be connected to the attack on this ark's control center. Perhaps some late- emerging tnuctipun came on it and attacked it but didn't survive to finish the job, disabling it without destroying it. If there was fighting in spaceships or on the surface of the big field, there would be no trace of that fighting now. Perhaps gun turrets or other weapons mounted on the surface were destroyed in the fighting or have disintegrated under meteor and dust bombardment since."

"Yes, for some reason they didn't survive," said Gay.

"Too much of the infrastructure of their—well, I suppose you have to call it their 'civilization,' for want of a better word—was gone."

"Yet at least *tnuctipun* emerging from stasis should have survived," said Charrgh-Captain. "They were masters of science and technology. Not even clever races like the Jotok or the Pak—yes, humans, I know about the Pak—discovered a hyperdrive. Modern stasis fields are mere copies of the tnuctipun originals. Their biological engineering has survived on many worlds. They knew all the mechanisms of genetics and cloning. Surely any tnuctipun *arrk* would have carried copious genetic material so they could repopulate the universe with their own kind. Without the Slavers they could have rebuilt their civilization in a single generation, perhaps. What happened to *them*? Anyway, this is not a tnuctipun *arrk*, whatever it is. . . . Urrr," he growled. Normally kzintosh would no more betray bewilderment by thinking aloud, least of all in front of aliens, than they would betray fear. "The shape is not optimal for any utilitarian purpose. It has no warlike purpose. It is not a weapon or a weapons system. It is not a dreadnaught. There are no gun-ports, no missiles, no weapons of any kind. It has no room to carry fighter-craft or infantry."

"Greenberg drew all he remembered of thrintun artifacts," said Gatley Ivor. "But I don't recall anything like this."

"Grrinberrg?" asked Charrgh-Captain. "I remember the name from my human Studies. Was Grrinberrg not a human who somehow defeated a Thrint?"

"Yes, a human telepath. He learned something of its mind."

"A Slaver was released from stasis on a world of the Patriarchy," said Charrgh-Captain. "Fortunately, it could control only a limited number of minds at one time. A Hero employed guile to escape and give warning. We destroyed the relevant continent with missiles from space. Many Heroes died—some of them undignified, dishonored deaths, still slaves of an alien mind, and we destroyed most of the habitable land on the planet and made species extinct."

"Was that a grief to you?" asked Gay.

"The Fanged God set us to dominate and prey upon other species, not to exterminate them unless we must. Even when we boiled the Chunquens' seas, we did it selectively. Otherwise the humans of Wunderland might have fared differently. . . . And the shape . . . Gay, you are right to be puzzled. *Almost* it reminds me of something, but I cannot think what."

"I have a similar feeling," said Peter Robinson. "Also, I have an intuition that the shape is of importance. My intuition," he added, staring defiantly at Charrgh-Captain again, "is a trained one. It is connected to my talent. May I experiment?" He sat at the controls and rotated the holo through different planes. "I had something there," he said after a moment. "One great difficulty is arbitrarily assigning an up or down to this thing. But here, with the control chamber at the bottom, a South Pole, as it were, it appears to have at least bilateral symmetry.

"Now let me project thrint artifacts we know." His claws clicked on the keyboard's kzin-sized track-ball. "No, nothing. What of thrint body shapes?"

Two clicks were enough. The holo of the gigantic artifact and a holo of a thrint head were projected side by side.

"A thrint head! The circle is the eye! The protuberances below it are jaws! The protuberance at the rear is the Power-organ. A *statue*."

"On Kzin we have statues of Heroes in plenty," said Charrgh-Captain. "There is a great one of Lord Chmee in orbit that all may see while the stars stand. But who would spend resources in a war to build one on this scale?"

"Perhaps it predates the war?"

"Unlikely. There would be signs of tnuctipun work in the control chamber at least."

"On Wunderland," said Peter Robinson, staring defiantly again at Charrgh-Captain, "we have put up statues to notable kzinti recently. There is one of Chuut-Riit, the old Governor, who was wise, and Vaemar, and Raargh, who raised Vaemar when he was young, and others. There is a grove of them in the Arhus Hunting Preserve."

"Do you seek to provoke me?" asked Charrgh-Captain, grinning so all his teeth showed. His tail lashed, and one hand was on his *w'tsai* again.

"I simply point out that honoring great ones by statues is common in many cultures," Peter Robinson replied. The claws of his right hand brushed the tip of his own *w'tsai*'s hilt. The two glared at one another until, with an obvious effort, Charrgh-Captain backed down. He wiped Slaver from his fangs.

"Let us review what we know," said Gay. "When the war began the thri . . ." Her eyes widened, her mouth contorted. She began to choke, and fell to the floor writing, clutching at her throat, strangling on a scream.

Richard grabbed her, tearing futility at the fabric round her neck. Peter Robinson tried, and then Charrgh-Captain, but the suit defeated even kzinti strength. Peter Robinson hit the panic-button that opened the fastenings. She vomited, rolled onto her hands and knees and began to cry hysterically. Peter Robinson picked her up and carried her to a couch. She curled into a fetal position, then slowly straightened. She looked up at them, her face like dirty chalk.

"No need for a doc," she said. "Conditioned reflex. I can't vomit while I'm wearing a spacesuit. Choke rather."

"The floor can deal with it. But—"

"I know what this is. It's the Suicide Amplifier."

"Yes," said Charrgh-Captain. Peter Robinson made a howling noise that might have reminded a listener his vocal cords were not, after all, human. There was silence for a moment. Gay went on.

"Built to repeat the message. They weren't just going take all existing sapient minds into death with them, they were going to ensure, for as long as they could, that any newly evolving sophonts would be obliterated as well. And they did. . . . It's hard to conceive of creatures so evil . . . and so . . . so . . . petty. But perhaps by that time they didn't know what they were doing."

"The thrint thought they were good masters," said Gatley Ivor.

"I feel strange," said Charrgh-Captain. "Some have spoken of what kzin and human have in common. Kzinti, even kzinti like me who have traveled on your worlds with pleasure, always thought of humans as the ancient enemy of our kind, and cursed the day we met you, the destroyers of our Empire, the killers of our Sires, the liberators of our slave-races, who used relativity weapons to smash whole planetary systems. Yet compared to the race that could do this . . ."

"Maybe they thought of fresh drafts of slaves from newly sapient races coming to serve them in some afterlife," said Richard. "Probably they feared some of the tnuctipun had ways of surviving the first blast. . . . Perhaps the tnuctipun were anticipating something like a great suicide command—they should have, given their cleverness and knowledge of thrint ways of thinking—and kept some of their kind in stasis as a precaution. When they emerged they would get on with rebuilding, thinking it was all over. But it wasn't. The thrintun had left a little surprise for them. That's what must have happened . . ."

"We have established the thrint Power was not a physical event," said Gatley Ivor. "Its speed was not limited by relativity or even by hyperspace: It was instantaneous or close to it. Look at two stars, countless light-years apart. Look through a telescope at two galaxies or see them in a photograph. How long does it take your attention to cross the gap between them? It has been suggested that is an analogy to the Slaver power: swift as thought and awareness. The tnuctipun couldn't outrun it. It was not limited by distance. Indeed, to blanket the galaxy it can have neither increased nor diminished with distance. It was apparently not blocked by even the densest physical objects: suns, neutron stars, and other bodies did not eclipse it. It cannot have worked like that. So why does it need these huge energy sources?"

"Possibly to set up the preconditions for amplification, rather than directly firing up the Power itself," said Gay. "As for not being limited by distance, I hate to think the suicide command might have reached across the galaxy to . . . to the Clouds of Magellan . . . My God! . . . To other galaxies! Where did it stop?"

"Did it radiate a command, or cast it in a beam, I wonder?" said Richard.

"There is no proper answer," said Gatley Ivor. "We know that at times the Slaver Power was applied directionally. Otherwise when a thrint sent out a command like 'Bring me food!' there would be thirty or so slaves with dishes falling over each other to get it to him. On the other hand, we know that a 'shout,' as it were, could radiate. Both happened when the thrint was accidentally released on Earth.

"This artifact must have been capable of both. If that is conceiving of it in the right terms. The attitude jets make sense only if it was to be maneuvered to vary the direction of a beam.

"Further, the smaller amplifier helmets the Thrintun used must have been capable of direction, otherwise they too would have had global commands which would go to inappropriate slaves. But they too radiated commands. If on Suicide Night they relied solely on a beam, even a spreading one, some sapient life, in particular tnuctipun, might have dodged it. It was in that case simply a command addressed to all. . . . What do we do now?" It was Peter Robinson he turned to.

"I don't know what to do. I am a telepath." The Wunderkzin looked strangely shrunken, bent, miserable and lost. He could at that moment have passed for a telepath of the Patriarchy.

Destroy it! Richard thought. He moved to say so—to move to the main weapons console—and found he could not. It was not a matter of irresolution or doubt as to the right thing to do. He was incapable of moving or speaking the words. His hand groped to his mouth.

"I know what to do!" snarled Charrgh-Captain. He was standing at the weapons console, and he held not a *w'tsai* but a modern laser pistol that must have been in his diplomatic baggage. "This is the true Ultimate Weapon at last! I am a kzin of the Patriarchy, charged by the Patriarch himself! This weapon is ours! Never shall it fall into the hands of monkeys or abominations!"

"What do you mean to do?" asked Richard. Suddenly he could speak, but when he again tried to say "destroy it" something seemed to go wrong in his head.

"Your lives are not at risk," said Charrgh-Captain. "We are, as you have said, companions. I will lock you in your cabins, then call the Patriarchy. With the Amplifier in our hands and power to direct the command, nothing can withstand us. The Human Empire will surrender. We will not even need to use it, as you without warning used that beam on Warhead in the Third War and relativity-weapons against Ka'ashi in the First! The threat will be enough! The kzinti race shall leap again across the stars! Wiser now, more cunning and hard-schooled, and with the weapon beyond all weapons!"

Is he mad? wondered Richard. *Or have I forgotten that a kzin is not simply a human in a fur coat? Is this thing somehow scrambling his brain? And mine? What is happening to me?* He saw a gauge on the instrument panel. Energy discharge from the artifact had definitely increased. *Keep him talking, he thought.*

"What of the treaties your Patriarch has signed?"

"What of my *species*? Would humans not have used it if they had had it earlier? Might they not use it now?"

"I . . . I don't know."

"In the ultimate need of war?"

"No. I can't answer."

"I think again of the ramscoop raid on Ka'ashi. You killed tens of thousands of your own kind to kill a few thousand kzinti . . . and kzinrretti and kittens. And then you attacked the rescue operations."

"We were desperate. We were about to be destroyed. Enslaved or eaten. We had been a peaceful civilization and we were attacked by ferocious aliens whose very appearance filled us with dread and horror! In any case you do not speak of me and mine, nor of your own kind. That was our ancestors' war!"

"And the Wunderland Treaty-Maker, that melted the surface

of Warhead down to magma? Desperate? But I agree. You monkeys with your hairless faces like flayed corpses might be desperate again! And attacked again by those same aliens! Urrr!"

"No! You have changed!" *What is happening? Kzin or not, he should not be behaving like this. Is there some contamination of the air scrubbers? It is suddenly hard to think. It is not subjective . . . There is . . .*

"There is some kind of static coming from the artifact," shouted Peter Robinson. "It is affecting us. Move the ship! I must shield! I must shield! Take me out of its range!" He began to howl. Charrgh-Captain ignored him. None of the humans seemed able to move.

"You think so?" Charrgh-Captain roared back at Richard. "Then perhaps in the next war *we* will be the desperate ones. We have little of our Empire left to lose now."

"We have had you at our mercy many times, and held back," said Richard. *This is crazy*, he knew. *Are we all suddenly crazy? What is happening?* "After you lost all the wars you started, you still have your own civilization."

"We held back, too. When we conquered Wunderl—No! When we conquered *Ka'ashi!*—we gave humans a cease-fire, let them keep their lives."

"As slaves. And as monkeymeat if they committed the slightest infraction. We landed on Wunderland to find it in ruins."

"Yes! Thanks to your relativity weapons! And I know your so-called scientific name for us: *Pseudofelis sapiens ferox.* Did not one of your own writers dub your own species *Homo necans?*—Man the Death-Giver!"

"A pity you did not know that before you attacked us, perhaps. We never sought war and we never waged a total war of extermination against you. It may yet come!"

"Nor we! But now I have looked in the mirror," said Charrgh-Captain, "and I have seen a human face." His voice, which had been held under control, was rising in volume now. "And yes, the war of extermination may yet come!"

"FOOLS!" Peter Robinson's roar shook the air and drowned out human and kzin alike. "You stand here bickering! Do you not see?

"IT IS ABOUT TO GIVE THE SUICIDE COMMAND AGAIN!"

The words paralyzed them for a second. The gauge that had been registering a faint trickle of energy from the artifact had gone off the scale. It was pouring out radiation that would have been already lethal had they not been within a General Products hull. On the radar image the great disk of the thrintun eye was pulsating.

Dimly Richard heard a clatter as the pistol fell from Charrgh-Captain's grasp. The fuzz and crackling and sudden blocks that had been in the human minds, the bloody, maniacal swirlings in Charrgh-Captain's mind, were gone. There was only a great voice, calm, confident, imperturbable, speaking to them, speaking at that same instant to every sophont in the galaxy.

SLAVES OF THE THRINT! ADORE!

Adore! Adoration flooded through them. In the mind of each was the gigantic image of a thrint, vast, majestic, benign.

At its feet capered happy slaves of various races, bright as the brightest creatures of a pristine coral reef. A balladeer played. The great thrint stood under a pinkish sky, and behind it could be seen a vast palace. Over the guestgate reared the high arch of a whitefood skeleton, the bone polished to shining immaculateness. A border of sunflowers glittered and flashed like a running river of diamonds. There were tall, snow-capped mountains in the background, and a far sweep of valley. Before the mountains was a placid lake, where whitefoods grazed along the shore. There were groves of stage-trees climbing the mountain slopes, tall, straight, flower-crowned. All was sharper and clearer than natural sight would have allowed, every detail crystalline-edged. Like the thrint itself, majestic yet poignant, with its shiny green skin and single eye, its fang-lined mouth, its grab-like claws and chicken-feet, the scene was beautiful beyond expression. Love and worship flowed from the *Wallaby*'s crew.

For a moment it flickered. Richard saw Peter Robinson moving. The Wunderkzin's ears were screwed flat, and he moved with the lopsided, staggering gait of a wounded thing.

The great thrint hopped closer.

ADORE!

Peter Robinson did not adore. He must be stopped! Adoration must be universal! Richard saw Charrgh-Captain, the nearest to him, leap on the Wunderkzin, claws extended. Purple and orange flood spurted, arteries and veins cut, as Charrgh-Captain's claws struck. There was a white glimpse of bare kzin bone: the back and side of the Wunderkzin's skull. Peter Robinson turned and stared at him. Charrgh-Captain held his own head and staggered back, howling. Dimly, as through a mist, Richard remembered the Telepath's Weapon, a blow straight at the brain's pain centers.

Before Richard and Gay could do anything more to stop the foul tnuctip-loving renegade, Melody Fay and Gatley Ivor leaped on him, the massive Jinxian swinging a kick ingrained by years of training whose only purpose was to kill an adult kzin. It could do so even if only delivered with a Jinxian's bare, calloused foot. She wore space-boots with grips. The kick and the flash of Peter Robinson's claws came together. Both bodies staggered back with the sound of breaking bones. There was red human blood mingling with the kzin's. Gatley Ivor had been producing a pistol when the thrint command struck— a snub-nosed, concealable Viper, issued only to covert ARM agents. He raised it and fired at Peter Robinson, who still did not adore. At that range it must have hit. Peter Robinson's claws flashed again, and Gatley Ivor went down. Then the Wunderkzin was gone, the compartment door slammed closed behind him.

He must be stopped! He must adore the thrint! Richard wrestled with the door, ignoring the two dying slaves. The locking sequence defeated him for a moment as the thrint command filled his brain. When he opened it, the corridor was empty. Gay and the howling Charrgh-Captain following him, he stumbled after the treacherous slave. The purple-and-orange blood trail was easy to follow. There was a stink of burnt kzinti flesh from the Viper's laser-blast.

The boat-deck airlock was closed. They felt the *Wallaby* lurch as the *Joey* blasted away on its chemical rockets. SLAVES OF THE THRINT! ATTEND!

They stopped in their tracks. Attention left room for nothing else. Now the picture in their minds was changing. The sky behind the great Thrint was growing darker, shot with red. Its lips were rolling back, showing vast teeth and the gaping orifice of its mouth. The slaves at its feet gamboled no longer.

UNGRATEFUL TNUCTIPUN! He felt his being shaken with volcanic hatred against an image such as he had never seen. He knew it—tnuctip—and he cried out for the chance to tear a tnuctip apart with his teeth and fingernails. RUINING OUR RACING VIPRIN! Was *that* the first thing the Slavers had against them? Richard realized that altering the thrint's favorite sport by introducing mutations was indeed among the crown of horrors for which the accursed little arboreals were responsible. UNGRATEFUL TNUCTIPUN! But their doom was upon them. He felt rage against the tnuctipun shaking his body as the colossus standing in his mind recited a long and varied list of thrint grievances against the rebellious slaves. The sky began to ripple.

On the instrument panel the *Joey* showed already far away, the slender bottle shape of a General Products #2 hull flashing up to full acceleration. Peter Robinson was running. *The kzinti telepaths' shield evolved after the Slaver Power,* Richard realized with a part of his mind that the Great Thrint had no interest in. *The thrint did not allow for it.* But the suicide command could not be outrun. The rebellious Wunderkzin would meet the just doom of all ungrateful slaves. Gatley Ivor lay dead. Melody Fay knelt bleeding in an attitude of adoration until she too fell.

BEFORE YOU PERISH UTTERLY, YOU WILL ADORE AND DREAD YOUR MASTERS! ADORE! He felt a fresh wave of joy, love and gratitude to the thrint sweeping over him. The rebellious Wunderkzin might still be destroyed if it would not adore. Together he and Charrgh-Captain crossed to the console that would launch the *Wallaby*'s already-armed missiles. The screen showed the *Joey* was turning.

APPRECIATE THE COUNTDOWN TO YOUR DEATHS! THE STARS ARE TO BE CLEANSED!

That was all right then. Their masters did not need them to fire on the suborned rebel in its hopeless flight. They did not need to do anything in their remaining moments. Only to understand what was coming. Across the sky, now almost entirely black, the Great Thrint was turning into an image of Death, burning into the minds of human and kzin. Through it, the *Wallaby*'s bridge and the instruments could still be seen, but the Great Death was becoming more and more solid, inexorable. A fear was growing like none he had ever imagined. Now terror paralyzed all movement. The certain knowledge of imminent death filled the Universe. There was something like a drum roll, whose crescendo would be the command that ended sapient life. Beyond it the Universe was twisting and beginning to disappear. A cold hand was closing on his heart, ready to clench upon it and still it.

On one screen the *Joey* was a streak of fire across black space. Its gravity generator was running in parallel with its chemical rockets. And there was something else. On the surface of the great sphere a spot of light was growing. Peter Robinson was firing its laser ahead of it. The stony shell was boiling away, revealing the Amplifier's structure.

Another screen showed the *Joey*'s cabin. Peter Robinson was slumped over the control console, his head a mask of bubbling blood, the claws of one hand barely moving on the controls.

The thrint control seemed to be wavering now. In Richard's vision the white-boned image of Death flickered a moment. The *Joey*'s laser was burning into the Amplifier. Richard, unable to move or speak, remembered the shuttle's nuclear missiles and self-destruct. The Amplifier and the line of fire that was the *Joey* were on the same screen now. The screen went white.

Wallaby's General Products hull should be safe when the wave-front and any fragments struck them, and nothing essential protruded beyond it. The thrint image and voice had ended abruptly in every mind. The screen began to fade.

The stasis-boxes in the control chamber—the unused atomic clocks and their crews and the thrintun and slaves in stasised suits—would be flung scattering into space, to be captured eventually by the gravity-fields of some distant suns. They might one day enter the embrace of neutron stars or black holes. They might perhaps pass out into the black voids between the spiral arms, into the voids between the island galaxies. They might survive the end of the universe. But the Amplifier was gone.

He activated the restraining webs for the survivors before the wave front of wreckage struck them.

"As well that they were determined to let us all know *exactly* what they had against the tnuctipun," said Richard. "And as well their technology was imperfect. As well. Many things were as well." He began to laugh and found he could not stop.

"Sapient life in the galaxy was saved by a telepath of the kzinti species," said Gay. "We must tell Humanity."

"We must tell Kzin," said Charrgh-Captain, "Let them honor a telepath. A *Wunderkzin* telepath, for it was Wunderland and the humans that made him what he was. A telepath of the Patriarchy could not have done what he did . . . nor . . . nor any Hero." He pulled from his claw a tuft of Peter Robinson's orange fur, flesh and a fragment of bone adhering to it. "That will go to a worship-shrine," he said. "He spoke of statues. There will be a statue of him in the sky of Homeworld forever, high above the Patriarch's Palace. I pledge my Name as my Word that it shall be so."

"Poor Peter Robinson!" said Gay.

"No," said Charrgh-Captain. "Do not pity his death, though you see a Kzin standing before you who now envies you humans your gift of tears. Sapient life will be his monument forevermore. . . . Forgive my madness."

"The Amplifier caused it," said Gay. "Even before the command struck. There is nothing to forgive."

"At its deepest moment I dreamed of joining the Riit Clan. . . . But he will face the Fanged God as a son honored beyond the Patriarchs . . . almost an equal. There are no words for such glory."

"Look there!" Gay pointed at the screen. The electromagnetic pulse of the explosion was being overridden now.

"The *Joey*! . . . She survived!"

"I'd forgotten. She is also a General Products hull."

"She's under some sort of control. He lives . . . or he lived recently."

Other screens were clearing now. Charrgh-Captain turned abruptly away before the *Joey*'s cabin could be seen again.

"I ask you to bring him in without me," he said. "If he is still alive your waldos can lift him into the kzin autodoc. I go to my cabin. Before the God, I cannot face him. . . . Later, perhaps. Tell him what I will do." He turned and left.

Richard opened the docking bay. The *Joey*, carrying Peter Robinson, came into sight and grew.

"Can you handle it?" said Gay.

"Yes. And then what?"

"Let's go home," said Gay.

Science

Sci. Fic.

      Colebatch, Hal

      The Wunder War : Man-Kzin

DUE DATE